The Scalpel

Feral Space 1

James Worrad

Cover art by Duncan Halleck

James Worrad
Visit castrumpress.com/james-worrad/

ISBN: 978-1-912327-20-1

Printed in the United Kingdom
First Printing: January 2018
Castrum Press

1. Rig

One

SWIRL TOOK A COMPACTION BARREL OUT of the crate and fitted it to the pistol grip.

"You should take one," she said to Lyreko over her shoulder. "Idiot."

His laughter rattled against the storeroom's gunmetal walls.

"Funny thats," he said. "Funny the missy calling everyone feral be the first to lift a gun."

"*Because* you're all feral."

"Meet-up's slap-middle of the Strip, tune?" She felt his breath upon the back of her neck. "Say the rig-pigs stop you with that gun? You explains thats?"

"A risk, granted." She checked the pistol over. "But we should be acting. Vartigans have us *reacting*. Reacting in an open space with no weapons. They're ex-soldiers, Lyreko. Bred soldiers. You're neither."

"Think I can't handle?"

"I know you can't, sweet."

Lyreko's arm drifted around her waist, his chest resting against her shoulder blades. Solid, warm.

"Okay, takes it," he whispered. "Pigs never check anyhow. But I've lived the rig life twelve year, and no one fucks on the Strip. Respect. Respect only a cramp fuckin' life provide." He parted her chin-length dreadlocks and brushed his lips against her neck. She shivered, relaxed, watched his pale fingers surround the darkness of her fist. Their tips caressed the gun as much as her own skin. "Vartigans just wanna deal, you tune?"

"Deal? They've kidnapped our pusher."

"Ever known a kidnap that wasn't?"

She turned around in his arms and faced him, brushed her lips against his.

"Lyreko," she said. "I've had... intimations."

"The Delighted Ones?" The tanned patch of skin around his left eye was a calm pool within a frown. Dermal reconstruction: you got what you paid for.

Swirl nodded. She gripped the pistol tighter, barrel pointed at the floor, safety on. "It may well be nothing to do with this meeting. But these..."

"Intimations."

"They point toward something *now*. I can't tell you anymore."

Lyreko stepped away from her. "Then you don't needs a gun." His expression was blank as ammo.

She dropped her pistol into the crate behind her, never taking her eyes off Lyreko. "Love your business face."

"This? My *belief* face, girl. Cuter."

Lyreko smiled, stroked her chin and walked out of the storeroom. The door closed behind him.

:He's disgusting: Sparkle sent.

"Shut up," Swirl replied to the warmth rising in her mind. "If you don't like me and him, you can always go to the villa, Sparkle."

:The anthropologist in me can't stop watching,: Sparkle sent. *:You better not be falling for that feral.:*

"He's a comfort," Swirl said. "An ally. Nothing more."

:I'll concede he helps. But whenever he's around, you hog the driving seat.:

"You could take pleasure in him too," Swirl said. "I wouldn't mind." A joke, of course.

:Words can't express...:

Swirl had ceased listening. She gazed at her palm. No arguing with the matter: the skin blemish there had become even more defined, more undeniable since last night. Two arrowhead shapes with a dash between them: the Divine Eye.

Their symbol. *Them*. Could they be watching now?

Swirl shivered. Three years since leaving Harmonic space, two years of it upon this rig-ship, and she'd never known the like. She'd never expected to know the like her whole life. Divine attention. The Delighted Ones.

She knew Sparkle gazed at the blemish through their shared eyes, too. Knew her to be just as frightened.

"Sparks," Swirl said. "You're getting cranky in there. Why don't you be ascendent when we hit the Strip? I can always step in if things get involved."

:Thanks, Swirly-girl.: Sparkle sent. *:I mean it. I'd really like that.:*

"What are sisters for?"

"WHAT'S WITH THE BEAST?" Hargie Stukes asked.

The barkeep looked at him and frowned. Not at the question—Hargie wasn't so drunk he was seeing things—but that his only customer had spoken. Just that kind of bar.

"That?" the barkeep said. He nodded at the backstreet taxidermy job leering from between the snacks and contraceptive serums on the high shelf behind him. Piebald and canine, the stuffed beast was a muscled thing. Its fangs were bared, though a couple had long since fallen out. A short life spent belly-to-ground, no doubt, snarling at every passing crotch. "That's a Jaqruzzil."

"Name's familiar," Hargie said.

"You've been drinking them for two hours," the barkeep said.

Hargie grimaced. He snatched up the bottle and scoured the ingredients list. No dog therein. Transpired *Jaqruzzil* was the brand name.

His last beer. Hargie hadn't a single rupee to piss on, or near-as-damn. Worse: two, maybe three hits of jumpjunk left in the cockpit. Two weeks his baby had sat on the landing pad and not a sniff of a job.

Was this it? Trail's end a-nearing? He'd seen his kind out of junk and all hope to get more. Street trash, shambling, their eyes red and dreaming of lost stars.

He shivered. He looked up to see the barkeep studying him.

Hargie pointed the bottle's lip at the stuffed animal. "Product placement, huh?"

"Local, actually," the barkeep said. "Local beer, local mutt. One named after the other."

"That so?"

"Walk to the edge of Import some time and look out: nothing but Jaqruzzils fighting and fucking," the barkeep said.

"Good to know *something* goes on around here," Hargie said. "Eh, big man? Ha."

The barkeep didn't smile.

Hargie did, soft and reassuring. Had to be careful as a traveller, as a bubbleman. Always remember locals everywhere thought their shithole world an Elysium.

Chances were he'd already done quite enough to piss this town off. He couldn't remember. He'd gone crazy these last two days, drunk himself atavistic. Faced with financial and narcotic ruin, he'd adopted the doctrine of the cornered animal. What else? He'd always been his own worst enemy. The enemy had won.

"You smoke?" Hargie said. He pulled out his pack and gestured toward the front door.

"It's all right," the barkeep said. "We can smoke here." He took a straight and lit it with his finger.

Hargie did likewise. Good ol' neuralware. "You're a scholar and a raj, sir."

"Story is," the barkeep said, "someone dumped a shipment of tiny dogs here long ago."

"What, like a big freighter?"

"No, man," the barkeep said. "This was like... two kay ago. Golden-olden shit. Wasn't any Freightways back then. Just..."

"Bubblemen," Hargie said.

"Yeah, guess. Anyway, the dogs' descendants adapted to the high gravity. Out beyond the spikes, I mean."

They could always tell, Hargie thought. Collar up, neck hidden, and still they knew. Hargie had the wide brown eyes of the old bubblefolk: tan skin, strands of their crimson in his brunette mess. Yet so did lots of other people. How'd they always tell?

He swigged. Maybe the slouchiness. Maybe that.

"Impressive," Hargie said. "Whole species born from a little bubble's hull."

"Guess inbreeding wasn't a problem here," the barkeep said.

"Guess not." Hargie hid his grin behind a sip of *Jaqruzzil*.

The front door hummed open and four guys stepped out of the night. The largest one, in some kind of peaked cap and navy uniform, had that camp strut tough men got when they meant to get tough. Hargie chugged down the last of his last beer.

"No one scrap-mouths Import," Uniform said. He strutted right up to Hargie's stool and slapped a gloved palm on the bar. Liquid splashed Hargie's cheek. "Hear me, Captain Fucko?"

King around here, then. Yet walk a mile, and no one there nor beyond gave a fuck, and that truth forever stung an asshole. He made examples of those passing through. Demur, and he was paid.

"I tune," Hargie said. "I'll keep it in mind, sir."

"Don't ratshit me," Uniform said.

His pals crowded around. Hargie sensed the barkeep move back.

"What say I buy you all a drink?" Maybe he could open a tab here. Stranger things had happened. Hargie turned to the barkeep. "One beer, please. Four straws."

The smallest tough laughed at that, then stopped himself. A positive sign.

"Fucking bubble-turd," Uniform said, and he yanked back Hargie's collar, exposing a chrome stud on either side of his neck. "We *heard* you. Saying shit about... about watching Jaqruzzil's hump being the only fun in town. Well, screw you! Outworlder motherfucker warp-jackal fuck."

Hargie looked at the barkeep. "This place bugged?"

"We're a Totalist town, little guy," the barkeep said. "No one tell you?"

Totalists. Their eyes recorded everything all the time, all of it shared on some local cloud. There existed as many reasons to totalise as there were Totalist communities, but the general idea was to create some pioneering communitarian utopia. The flaw, as far as Hargie's philosophy went, was that everyone could see you whack off. A person's retinal cameras were their own business, damn it.

"And you had such honest eyes," Hargie told the barkeep. "Makes me weep." He turned back to Uniform. "I'm drunk," he told him. "I apologise profanely. Profusely. Ah, you tune what I mean."

"That Jaq comment's the least of it, dickhole," one of Uniform's guys said. "Town's been watching you two whole days."

"Oh," Hargie said.

"You pocketed stuff from the store," the shortest guy said. "My kid saw you."

"Old Annu," the fourth said, "found you, you... urinating against her generator."

"Think I remember that," Hargie said. "She got quite the show." He thought a moment, then looked at them all. "Uggh..."

"No one was impressed," Uniform said.

"Next time, use wide shot." Hargie smiled amiably.

No one smiled back.

"Smoosh," Hargie said, "I'll leave, tune?" He put on his lucky green hat with the flaps and the silver badge and got up from his stool, all five foot two of him. "Leavin'..."

"Exit denied, bubble-turd," Uniform said. Hargie saw his uniform was for some takeaway chain with a military image. "Import's got a certain punishment for shitscum like you."

"I see."

Hargie grabbed his empty beer bottle, screamed, and swung it down on the bar top. It bounced out of his hand.

The bar fell silent a moment.

"It's plastic, moron," Uniform said.

"Yeah," Hargie said. "Yeah."

"Grab him, boys."

Ten minutes later, Hargie stumbled in the cold smelly night in nothing but his underwear and his lucky hat with the flaps. Damn it, something in this planet's atmosphere reeked. His bare feet slapped tarmac.

"Guess where we're going?" Uniform asked, strutting ahead of Hargie and the cronies holding him.

The edge of town. Black out there, beyond the last lights. They were joking. They would just give him a roll, a kicking, and be done. He'd take it. He never let idiots embarrass him into calling the authorities.

"Gonna shoot me? That it?"

"You see a gun?" Uniform said.

"Fuckin' *wish* we'd have shot you!" the guy holding his right arm said.

Bad craziness, Hargie thought. No jape. These Totalists were simply perverts, sadists. Screw embarrassment: he logged onto the local memestream and alerted Import security. A window popped up at the bottom right corner of his vision: was his call regarding police or takeaway? The logo above the window showed a cartoon Jaqruzzil dressed like the uniformed guy.

"Nice try," Uniform told him. "All Import's watching this. Or will do. Think about that. While you *can*."

Hargie wouldn't pee himself. He wouldn't let them see him piss himself. He was surprised he still had some pride, some fight.

They walked past the last building at town's edge, into the broken ground that lay before the big spikes. Hargie could see two of those spikes just ahead: obelisks looming forty feet into the night sky, their blade-like silhouettes outlined by stars.

They stopped just before the spikes. Hargie's feet stung. They bled. Uniform pulled out a gun.

"Hey, now, wouldya look at this," Uniform said, waving the pistol. His pals stepped away from Hargie and laughed.

"No," Hargie said. "C'mon."

"Keep walking." Uniform nodded at the darkness beyond.

"You're screwing," Hargie said.

"I'm cleaning house, jackal. Move." He raised the gun to Hargie's throat.

Okay. Bad crazy, but okay. Hargie limped off toward the dark. He'd risk the dark, sit out there and run back in once these toughs got bored. They'd get bored.

His feet were agony; he couldn't see where he trod. He passed the line of spikes.

Something barked in the darkness. Hargie froze.

"Walk," Uniform called to him. Hargie wanted to scream at him to shut up. He began walking again, realised he walked like some primate: a loping gate. Everything heavy. Heavier...

"Boy got a weight on his shoulders," one of the guys shouted. Laughter all round.

Gravity. He was leaving the obelisks' dampening zone, entering the world's real-and-natural.

"Gravity won't kill you, little man!" Uniform called. "Just slow you down. The Jaqruzzils *love* that!"

Hargie dropped onto all fours. He didn't move. Fuck 'em. He wondered whether, secretly, he'd been grasping for something like this all along. Suicide on instalment.

"Shoot me!" he shouted. Whimpered. "Shoot!" It hurt his chest shouting that. *Sorry, Mother*, he thought. *Sorry, Father...*

"So endeth the lesson, bubble-turd!" Uniform shouted. "Goodnight!"

"Don't mess with the good guys!" shouted one of his pals. "Don't mess with Import town!" They whooped and laughed as they headed back.

A lesson. The whole town watching. All those good guys. Taught the villain the error of his ways. Probably watch it every holiday for the next twenty. Good guys dispensing homespun justice like some cutesy memestream drama. A plague on the galaxy, good guys, a plague.

Hargie turned around on all fours and crawled back, breathing hard, his muscles burning. A howl came. Somewhere behind. Closer.

He shuffled faster, tried not to think of the stuffed beast in the bar fang-deep in his ass and balls. Almost ran the last part, collapsing in the dust somewhere between the spikes and the lights of Import. They didn't come in here, he told himself, the gravity...

Breathing easier now, his world lighter. Remote from his body. He felt only one thing: a kinship with beasts.

He saw the silhouette of a figure gliding silently, silently, toward him. Too tall for a man, too slender. The silhouette grinned. White fangs.

Hallucinating of course. The drink, the fear. Had to be.

Damned galaxy, Hargie thought. *Everyone always seeing things their own way*.

The night blurred.

SWIRL HAD TO WONDER at it. For all Sparkle's disgust at feral humanity, she seemed eternally at ease talking to them. Good at it, too. Better than Swirl, at any rate.

"Oh, I know all about having a penis," Sparkle was telling some stranger called Crowbone, and anyone else listening in the busy public cable-pod. "Don't explain the story for my sake."

The man's mouth, nestled in its beaded goatee, fell slack. He scratched his shaved head. "What?"

"We've a machine for it, back in the Harmonies," Sparkle said. "Takes days, mm-yes. Turns out I'm hung like a freighter's undercarriage when you switch my chromes. Who'd have thought?"

"You can't just *drop* that shit on a stranger, girl," the man said, curling up with laughter. "No way."

"Prefer I eased it in gentler?"

The man Crowbone cracked up at that. Even Lyreko beside her grinned, despite his obvious territorial posture.

Sparkle snatched a look at herself in one of the pod's windows, her reflection a translucent ghost against the black backdrop of deep space.

Being currently head-descendent—watching from the back seat, so to speak—Swirl's viewpoint was dictated by wherever Sparkle chose to point it. A lot of the time, that was Sparkle's nearest reflection. She'd been like that since they were kids. Swirl watched as Sparkle checked the two absurd pigtails she'd insisted on having their dreadlocks bunched into. Of late, Sparkle had been pushing to change the locks from their current ice blue to 'fun' pink. Not a chance.

"Gotta ask," Crowbone said, and Swirl could see it coming. "How's a dick rate compared to, you know..."

"Less hassle, less fun," Sparkle said.

"Figures," Crowbone said, almost melancholy. He looked to Lyreko. "Please tell me you knew about this. Please."

"Sure," Lyreko said, relaxing now that this other male had included him. "Smoosh with thats too. Means Swirl knows what to *do*, if you tune..." He stretched his arm around the back of Sparkle's seat. Sparkle took a breath and sat forwards, away from him.

The men picked up on it, Lyreko most of all. One of 'Swirl's' cold moods, he'd think. Again.

:Appreciated, Sparkle,: Swirl sent to her sister. Damn her.

Sparkle didn't reply, not even in their head. She stared at her reflection once more, as if she knew it irritated Swirl.

Forget her. Swirl made good use of their gen-altered irises instead: she could turn her full focus toward the edge of whatever Sparkle stared at—typically herself—with no adverse effects on either user's view.

She chose to take in the pair of mile-long chains far beyond the window, each running parallel with the cable pod and festooned with hundreds of spacecraft. Ingenious as it was crude, the 'rig': smaller ships tethering themselves to a main unit and donating their engines and computing power to the orbital journey around the Eucrow system, breaking off at their desired destinations. How like the feral worlds, making the best from what scraps they possessed. Swirl watched a tethered hauler discharge its old-fashioned thrusters against the black beyond, a single twitch in the rig's endless slouch.

"We're here," Lyreko said, standing up. "Let's dust."

The pod docked with the rig's core, and the door whirled open. Passengers poured out into the gunmetal terminus. Dock loaders, bubblefolk, a few rich kids from Luharna or Psiax. All hungry to squeeze whatever fun from the Strip. Sparkle's acquaintance, Crowbone, nodded and vanished into their mass.

Lyreko stopped beside a drinks 'n' hox machine. "Eyes up," he said to Sparkle. "This the place."

"No Vartigans," she said.

True enough. Those brutes weren't difficult to spot: white-skinned and blond, their faces tattooed so as to put some distance between themselves and their clone factory past.

"Using friends, maybes," Lyreko said, eyeing passersby.

Swirl felt Sparkle reach into her jacket.

:I didn't bring the gun,: Swirl sent to her, *:We get a situation where you wish I did, let me take over:*

"Obviously," Sparkle said.

"What?" Lyreko's eyes searched her.

"Nothing."

Lyreko frowned. "Just gots messaged," he said, staring into the mid-distance. "Sender unknown."

"What's it say?"

"Nothing." He looked at Sparkle. "Just a directional."

"Share it, then," Sparkle said.

Lyreko stared at nothing again, blinked.

Sparkle pulled a handheld out of her jacket and turned it on. Their shared brain's structure couldn't access the primitive neuralware feral humanity used. The sisters played it off as an allergy. Whenever they used their handheld in public, they got the most pitying looks.

The handheld's screen displayed a map of the Strip's length. An arrow flashed on the map at their current location, pointing north.

"This some ratshit," Lyreko said, suddenly uptight. "A trap. Our man's dead alreadys."

"Smoosh, tough guy," Sparkle said. "That's what you say, right? Smoosh? Keep it smoosh, prick. Fuck's sake..."

Lyreko side-eyed her. His pride chipped at, of course, but more than that. Swirl never swore. Sparkle always did. Lyreko knew nothing of Sparkle.

"Where's this arrow goin'?" Lyreko muttered. "Shit, they were meants to meet us *here*."

"Perhaps we need a little perspective," Sparkle said. *:You had better step in,:* Swirl felt her send. *:Five minutes:*

:Of course,: Swirl replied.

Their shared body tensed—that uneasy second where neither sister had possession—and then Swirl felt control return. She reached into her jacket and pulled out a silver cylinder. She flipped it open and shook a leaf into her palm: blue and transparent, its veins luminous with mauve serum. She tore it in half.

She placed half onto Lyreko's waiting tongue. "The Delighted Ones guide you," she said.

Swirl's eyes replied to Lyreko's fear—and, yes, weakness—with reassurance. Swirl was good at this. Sparkle exceeded her at making friends and fitting in, but it was Swirl who breathed ritual, who engendered reverence for the Hoidracs' narcotic gift, whomever she sold it to. She was more than just a supplier to her buyers here on the rig. She was a priestess, a hierophant of the access hatches.

Lyreko's face softened. "That's the shitsy," he said. "Right there."

No reverence, Lyreko, despite her work on him. Swirl swallowed the other half of the leaf, its surface smooth and tasteless. An act of solidarity: her tolerance for leaf, shaped from birth, exceeded such doses.

Swirl strode on, following Lyreko. She could picture his mental state well enough: the geometry of his own ego made manifest, blending into the tumult of all the heads around him. Mildly psychic, primitive societies might deem it.

:Forget something?:

Sighing, Swirl allowed Sparkle to ascend, felt her limbs succumb to her headsister.

"We're on a night out," Sparkle told Lyreko as they left the pod terminus. "Start acting like it, hmm?"

The Strip was a hexagonal tube half a mile in length. On each of its six planes—up, down, sides—heaved crowds of people making their way between shops, bars, and clubs. Music punched through the stink of fried carbohydrates that rose from stands, the fast food and faster tunes of a hundred human worlds. And everywhere movement, catcalls, laughter, parties of friends strutting along one plane then turning, strutting onto the next. Traffic was thickest at these points, as pedestrians manoeuvred into oncoming crowds at ninety-degree angles to themselves. A trail of searchlights floated in the air along the strips' lateral centre, held between the artificial gravities of all six planes.

A thousand enemies could lie in wait here inside the Strip, shrouded in neon, heat and bustle. *Caution*, Swirl thought, *always caution*.

"Party!" Sparkle yelled at everyone passing. "Raise this motherfucker, people!"

People whooped back.

"Little tourist girl," Lyreko said, trying a smile.

Sparkle didn't reply.

:Could you at least smile at him?: Swirl sent. *:For me?:*

Swirl felt their face make a sarcastic-feeling grin. Lyreko's frown confirmed it.

They walked on, turned right. Swirl felt the lurch as she crossed from one plane of the strip to the next, like climbing a step and suddenly the step 'wasn't there.

Lyreko halted. "Arrow says it's over there."

Things were quieter, moderately, at this end of the strip. Behind a rundown casino lay a derelict kiosk that once sold adrenoslurps. Behind the derelict kiosk that once sold adrenoslurps lay a thoroughfare no one passed through on account of the casino's trash. Under the casino's trash lay a manhole with the cover loosened.

"Bomb," Sparkle said. "I'm calling bomb."

"Varts ain't dumb," Lyreko replied. "It'd be slaughter."

"Yes," Sparkle said. "Because that doesn't sound like clone soldiers, huh?"

They stared at the manhole for some time.

Swirl received a message from Sparkle: *:If you wanted to ascend right now, I'd be entirely happy with that, sister-my-love.:*

She did so.

"Right," Swirl said to Lyreko. "You hang back."

"No way," Lyreko said. "Tag with you, all the way."

She smiled. "Thanks."

The pair of them sauntered toward the manhole. Swirl wondered whether blast victims ever saw it coming.

They shifted the manhole's cover to one side. Blackness below. Stale air. An aluminium ladder ran down a concrete wall into the gloom.

"Be just a 'con unit down there," Lyreko said. "Ten foots by ten. No tunnels or shit."

"Help me down," Swirl said.

"Swirl, I—"

"It'll be a corpse, Ly, a message," Swirl said. "If it were anything else, we'd know by now."

Lyreko nodded, looked around. "Make it quick."

Swirl clambered down the ladder. She almost stumbled over a box on the bare concrete floor. She switched on the light of her handheld, pointed it at her feet. Next to the box lay a body: their pusher. No visible wounds. She leant down, felt a pulse. A medicated slumber, most likely.

The box wasn't sealed. Gently, she pulled back the box's flaps and gazed inside.

A face gazed back, flat and eyeless. A stack of them: flayed, one atop another, real human faces. Bloodless and laminated, the top one reflected the handheld's light. Swirl recognised the DNA helix tattoo. Baron Jape, the Vartigans' leader.

:These Vartigans certainly know how to apologize,: Sparkle sent.

Swirl ignored her. A rolled-up note sat next to the faces. Ink and paper. An anachronism in feral space, though not at home...

"Swirl?" Lyreko said from the other side of the counter, "We smoosh?"

"Surprisingly so," Swirl said. "I think."

HARGIE STUMBLED TOWARD the landing pad, lucky hat flaps flapping and underwear rippling in the morning's breeze. Townsfolk grinned as he passed. No one said shit. No one looked surprised. Which figured, but only made his mood worse.

He tried to ignore them. He tried to ignore his stinging feet. Strange dreams he'd had, lying in the dust last night. He couldn't recall what. But they'd left him... uncomfortable.

He cheered up—almost—when he saw his bubbleship out on the pad. No graffiti on its orange-brown hull, at least: the townsfolk were clearly too virtuous for that. Lumpishly spherical and five storeys in height, *Princess Floofy* was as large as bubbleships dared to be.

And a bay chock-full of nothing, of course. Memories, maybe, which never filled a belly.

He stumbled into the shadow of *Princess*, the drop in sunlight causing him to shudder. It was then he noticed two silhouettes standing beneath the opposite side of the ship's underbelly.

Hargie stormed toward them, his face a grimace, his feet throbbing.

"One last visual, huh?" he said to the two figures. "Here you are." He gestured at his underwear. "Or a lecture, that it? Come on: drop that homespun A-bomb. Blow my mind."

The two men stared at him, their faces still as concrete. The closest seemed in late middle age, with grey in his slick hair and well-clipped beard, but there was a vitality in his bearing that bordered on incongruous. Tall, too, spindly. The square collar of his suit was of a fashion three decades in the grave.

The second, younger, was built like a frigate's shithouse, stocky and foreboding. He wore an orange t-jacket and fluorescent green shorts. That explained his grim face. Hargie wondered if the young man let some disinterested party dress him each morning.

"You're, er... not townsfolk, right?" Hargie said.

"No," the older man said.

Hargie laughed, whistled, made a show of a shrug. A job, maybe. Dared he dream? "I know what you gentlemen are thinking," he said. "Why's this lunatic dressed like a, a caveman?' Well—"

"No," the older man said.

"—since you're wondering I, er..."

"We wish to book passage to this system's orbital rig," the older man said.

A reprieve! Hargie shivered with elation, hid it in a shrug.

"Stukes." Hargie offered his hand to shake. "Hargopal Stukes. Hargie. This is my ship."

The older man regarded Hargie's hand. He smiled, nothing more. "A bubbleship," he said. Hargie couldn't place the accent. "A bubbleship."

"You know your star craft," Hargie said, nodding. *Congratulations*, he thought, *now see what you can do with these toy blocks*. Everyone knew bubbleships. Clearly some real dirt-huggers here, come adrift in a travelling man's world. Which, of course, would mean they wouldn't know a deal from a meal...

"I'll run you to the rig," Hargie said. "One lakh seventy. Usually it's two, but it's clear you respect the bubbletrade, so..."

"Could you travel full-speed?" the older man said. "What might you say to four lakh?"

"Carry your bags, sir?" Hargie said.

"We have everything. Could we leave now?"

"'Course." Hargie accessed his neuralware, and the gangway lowered from *Princess*' undercarriage.

"My name is Illik," the older man said. "This is my son, Doum. We're to meet my daughter."

Doum looked at Hargie, his expression blank as a rock.

Hargie smiled back regardless. "Family reunion, huh?" Doubtless a laugh riot. Creepy-doo-dee, these heads.

Short flight for tall money, Hargie told himself. *Lunch too*, his belly added. He could suffer coo-coo cargo for four hours. Came with the job. Hell, it *was* the job.

Hargie gestured at the gangplank, and Illik embarked.

Doum turned to Hargie. "This ship," he said, his accent his father's, rolled in gravel. "A name?"

"*Princess Floofy*, friend," Hargie said.

Doum looked at the hull. His frown softened to resolve.

"So be it." He made his way up the gangplank.

SWIRL GOT UP, THREW on some clothes. Lyreko's place—their place—looked a mess again. A cramped mess. Always. Away from home, beyond the Harmonies' borders, out here in the great spaces of feral humanity, mess was the norm. An endless war. That fact was the clearest refutation—one that could be shoved in the faces of contrarians like Sparkle—against the insipid argument that life could ever be as good here as it was in within the Harmonies. Life was clean there. It had purpose.

She breathed out long. Lyreko's place. One primitive hatchway in and out. Dead end.

Mess was getting to Swirl and to her sister: clutter for Swirl to obsessively clean, filth for Sparkle to reel from but never do anything about. Trouble was, of late, both had ceased acting on their horror. They merely beheld it. It occurred to Swirl that neither of them had articulated this change to the other.

She washed her face in the sink, cleaned her pores with a dermshell, vibed her teeth. She thought of the faces in the box. The note.

The flayed Vartigan faces had proven a sort of handshake, the note accompanying them an invite. Three hours hence, they'd rendezvous with whoever had offered both: lot A574, out on the sunward chain's far end.

The matter ate at Swirl. Not the fact that parties unknown had chosen to flay her enemies' faces, nor that they now directed her to as remote a location as one could find on the rig—if anything, the former justified the latter—but that it coincided with the blemish, the symbol on her palm.

She studied it now under the basin's bleached light. The Divine Eye: clear as on a crest or monument. She had heard of this phenomenon, these sudden blemishes. She knew their ramifications.

Thus far in their reluctant travels as penal *flaneur*, Swirl and Sparkle (well, Swirl) had been a wandering pair of eyes exiled ever-outwards, desperately trying to find something that might spark forgiveness and a return home. The symbol proclaimed them an active tool, a hand for some purpose known only to the Hoidrac, the Delighted Ones.

But what? No amount of leaf ingestion offered any insight. Worse, she couldn't comadose on the stuff—couldn't drift into the limitless Geode—this far away from the Harmonies. Leaf's potency increased with proximity to home.

Swirl missed the Geode.

Lyreko stirred in bed. Their bed. His bed.

She didn't look at him. She wondered what Sparkle was doing. Asleep, most likely, or kicking back in the villa. Sparkle was spending a lot of time in the villa. She rarely let Swirl forget the fact.

"Morning, sunlight," Lyreko said, rising, sauntering close to where she stood at the basin. She felt his arm slide about her waist.

Swirl stared at the basin. She brushed away Lyreko's arm and stepped from him.

"This is not working," she said.

"What?" He squinted.

"Us. I'm no longer... comfortable."

She studied his limbs' movements, couldn't watch his face. They tensed with all that discomfort of intimacy abruptly denied, stirring then bringing themselves to heel.

"It *has* been fun," she told him. "But it's gone further than I'd like. Than it should have."

"No," Lyreko said. "Don't be freaking. Not todays."

"I'm sorry, Lyreko," Swirl said.

"This another mood," he said.

"What?"

"You flips all the time. Go cold, switch." He pointed a finger at his temple. "You be sunlight later."

"No." The forcefulness of it surprised even Swirl. "I won't. Not remotely."

His expression shifted, lightened. "Bitch," he said. "Can never tune who you are. Know that? Who the fucks are you?"

"Someone you're far too dull to comprehend."

She moved to step away, but Lyreko threw a palm against the mirror behind her, blocking her path. Swirl grabbed his arm and spun him around. She locked Lyreko's elbow, forcing him to his knees.

"Deep breaths," she told him. "Calm. We're allies, friends. But it's over."

Lyreko struggled and she pushed at his elbow. He groaned.

"Ask yourself what you'll do without me, Lyreko," she said. "Think you'll get your own leaf, hmm? Where would you even start?"

He ceased struggling.

"Smoosh," he said. "'Kay."

"Imagine your life *without* leaf," she said.

"*Okay*."

"Now go," Swirl said. "Give me my space."

She let go. Lyreko leaped to his feet and spun to face her, fists clenched, red-faced save for the patch around his eye.

"Interesting," she murmured. "Let's see how that works for you."

He stared at her. Feral eyes. Then he stormed away, the hatch-door slamming behind him.

:Everything fine?: Sparkle sent.

"Listening in?" Swirl said.

:No,: Sparkle sent. *:I was on the beach and the sky began to grey.:*

"Oh," Swirl said. "Set off the adrenalin alarm, I see."

:Only a little,: Sparkle sent. *:But enough for me to venture out and risk a UFC.:*

"Sorry?"

:Unexpected Feral Cock.:

"Well, rejoice," Swirl said. "Your liberty is at hand."

:Pardon?:

"Lyreko and I are over." Swirl slumped down on the bed and tried to work a boot onto her right foot.

Sparkle was silent awhile. *:That's... unexpected,:* she said eventually.

"Is it? Is it really, Sparkle?"

:What are you insinuating?: Sparkle sent.

"What I'm *saying*, Sparkle, is any affection is doomed out here. Every time one of us picks up a toy, the other spits out her dummy and whines." Her damn boot refused to go on. 'We're cursed, living out here."

:I was happy for you.: Sparkle sent.

"No one's here," Swirl said. "May as well speak it."

"I was *happy* for you," Swirl felt her lips say. "In my way."

"Sparkle," Swirl said. "Why is it you're always the last one to realise you're miserable?"

"Because I take pompous questions like that in the spirit they weren't intended," Sparkle replied.

Swirl said nothing. She finally buckled the damn boot and set to work on the other.

"Swirl," she felt her lips say. "Let's be realistic here. And you know how much I abhor that, so you know I must be serious. We're never going to have an authentic love life out here in the feral spaces, and not because we're a Triune lost amid monominds. Ferals are simply not long-term prospects."

"We're not a Triune," Swirl said, pulling her dreadlocks into a ponytail. "Not anymore."

"Exactly. Even back home we'd be damaged goods. With Pearl tethered—"

"We do not talk about Pearl," Swirl said.

Swirl felt her lips readying to speak. Then they loosened.

"We do not talk about Pearl," they repeated eventually.

Two

HARGIE SHUFFLED OUT OF THE DOCKING PIPE and onto the bay floor. The rig's scrubbed air filled his nostrils. Not an ideal night's sleep, that, lying in the gravel back on Import. A four-hour flight hadn't helped. Maybe he'd grab a couple of hours after lunch while his passengers got up to whatever nefarious pursuits awaited them. Clothes shopping, hopefully.

"So that was bubble travel," Illik said behind him.

"Afraid not, sir," Hargie said, smiling at the old man and his son. "Real bubble jump's for between systems. That was just sub-bub. G-wave."

"I'll get to experience it later, then, when we leave," Illik said.

"Leave for where?" Hargie said.

"Qur'bella sector," Illik said.

Hargie nearly had a coughing fit.

"Are you fine?" Illik asked. "You can take us, yes?"

"That's months away," Hargie said.

"You have other plans?"

Hargie shrugged. "Depends on the food court here..."

"My son and I pay assiduous professionals well." Illik studied Hargie's expression. "That would be you, Mr. Stukes."

"Right," Hargie said. "I mean, yeah, that's a given."

"Well?"

Hargie looked at the two men. The lakh would be useful. But weeks in a cramped bubbleship with Professor Strangenuts and his ogre child?

"Okay," Hargie said, "but I have to take someone along for the journey."

"Who?" Illik said.

"Anyone." Hargie cleared his throat. "What I mean is, to justify such a long journey—"

"No one," Doum growled.

"As my son says," Illik told Hargie.

"Six lakh," Hargie said.

"Twelve," Illik said.

"Erm. Okay." Illik was insane, clearly. "You drive a hard bargain. Pay me eight now, rest later." He'd take the eight and run.

"Mr. Stukes," Illik said, his face cracking to a grin, "we were rather hoping you'd come along. We've a fascinating business, my family. A business, yet a sort of game. Besides..." He placed a hand on Hargie's shoulder. "I wanted you to meet my daughter."

Father and son chuckled.

"Twelve lakh now," Illik said, "'twelve lakh later."

Hargie blinked. A man with twenty-four lo-los could quit the bubble game for a year. Kick back somewhere, let the jumpjunk pour out. And, well, this talk of a daughter, the knowing chuckles? Maybe generosity ran through the family. It had, well, been some time...

But why? What the fist-thrown-fuck was their game?

Hargie looked at the two men. In times like this, when uncertainty hovered, Hargopal Stukes fell back on the ancient bubblefolk philosophy of empathic rationalism. Empathic rationalism argued that, given the vastness of all things and the super-numerousness of human individuals therein, the overwhelming likelihood was that you and your worldview sat somewhere in the overall average, deep in the bell curve. You were nothing special. Statistically, then, the opinions and temperament of anyone you met would almost certainly resemble your own.

He didn't know if its logic stood up, not really—life had beaten him almost agnostic on the matter—but Hargie still lived and breathed, so...

So the question was why would *he* behave like Illik and Doum, if he *were* Illik and Doum? Well now... if Hargie were super-rich, he probably *would* throw credit around like confetti. Why ever not? And if he were pretending to be super-rich, it would be because he was either trying to rip someone off or make them look foolish, likely both.

Risk oft spewed reward. And he'd nothing else to do. That idiotic bubblefolk need to fill a hole. Bet high.

"Fifteen now, fifteen later," he said.

"Done," Illik said, and offered his thumb tip. Hargie pressed his own against it and let fifteen—fucking fifteen!—lakh into his neural account.

SAT IN THE CABLE POD, chewing his last bite of noodlurrito, Hargie questioned his reasoning. Life had made him gullible by heritage, cynical by experience. He knew that. Arguably it was the manner of all bubblefolk. Looking at Illik and Doum—sat either side of him in the otherwise empty pod, dammit—he wondered if he'd become the very blueprint of his people's idiocies.

"Anthropology," Illik said out of nowhere. "That is our business here."

"Anthropology," Doum repeated. He studied the stars beyond the windows.

"Tell me, Mr. Stukes," Illik said, oddly chattier now. "Do you take an interest in the ways of other peoples?"

"Be dead if I didn't," Hargie said.

"Ha." Illik slapped his palm on Hargie's knee. "Mr. Stukes, today we encounter a mysterious people in possession of an enigmatic narcotic. My daughter walks with them, observes them."

"This a drug deal?" It made a kind of sense.

"For them, yes," Illik said, gazing at another cable-pod passing the window. The pod's four corner-cables had a strange stillness as it passed along them, unlike any on a world. "But for us this is..."

"Anthropology," Hargie finished.

"Yes, Mr. Stukes." He squeezed Hargie's knee and let go. Hargie wasn't cozy with this sudden leg tendency. "But you'll get your money, have no fear."

Doum grunted. A laugh? Yes: mockery. As if these men found wealth and barter a joke. Like Hargie was a dumb mutt and they kept feigning to toss a ball.

Their cable-pod approached the outermost ships of the rig's sunward chain now. The sun's edge rose over their hulls, dappling their supra-graphene features gold.

"The ship we're visiting," Hargie said to Illik. "Your daughter's, is it?"

"No," Illik replied. "Hers is elsewhere. The ship is rig-owned, confiscated from a bankrupt, I imagine. A public area."

Smoosh. The rig's equivalent of a dark alley, one with generous storage space for bubbleman corpses. Well, Hargie still had his neuralware. The rig's security was but a call and a cable journey away. If, y'know, they'd bother.

The ship lay ahead. A system corvette, a hundred yards long and a century old. No lights.

"Come," Illik said to his two companions. "Illumination awaits us."

The three of them stood before the cabin-pod's doors, Illik in the middle. The pod connected with the ship's docking unit, and the sudden inertia danced with the fear in Hargie's belly. The noodluritto, too.

The doors whirled open, and they stepped into a near-darkness. The air smelled of dust and sealed packaging. A tight cargo bay.

"Lights," Illik said.

The lights came on and two pistols stared at the three of them. They were in the hands of two shitscum, rig-gangers by the look of 'em. One man, one woman.

"Don't move," said the man, pale-skinned with a bad derma-job around his right eye that left it smoother and browner than the rest of him. "Gonna frisk."

"Feel free," Illik told him. "You'll find we are unarmed."

"Silence," said the woman. Short blue dreadlocks and skin dark as skin got.

The man worked them over like an octopus. His palms trembled.

"Smoosh, Sunlight," he told the woman once he'd finished. He strode back to her, trained his gun on Hargie and his clients once more.

"We were meant to wait for *you*," Illik told the gangers.

"Thought we'd come earlies," the man said. "Sorry if we're causing any, y'know, discomforts."

"Oh, you needn't have worried," Illik said. "We always see to our own comfort. Always. Hello, Zo."

"Hello... daddy."

The voice—female, amused—came from the darkness behind the gangers. The male ganger spun around in its direction, but not his comrade, the blue-haired woman. She grimaced, sure, but kept her piece on Illik. Impressive, Hargie had to admit.

A young woman stepped out of the dark. She wore some soft black body armour, and her hair was cut like the singer from Mute Elation: all shaved but for a black fringe and two short pigtails jutting upwards and outwards. She had two pistols trained on the two gangers.

It occurred to Hargie that the cable-pod doors were still open behind him. With the ganger-woman's pistol trained in his direction, it would be dopey to run, of course. But should everyone's attention be taken elsewhere—a gunfight, say—discretion was but a back-step and a button-prod away.

"Well," Illik said, "what a comfortable diorama this is."

"So," the male ganger said, "how cans we help you?"

"I was hoping my daughter's gift, the violent effort she went to, might assure you of our good faith," Illik said.

"The faces?" the male ganger said, his gun trained on the girl. "A food hamper would have cut it."

"Zo here has observed you a while," Illik continued. "It seems you are purveyors of a product we wish to procure. That is what you *do*, is it not?"

"Guess," the man said.

"Then you shall lower your pistols, Zo shall do likewise, and we can talk." Saying that, Illik nodded to Zo and the girl, quite casually, holstered her pistols. Too casually for Hargie's liking.

The male ganger nodded and holstered his gun.

The female ganger didn't.

"Who do you represent?" she asked Illik, her voice clipped, accent plummy. Hargie couldn't place it.

"We're a family business," Illik said.

"It's smoosh," the man-ganger said to the woman. "Stow your piece."

The woman ignored him. "I control the... 'product,'" she told Illik with a vicious sneer. "I do not bless just anyone with it."

"We pay very well," Illik said. "Ask our bubbleman friend here."

All eyes fell on Hargie. He pulled out a cigarette and lit it.

"My advice?" he told the gangers. "Push for five. Settle for fifty."

The ganger-woman squinted at him. She returned her gaze to Illik.

"It's not the money," the ganger-woman told Illik. "It's the product itself. The gift which it bestows."

"A fascinating attitude," Illik said, and for the first time he sounded genuinely surprised. "If enigmatic. Where *are* you from?"

"That's my business," the ganger-woman said.

"The same place this 'leaf' comes from?" Illik said.

"Who's asking?"

"I would be fascinated to know," Illik said. "We've a sympathy for those who recognise money as a bauble and a weight. Credit merely paves a way, does it not? We feel your leaf could be important. It may have important work to do."

The woman kept her stance a while, either considering Illik's words or some inner counsel, then lowered her pistol. "Fine," she said. "But one condition."

"Name it," Illik said.

"I come with you," The woman said. "See your operation."

"That may be problematic," Illik said.

"Meeting over," she said.

"Fine," Illik said. He sighed; he smiled. "Fine."

"Sunlight?" the male ganger said to the woman. "You're leaving?"

The woman ignored him. "It's a deal," she told Illik.

"Wonderful," Illik said. "I believe there's a custom in moments like this..." He offered his hand out to shake. The woman took it, and reality exploded.

The room filled with what at first Hargie took to be light, intolerably bright blue light. But it consumed all detail, in all five senses. The taste of Hargie's cigarette vanished. The *idea* of tasting a cigarette remained, but the sense was gone. Same for everything else. Everything concept, essence. Hargie's body became abstract, more pure, more authentically *Hargie* than it had ever been, and yet physically not there at all. Everything a mirror: mirrors down to the very atom, reflecting and reflecting and reflecting beyond the horizon of awareness.

What was this? What in—

The male ganger had bloomed into an intricate star system of thought and feeling, one seized by a vast and sudden terror. What the fuck?

But that was as normal as this strange new crazy got. Illik and his two children weren't even *there*. They were voids, silhouettes of nothing. The blue light all around seemed to snap and prod and test their non-existence, a limitless beast furious at these three vacuums' affront.

And the woman, the ganger woman. She was a sort of... well, a *binary* system, a tree trunk rising into two boughs, branches and twigs intersecting in a complex matrix. And there, falling into the trunk, into the very depths of her, a sliver of Illik, a slice of his nothing-silhouette, somehow recognisably *him*.

An elongated figure, horned, appeared out of the haze. It had no eyes, no features save a fanged and grinning mouth. And yet it was the only thing that made any sense here, because Hargie had already met it, he just couldn't place where. The figure darted around the vacuum-people and the ganger-star-systems and rushed straight at Hargie.

Hargie felt the air punch out of him as he hit the cabin-pod's floor. Things were back as they were supposed to be. No more blue light. He could see and hear. He could feel pain.

Clambering, he brought himself back up on to his haunches. The light—the regular electric light—had gone out in the ship's cargo bay. His ass hurt. Had someone just pushed him into the cabin-pod?

Lightning sliced the darkness, followed by the familiar hammer-on-metal *tonk, tonk* of compaction rounds. Someone was pulling a trigger.

Hargie accessed his neuralware and commanded the pod doors to shut, requested to disembark. He leaped up onto the seating away from the door's shrinking metal iris. Something blue blurred through the dwindling gap, rolled along the cabin-pod's gangway and spun around, pointing a gun at the door. The ganger woman.

"Close the door," she told him.

"I was!" he said. "You slowed it!"

A round bounced off the closing metal, then the door sealed shut. The warm *clunk* sound was bourbon to Hargie's ears.

He turned to see a pistol muzzle trained on his head.

"Don't move," said the woman. She stood half a foot taller than him. "Don't say a thing."

He didn't even nod. Wisest course.

The cabin-pod disconnected and lurched away from the ship. The woman seemed ready for Hargie to use that lurch, but no way. He wasn't gonna do shit.

"Face-down on the floor," she said. "Slowly."

Hargie lowered himself onto the gangway floor, heard her stand up. A gun *behind* your head always felt worse. Just like Father...

"I'm not one of them," he blurted.

"I know that." She paused. "He said you were hired."

"I've kids," he lied. At least he assumed he lied. "Please, lady, imagine how they'd take it."

The woman shrieked.

Hargie flinched, but nothing happened. "Yeah," Hargie said, uncertain. "Something like that, I guess..."

His confusion subsided when a hand, mummified and steaming, fell in front of his face.

"Was still in my palm..." she muttered.

Illik's hand, then. They'd been shaking hands when it all went freak-o. Illik must have... well, exploded? Illik's burnt aroma filled Hargie's nostrils. He was too frightened to be sick.

"What happened just now?" Hargie asked the woman. "All that weird shit? That happened, right?"

"You're a bubbleman," she said.

"Yeah," Hargie said.

"So you've a ship?" she asked.

"Uh-huh."

"Get up and sit over there," she told him.

"Thank-you-sir. Lady." He did.

She sat too, on the seats facing his, gun still pointing. She inspected the palm of her other hand. "Listen," she said, "I want to get off this rig."

"Heading that way myself," Hargie said.

"I'll pay. Pay good. I'm merely pointing this gun for now."

"Call it a retainer," Hargie said.

"And don't neural security," she said. She winced. "There's a block-fi, localized, I got..." she sighed and muttered something like 'lyric oil' or 'leery-co'. She looked painfully sad.

"You hurt your hand," Hargie said.

The woman almost replied, but then the pod lurched to a standstill. It near-threw them out of their chairs. The woman sat back upright and trained the gun on him.

"See?" Hargie said with a smile. "Not a funny move on me." He just wanted out of the pod. He'd evade her later.

She sensed truth in his words, Hargie was sure. Leastways, she got up and went to see why the pod had stopped.

Hargie could have told her: the weirdos must have cut the power. But she'd figure that soon enough.

The woman stared out of the end window, back in the direction of the old corvette. She muttered something in a tongue not Anglurati.

"A problem?" he asked.

"It is a chase now," she said, still gazing out.

Hargie stood up and looked. He couldn't see anything unusual.

"What?" he said. "No other pods out there."

"They're on foot."

Hargie ambled to the window, a liberty the woman seemed too occupied to take offence at. It was then Hargie saw it: a black figure walking along the bottom left cable like a tightrope walker. No net save the endless void.

"They can't get in here," Hargie said.

"Not the plan," the woman said. "They've a gun."

"It'd bounce off the glass," Hargie said.

"Press a compaction muzzle hard against it, fire on full power and tell me again."

"Right," Hargie said. "Wouldn't that kill them too? Maybe?"

"Look at them, idiot," she said. "Do you think self-preservation their key skill?"

The figure was a little closer. The daughter. Hargie recognised the black bodysuit, now complete with helmet. Her progression wasn't fast—why should it be?—but it was the diligence that unnerved, the casual comfort.

"Surrender?" Hargie offered.

"Idiot," the woman said.

"No, really," Hargie said. "We just drop the gun and wave to her."

"Good idea," she said. "Let's wave with her dead father's burnt hand over there."

"Point taken."

The woman stomped away from the window and began to pace around the cabin-pod's interior, her head down. She was like a... well, *caged animal* wasn't the sort of imagery Hargie needed to contemplate right then.

The woman growled to herself. "Oh, fine then!" she barked at no one. "Why *ever* not!"

"Why what?" Hargie asked.

The woman ignored him. She appeared to freeze up a moment, rocking on her heels. Then she spun to face Hargie. She gave him the loveliest smile, a railgun shot through Hargie's heart. He wouldn't have thought her capable.

"Hey," she said. "Could you hold this a moment?"

She offered him her pistol. Confused, he took it.

"Thanks," she said. With that, she pulled a handheld from her jacket and started scanning the fixtures.

What was this? Hargie had the gun now.

He had to think this over.

Yes, empathic rationalism, the way of his forefathers. He looked out at Illik's daughter. If he were her, what would he do? Vengeance. Sheer bloody vengeance, no matter who got in the way. Like he was long meant to be doing, he thought.

He turned to face the woman, who now had her back to him, bent over, trying to dislodge a seat cushion.

Shoot her. Just shoot her. She wouldn't know. This was a him-or-her scene, bet your ball sack, Jack. He could... well, he could lift her body up to the window and Illik's daughter would know, and she and her brother would see Hargie was on the level, that he honoured their father or at least his money. Really, what choice was there?

He lifted the pistol and aimed. Then he positioned himself in a dramatic pose so that Illik's daughter—Zo, was it Zo? Lovely Zo—would see him shoot.

Wait. He might shoot through the hull. No. No, velocity too low. She'd already used it just now in the cargo bay, no problem.

Shoot her. Stop groping for excuses, shoot. Hargie aimed again. Cry later.

Wait. Why'd she pass him the gun, anyhow? Which was to say, if *Hargie* were *her,* why would he pass a damn gun? Good question. Well... well, there must be a lot of elements Hargie wasn't privy to. Elements that would make undeniable sense if Hargie were her. But what?

She trusted him, he realised. Trust.

Hargie lowered the pistol.

"What are you doing?" he asked her.

"This model of cable-pod," the woman explained, "is built in a certain system." She got the cushion off and threw it to one side. "There's a regular world there, and another where humans have fixed themselves to breathe 'dioxide. For that system's rigs, then, the life support needs to be a little more hands on. Mm-yes." She stood up and pointed at the seat with her good hand. "Could you shoot this off?"

He offered her the gun.

"Oh no, I'm useless with those things," she said.

Hargie didn't know what to say to that. He set his mind to the task. There was a lid on the white metal of the seat, with an inbuilt lock. Hargie braced, then fired. He fired again. The lock flew off.

"Thank you," said the woman, and she knelt down once more. She flipped open the lid and waved her handheld over the tiny processor inside. She ran a hack. Had to feel sorry for her, using a handheld in a neural age. Allergic to the 'ware. Shitty deal.

"Sit down," she told him.

The cable-pod began to roll forward. Hargie had expected to be thrown back in a sudden burst of momentum. No such. A tortoise-crawl.

"Engine damaged?" he said, sitting down.

"No," she replied, sitting next to him. "I've uncoupled our air supply. That's what's propelling the pod now."

"Clever. I think."

"Best to stop talking now," the woman told him. "Not much air."

Hargie opened his mouth. Then he closed it. The pair of them gazed out of the rear window. Illik's daughter wasn't out there on her tightrope anymore. Hargie looked quizzically at the woman.

"Whoosh," the woman said and she made a tiny Illik's daughter of her hand, cartwheeling off into a figurative eternity. Nasty.

The woman put her palm out and waited. Shrugging, Hargie gave back the gun. In return, the woman picked up Illik's scorched hand—her earlier squeamishness had vanished—and placed it in Hargie's jacket pocket. Hargie shuddered.

She smiled. "Analysis," she said.

An hour or so later, Hargie was surprised to find he still lived when the cable-pod docked with the rig's terminal zone. The pair of them lay on the floor by then, gasping for breath.

"Sparkuh..." the woman said as the doors whirled open and air rushed in.

"Whu..." Hargie said.

"Sparkle. Name's Sparkle. That's the name. Sparkle."

"Oh."

"Sparkle."

SPARKLE HAD TO HAND it to that little slouching rodent of a man: he was a sort of artist. Somehow he'd manipulated the innards of his ship into a compelling abstract portrait of the feral mind. An installation piece in dust, gloom, and mechanical odour.

"Cockpit's through here," he told her, pointing to a bulkhead along the corridor. "But feel free to kick back in the lounge."

Sparkle had seen the lounge. It boasted a table, whose apparent sole function was displaying various planets' takeaway wrappers, and a large brown object that had recanted its sofa origins.

"Er..."

:Stay with him in the cockpit, idiot,: Swirl sent to Sparkle.

"I'll come see where it all happens," Sparkle told Hargie. "If it's all the same to you."

"You pay, you say," he replied. He looked at her a moment. "You're still paying, right?"

"Please, I'm not all pistol-whips and glares." She patted the pistol in her jacket pocket, if only to keep Swirl happy. In truth, she was surprised the man hadn't demanded it off her now they were aboard. "One lakh fifty. Another seven on reaching Calran."

"Appreciated," he said as he placed his thumb on her handheld and accepted the down payment. He had to be half a foot shorter than Sparkle. "Those people back there, no idea who they are. Just a job."

"You said." Sparkle flashed him a smile. "And I believe you." Smiles were free, after all.

They reached the bulwark and the cockpit hatch whirled open. The oppressively gloomy theme continued inside. Driest air, a tomb. The little rat stepped through and the lights shrugged into life.

The cockpit was geodic in shape, a mausoleum of gunmetal plating, pipes and dials. She had thought the rig vile, but here was a display of bare functionality so wanton as to leave Sparkle profoundly, desolately homesick. But all this was a mere frame for the... *thing* at the cockpit's epicentre.

It took Sparkle a moment to realise it was a chair, presumably fashioned by some dentist with pretensions of gynaecology. Or torture. It had ribcage-like rows of manacles on each arm and leg rest—the leg rests horizontal with the floor and slightly splayed—and a neck brace blemished with holographic displays. Two brutal needles on robotic arms rose from the chair's back.

The little rat hopped into the chair. None of its features moved, thankfully.

"Where do I sit?" Sparkle asked.

"The lounge," he said. "Typically. But there's like this fold-out chair in that pile over there."

Sparkle walked over to the 'pile,' an aggregation of detritus leaning up against a dank metal wall. She began to search through it.

:Never turn your back on him,: Swirl sent.

:Trust me, Sis. For once?: Sparkle sent.

:Forgive my cynicism, Sparks, but you handed him our gun earlier. Remember that? He tries anything, I take the reins.:

:I can handle myself...: Sparkle sent.

She put her hand on something like putty. Old chewing gum trapped between two wooden boards. "Ugh..."

:You have my fullest confidence,: Swirl sent.

:Fuck you.:

Sparkle pulled out an offensively ugly folding chair, opened it, and placed it to the right of the man's own seating abomination. She wiped the fabric seat with her chewing-gum hand and sat down. "Well, go then," she said.

The little rat shrugged and squinted, and metal closed around his arms, legs and throat.

"Think I could have some sort of visual here?" Sparkle asked.

The man squinted again, and a holographic screen flashed into life before Sparkle. The ship's prow view: the sterns of other craft directly ahead, each with a flex-pipe trailing into the rig. Each fixed to its great frame. Beyond all that lay a blackness peppered with light.

"Name's Hargie, by the way," he told her.

His loathsome ship released the flex-pipe and broke away from the rig.

PRINCESS FLOOFY travelled two klicks out. Far away enough to bubble, which was seldom all that long. His veins nuzzled for that sweet hit of jumpjunk.

He had everything laid out in aug-real, his neuralware providing a set of windows—ACC, TORQ, GZG—that floated before his eyes.

At forty klicks from the rig, Hargie shut down the engines and applied counter-thrust. *Princess Floofy* hung in the big empty.

"Have we stopped?" Sparkle said. "Why have we stopped?"

"I'll need more than money," Hargie said.

Sparkle's brow creased. "I'll shoot you."

"Save a round for yourself. You ain't a hope of shifting this baby. Or calling for help. You'll find dry supplies in storage, cold takeaway in the lounge. And my corpse, of course. That's what? Three months."

She kept her face blank. "What is it you want?"

Hargie let the moment hang a while. "The deal."

Her eyes went wide. She fumbled the pistol out of her pocket, nearly letting it fall. So artless compared to earlier. Scared. She pointed the muzzle at him.

"I mean the deal with what happened back on the corvette," he said. "The freaky shit. The blue light."

"Yes, well," she said, relaxing. "I can see why that might stick in your mind. But first tell me everything you know about your employers back there."

"Their kink for not shoving guns in my face comes to mind."

Sparkle lowered the pistol.

"Appreciated," Hargie said. "Like I said: I know almost zilch. They're a family. They wanted to meet you. They're rich without due care or attention. Oh, and father supposed meeting you would be a kind of... anthropology."

"Anthropology?" She let the word float, as if studying it.

"Now you," Hargie said.

She settled back in her seat, looking up at the ceiling as if she was about to faint. Her limbs tightened, seizing up.

When she looked at Hargie again, it was with a stare that pierced. "Do you know of the Harmonies?"

"Never travelled that far along the spire," Hargie said. "No call for bubblefolk, way I hear."

"We are a star-nation nurtured by gods," she said. "Real gods, not some fancy of an infantile culture. Their vision guides us."

"I'll level with you," Hargie said. "This ain't a cracking kickoff."

"You don't believe me?" Sparkle said.

"Throw a unicorn in the mix, see if that works," he said.

"*Aliens*, then," Sparkle said. "Aliens who achieved a singular godhood aeons ago. We call them Hoidrac, 'the Delighted Ones': they are keepers of a dual reality, our own and the Geode."

Her face: so cold, so alien without her smile.

"I have no idea who your employers were back there," she said. "But I know this much," and a sober pride filled her eyes, "the Hoidrac care who they are. They acted *through* me, you see." She lifted her hand, now wrapped in medibands. "This wound opened a brief portal between here and that other real. In that sacred moment some, some... *essence* of your employer fell into me. I've no idea what. I cannot feel it now. But clearly the Hoidrac want it. I have to get home. To the Harmonies."

Hargie took a long breath, then laughed.

"WHAT, YOU'VE A BETTER explanation?" Swirl said. Her lips rolled back with anger, but she controlled it.

"Try this," the bubbleman said. "Those freaks back there drugged the shit out of us and, I dunno, recorded it all so they could jack off of an evening."

He gave Swirl a look. "You know, Sparkle... you may still be coming down. Just sayin'."

"Idiot," she said. "His burnt hand is *still* in your pocket!"

"Oh yeah," the bubbleman, Hargie, said. He frowned at the thought. "Well, a prosthetic, maybe. A gen job."

Swirl groaned and fell back in her chair.

:A noble attempt,: Sparkle sent, *:foiled only by the fact it was shit. You've had your shot at the holy angle, Sis. Now let me try, eh?:*

:But it's the truth, Sparkle.: Swirl sent.

:Your point being?:

Swirl gave up, and Sparkle took control of their body once more. Whatever. Swirl was in no mood to reason further, especially with that ignorant smelly feral.

"Look," Sparkle said to the cretin, "it's obvious you think I'm mad. Fine. Maybe I am. But people want to *kill* me, Hargie. You saw that yourself." She leaned forward, eyes widening. "*Please*... I need your help."

:Oh, very classy,: Swirl sent to Sparkle.

:Give it a moment.:

"You're still going to pay me, right?" Hargie said.

:See?: Sparkle sent. "Of course," she assured him.

"Sorry about your friend," Hargie said.

"What?" Sparkle said.

:He means Lyreko, Sparkle,: Swirl sent, *:Lyreko, remember? Damn you.:*

"Oh yes," Sparkle said aloud. She looked down at her own knees. "I haven't really... processed it yet, you know? But he will be with me always. Always."

Swirl seethed.

:The greatest tragedy of my life, Sparkle: she sent, *:is I cannot punch you in the face without hurting myself.:*

YOU DUMB BASTARD, Hargie told himself. He'd rather she'd just pay cash than this eyelash game, this pulling at pity. *Think you've got me on a string, don't you, girl?* Only she did. Just not the one she thought.

Atonement was a bitch.

The cockpit bit at his neuralware. An alert.

"Are you fine?" Sparkle asked.

Hargie ignored her. He closed his eyes, spread all his senses across a light-minute radius.

"Fuck..." he muttered.

The vast orbital rig's engines had died. All its engines: every single fusion source in every ship attached to the thing. Impossible.

"Hargie?"

Ten thousand locked rooms, dead locks, air con dying...

"We have to go back," Hargie said. "Gotta help."

"What are you talking about?" Sparkle said.

He changed her screen to a viz of the rig, stats listed on one side.

"What?" Sparkle said. "How can that even happen?"

"EMP, maybe." But pulsers didn't come that big. That *good.*

Hargie recalled something. He brought up cartography. Yes: a rock belt, deep and thick and vicious.

"Heading for rocks," Hargie said. "Shields gone..." It would look like an accident.

"We are not going back," Sparkle said.

"Not up for debate," he said.

"You mistake me." She pulled out her pistol and aimed at his head. Again.

"Thought you were useless with those." Damn it, she was, wasn't she? Some fucking consistency from the woman. Was that asking too much?

Her expression had shifted again, too, the warmth all gone. "I adapt," she said.

The animal in Hargie screamed to do as she said, just run. He pictured the round going through his temple. Then he pictured humans stumbling, shouting in the dark. Kids asking mothers questions they couldn't answer. Scores of them. Right now, happening now.

He grit his teeth. "I die, you starve," he said. "Did we not just have this conversation?"

"This primitive pile of filth?" Sparkle said, eyeing the walls. "I'll find a way. You have no idea how capable we are in the Harmonies."

"Who-blinks-first, huh? I can play that—"

A feeling went through Hargie like he was one big funny bone. A warning symbol flew into his vision.

Explosion. Small craft. Five klicks distant, between *Princess* and the rig.

"What?" Sparkle said. "What's... give me a, a visual."

He did. He pulled another up for himself, a window that obscured the earlier warning sign still floating in his vision.

Princess Floofy simulated what it could: plasma, debris, the prow of a small black ship, the image too blurry to judge its make. All about the wreck, grey blotches; some objects *Princess* couldn't process.

"Whatever's neutralised the rig is now killing any witnesses," Sparkle told him. "Anyone trying to escape. Run. Run, you rodent!"

Damn it. Hargie engaged the bubblecoil. He felt the twin hypodermics sink into his neck studs, felt the sweet quantum rush, the junk. Forgot the dying. Home again. *Princess Floofy* punched a gravitic tube through reality and scarpered out of the Eucrow system.

Three

EMISSARY MELID PROPELLED HERSELF ALONG the access tube, handrail to handrail, bulkhead to bulkhead, floating headfirst in a fresh uniform with a dignity more performed than felt. Her first time upon a true Instrum-craft. A serious matter, doubtless.

She stopped herself before the entrance to the social core. Too quickly, in her nervousness. Her palms and wrists strained against the handrail, against the halted momentum.

She opened her awareness to the craft's local kollective, that ceaseless confluence of its crew's streams of consciousness. They were waiting for her and, in so doing, had already sensed Melid's trepidation. Inevitable, of course. Such was life. She hoped they would pick up on that last sentiment too.

She floated through the entrance. Inside, the core was spherical, some seven meters in diameter and, unlike the social cores of home, plated with rectangles of scarlet metal.

Its current occupants were equally imposing in the subdued light: Craft-Emissary Gei and Field-Instrums Zo and Doum. Black uniforms all, tight and glistening. They had all chosen seat-pits that ran along the social core's equator. All sitting the same way up, like a meeting on ancient Earth.

"Welcome, Emissary," Gei greeted her. He emoted a professional warmth.

The other two said nothing. They emoted nothing.

"Craft-Emissary." Melid took a seat-pit on the other side of the equator, facing them. Its muscleform padding coiled around her back and haunches, fixing her in place.

An odd sort of humidity to this core, Melid thought, hotter than that of civilian installations. Perhaps the Instrum preferred it that way. They had a 'way,' all right. This meeting, whatever it was about, could as easily be held through the ship's own kollective. Yes, over-reliance on such communication led to softness—unquestionably—and from there on to the erosion of individuality itself and subsequent kancerisation. But there was something about the Instrum's insistence on face-to-face encounters that went—

She reined in her thoughts.

"Uploading Domov," Gei said, choosing not to comment on Melid's sentiments. Experienced enough to pay no mind, Melid thought. From Instrum Zo—with her hair cut in such a brutal manner it simply had to be part of her field cover—Melid sensed a well-muted but increasingly pulsing distain. Doum, muscles bulging beneath his uniform, remained a curious blank, a dull throb.

The Domov materialised at the epicentre of the core, head-relative to its audience. A male figure with shaved head and high cheekbones, its assigned appearance was the Konsensus citizen archetype: lithe with pale skin and epicanthic eyelids. It, too, wore a black uniform.

Domovoi-composite, name-assigned 'Conybeare,' it said. Am non-aware aggregation: all situation-aware individuals, all situation-relevant information combined. Situation restricted, foremost level.

It turned to face Melid. Emissary-inactive Melid, it said, Instrum selects you: coordinate situation in-field. Reason: locality, prior experience. Emissary status activated. Effective immediately. Prepare receive: full-status plus records.

Her 'prior experience'? A Scalpel incident, then, those mysterious beasts of the void. Melid had thought the like might never come.

The situation came wave by wave, through the receptors of Melid's spinemarrow and up through the hypothalamus. Higher, higher into her awareness.

Illik was dead. She recalled him watching the great scalpels bathe amid the stars, their distant silhouettes flickering in the light of a pulsar. Later: Illik's whispered words, his wisdom. His touch.

She looked around the core. The others studied her emotional responses: Gei with objectivity, Zo with... *hunger.*

Melid held back her tears, let them become anger, and then anger became resolve. This sudden reveal, she sensed, was no accident on the part of the Instrum. It was a test.

"Understood," she said.

The situation congealed in her consciousness. An encounter aboard this star system's local 'rig': an explosive singularity resulting in Illik's death, two escaped Worlders (and Zo's failure to terminate them. Melid felt a childish glee at that, and did not care if Zo and everyone else knew she did). Also, some form of drug. Illik, it seemed, had believed this drug and the Scalpels in some way connected. Strange. Interesting.

It got more so: a Scalpel apparition had occurred.

Having neutralised the fusion cores of the Worlder rig, an Instrum-craft (Hunter-Killer class) had turned its attention to the two fleeing individuals in their small craft (a '*bubbleship*' in Worlder language, weaponless, but jump-capable).

The Hunter-Killer had achieved target-lock but, at exactly that instant, a Scalpel (apparition-type 9) had manifested behind the H-K and discharged its inscrutable weapons.

Remarkable. A rarity against any vessel. Unprecedented against a Konsensus craft.

The Hunter-Killer's prow had survived intact. Crew could yet still live. Yet the H-K's Craft-Emissary, for reasons unclear, had elected to lock off his craft's local kollective from the Kollective-at-Large. Curious, that. Unnerving.

"Thoughts?" Gei asked the room.

Melid looked around her. She knew what everyone in the social-core thought of her: trained but untried, a maladjusted Scalpel-chaser from Silvercloud kollective.

"Examine," she said, visualising a Hunter-Killer so the rest would too. "*Bubbleship* trail lost. Wreck only lead."

Was it worth chasing two ignorant Worlders, despite their connection to this drug of Illik's? A Scalpel had never attacked a Konsensus craft before, had never so much as acknowledged their existence. Illik would have understood.

The others noted her compulsions.

Contamination possibility, the Domov Conybeare, told her.

The room felt its meaning. The Hunter-Killer must have had a good, and singular, reason to lock off. After all, it had been compromised by an inhuman force. Any cadre investigating might have to be vaporised along with the wreck.

"I volunteer," Melid said. "Take Zo, Doum. Others." She waited for Zo to emote the barest sliver of fear. None came. Field-Instrums were a most singular bunch.

Agreed, Conybeare said.

Later, alone, Melid wept.

She closed her eyes and diluted her personality into the Kollective-at-Large, that vast sea of minds. Her emotions shrank into a comfortable and familiar inconsequence. Melid was but a grain of dust inside a nova, a nova with purpose. Compared with the arc of Konsensus history—and its future—her selfhood was inconsequential. She was just a tool.

An instrument.

"HARGIE?"

Sparkle knocked again. No answer. She stood by his cabin door, uncertain what to do next. The steel corridor echoed with machine noises: engines, life support. Faint, constant.

:Leave it, Sparkle,: Swirl sent. *:You're bothering him because you're listless.:*

:He's our pilot,: Sparkle replied. *:We need him on point. Or whatever the term is.:*

:Not mid-transit. Another three days until we come out.:

"Don't remind me," Sparkle said.

"Hey." Hargie's voice from behind the door.

"Hargie?" Sparkle said.

"What ya talking 'bout?" Hargie said.

"Nothing," Sparkle said. "You all right in there?"

"Not now," he said. "Go away."

:Do as he says,: Swirl sent.

:Maybe.: Sparkle sent. *:It's just, well... a thing I read about. They inject quantumphetamine to bubble-jump. Those needles in their necks...:*

:And?:

:They come down bad.: Sparkle sent. *:Depressed.:*

:Such concern for a feral.: Swirl sent.

:Least I don't fuck them.: A silence in her head followed, quiet as the corridor she stood in. *:Sorry. No call for that. Lyreko was a good man.:*

:No, he wasn't,: Swirl sent. *:We both know that.:*

Sparkle looked at the cabin door and shook her head. "Fuck this moron."

She walked back down the corridor and entered the lounge with its overhead strip-light. She fell on the dilapidated sofa-thing. Swirl had gone on a formidable cleaning spree in there, much to Sparkle's relief, though she'd never admit as much.

:Must be horrific,: Swirl sent.

"What is?" Sparkle said. "Use our mouth. Easier."

"One mind, one skull," Swirl said. "What does he—any of them—do about that? You know, all those thoughts and doubts. Like being trapped on an empty ship."

"Right now I can see the benefits," Sparkle said.

"Woman," Swirl said, "you are getting seriously cranky,"

"And who beat the fridge up yesterday morning?"

"It wouldn't close," Swirl said.

"Well, it's certainly closed now." Sparkle pulled her dreads back, held them in place with a band from her pocket. "Door falls off otherwise."

"What *is* your problem?" Swirl said.

"I'm *bored*." Sparkle said.

"How about we watch something on the handheld?" Swirl said.

"Same old shit."

"Early dinner?"

"Same old shit." Sparkle said.

Their shared lips didn't move for a while. Sparkle fixed her ponytail.

"Well," Swirl said, "I could always go to the villa for a half hour, let you... you know."

"*No*."

"It's just if we schedule for that round about now, we—"

"*No*," Sparkle said. "And you know why? Because you want me to fucking 'schedule' it. I mean, shit, what's next? List my fantasies in bullet point?"

"Forget I said anything," Swirl said.

Sparkle slapped her forehead. "I cannot... I *will not* believe we're reduced to this conversation." She sighed. "Five days. Five. If it wasn't for that bipolar dickhead's neuralware, there'd be things to do on this ship. To occupy us. I mean, what does he expect his passengers—"

"Sparkle—"

"How much leaf do we have left?" The question she'd wanted to ask. She braced for the answer.

"No, Sparkle," Swirl said. "We have to ration."

"I'm going to murder someone," Sparkle said. "Anyone. I just am. Murder them right in the face."

Sparkle felt her lips twitch. Her vision blurred.

:Let me use our arms,: Swirl sent.

Sparkle let her. She closed her watering eyes and felt her hands grasp her shoulders. They embraced her with a hug.

:It's all right, Spar-ki-dar, it's all right.:

"Haven't called me that since we were children..."

:Love you, sis.: Swirl sent.

MEMORIES. BEDCLOTHES. How long had he lain there, waiting for the bedroom to feel truly real again, for any of it to matter?

Hargie picked at his nose, inspected it, rubbed it into the headboard. He thought of that bright day back when he was... what? Twelve? Why think of that?

Flags, snapping and dancing in the breeze. Sunlight baking the tops of bubbleships. So many colours. He hadn't seen flags before that day. Not a bubblefolk thing. Not for centuries.

He hadn't stood next to Father as he spoke. He, his mother and his sister had watched from the crowd—so many bubblefolk that day—and had thought nothing of that. Only as an adult had Hargie understood that Father had no time for dynasties. Had never wanted to rule, just do what he could. Anything else put his family in harm's way.

Father made the crowds cheer at any word starting with 'bubble', made them hiss and rattle at 'Freightways' or 'Raichundalia'. He didn't appeal to anger. He appealed to a reason arising from anger. There were non-bubblefolk in the crowd. Supporters. Media. A fine day. Go figure.

Arise. A people once great can be so again. Had Father said that? Or was Hargie filling a gap?

Arise. He knew he should. He activated his neuralware which, he told himself, was like arising. The destroyed ship back at the rig was bugging him, had bugged him all morning now. He wanted to know the make. Hargie knew just about every make of ship, was still his twelve-year-old self in that sense. He brought up *Princess'* augmented footage on his 'ware.

A black, sleek prow. Rest of the ship nothing but an explosion. He ran the timeline back.

Before the explosion occurred, no ship had existed in that patch of space. Nothing. *Princess Floofy*'s AI had messed up, surely. Maybe some glitch leaving *Princess* blind to anything in its own wake? Ships didn't just materialise out of nowhere, certainly not with the express purpose of obliterating themselves.

Some poor bastards with a cheap detritus field. Had to be. Hit a rock. Shit for luck.

But a ship like that, with a prow like that? Hargie would have seen it on the rig. He'd remember something with that prow.

He removed deep space from the image, transed the exploding ship into a 3D model that floated before his eyes. Something wasn't right. The explosion had a trail on its underside, long and straight, as of something tearing through, dragging the trail and shrapnel with it. A projectile.

Couldn't be a micro. The rig wouldn't have handed out shipping lanes with super-fast rock. So a weapon. Someone cleaning witnesses, just like Sparkle said.

Out through the underside, in through the roof. He followed the trajectory up, up above the sharp black ship, up to whatever had fired. Hargie felt an exhilaration he hadn't in days.

Nothing. Damn.

Wait: red shift. Take the light from the stars and intensify. Up, up.There. A silhouette. Tall, thin, a humped back.

If this were a ship, if he wasn't seeing things in nothing, then it looked like nothing he knew. No one built craft on a vertical axis. The silhouette reminded Hargie of something. What were those creatures he'd seen in that market on Rashik Ben, bobbing about in their tank? Seahorses? That the name? The silhouette was a seahorse, a seahorse with a sail down its back. Something about it... the shape itself... beautiful...

He ran the film back, played it slow. A corona of grey—that stuff *Princess* couldn't process—then the silhouette, then another corona, then gone. Deep space.

Hargie swallowed his ship-spotter pride and decided to run the two unidentified objects through a shared database he'd downloaded off the memestream. The prow of the exploded ship matched no design it carried, not even any conversion job.

For kicks, Hargie ran the image through the crank files: eyeball sightings of unidentified stellar objects. Transpired black diamond-shaped hulls were a running theme in boozy oddball spacer world: a whole stream of illustrations and 3D models fell into Hargie's vision, plus sketches of bizarre alien occupants, often with shiny black skin, thin bodies and faceless heads. Gibberish. Ratshit.

He took the other ship, the attacking silhouette, and put that in. No point running that seahorse motherfucker through official designs. Just for kicks, just to keep this new energy in him rising.

Just one file: a charcoal sketch found in the bubbleship of a suicide. A seahorse-shape, anorexic, with a spiny sail down its back. Horns, too, atop its head. It sent a shiver through Hargie. He wasn't sure why. Some dream, maybe, beyond recollection.

More. Photo-images of the bubble suicide's cockpit. None of the body, which Hargie, in his mood, was thankful for. But all over the walls of the 'pit, one word again and again in oil. *Foozle*.

Ice water ran through the marrow of his spine. Foozle... the Great Foozle. The beast itself, the vacuum-made-flesh. He made the ward-sign over his chest with his right hand (always use the right hand). He winced, couldn't help himself.

A knock. Hargie jolted.

"Hargie?" came Sparkle's voice through the door. "Hargie, I was going to make food. I know it's early, but..."

His heart hammered like a pulsar. He took a deep breath.

"Hargie?" she said.

"It's fine."

He looked at the sketch again. Foozle. Shit, he didn't hold with that stuff.

But, shit, who was this woman, anyway? Mass murder and shadows trailing in her wake. Something unnatural about her. Creepy. Hargie couldn't put a finger on it.

"You don't want me to zap some noodles for you, then?" she asked.

Fuck no. "Not hungry."

"No problem. We'll schedule dinner for later, shall we?" She paused. "I can wait."

Hargie gulped.

MELID STUDIED THE HUNTER-Killer's wreck. Her consciousness, merged with the hauler's sensors, had a clear view of the wreck's upper surface.

The entire aft had disintegrated. The cleanliness of a Scalpel's attack always impressed Melid. It was how they had earned their name.

Life support had held out in the prow. Melid studied the severed wound: it had been sealed off, but the outlines of torn rooms and tunnels were visible beneath the ever-growing layer of solidifying hoxnites. Other sealant clouds had drifted off into space, searching for the half of the wreck that no longer existed.

There were patches of Unreal: the energy that emanated from Scalpels, if energy it could be called. The Hauler's sensors could not replicate the image of it (nor could Konsensus eyes and brains, worryingly), instead displaying featureless grey patches here and there about the prow's hull. The patches shrank and grew, as if breathing.

The four Assault-Instrums floating beside her rippled with an anxiety bridled only by their training. Melid hoped her knowledge of the Scalpels might allay that anxiety, lend the cadre some facts she might cling to. It was all Melid had herself.

"Ready," said Doum to no one. If the two Field-Instrums were nervous, they kept it bound within their own individualities. Leastways, it didn't show in the cadre's local kollective.

Melid opened her eyes, and the vision of the wreck disappeared. It was replaced with the tight interior of the hauler bay and Zo's face staring at her.

Zo thought Melid a liability, cargo at best. Melid couldn't mistake the sentiments rising from the Field-Instrum as anything else. Zo's grin, at least, vanished when the muscleform of her black encounter-suit grew a helmet over her head.

Melid's did the same, and for a moment her world became tight and lightless. Then the air supply kicked in, followed by the suit's area-awareness, and she felt as though she wore no suit at all.

A dull thud: the Hauler's airlock connecting with the wreck's.

The muscleform airlock stretched open. Beyond it lay an access tube. No lights.

The first two Assault-Instrums swam through the airlock, their rifles' barrels pointing ahead. Five seconds passed, then Zo and Doum followed.

Melid's turn. She could feel the two remaining Assaults behind her, their patience melting to concern. She took a breath, accessed her suit's thrusters—no scenario for handrails, this—and propelled herself forward, into the access tube.

She adjusted the suit's awareness, adding a little infrared. Better. The access tube appeared unaffected by the Scalpel's touch. But for the dead lights and detritus—food pouches, mainly—it could have been any craft.

She visualised aiming for the Craft-'Emissary's cockpit, and the cadre acknowledged her order.

The two Assaults ahead intimated a door was jammed.

Blow it, Melid directed.

They fixed a charge, and everyone curled into an embryonic position, the muscleform of their suits hardening into armour. Melid didn't even sense the blast. She only knew it had worked when a flat grey nothing glared from behind the door's shredded muscleform.

The entire cadre rippled with apprehension. Even Zo and Doum.

Proceed, Melid directed. The two forward Assaults propelled through the doorway, rifles ready, Zo covering them with her pistol.

A severed hand floated past Melid. Bloodless, freeze-dried. No sign of its owner.

The tube was illuminated by fluctuating patches of Unreal, the metal plating of the walls riddled with pools of flat grey. Scalpel-energy, the Unreal, was actually a strange kind of blue light, if Worlder reports were to be believed.

But to Konsensus eyes it wasn't replicable; the brain's kollective program simply couldn't render it. Alien, utterly alien.

Avoid walls, Melid directed. The cadre didn't need to be told. They floated through, thrusters at lowest setting, limbs tight to their bodies.

A muted thud rang down the tube, shaking the bulwarks. The tube began to revolve around the cadre.

Air discharge, weapons section, Conybeare's calm voice stated in her suit's com. *Wreck in spin.*

Move, Melid ordered.

Thrusters on full now. The tube's walls circled around her in swirls of flat grey and gunmetal. Diving forward, limbs in, diving, diving. Neuro-static stabbing at her mind, shouting over coms. Then nothing. Someone's terror cut short.

They gathered in the gloom of the large multi-junction at the tube's end. No Unreal there. Headcount: two Assaults, then Zo, Doum, Melid.

She thrust around to face the access tube they had come from. Where were the rear Assaults?

Just one, accelerating toward them in what seemed like panic. But they couldn't *feel* that panic. They felt nothing from their comrade.

"Report," Melid said, using the vocal com.

The panicked Assault—Sen—applied counter-thrust, coming to a stop just before the others.

Sen stared at them through the glassform lens of her suit's helmet. Her eyes were wide, weeping. She held her right hand behind her back.

"*Est nisi cadavera quae lacerantur*," she said, "*aut corvi qui lacerant.*"

Gibberish. Sen was just... making sounds.

"What?" Melid said over her com. "Not understand: Kollective disconnect." Communication by voice alone was frustrating, nigh-impossible.

Sen raised her arm before her face and stared. No hand. Merely a wrist. No cut, no suit-rupture. The stump smouldered blank grey.

"*Aut corvi qui lacerant,*" Sen repeated, her voice shaking, trying to be understood. Unconnected, like a breathing corpse.

Conybeare, Melid called out to the Domov, *injury*. "Med cadre req—"

Sen's head flew off at the jaw, tearing off the muscleform helmet that contained it. Sen's body cartwheeled backwards.

Necessary, Zo sentimented to the rest of the cadre, checking her spent pistol.

A mercy, Melid thought. Yes. She watched Sen's head sail down the contaminated tube, blood trailing behind it. It hit a patch of Unreal on the wall and vanished. The Unreal had *swallowed* it. The other Assault must have been swallowed whole. But where to? A chill passed through Melid.

Onwards, Melid ordered them all. It was all she could think to do.

The tube leading upwards was uncontaminated and utterly dark, were it not for the 'cadre's infrared. They stopped before the hatch to the Emissary's pit. Air in there, Melid's suit informed her. A heat signature. No konnection.

Sphere, Melid ordered one of the two remaining Assaults. He fixed a field-charge to the hatchway and activated it. A transparent bubble—oil-patterned—bloomed out of the charge, covering the hatchway. Air pressure now assured, the two Assaults opened the hatch. The others covered them.

Silence. At Melid's direction, the cadre entered.

The Craft-Emissary—male, ageing—lay in his pit, fixed in place by a rippling corona of shiny black muscleform. Giant black spinal columns ran out from the pit in all directions, rising up the walls of the core and disappearing into armour-plated sphincters, all of it lifeless, inert.

"Who there?" the Craft-Emissary said. No emotion or sentiment arose with his words. His face was a talking death-mask, capable of words alone.

Melid thrust toward him until she floated directly above. His eyes showed no recognition.

"Rescue-cadre," Melid told him. "You blind?"

"Yes," he whispered. "Diskonnected. Insane. Useless."

"What happened?" Melid asked.

"Craft nervous system: compromised. Disabled self from Kollective-at-Large."

Melid spied grey scalpel-energy flickering between the spinal discs of one of the columns.

"Before," the Emissary muttered, "before attack. Targeted bubbleship. Tracker-missile. Connected."

"Trail established?"

"Yes," he said. "Tracker-information stored. Remove, take."

"Yes, Emissary," Melid told him.

She braced herself for the required duty. Melid shaped the muscleform on her suit's index finger into a spike.

"I honour, Emissary," she told him. She drove the spike into the front of the Craft-Emissary's skull. Prizing her thumb in, she cracked the skull wide.

She could feel it: spherical, hard. The brain's kollective-organ. The information it held. Somewhere out there, a tracker device spoke of the bubble-ship and its occupants. Broadcast their every move.

A hunt, then. A hunt.

2. Desolation Row

Four

HARGIE FELT THE NEEDLES PULL OUT OF HIS neck-studs seconds after *Princess Floofy* broke through into regular space. Not even a shudder. Coming out of a bubble-jump was a lot easier than going in.

He checked his heart window: fast, but subsiding. Two more years and he'd have to buy another chainweave lining for his aorta. He felt drowsy, juice leaving his system, but not tired, not exactly. He'd drop Sparkle down on Desolation Row or wherever, take her lakh and fly the hell out. Sleep then.

"Hey," came her voice from behind him. His pulse signature on the heart window.

"Hey," Hargie said. He put his recent research, all that Great Foozle cackaroo, out of his mind.

He heard the door whirl and footsteps cross the floor. Sparkle wore a long t-shirt, her trousers seemingly having vanished. She was slouchier than he'd ever seen her, her arms crossed and shoulders hunched. She didn't look at him, just stared at the bare wall of the cockpit. 'She had something in her right hand.

"So," she said. "The ship made a different sound just now. Are we there?"

"What's with the dress down?" She had good legs: smooth, stately. Between all the gunfire and depression, Hargie hadn't noticed.

"Only one set of clothes when we ran, remember?" Sparkle said. "Rest is in the cleaner."

"Borrow some o' mine."

She grunted in an annoyed sort of way. "I really don't think they would fit me, do you?"

"Suppose not." Tall people: fuck 'em. "But, yeah, we're in the Calran system."

Upon hearing 'yeah,' Sparkle took the thing in her hand—a box—and opened it. She poured something into her palm and put it to her mouth. She swallowed. Her slouch melted into something more tranquil.

"High-fucking-time," she said. "This ship's an oubliette nailed to an engine."

"Can I quote you in our brochure?" Hargie said.

"You've a brochure?"

"With quotes like that? No way."

She laughed. "I've only seen Calran once before," she said. "Could we bring it up on a screen or something?"

She smiled and turned to face him. Whatever support she'd worn earlier was clearly now spinning around in the laundry room. Hargie had never understood other men's taste for lingerie. A woman in little but a tatty old top was a far more sensual prospect. That softness beneath. That... freedom...

"Doesn't matter if we can't," she said. "Just be nice to see. Wonder of the galaxy and all that."

"Erm, yeah..." He lifted his legs out of the supports and leaned forward into a hunching position, pretending to work on some dial. He didn't feel drowsy anymore.

He used his neuralware and brought up a panoramic. At once, the walls, floor and ceiling of the cockpit transformed to deep space.

Sparkle walked on stars. She looked down. For a moment, Hargie thought her lost in some thought, some sad memory. But then she grinned, and Hargie knew she stared in wonder. He hadn't seen that much lately.

He stood up, adjusted his lucky hat with the flaps, and gazed where she did.

"There it is," he said.

There it was, rendered in VR by the ship's sensors: Calran, the broken world. Desolation Row. He magnified it, and the planet filled the cockpit's floor.

Like all the great wonders of the universe, humans had nothing to do with it. Not at inception. Calran—not that anyone had called it that back then—had been an ordinary enough rocky planet until the Gerontic culture interfered. Not that they'd called themselves that. No one knew what they'd called themselves.

The planet's inner molten core lay exposed to the galaxy. The outer core had, presumably, just boiled away into the void long ago. That was marvel enough, of course, planetary cores being the ultimate shut-ins, yet Calran's thick, tanned crust had stuck around. Its tectonic plates hovered over the core at various heights, as if the planet was exploding in freeze-frame.

Humanity was apparent all over Desolation Row, but you had to squint to see it. Transport pipes, some thousands of kilometres in length, jutted out diagonally from one continental plate and then rose or fell into another, black hairlines warping in the core's heat waves. Traffic lanes of tungsteel-plated flyers went about their commute, their silhouettes like impurities in the yellow core's furnace. No piece of the crust's jigsaw was without gravity spikes, whole mountain ranges of them, each dwarfing the spikes back on Import. No overall plan, just gravity wherever it was needed. Some speckled the surfaces of the dusty plates; others lined their edges like the spines on some beast's back.

Sparkle whispered to herself, something in her people's tongue. She gestured to Hargie. "There. What's that?" she said, pointing at some detail.

He walked over to her and looked, saw a large shadow trawling high above all the commotion like some idle bird of prey.

"A fearzero," Hargie said. "Jugurtha class."

"A warship," she said.

"Yep. A bubble-drive can only propel a small ship like *Princess*. Fine to raid a system with, not enough to hold it." He smelled perfume on her, sweet and regal. He wondered where she'd got it from. "For that, you build a big-ass fearzero and squat where everyone can see you have power. In this instance, the Clan Combine. They rule here."

"The Freightways," she said, never looking up. "Mm-yes, a fearzero could fit in a Freightways box, I should think."

Hargie felt hot coals in his belly. "Well," he said, "those bastards are rewriting everything..."

She'd stopped listening, taken in by some detail of the fractured hemisphere below, lost in it: searching for a beauty Hargie couldn't comprehend. Her eyes watered, and he couldn't believe he'd feared her before.

"All yours, my lady," he said. "Which part do you wish to be taken to?"

She looked up. "The Freightways," she said.

"Freightways?"

"The one in orbit," she said. "I can direct you if you like."

"I know where it is, woman," he said. He shook his head.

"There a problem?"

"For bubblefolk, just a little. Freightways are crushing our way of life." He shrugged. "No biggie."

"They'd hurt you?"

"No; they'd be especially nice to me," he said. "Like all poisoners. Hang a mo-mo: how come you know about makes of cabin pods but not that?"

"I'm a polymath," she said. "Just an unorganized one." Sparkle gestured at the vivisected world beneath their feet. "We've come this far, Hargie, it—"

"And here I stop," Hargie said. "I'll drop you on Desolation at a plate-station, you can roll on from there."

"But—"

"I'll take fifteen percent off, how's that?" Hargie said.

"Harg—"

"Twenty."

"Hargie-I-can't-pay-you," she blurted out.

The words slapped the next offer out of his mouth.

"You can't pay me." Now he said it it made consummate sense. Why had he entertained anything else?

"Not personally," Sparkle said. "I'll need to speak to Fractile."

"What?"

"Regional leaf-coordinator," she said. "My dealer, you would say."

"And he's at Freightways?"

"The import zone there," she said. "Best place for his work."

"Obviously." Hargie closed his eyes. He didn't need the money now, Illik and his family had seen to that. He could relax for a year, let the jump-juices drain out. Man, that's where he belonged. But with that extra? Open a bar, maybe. Avoid bubblefolk.

"Well?" she asked.

He'd be rid of her, too. Rid of the shadows clinging to her. Rid of the dangers, her inconsistencies and ever-encroaching physicality. *Yes, do it,* Hargie thought. *Do it. Swallow your long-shrunken pride, spend an hour in that monstrosity, take the pay and fly on.*

He opened his eyes and looked at Sparkle.

"We couldn't call your dealer man?" he asked. "Get him to pick you up from Desolation?"

"He doesn't trust communication devices."

"Course not," Hargie said. "That'd be crazy."

MELID WATCHED THE SCALPEL bask. A Great-Sail, type 2a. She knew that without having to consult the Kollective-at-Large. All her own mind.

Illik floated ahead of her and the other students, his vac-suited form a silhouette against the filtered light of the blue giant, the Wolf-Rayet star.

"Note the Scalpel's draconian head," came Illik's voice through her suit's comms. He spoke in Anglurati, the Worlders' trade language. "Famous, of course. The dracocephalic archetype surfaces in every known human culture. Increasingly so, the farther up the galactic spire one travels."

Oh Illik, people would express back in Silvercloud, *many-words, little-emotic. Too long with Worlders.* Difficult, keeping up with his vocalisations. But worth it.

Melid pressed for a question.

"Melid," Illik said, exuding a mannered warmth: pride, perhaps, though not quite.

(And that part nearly burst the memory, caused Melid to perceive her body in its foetal position, hissed at by unceasing vapours. She had been too young then, in the memory—seventeen—to have had the full measure of Illik.)

"We watch with eyes now," she said. "Konsensus eyes... inferior." Melid faltered. She emoted apology, for Illik to carry on. "Illogical."

"Beyond illogical," Illik said. "A phenomenon that hints at some fundamental difference between observers, between standard humanity and we the improved. The Konsensus mind should be inferior in nothing. Yet in observing a Scalpel-beast, it would appear that we are. A disquieting thought."

He spun around with his thrusters to face his students.

"A disquieting thought each of you may consider from time to time," he said, "dispersed as you will be across the stars. *Happenstance*—that's a Worlder word, look it up—has placed your home kollective beside an oasis to these beasts."

Behind Illik, the great shadow loomed, framed in coldest blue.

"Are they an illusion, these entities?" Illik said. "Or more real than we can hope to perceive? Are we, if they note us at all, an illusion to them?"

The Scalpel turned away from the sun: no shadow now. Illuminated.

"Either way," young Melid said then, speaking Anglurati to impress Illik, struggling for her words not to be swallowed by her own wonder, "an illusion with teeth..."

The reminiscence eroded, a dust falling from her immediate perception into the depths of long-term memory. Warm vapours blasted at her limbs. She was floating inside an ablution sphere. She'd needed to refresh, clean herself.

Conybeare the Domov was calling at her, had interrupted her reverie.

"Yes?" she said. She allowed Conybeare's generated face to appear inches from her own. Its perfect skin freckled in the sphere's many vapour-jets.

Grav-buoy confirmation, it told her. Target signature arrival: central Calran sector.

Melid had thought it unlikely their quarry would re-emerge in the sector's most Worlder-populous system; but Conybeare, being a distillation of all personalities and information pertaining to the current concern, had been proven correct. Naturally.

Seven hours, Conybeare said before Melid had a chance to vocalise her next thought.

"Will prepare," she said.

You reverise, Conybeare said. Illik memories.

"Downtime," she replied. "Problem?"

Four times this journey, Conybeare said.

"Yes," she said, annoyed. "Strengthens. Resolves." In theory, one was used to the truth that the Konsensus could—should need warrant—inspect your memories. But as a citizen, a utile, it rarely occurred. Here, amid an Instrum concern, on an Instrum craft, it was a matter of course.

"You doubt?" she asked Conybeare. "Doubt me?" She felt childish. Children whined over their memories being inspected, not emissaries.

Doubt: human-term, the Domov told her. Domov not self-aware.

"You read mind," Melid said. She was tiring of her shower. "Why need speak?"

Human complete-read impossible, Conybeare said. Distance between mind and mouth. Border zone. Talk quantifies. Besides: feeling-statement is benefit. Benefit to you.

"Fine," Melid said. "Illik's death an emptiness, uncertain how fill. Ever. Angry: at him, me, killers." Her emotions wanted to emerge as a frown, a glare. She controlled it with a bitter smile. "Consolation in revenge. Maybe that." She switched the jets off and floated in silence, water droplets transiting from her in all directions.

Noted, Conybeare told her.

"And I finish Illik's work."

Present concern has use of all Melid say, Conybeare said.

Melid stared at the generated face. "Enough? Enough words?" She activated the dryers, and the inside of the ablution-sphere roared. Conybeare vanished.

A minute later she opened the sphere and floated out. All the other spheres in the ablution core lay empty, but at the end opposite her own a stocky male figure had stripped itself of clothes.

"Instrum Doum," Melid said, drifting toward him before catching herself on a handrail.

"Emissary," he said, staring ahead.

The pair of them ignored each other's hypothalamic frenzy at seeing one another naked for the first time. The mandates of the higher mind—duty, rank, mission—crushed animal curiosity soon enough.

"Amongst Worlders soon," Melid said.

"Emissary."

"My first encounter," Melid said. "Conversed with Worlders, Doum? Much?" She knew he and the others had posed as a 'family', a Worlder phenomenon.

"Converse, no," he said. "Illik, Zo do that." A sadness rippled from him. "Now Zo."

She placed a palm on Doum's brawny shoulder. "Miss Illik too."

He looked at her hand, then at her. "Have to shower, Emissary. Also now masturbate."

"Of course."

He floated away to one of the spheres. Melid propelled herself to the clothes holders and began to dress. Odd; she was finding meeting Worlders a more terrifying prospect than the high gravities of their worlds and stations. Talking corpses, Illik had once described them. Corpse-talk...

"Conybeare," she said. She somersaulted gently as she pulled a bodytight over her thighs.

Emissary, came Conybeare's voice.

"Read me," she told it. She visualised Assault-Instrum Sen back on the wreck, the gibberish she'd muttered after being contaminated by the Scalpel-energy. Before Zo terminated her. "Translated? Possible?"

Yes, Conybeare said.

"What language?" Melid said.

None known. Contains known elements: Worlder Anglurati, our moticjiang.

"How translate then?" Melid said.

Work backward. Anglurati and jiang share common ancestor. Believe called 'Anglush'.

"She spoke *Anglush*?" A tongue of old Earth.

No: Anglush ancestor, Conybeare said. No records. Kollective attempt reconstruct. Imperfect, but 41% satisfied.

A long way back, Melid thought. Ancient beyond ancient. Had the Scalpels roamed between stars even then?

"Understood," she said. "What say?"

ALONE IN THE BUSY MALL, Hargie felt like an impurity, a freak. The walls were laboratory white, the air and grav better than most worlds. And the crowds? Clean, rich. They strode with a triumph both ignorant and unearned. Space travel was a shuttle and a freight-jump to these people, these winners. A wait.

Where was she? His clothes hadn't felt so worn and, yes, dirty till now. Rags amid the suits, a bruise on the pristine skin of the Freightways mall.

Sitting down near a fountain, he opened a can of updates and drank back the silver milk. A giant screen above the escalators showed a freightbox in operation, accompanied by the sort of music normally reserved for documentaries on the Big Bang Fifty cargo ships glided into a vast silver box hanging in space. In turn, this box slotted itself into the mouth of an even bigger silver box with a Freightways sign on the side. Everything glowed white and, the next thing the viewer knew, some actors playing a family smiled down on a foreign world. The Freightways insignia materialised above them. Hot shit.

He went to pull out a cigarette, then remembered he wasn't allowed. Ah, but he'd be gone soon. Grab those rupees and run.

A notion struck him. He looked around to check that Sparkle wasn't approaching, and then accessed his neuralware. The can of updates had provided his personal 'ware with region-specific hoxnite-patches. Nothing remarkable. He brought up his contacts window, selected and called.

Aewyn Nuke answered. He seemed to be walking down a pipeway somewhere inside one of Calran's crust fragments. Hargie's view of him bounced up and down to compensate.

"Nuke, you loathsome prick," Hargie said.

Aewyn laughed, revealing his sharpened teeth. "You fuckin' knows it," he said in that sing-song accent of native Calranese. "Man can't go around being a prick in this life. Got to be loathsome too if he wants to get by, isn't it?"

"It's those loveable pricks ruin everything," Hargie said.

"Amen! Fuckin' amen, brother Hargopal, you walking turdpurse of a human being. What can I do you for now?"

"I'm in system, dropping a delivery. After that," he looked around, "I may require one of your girls."

"Oh," Aewyn said. He stopped walking and smiled at Hargie. "Like that, is it?"

"You know me," Hargie said. "Lucia free? She was ideal last time."

"Fraid not, you giddiest cock-moth of a reprobate, you." Aewyn squinted, probably checking his own neuralware. "How about Sophi? Right next door to Lucia, all the same kinks. Lush as fuck."

"Works for me," Hargie said. "I'll be there within twelve, ratshit permitting."

"Sophi waits with open limbs," Aewyn said.

"Reassuring. How much?"

"Nothing." Aewyn shook his head. "I owe you. Big style, you fucking twat."

"Not as much as your bookies," Hargie said.

"You know me implicitly. Talk later, eh?"

"Over a bar," Hargie replied. "Then under." He switched off.

Sparkle was walking, almost stumbling, toward him, shopping bags in hands. He hadn't recognised her at first.

"Hey," she said. "Check me out."

She'd got her dreadlocks toned pink, up in two plastic-flowered pigtails. New coat, too: burgundy and furry. The stumbling was due to a pair of bright red imitation loopy-scoops her feet were clearly not happy in. The overall effect was of a woman who'd fallen through a boutique when the gravity shut down.

"Got paid, then?" Hargie said.

"What makes you say that?" Not a trace of sarcasm.

"Thought you'd no money," Hargie said.

"Hargie, I've wore one set of clothes for a week," she said. "I had to run, recall?"

"Those days are over," he said, eyeing her loopy-scoop shoes. "So what did Fragile say?"

"Fractile," Sparkle said. "Haven't spoken to him yet."

"So why I been sat here so damn long?"

"Because you'd have been judgmental if I'd taken you shopping." She started rooting through one of her bags. "But fear not, I've got you a present..." She pulled out a coffee mug with a flourish. It had the Freightways logo emblazoned on it.

"You're shitting me, right?" Hargie said.

"Yes, I'm shitting you. Clearly." Sparkle put the mug away. "Got you a carton of smokes."

"My admiration shines eternal," Hargie said.

"You're unhappy because I haven't paid you yet, aren't you?" Sparkle said.

"What's that word for what you're doing now? Telepathic? Telekinesis? Can never remember."

"Fine," Sparkle said. "It's just Fractile doesn't like me when I'm... like I am now. To visit Fractile I'll have to, I don't know, sort of... get in a mood. A business mood."

"I don't care if you get in a mouse costume," Hargie said. "Just pry my pay outta him."

Sparkle stared at the top of Hargie's hat, or some point beyond it. She blinked, and all the ditziness in her face sharpened to a frown. "Business mood," she said. She inflected the words with disdain.

"Okay." Not for the first time, Hargie was a little freaked out by this woman. Her weird damn drugs.

"Fractile's got a cargo hold up on the import levels," Sparkle said, her words clipped. She turned around and walked. "Keep up," she said to Hargie over her shoulder.

Hargie sighed and stood up.

Sparkle stumbled, nearly falling, on her left loopy-scoop shoe.

"Ruined the mood there," Hargie said.

"Shut up," she said, working herself into a stride once more. "Ridiculous shoes," she mumbled to her feet. "Idiot..."

SWIRL AND HARGIE FOLLOWED Fractile's bodyguard along the tunnel, their shoes a broken rhythm on the central walkway's grill. Countless transparent bags of what looked like saline circled all around them, carried along on segmented steel conveyor belts that traversed the tunnel's walls, floor and ceiling. A dry antiseptic breeze filled the tunnel, its source some hidden but audible machine. Everything was cool and alloy and fierce.

Swirl had pictured this meeting for a little under a week. She had considered every likelihood, every argument and counter-point. What she hadn't pictured was having to carry shopping bags. Or wearing shoes designed by idiots who clearly found walking a universal affront. She had thought it the decent thing to do, allowing Sparkle leisure time after being cooped up. But give Sparkle a little leeway and she took a whole parsec.

:Please tell Shine he's a rectum,: Sparkle sent. *:That's all I ask.:*

:I won't be talking to Shine, will I?: Swirl sent back. *:I'm dealing with Fractile.:*

:Don't see how that stops Shine being a rectum...:

:Sparkle, please. Let's not have a raging argument in our head while ferals are about, eh? You know what happened last time...:

Sparkle sent nothing.

"So what's with all the water bags?" Hargie was asking the bodyguard, who seemed the local flavour of thug. Neither man had offered to carry a single shopping bag.

"Ask the man himself," the bodyguard said, pointing at someone on the walkway ahead: Fractile, sat by a little makeshift table with a glass of wine. A shadow at this distance, Swirl only recognised him from the blue light of his trademark monocle.

"Word to the wise," the bodyguard said to Hargie. "Boss real cranky right now. Bad news and all." He stepped back and let Swirl and Hargie walk by.

"Greetings," Swirl said, walking up to Fractile. "It's Sparkle here."

She put the shopping bags down and hooked a thumb into her belt. With her fingers flat across the buckle, she used them to spell out:

It's Swirl talking now. Sparkle our current handle.

"Sparkle!" Fractile said, offering his elegant milk-toned hand to her. "Always a pleasure."

Fractile used his own fingers against his wine glass to spell out:

Shine tells me he's pleased to hear that.

:Finger-sign that Shine's a total cavity,: Sparkle sent to Swirl. *:Please, Sis.:*

:Shut up,: Swirl replied.

"Who's your bubbleman friend?" Fractile asked. He squinted to see, the piercings of his monocle pulling against his left eyebrow and cheek.

"Hargie Stukes," Swirl said. "He brought me here."

"Pleased to meet you, Mr. Stukes," Fractile said, offering his hand again.

"Back at you," Hargie said, taking it. He gestured at the countless transparent bags making their way along the corkscrew of belts all around.

"Shark embryos," Fractile explained. "For the terraforming market. There's money in emerging ecologies."

"I'll bear it in mind," Hargie said.

Fractile turned back to Swirl. "You're a long way from home. How is life on that rig of yours?"

"Inadvisable," Swirl said. "It's been annihilated."

"I'm sorry to hear that... Sparkle," Fractile said. "And surprised. Now why has it not been reported in the news, eh?"

"Distance, maybe." It sounded stupid to her even as she said it. News would have got out by now. "That's why I'm here. I lost the last consignment. Went up with the rig. So no more market either."

"Clearly," Fractile said.

"And... I've no more leaf, Fractile," Swirl said. "Not personally. Swallowed my last this morning."

"In other news," Hargie said, "she said you'd pay me. Sir."

"Oh, cruel mistress happenstance." Fractile sighed and watched the embryos pass by. "Would you believe it? I'm wholly leafless myself."

Swirl stuttered, couldn't find the words.

:*What the eternal fuck?*: Sparkle sent. :*Utter shit. He's the sector's major dealer! It's SHINE, Sis. He's playing with us, pulling his brother's strings and—*:

"This comes as something of a surprise," Swirl said. She felt sweat break on her hairline. She'd never imagined this. No leaf. The very rim of hell.

Sparkle says, Swirl finger-signed to Fractile, ***Shine is making you lie.***

Shine says, well she would, wouldn't she? Fractile finger-signed back. ***And Radiance also says hello.***

"Freightways," Fractile said to both Swirl and Hargie, "or perhaps their owners, Raichundalia, have informed me our enterprise's next consignment has been postponed. Unusual, don't you think, for a company that prides itself on honouring customer shipments? Health considerations, apparently. I dare say I'll be hiring bubblemen smugglers in future. Never ideal." He eyed Hargie. "No offence, my boy."

Hargie said nothing.

"Are you telling me," Swirl said, "there is absolutely no leaf? Not anywhere in the entire sector?"

"Not entirely," Fractile said. "My chief buyer down on Desolation Row—Valatka 'Pa' Nuke, patriarch of the Clan Nuke—is sitting on a fair amount. Oh, I can buy it back, naturally, but at a price he knows I can't afford.

Due to a previous misunderstanding, he would delight in breaking my back." He grinned ruefully, then sipped his wine.

"I see," Swirl said.

Swirl finger-signed again: ***Am being followed by people unknown. I've something of theirs imprinted on my psyche-mandala. Need you to look.***

Fractile grinned, put his glass down on the table. "But enough of this trouble, eh? My, Sparkle, you've clearly been looking after yourself. Exercise, is it? Perhaps you'll stand up straight and allow me to inspect your figure."

"Of course, Fractile." She did so.

Fractile adjusted his monocle and a light came on. He leaned forward and looked Swirl up and down slowly. "Ah... yes, yes..."

"Erm..." Hargie muttered. "This some kind of thing back in the Harmonies?"

Fractile ignored him. He switched his monocle off and leaned back.

You've a sliver of nothing inside you, Fractile finger-signed. ***Unnerving. Agents like ourselves have (occasionally) observed humans whose psyche-mandala are non-existent. No one knows who they are/where from.***

That all? Swirl signed.

All I can give. To learn more you must comadose. You need leaf.

:Tell me about it,: Sparkle sent to Swirl.

"Okay," Hargie said. "That's about all the snubbing and leering I can take. Mr. Fractile, I'm owed. I brought your friend here. It took days, it took an entire solar mass of patience. You owe me. Now, sir."

Fractile's face twitched. He stared into the mid-distance, then smiled.

"Do I?" he said to Hargie, and a strange look came to his face. "Do I, now? Let's see: firstly, I didn't request your services. Secondly, this is a quasi-illegal operation so you can't throw lawyers at me, whom I doubt you could afford anyway. You seem to have no gun, either." He leaned forward, his body language tighter, predatory. "Note my man, Esebius there, does. Mr. Stukes, ask yourself what's to stop him using it, eviscerating your corpse and feeding the goo intravenously to all these budding little apex predators?" He waved at the million embryos all around. "In light of all that, sir, you may want to consider sticking your feral tail between your legs and loping the fuck off."

A pistol whirred ready behind them. Hargie said nothing.

:That was Shine saying that,: Sparkle sent to Swirl. *:Fuck, Swirl—they're struggling against one another.:*

Fractile shook his head, his hands spasming. "A-apologies," he said. "Truly. But I... stand by what I just said..."

:Sparkle, you're right.: Swirl sent. *:By the Eye, you're right.:*

Leaf withdrawal. You heard stories.

"Bad's mine, Mr. Fractile," Hargie said. "I'll leave you all now. I hope your drug acquisition problem sorts itself out, truly, but it's late and I said I'd meet a pal from the Clan Nuke." He turned around and began to walk away.

"Wait," Fractile said. Swirl said it too.

"What?" Hargie turned around. "You can keep that carton of smokes, Sparkle, it's no problem."

"Droll, Mr. Stukes," Fractile said. 'I salute you.' He looked the feral up and down. "You have connections with the Nukes?"

"A man bubbles through Calran, he'll meet the Nukes sooner or later." He pulled a pack of cigarettes out of his jacket. He flipped open the pack, pulled out a cigarette and lit it with his finger.

"Hey," the bodyguard said.

Fractile waved the bodyguard silent. He gave Hargie a piercing, monocled stare. "I sense a notional deal about to colour the air," he said.

"It's like you know me," Hargie said. "All right; if I roll down to Desolation bartering for the weight you originally sold, they'll know you're pulling my wires. All doors close. But one case? That's just Hargie O'Smalltime. Enough to tide you both over until that embargo or whatever is done. Be back in forty-eight."

"And your price?" Fractile asked.

"Aside from the lo-lo to buy the stuff? Let's say... double the price Miss Loopy-Scoop here said you'd pay me."

Fractile looked at Swirl.

"Twelve lakh," Swirl said. "A liberty on my part, admittedly."

"Doubtless," Fractile said. He looked back at Hargie. "Quite the invoice for one mere case."

"Dealer's market," Hargie told him. "Dealer being me."

"Would you be happy with half of that in state-of-the-art shark 'embryos?"

Hargie breathed out a cloud of smoke. "Who wouldn't?"

"Done," Fractile said. "But I insist Sparkle accompanies you, my reasons being twofold. Firstly, once her leaf withdrawal emerges, it'll help to convince your Clan Nuke friend of your sincerity. Secondly, Sparkle can kill you easily, weapon or not. She doesn't talk about that particular skill set but trust me, it's there. More importantly," and he met Swirl's eyes, " she knows what hand feeds her."

One larger than yours or mine, girl, Fractile finger-signalled against his wine glass. Or perhaps it was Shine doing that.

:Lend me use of our signalling hand,: Sparkle sent to Swirl. *:It's imperative I call them both pricks.:*

Swirl ignored her.

Fractile pulled a handheld out of his robes and pointed it at Hargie. "I'll give you two lakh for the purchase itself and half your payment now. Embryos later. The purchase payment will only transact upon your finger touching Nuke DNA."

"Smoosh," Hargie said. He squinted. "You two related?"

"No," Fractile said. "Why would you ask?"

"Neither of you use neuralware." He nodded at Fractile's handheld and then put his finger on it. There was a bleeping sound as the transaction went through.

"We're both allergic," Fractile said.

"Really?" He shrugged his shoulders. "Huh, what are the chances?"

"Indeed," Fractile said.

Fractile finger-signed to Swirl: ***If you've made a feral aware of our (Triune) nature, our world's high mistress might not be forgiving.***

Relax. He's a(nother) idiot.

"Come on, Hargie," Swirl said. "Let's go. Something about the cold predators in here is making me sick."

With that she turned around and began to walk away.

:Swirl,: Sparkle sent.

Swirl sighed. She turned about, walked back, picked up the two shopping bags and walked off again.

:Damn it, Sparkle,: she sent, *:you ruined our exit.:*

THIS TOWN IS NOUGHT but corpses and the crows who feed upon them.

Melid rolled the phrase around in her head as she floated through the hatchway. What did it mean, this snatch of a forgotten language mouthed by a contaminated Instrum before Zo blew her head off? What had she meant? Or had something spoken through her?

She shook the thought off; it could so easily consume her, as it indeed had done these last twenty hours. Melid had matters to attend to. Field-Emissary work.

The male Assault-Instrum guarding the hatch—its muscleform stretched to fit a foreign counterpart—floated to attention. He urged a deferential caution: what lay beyond the hatch was not to be faced lightly.

She emoted her regard, then said: "Open."

The hatch whirled open and gaudy yellow light shone through: the chosen illumination level of most Worlders. Melid took a deep breath and grasped the two handles on either side of the hatch. She lifted her legs up and then forward. Halfway through, her horizontal glide became a vertical fall.

Weight. It took her by surprise, despite her suit, despite preparation. Her left hand slipped off the handle and she hung by her right, swinging in the Worlder-craft's corridor. Undignified. At least Zo wasn't there to see it.

Melid let go and hit the floor of the corridor. She couldn't believe a drop of one meter could ache so. The universe pushed her against the floor. She breathed deep, remembered her training. Adjusted to up and down.

Who could live like this?

Melid's suit was already compensating, its muscleform fibres hardening on her thighs and lumber. Tentatively, she took her first steps. She made her way toward the open door of the cockpit.

Doum was already in there, his pistol aimed at the pilot's head. Melid now understood why Doum enjoyed field work amongst the Worlders. He was short, stocky, his movements a joke in the buoyant milieu of the Konsensus. Doum didn't need a suit—as a field instrument he'd been gene-fixed long ago to handle gravity both natural and replicated—but Melid had to wonder if he'd needed much G-F in the first place.

The pilot's eyes darted toward her, clearly too frightened to turn his whole head. At least he *looked* frightened. Melid felt no emotion, no thought or imagery, emanating from him. She knew this would be the case; Worlders were base creatures without spinal receivers or kollectivised brains. But to actually meet one? Unnerving.

"You are cargo-shuttle pilot Morley Saito, yes?" Melid asked.

For a moment he didn't answer, and Melid thought she had spoken gibberish. With no moticjiang, no way of radiating emotion or intent, one had to fit all meaning into vocalisation, create baroque sentences.

"Look," Saito said, "this is an empty haul, just going to a pick up at Freightways. Nothing for you here, Ma'am. I swear."

"Huh." She looked at Doum and smiled. "A lie. My very first... lie." She was surprised to encounter one so soon. Fortunately she had a level three grade in ironics. A Field-Emissary had to.

The pilot's face wrinkled up. Disgusting. A puppet, an imitation of a human draped in rolls of needless fat.

"Pilot Morley Saito," she said. "I would like you to unbutton your jacket. Would you do that?"

Saito's eyes rolled from Melid to Doum's pistol. He nodded and undid the buckles on his jacket. Chilling, watching corpse hands move. Yes. A living, talking corpse.

"Thank you, Pilot Morley Saito." She took out the circular piece of film from her pocket and activated it. "You do have cargo. We know that. We are not interested in taking cargo. You must not let that concern you." This Worlder talk was difficult. "However... we do want to *use* your cargo." She slapped the film disc onto the corpse-man's chest and watched it sink into the skin.

Saito yelped and clutched at his breastbone.

"See?" Melid told him. "No pain."

"Please," he said. "Just take the cargo."

"I said," she hissed the latter word and the corpse-puppet winced, "I said we do not want to take your cargo. Did I not? Pilot Morley Saito, in forty-five minutes you will experience a natural-looking and fatal cardiac arrest. Is that the term? Have I got that right?"

The 'pilot's eyes went wide, his puppet face a parody of horror. Amusing, in a morbid way. "Please..."

"In fifteen minutes Freightways will contact you, as you are surely aware. You will behave as if nothing is the matter. Perhaps a joke or two. Be creative. You've already proven you can lie."

The pilot gulped, his Adam's apple like a bubble rising up a sewage pipe.

"Then you'll give me a cure," he said. "An antidote. Right?"

"Has it occurred to you we know your name, Pilot Morley Saito?" Melid said.

He twitched, no doubt surprised by the call coming through to his nervous system's primitive computer. His neuralware.

"Best answer that," Melid said. "We'll wait."

"Hello?" the pilot said. His eyes went wide again. "Miki? Miki, darling? What's the... who's that with you?"

Worlders reproduced by inseminating one another and spewing babies from their vulvas. Monstrous. But it made Worlders weak, creepily obsessive about their own creations. The Instrum had long known to use that.

"Okay... Miki, listen to me... Just be nice to the lady. Yes, she *is* a nice lady, isn't she? Yes, yes, she *is* a friend. Oh, ice cream, huh?" The pilot made a face that caused Melid to think the film disc had acted early. "Okay... okay... listen to me, Miki-Tiki... I love you, hon. Always will, forever. Ever and ever. Bye bye, girl... bye..."

He began to sob. Sickening leaking corpse. Melid wanted to hit it, stop its noises, its mockery of suffering. You could hurt Worlders and never feel their pain. Do anything you liked.

"I promise you," Melid said, "no harm will come to your daughter. Not the slightest bruise. But you have to convince Freightways that everything is fine. And then you have to die. Most people do not know when they will die. You do, Pilot Morley Saito. Sculpt death into something noble. Save your child."

"There's a place in hell for you," he said. "When *you* die."

"No," Melid replied. "I'll just cease to be. As will you. We have to wait in the cargo bay now. Can we trust you to behave?"

"You'll kill her," he said.

"No; we'll erase her memory of these last few hours," Melid said. "We can do that."

"And how do I know that, bitch?"

"What choice do you have, Pilot Morley Saito?" She lifted a box of tissues from the dashboard and threw them on his lap. "You'll need these."

Melid and Doum left the cockpit. She felt a lot better now she'd adjusted to the gravity.

When they reached the cargo bay, Melid called to Zo down on Calran with the girl.

"Terminate."

Ironics-in-the-field—or 'lying'—was a lot easier than she thought it would be, Melid realised. Perhaps she was a natural.

"YOU WANT JUST A SCREEN or the entire cockpit walls?" Hargie, piloting *Princess* from his seat, asked Sparkle.

"I don't care," she said. "Neither. Just get us to Desolation. Calran. Whatever it's called."

"Still in your business mood?" Hargie said. "Prefer you dazzled and awed. What happened to that?"

"The leaf talking, the drugs. Just fly the ship. Sooner we can part ways."

"Sure," Hargie said. *Finish the job. Think of the shark embryos.*

Two shapes moving together, coming out of Freightways traffic. Trailing *Princess Floofy*.

Falcatta ships.

"Shit."

Hargie's neuralware registered a coms call. He answered. "*Princess Floofy* to unknowns: who is this?"

"*Princess, er... Floofy,*" came the voice, "*this is Freightways security. We're authorised to order you to turn back and dock with, er, dock 7a90. Please respond.*"

"What's going on?" Sparkle asked him.

Hargie ignored her. "Freightways security, please explain."

"*Just a random check, Floofy,*" the voice said.

Fucking Falcatta. Descendants of rapists both human and robo-medical, courtesy of every faster-than-light-hungry human power in the galaxy. They had the bubble-gene; difference was, they whored it to scum like Freightways.

"Security," Hargie said, "I'm wondering if, when you say 'Floofy' what you mean to say is 'bubblescum'. Freightways won't like me filing a discrim. Too many 'random checks' in the news, tune?"

"Hargie?" he heard Sparkle say.

The voice came over his neuralware again: "*Floofy, this is a random check, I assure you. Step up in security.*"

"What? 'Bubblescum'? That what you said?"

"*Floofy! Damn it...*"

"Step up in security?" Hargie said. "Why can't you tell me what it's about, Falcky? Too busy priming your tazers and nightsticks? That it?"

Another, angrier voice came over the neuralware: "*Shut the fuck up, bubblefucker! Turn around NOW before we fill that piece of junk's asshole with compaction fire!*"

"Bubblefucker?" Hargie said. "You call me that? You call my recording facilities that?"

"*I'll call you motherbubblefucker, cocksucker!*"the angry voice said.

"I bow to your expertise," Hargie said and he laughed. "Stretching your mouth around Freightways' each morn and all..."

"Hargie?" Sparkle said. "What *is* this conversation?"

"*Motherbubblefucker, I will SHOOT you. I will shoot you this MINUTE if you don't turn that rusty dogturd around and acquiesce.*" There was a pause, then the sound of the angry dickhead talking to someone. "*What? Fuck him. I'm the man here, Jensin, don't forget that.*"

Calran wasn't so far away now. Fuck 'em; he wasn't Freightways' bitch or these asshole 'Falcattas'. Random check, Hargie's ass.

"Security," he said. "Apologies, will comply. Just, you know, joking and shit."

"*Oh, learned your lesson now, bitch?*"

"Clearly," Hargie said.

"Hargie?" Sparkle said. "Could I have that visual now, please?"

"O' course, lady," Hargie said.

The cockpit walls turned to deep space, Calran's ripped crust dead ahead.

With a blink Hargie jettisoned a chuck barrel out of *Princess'* aft. The comm disconnected with a squeak. Hargie accelerated the sub-bub drive and *Princess Floofy* shot off.

SWIRL LEAPED UP FROM the foldable chair. Calran was filling the front hemisphere of the cockpit at an alarming rate. She spun around.

The vision of deep space on the back wall stretched and grew, as if a giant magnifying glass had materialised over it. The stars stretched into lines.

"What's that?" she said.

Hargie said nothing.

:Chuck charge,: Sparkle sent. *:At least I think. One-shot gravity wall, used to repel detritus, or, more usually—:*

An alarm cut her off.

Swirl spun about to face Hargie's chair. "What's that?"

"Missile," Hargie said.

"Missile?"

:Missile!:

"MISSILE," HARGIE REPEATED. Electropulse. Only one of its salvo to get through the chuck-wall. *Lock on, Princess* told him, *detonation in eight.*

Hargie tensed and bubble-jumped. His veins were awash with ticklish pleasure, the jump-juice kissing each nerve. Ten seconds would do it. He stayed in for fifteen. "Oh, yeah..."

Princess Floofy came out of the hyper-tube back into real space. The missile had lost lock. Calran was closer.

The two Falcatta ships had vanished. Bubble-jumped too, most likely...

Damn, but this was fun! Damn!

Woman's voice. Hargie couldn't make it out. A passenger maybe.

:SIS! LET ME TAKE OVER, Sis! Please! We're about to die!:

"No, we're not," Swirl told her. Damn her sister. "Hold on!"

The swap from pale white bubble-space to actual, the change of ship direction with no sensation of momentum: all made her feel ill.

She felt her lips move: "He's suicidal!" Sparkle shouted.

"Don't do that!" Swirl said. "Idiot, your paniiiciiinuh..."

Using their shared lips simultaneously.

"Scuuurewyouuustoppppaanifuuuc..."

Swirl felt her legs move. She stopped them. Her body froze. She had ascendency here, but it took all her concentration.

:Sparkle, stop it, you idiot!: Swirl sent.

:Kill us!: Sparkle sent. *:He'll kill us!:*

Muscles fighting one another, Swirl and Sparkle's body hit the cockpit floor.

THE FALCATTAS POPPED into reality again, *pop, pop*. Either side of *Princess*, forty klicks distance. Juddery joy in Hargie's belly.

Ohhh, fun time.

He bubble-jumped—a brief flash of hyper-tube, joy bursting in his bones—and he popped back into real space again, five m-k behind the two Falcattas.

Grinning, he opened the tubes and fired. Forty-eight warheads straight at those dickheads, twenty-four apiece.

He sent a com: "Eat-shit-you-falky-pissflasks! Eat shiiiiiit!"

He laughed, all crazy, all *fun-fun-yeah*!

The Falcattas' bubblecoils would still be re-charging. No jump for them, no jump!

The two Falkies schlepped into evasive manoeuvres—a pussy dance, real minuet. Coming to terms with imminent death.

Too close to Calran to jump. *Princess* passed Gully Bay, the outermost crust-island.

Flyer traffic below, ahead. He checked GZG: the Falcattas had realised the missiles were just nixies, phoneys. *Yeah*, thought Hargie, *like bubbleships carry forty-eight missiles*. Dumbest fuckwipes.

Hargie drove *Princess* between two flyer lanes, straight through. Falcattas were brutes, but they knew who fed them; Freightways wouldn't appreciate missiles thrown around innocents. Not in their public name. All suited Hargie.

Past Dai's Crust, past the grand tube nexus, lower, lower, ever closer to the core. He felt *Princess*' sensors compensate for the heat and light. Sensor range dropped way down this low to the furnace, targeting ranges too. No missile would function this close.

Hargie spied his own target: Hailmogambo, the lowest crust. Home to Clan Nuke. Somehow even the traffic around its blackened mass looked seedier.

He felt a blip enter *Princess*' sensor radius, immediately followed by a fired-upon warning. A Falcatta, still on the scent. Nice work, damn it.

They were passing close to Hailmogambo now, its baked wall rushing by, a blur of rock, lights and tunnels. The Falcatta sent a com request.

"Princess Bubblescum," Hargie answered. "How may we hinder?"

"*Congratulations, boy.*" The angry voice. Trust Hargie's luck he wouldn't be the one to lose the quarry. "*You've graduated to lethal force. I'm talking compaction rounds here. Now, ACQUIESCE, or you're gonna wish you ran down your mom's leg.*"

"Falky," Hargie told him, "'you're outta range."

"*I got the top speed here,*" Angry said.

"I got the acceleration," Hargie said.

"*I got the guns and you're running outta space.*"

"I got plating and you're outta luck."

Hargie decelerated and pulled up. *Princess Floofy* swung herself under the belly of Hailmogambo.

What a sight: endless lake of fire below, upside-down mountain ranges above, their summits molten saffron. No way a Falcatta would follow under here. They were bubbleships in only the loosest sense, had swapped insulation and cargo for high speed and weapons.

He brought up the map.

Damn it, he was already coming down.

DEEP BREATHS. SWIRL could always get the best of Sparkle with deep breaths. Whenever Sparkle panicked or raged or sulked, she went straight for the limbs. Never the lungs. She hadn't the physical subtlety. Swirl merely had to apply enough counterforce to the limbs to keep Sparkle in check and then focus on slowing their shared breathing.

:Sparkle,: Swirl sent, *:We're safe now. Safe.:*

Sparkle just breathed with her. Fine. Progress.

:Sparkle... listen to me. Never do that, OK? Not amongst the ferals.:

:I panicked,: Sparkle sent.

:Clearly.: Swirl looked up from the floor. Hargie was in his pilot seat still, frowning, chin buried in his chest. *:I don't think he saw our... seizure.:*

Swirl took in the hellscape all around the cockpit's walls. Calran's exposed core filled everything below. The sky was a smouldering continent. They were flying up into one of its charred canyons.

Swirl felt her limbs move. She held them back.

:Deep breaths, Sparkle,: she sent, *:deep breaths...:*

THERE SHE WAS: SOPHI. Looked like Hargie had needed her comforting limbs after all.

He sent a ping: *Princess Floofy*'s ID.

With a brief hurricane of steam—soon evaporated—Sophi's great doors slouched open. *Princess* entered.

Five

TWISTING, BOILING, simmering, still. Voices chanted "Ashemi."

Then silence.

A great chamber above, blue stone, vaults rising into blackness. Incense tumbling, snaking upward through air. No scent.

Clearly, the Ashemi lay on his back. He could not tell whether he lay on stone or wood, or if it felt warm or cold. He knew his sense of touch to be nonexistent. This new body was no body.

Slowly, he sat up. He did not need his arms to do this, his new back being more than strong enough. Voices muttered, prayed, offered blessing.

He was encircled by men and women, their collarbones lacerated and bloody in the dim light. Behind them stood others in eyeless masks, snouted and horned. They held swords of night-black wood.

He sat waist-high to them. He'd woken upon an altar.

Directly before the Ashemi, at his feet, stood a woman: dark, old, her grey hair in dreadlocks.

"Ashemi," the woman said. "Zahrir offers humble greetings. Please forgive the laxity of our wassail. We had but short notice."

As it should be, the Ashemi thought.

"A mirror," he said.

The old woman's lips quivered a moment. "Of course, your Ashemi."

He stood up. The lacerated people stepped back, bowing. He felt nothing in his limbs as he rose, and even less for these people. He stood a half-yard higher than any of them.

Two of the masked attendants brought forth a body-length mirror, its ivory frame carved with swirls, with dreaming eyes. The Ashemi studied himself.

His eyes, quite lidless, were of blue glass. His face, long and slender, was carved of alabaster. His eyebrows and sockets were gilded gold. So too his lips, which were bowed in shape and gently cruel in expression. All framed by a mane lengthy and black: silk braids, crow feathers, leather strips, clasps and pendants. Acceptable. They had chosen an acceptable vessel for him.

"More leaf," he said.

"Yes, your Ashemi."

The old woman pulled a handful of the Geode leaf from out of her robes. The Ashemi opened a hand—fingers black and bone-like, patterned with gold and rising to silver claws—and accepted the leaves. He crushed their translucent purple forms and, opening the seal on his iron and alabaster chest, poured the leaves into the heart-furnace. The blue flames crackled and rose in both realities: here and the Geode. He could feel it.

The Ashemi studied his face once more. His body was no body. It was a sculpture possessed.

"You are all wondering why I am here," the Ashemi said, his gilt lips unmoving.

"Your Ashemi," the old woman said. "We would be honoured to know."

"It regards the matter of Pearl-Swirl-Sparkle Savard," he said.

The old woman hesitated, her mouth quivering in a way the Ashemi had already come to disdain.

"I see," she said eventually.

"SAFE, SAFE."

All Sparkle had gotten out of Hargie these last hours. He seemed comfortable, at least. He lay there grinning, hovering on dribbling. Every few minutes he'd moan happily.

Through the walls the outside world appeared black. It had been nothing but steam an hour ago, the product—Sparkle presumed—of an army of vapour cannons intent on cooling *Princess Floofy*'s frightful hide.

"Have we been captured?" Sparkle asked. Swirl had let Sparkle ride ascendent in the body a while. Find her calm, she'd said. Not that Sparkle needed to.

:I don't think so.: Swirl sent.

:Wasn't asking you, Sis,: Sparkle sent.

:It's probably a hideout of his, like I said. He flew in here, after all.:

:Little rat's probably got holes all over the place.: Sparkle sent.

:Little rat saved us from capture.: Swirl sent. *:Show some respect.:*

Sparkle shook her head. "Freightways were just following procedure," she said out loud. Why not? Hargie was insensible. People always assumed she talked to herself anyhow. "Hargie... lost it."

:Presume nothing,: Swirl shot back. *:We have no idea how far up this all goes. The spindly family might be working for Freightways.:*

"Your paranoia's an eternal delight, dear," Sparkle said.

:May I remind you we are—well, I am, at least—a foreign agent in feral lands? Ask yourself what an edifice even half as organized as Freightways might discover. Hargie Stukes did us a great favour at immense risk to himself. Remember that, Sparkle.:

Sparkle scrunched her nose, breathed out long. The walls remained as tediously black as they'd been this last hour.

"You bloody like him, don't you?" Sparkle said.

:You're absurd,: Swirl sent. *:He's just earned a modicum of professional respect.:*

"Funny name for it." She stood up and stretched her legs.

:Not my type.: Swirl sent.

"He's feral." Sparkle said.

:Not my feral *type. Doesn't even own a gun. Anyway, why are you so interested?:*

"Just think it's funny, is all." Sparkle looked over at Hargie and spoke loudly: "Hilarious."

No answer. Sparkle noticed a shaft of light beyond Hargie's chair, rendered in VR. She looked up at the cockpit's ceiling. A circle of light above. Growing.

"We're rising," she said. "Climbing up some tube."

Progress, at least. The sisters had assumed they waited in a dark cavern or some such.

"Wonder what's at the top," Sparkle said. "Or who." She wandered over to Hargie and shook his elbow. "Hargie? Who's at the top, Hargie?"

He rolled his head away from Sparkle. "Not me, pal. Sure not me..."

"Hargie?" Sparkle said.

Hargie passed out.

They came out in a supermarket-sized square vault, its tanned, scratched walls half-illuminated by strip lights. Spaceship parts lay in organised piles. Something like an altar—a console, perhaps—built of tungsten pipes squatted directly ahead some thirty feet away. A thin blond man in a long jacket loitered behind it. Hargie's seat began beeping.

:He's trying to talk with us,: Swirl sent. *:Wake Hargie.:*

"You've a fusion bomb, I take it?" Sparkle asked.

Sparkle looked down at Hargie's seat. A light kept winking on its right arm, just below a button that read MANUCOM. She reached for it.

:Sparkle,: Swirl sent. *:That could be the ignition for all we know.:*

Sparkle pressed it.

"Hargie-boy," came a voice. "You in there? Oh, I see. Juiced-out, is it? Come on, H-bomb: wake up. I got five rupees here and me cock needs sucking."

The man on the altar waved at them. For a moment Sparkle felt exposed. But the man was waving at *Princess Floofy's* opaque and ugly hide. When not in the depths of space, the cockpit's wrap-around was just plain unnerving.

:So…: Swirl sent. *:This man and Hargie have some kind of… understanding?:*

"Feral culture thing," Sparkle explained. "Heterosexual males cannot express affection for one another and thus rely on extreme irony. The males back on the rig were similar, remember?"

:Hmm. I sort of thought they meant it,: Swirl sent. *:What's a heterosexual?:*

Sparkle ignored her. The man kept calling for Hargie and saying feral things. She pressed another button beside the first. A mic popped out. There was a screeching sound and the man outside bent over, covering his ears.

Sparkle found a dial and turned it down.

"Sorry," she said. "Sorry about that."

"Oww," came the man's voice over the chair. "What I ever do to you?"

"Apologies," Sparkle said. "Who are you?"

"Where's Hargie?" the man said.

"He's here," Sparkle said.

"And you are?" The man said.

"Believe I asked first, sir."

He stood up straight again. "Aewyn. Let's keep it to tha'. Friend of Hargie's I is."

"What is this place?" Sparkle said.

"Mine." He waved a gloved finger. "Guessing Hargie's all jump-spazzed and cunted, right? Been zipping about, is it?" He laughed. "Naughty bastard, Hargie. Proper legend."

Sparkle covered the mic. "What do you think?" she asked Swirl.

:May as well tell him.:

"Yes," Sparkle said into the mic. "How long does he usually take?"

"Could be hours," Aewyn said. "I got stuff out here'll help. We'll have to carry him out, though."

"We'll come down to you."

"Right you are, love," Aewyn said.

Sparkle switched the mic off. "We can carry Hargie out, can't we?" she asked.

:Yes, I'm sure 'we' can,: Swirl sent. *:Put that ridiculous coat you just bought on, Spark-o.:*

"Why?" Sparkle said.

:So we can strap my gun under it.:

Sparkle went to their cabin—a box with stained plastic walls they'd both tried and failed to make habitable—and did as Swirl said.

"You know," Sparkle said, "Aewyn might be Hargie's leaf man." She adjusted the gun strap, put on her charmingly quirky and far-from-ridiculous furry red coat. "Just a thought."

:We'll play it stoic for now.: Swirl sent.

Back in the cockpit, Hargie hadn't moved. Sparkle noticed the chair's needles had retracted out of his neck studs. One relief, at least. She spent the next ten minutes unlocking the callipers around the man's limbs, Swirl offering useless advice the whole time.

"Right." She leaned into Hargie, lifted a flap on his pilot's hat and spoke: "Hargie. Hargie, we're gonna move now. I'm going to help you up."

Shouldn't be too hard. The man was smaller than her, after all.

"Right," Sparkle said. She struggled with getting her arm under Hargie's shoulder. "Right..."

:Sparkle,: Swirl sent. *:Lifting a fully grown man and facing up to a stranger: bit of a Swirl-job if there ever was one, don't you think?:*

Sparkle sighed. "All right. Ascend."

She did so. Swirl shoved an arm under Hargie's shoulder blades, the other beneath his knees, and lifted him. She turned and staggered her way downstairs. At the airlock's hatch, she had to put Hargie down in order to let Sparkle figure out how to get it to open manually. Then they were out, staggering down the gangplank toward Aewyn.

"Tell me where you want him put," Swirl told him.

"Please follow my exquisite arse." He turned and sashayed toward a doorway twenty feet away in the bare rock.

Inside were living quarters larger and tidier than aboard *Princess*. Aewyn led them into a bedroom, and Swirl dumped Hargie onto the mattress.

"Tidy," said Aewyn, which was apparently a word for pleased surprise. "Quite some biceps on you, girl. Been injecting adrenosmack or wha'?"

Swirl gestured at him that she needed to catch her breath. It gave Sparkle time to study the man. Same age as Hargie, maybe. Far taller. Probably what passed for a dandy around these parts, judging by his attire. His blond thatch was up in drooping spikes and his skin was tan saffron. He had a small tattoo below the left eye: a red diamond.

"Right," Aewyn said, and he pulled a light on a metal arm from the wall. He placed it over Hargie's face and switched it on. Hargie's still features shone blue under the glare. "Vitamin D," Aewyn explained. "Helps."

"What is this place?" Swirl asked.

"Lowest point in all Desolation Row," Aewyn told her. "If the old Regent didn't take a shine to you, he sent you down here, isn't it? Scratchin' out caverns. And if he fucking hated you, it was bye-bye: down that tube you just came up." He studied Swirl a moment. "Not that that happens now, mind."

:Ask him about the leaf,: Sparkle said. *:Ask him:*

"And you are?" Swirl asked Aewyn.

"Aewyn."

"You told me that," Swirl said.

"I'm a fixer," Aewyn said. "Bubble-fixer. Offer my girls to bubblemen wanting to keep a low profile. Act as middleman between them and local interests, shall we say."

"Girls?"

Aewyn gestured all around him. "You're currently inside Sophi. We call these caverns 'girls' as code; anyone snooping presumes I'm a pimp."

Anyone looking *presumes you're a pimp*, Sparkle thought.

"Then I thank you for your hospitality," Swirl told Aewyn. She held out a hand to shake.

Aewyn took it and kissed the knuckles. Sparkle could feel Swirl's muscles tense. Aewyn wore some hideous perfume.

"You've got a pistol, Aewyn," Swirl told him.

Aewyn let go of her hand, tapped the pistol inside his coat and grinned. His teeth had been filed into spikes.

"Course I have," he said. "Desolation-fucking-Row, isn't it?"

He went over to a shelf in the wall and picked up an applicator. "Should bring him up nice and slow," he said and he injected it into Hargie's neck. Hargie's lids fluttered. "I take it our boy did one too many jumps, yes?"

"Something like that," Swirl said.

"That's Hargie, all right." He grinned again, his fangs flashing blue in the vitamin light. "'Bubblejump emptiness': see it time and time again. So many bubblemen moving around the galaxy with nothing to hold to, see, living for that next superluminal hit, crashing out then hungering for more. Souls lost in the void." He gazed at Hargie and shook his head. "It's proper shit is what it is..."

:Absolute tragedy,: Sparkle sent to Swirl. *:Now ask him if he can get us more leaf.:*

Swirl groaned.

"You all right?" Aewyn asked.

"Quite fine," Swirl answered. "Hargie was going to meet a contact. Someone in the Clan Nuke. You know them?"

"Maybe." He looked her up and down. "No offence, love, but I've really no idea who the fuck you are. Get Hargie to call me when he rises from his tawdry abyss, eh? Just how I operate."

:No!: Sparkle's mind shivered.

"Of course," Swirl said. "He'll call you."

"Right you are," Aewyn said. "I'll be off then. Busy, busy. Help yourself to drinks, ammo and shady corners." As he reached the bedroom door, he turned around. "Top man, Hargie. Tidy to see he's found a good woman."

"I'm just a passenger," Swirl said.

Aewyn looked her up and down. He smiled his wolf's smile. "Best news I've had all day, tha'. Bye now."

THE CASTLE HAD MOSTLY disintegrated.

Fractile sat on a step at the top of what had been a full spiral staircase and watched the sky tear, slow as glaciers.

Fractile had heard of this kind of thing. Extreme leaf-withdrawal. But it shouldn't have been happening. Not to him. He'd still a slim personal supply. He was certain.

Shine cavorted on a walkway, a piece of the floating castle's walls now floating alone above a twilight sun. A stick figure at this distance, Shine bellowed something at Fractile, shook his fists.

How long had this been? Decades?

"He's losing it," came a voice behind Fractile, identical to his own.

"Greetings, Radiance," Fractile said. "And frankly... I had noticed."

Fractile shifted himself, looked up. Radiance, quiet Radiance, stood there: Fractile's double, save for his choice of green attire. Radiance stood at the top of the staircase, stark against the darkening sky. Evidently the room at the top of the stairs—the top of the tower—had dissolved away behind him in silence.

"We have to persevere," Fractile told his headbrother. "Help will come. One of our staff will find us. Wherever our body is..." He faded off. The tear in the sky had widened without him noticing. It rose from the golden horizon up, high into the deep belly of the atmosphere. Not that imaginary worlds had atmospheres.

Shine was calling something to the pair of them, his hands to his mouth. *Real one*, it sounded like. *Real one! Me!*

"Oh," Radiance said. "It appears Shine has fallen prey to..."

"The Big Lie," Fractile replied. "Indeed. Has for some time."

"We must pay it no mind," Radiance said.

"Remember our training," Fractile said. "We pay it no mind. We survive."

"We survive," Radiance said.

LIGHT. MOVEMENT. GUT pain.

A woman smiled at him.

"How was that?" she said. Fractile was certain he recognised her. Certain. But it seemed so long ago.

:What? What's happening?: Shine sent, to neither brother in particular.

The woman: pale skin, short black hair, lanky. The man beside her: shorn head, stocky. Muscular. A metal crate behind them: Eight feet by four. Fractile owned a great many. This was his hangar.

Warmth. He was bleeding. Belly shot. Without question. His body's upgrades had tranqed most of the pain.

"I ask you again, Mr. Fractile," the woman said. "Where did your recent visitors go? What were their names?"

He felt Shine pushing to take ascendancy. Fractile and Radiance held him back with ease. Shine's attempts were uncoordinated. Crazed.

"What?" Fractile said between deep breaths. "What is this?"

"We came to you in this very cargo container, recall?" she said, pointing at the crate behind her.

Yes. His inspection of the new cargo. He'd been frustrated by that, and Shine angry. There had been some delay, some trouble with the hauler pilot. Drunk, most likely. But the cargo had arrived, and that was when the man and woman emerged. The first Fractile had known of it was when Esebius' head had burst to pink steam. Then his fellow bodyguard's chest flew out, right across the deck. The big man had killed Fractile's personal assistant by driving her head between her shoulders. Remarkable.

"You must be terrified," the woman said. "We have injected your skull with a..." She squinted, as if placing the word out in her head beforehand. "Chemical nanomesh. With a thought I can shut down your senses. Condemn you to blackness."

Fractile thought to inspect her psyche-mandala. But they had smashed his monocle. Only the piercings that once held it remained, two rows of them along cheekbone and brow, useless and throbbing. His whole face had puffed up. He could almost feel it.

"Worse," the woman continued, "the mesh currently surrounding your brain can alter time perception. You've already felt that, Mr. Fractile. Must have seemed years, perhaps decades. The closest one can get to the state of death and still exist."

She smiled, finding something humorous in Fractile's ruined face. The woman reached out and grasped his chin, squeezing it as if inspecting a vegetable's freshness. "Do you know how long your season in oblivion was, Mr. Fractile? For us watching, I mean?" She leaned in and breathed the words: "Fifteen seconds."

She studied his eyes then, like someone rapt by the workings of an ancient clockwork mechanism.

"Nothing for us to put you through that again. Really. Doum here thinks we shall break you in the next minute. No point holding on in light of that. Far better to tell us. Where did your visitors go? What are their names?"

:If we tell them,: Radiance sent to Fractile, *:they still won't know of our secret nature.:*

:Sparkle is weak,: Fractile sent back. *:If captured, Swirl would hold out, but Sparkle, no.:*

Radiance fell silent.

"No?" the woman asked.

"You've... no idea," Fractile told her. "None. My masters will eviscerate you..."

She let go of his chin and blinked.

NOTHING LEFT OF THE castle but the step he sat on, Shine's piece of wall and Radiance's floor tiles. All three of them faced one another: close, floating in a blackness beyond black. No more skies. How long had it been since their torturer had held their chin and told them of the nanomesh? Centuries? There remained no way of counting. He could barely remember her face save for her thin and piercing gaze. Perhaps memory had invented even that.

Their castle was gone. It had been a refuge all their lives. Their own father, long dead, had helped them build it. His father had taught at Fractile-Radiance-Shine's Trinity House.

"It's me who's real, you know." Shine's voice. "I have the life urge."

"We are all real, Shine," Fractile told him. "Only unbelievers say what you currently vomit."

"I've been lied to all my life," Shine said. "How do you think *I* feel?"

It was clear that if they got out—when they got out—Shine would always have to be carried, cared for in their skull. He had seen it occur in other bodies' lives, had always pitied such Triunes.

"Shine," Fractile said. "Recite the truths."

"Fuck you, dream," Shine said.

"You cannot recite the truths?" Fractile said. "How do I, a dream, have more knowledge than my creator?"

Shine tensed. "The first truth..." He faltered.

"Yes?" Fractile looked over to Radiance and smiled. The ploy always worked with Shine.

Radiance did not even look up from his lotus position. When last had he spoken?

"The first truth is the woman has no measure of us," Shine said. "She speaks the great trade language, not Tu'la'lec. She assumes we are feral, then, and has no knowledge..." He looked at his brothers with a sneer. "...Of our trinity."

"The second?" Fractile said.

"The second truth is our very nature protects us," Shine said. "The woman believes we rot in sensory nothingness. She believes this because a monomind does not build places in the skull. A monomind is forever alone. Our castle is our strength." He looked around. "We find sanctuary in one another." He spat into the nothingness below.

"The third?"

Something like a week passed. Something like that.

"The third?" Fractile asked again.

Shine stared at him. "Fuck your truths! Begone! You are a lie!"

"The third truth, brother," Fractile said. "Say it."

"You are no brother!" Shine said. "You're a delusion! You will fade and I will live and—"

Radiance screamed.

The two others fell silent. They looked at him.

"We survive," Radiance said.

The ages passed.

"TWENTY SECONDS," A woman said. The Woman. "How *was* that, I wonder?"

Fractile moaned, his limbs shaking against the floor. He could feel Radiance holding Shine down.

"Their names," the woman said. "Your visitors, remember? Who they are, where they are going? Come on: so long ago, isn't it, Mr. Fractile? No harm in telling now. All we ask is closure on a matter of historical interest."

Perhaps she spoke sense. Perhaps... no, no. Hold fast.

"Answer," the Woman, that near-mythological figure, said. "Answer and we'll let you go."

Her smile twitched. She was a bad liar.

"Beast." Fractile coughed. "Beast of beasts."

His nose erupted. Blood pooled in his mouth. For a moment he thought he might drown, but somehow he coughed it up.

She held up her gloved little finger. Its black material had somehow sharpened to a razor point. A chunk of his nose cartilage—a tiny white square—rolled, then fell from it.

"Emissary," she corrected him. The Woman studied each twinge of his face, as if there existed something uncanny in a tortured man. "Beast-Emissary, if you like. Now, please—"

She stopped. There was a humming sound, a golden pallor, somewhere off behind her. The Woman looked to her minion, the Man. The Man primed his pistol.

The noise. What was that? A cutter, maybe? Someone trying to cut their way through a bulkhead...

:Hold fast,: Fractile sent to his brothers. *:Help comes!:*

The Woman gazed at him. "There's an urgency now," she said. "Please answer. No? Fine. I'm going to stretch your time perception all the way. Happy ages, Mr. Fractile."

She blinked.

CENTURIES OF WATCHING each other dissolve. Fractile had long lost form; he was movement, thought. Nothing else. He stewed in a blackness beyond black.

The time of form and of bodies had become personal legend. Too gaudy to be real. Of late Fractile had thought of one particular myth: the myth of the first coupling, his young body against the warm presence of a woman the same age. Abstract concepts, hard to combine and picture. She had held his face as they lay, whispered to him.

Had that really happened? It seemed a hypothetical notion. The young woman of that first-coupling myth was blurring with the ancient Beast myth. Sometimes he pictured the young woman's dark face in night's bedroom, telling him she loved him, but increasingly, her skin turned yellow-pale, her expression hungry. He would lie on the bed, in that lost myth-time, the woman caressing him, telling him she loved him. Slicing his face with a finger. He only had to say...

Lonely without Shine. Strands of Shine would pass Fractile occasionally, pass through his formlessness. Just memories, frayed impulses. Barely even that. Radiance had devoured Shine. It seemed millennia ago. Possibly was. Radiance would come for him, also. Fractile knew it.

Some ages later Radiance did come.

"Greetings, brother," Radiance said, or something like said.

"Greetings," Fractile replied.

"I'm going to tell her," Radiance said. "Tell the woman. I deserve to live and think. Will you try to stop me?"

"The truths must be held to," Fractile said. "It is our way. I must stop you."

"I am sorry that you are not real," Radiance said. "I should never have imagined you, brother. I should have suffered alone."

"Not real?" Relief filled Fractile. "That seems sense. Thank you, brother."

Radiance didn't devour Fractile entirely. He didn't seem to have the heart for it. He merely chewed off all Fractile's volition, his movement, left him a limbless observer squatting in Radiance's id. A good brother, Radiance.

THE WOMAN-BEAST STARED at them, placid image against the roaring sound. (Gunfire? Was that a thing?)

Radiance was mumbling something through their shared mouth. Fractile couldn't stop him. Fractile wasn't real.

"What?" she asked. "Deep breaths, now..."

"Swir—" Radiance stumbled. "The woman is Swirl."

"Her name is Swirl?" The Woman said.

"Her name is Sparkle." Radiance said.

"Swirl or Sparkle?"

"She... she's from Zahrir," Radiance said. "From Harmonies."

"The Harmonies?" The Woman said. "And the man?"

"Hargie... I think. A nothing, a bubble."

"Yes." The Woman looked over her own shoulder. The Man, the Beast's Man, had fallen back to the metal crate behind the Woman. "Harmonies," she muttered, nodding. "Beyond the Fugue. Where—" The Man fired a round over the crate. The Woman tried again. "Where have they gone?"

"Nuke..." Radiance said.

The Woman frowned. Then enlightenment came to her. "The Clan Nuke?"

Fractile could feel Radiance nod almost frenziedly. "Leaf deal."

"The drug?" She looked set to ask another question.

A round exploded against the metal crate and the Woman flinched, ducked. The Man fired back at whoever had shot the crate.

"Yes," the Woman said to no one. She took out her pistol and primed it.

Radiance grabbed at her. "Please, please... there's something..."

"Something else?"

:Don't tell her,: Fractile sent to Radiance. But it was quite useless. Fractile wasn't even real.

"Three," Radiance blurted. "Three of us here."

The Woman—that Beast, that Lover—gazed at him perplexed, then down at herself and over at the Man, still firing off rounds.

She gave Fractile an almost sad smile. "Yes, Mr. Fractile. Yes, there are three of us."

Fractile laughed, deep in the skull. The Woman lifted her pistol to it.

SPLATTER. THINNEST vomit all down the bowl. Dignity, dignity...

Sparkle stood up too fast, had to grab the towel rail. She breathed deep; then she moved over to the sink and rested against it. The bathroom was sandstone, riddled with scratches.

"You look dreadful," she told the person in the mirror. Dark rings circled her eyes. Withdrawal.

"*I* look dreadful?" her lips shot back. "Take a look in the mirror sometime."

Sparkle shook her head and picked up the mouth freshener on the sink. "Never gets old with you, that one, does it?" She took a hit of the freshener and gurgled.

:Foolishness is your area of expertise, eh, Sis?: Swirl sent. *:Seriously, though; not long now.:*

Sparkle spat into the sink. She didn't rinse the freshener out.

"Hargie hasn't even called his people," she said. "Man's a root vegetable." Her temples began to throb. "He'd yawn at gelding shears."

"He was walking about earlier," her reflection said.

"What?" A rush of excitement coursed through Sparkle. She hadn't felt like that for so long. "How did I miss that?"

"Happened when you were sulking in the villa," Swirl told her. "We had that argument about fingernail dirt and you stomped off, remember?"

"Right," Sparkle said. She noticed bile on one of her dreads. "And you're still wrong. But you could've mentioned Hargie."

"We were vomiting," Swirl said. "Hardly seemed the time."

Sparkle laughed. "See? You *are* funny. Don't put yourself down. Let's go talk to him."

"Please," Swirl replied. "Shower first, eh?" Their lips stopped moving a while, both sisters in thought. "Makes you think, doesn't it?"

"What?" Sparkle said.

"The scratches on these walls; all those wretches forced to toil down here, like Aewyn said. Just to carve out a bathroom."

"Just now," Sparkle said, "when I said you were funny?"

"Retracted, yes?"

"At speed."

She took a shower, put some new clothes on from out of one of her shopping bags and shambled over to the room Hargie slept in. The door lay ajar. She knocked on it.

"Hargie?" No reply. Through the crack in the door, she could see the lights were low but not off. "Hargie?"

Sparkle stuck her head around the door before Swirl could boss her not to. Hargie was sprawled face up on the far side of the double bed, his head propped up on a pillow. He wore just shorts, an old sports t-shirt and that stupid hat of his, cocked over his right eye. He was asleep.

:Let's leave him,: Swirl sent.

"Hargopal?" Sparkle said.

The bubbleman opened his visible eye, but he didn't look at her.

"How are you?" Sparkle asked. She made a sympathetic face.

He took a while to answer. "Better." He closed his eyes again.

Sparkle walked across the room and sat on the edge of the bed. "Has Aewyn called?" she asked him. "Hargie?"

He opened his eyes again. Blinked. Then he leaned away from Sparkle and fished something out of the bedside cupboard. It was a savage-looking cigarette, homemade. He lit it and took a drag.

"Hargie?"

"Yeah." He breathed out. The smoke was sweet, sinisterly perfumed. "Fixed a meet."

Sparkle felt like every muscle in her body had put its feet up and sighed. "Thank you."

:Well, that's a relief,: Swirl sent. *:Plan arranged. By the Eye... he's a state, isn't he?:*

Swirl's words bit at Sparkle. He'd climbed out of this fug right here, climbed out to help a stranger in need. Hargie wasn't a state. He was brave. That was the problem with Swirl: she couldn't see inside others' lives. No respect.

She studied Hargie a while. He stared ahead, probably watching something on his neuralware.

"Why are you always wearing that hat?" she asked him.

He said nothing, just smoked.

'I want to see what's under it," she said. "Come on."

Her hands drifted toward him, ever so slowly. Hargie made a lazy show of trying to avoid her, but he clearly knew struggling was futile.

She took off the hat, its faux fur warm, almost moist, between her fingers. Transpired he wasn't bald; a lot of the poorer feral males were that way. If anything, Hargie had too *much* hair. Two or three people's, in fact: black-brown with blond and reddish streaks. It reminded her of a calico cat she had once begged her parents for.

"Challenging," she said. "Yet prospects for improvement."

She pulled out her metal comb from the long pocket on her trousers. She play-acted approaching Hargie's locks with it, making the comb dance before him, mugging a sneaky face.

:Sparks, what are you doing?: Swirl sent.

Hargie squinted up at the movement, moaned and sighed a chuckle. He batted away her playful strikes. Grinning, she stopped, but kept the comb hovering. He kept his left arm up, a shield. The other he held out high and wide, protecting his cigarette from the theatre of war.

"Busybody," Hargie said, smiling, meeting her eyes. She hadn't met his eyes in days.

"Made you laugh," she said. "You laughed."

He made a lopsided smile, gazed away from her and back again. "Yeah."

"Hargie?" Sparkle said. "When's the meeting?"

"Tomorrow. Evening."

Sparkle threw the comb across the room, away from them both. She said 'fuck' in her own language. She dumped her face in one palm and rubbed her eyelids. Her temples throbbed again.

:We can hold on, Sparks.: Swirl sent. *:Come on; we've made it this far.:*

:We've never been this long without.: Sparkle replied.

When she gazed up again, Hargie was offering her the rough cigarette. It smouldered stronger on one side. She could feel its heat. "What is it?"

"Pooka," he said.

:No, Sparkle,: Swirl sent.

"Could it kill me?" Sparkle asked Hargie.

"Maybe choke on snacks." Hargie looked at it. "Aewyn leaves some. Helps comedowns."

"Pass it here." Sparkle had never smoked anything before. But on no account would she look an ingenue in front of a feral.

:Sparkle...:

She sucked on its... sucking end, took the gravelly smoke down, and immediately had a coughing fit. Hargie laughed.

"Monster," she told him between coughs, her throat rough as pig iron "Dying here." She handed back the cigarette and picked up the hat. It lay between them.

She turned the hat around, studied it. Green-grey, peaked, some metal decal on the front. Those long ear flaps. "Why do you wear this?"

"Luck." His nostrils twitched. "Sentiment."

"Did it belong to anyone?"

He stopped smiling. "You must be homesick."

"What?" She coughed again.

"You heard," he said.

"That's a deflection, Hargie."

"Yeah."

Sparkle looked over at the comb. She had a sudden need to lie down.

"I've got to lie down," she said. She did so.

:Should I go now?: Swirl sent *:I can go to the villa, it's really no problem.:*

:Don't be absurd.:

A minute passed. Hargie offered her the cigarette, but she waved no.

"I *am* homesick," she said to the sandstone ceiling. "Homesick means you can never relax. Two years. I can't sit down without the sense I'll have to stand up again." She glanced at him. "You get that, right? You travel."

"Used to standing," he said.

Sparkle laughed. She couldn't believe she laughed. "This is all right. I'm actually feeling all right."

:This stuff is strong,: Swirl sent. *:You know, we should really watch the news. Keep an eye out. Reconnaissance. We might be on it. By the Eye, we might be the top trender...:*

"It's the little things that knock my breath out," Sparkle said, reaching out to the cigarette and taking it. "Homesickness, I mean." She sucked on the wet paper, breathed out and passed back. She didn't cough this time. "I mean, everything's packaged here. Nothing's fresh. Vacuum-packed, laminated."

"Space," Hargie said.

:Sparkle,: said Swirl, *:Do you think we could look at the handheld? Seriously. Reconnaissance. The news...:*

Sparkle ignored her. "I've got used to the big things, oddly. The new language, different skin colours. The lack of any... well, theme."

She felt Hargie look at her. "All one tone where you're from?"

"Please," she said. "Zahrir's not some creepy backwater planet. We've two: birth-females dark as ember, birth-males pale as milk."

Hargie took a deep breath. "Always fucking with me."

"I'm not. I swear." She giggled. "Our guides, the Hoidrac, ensured it. Back during the Eighth Lavishment. There's variations of that sort of thing across many of our worlds."

"Why?" He stubbed the cigarette out on the sandstone cupboard.

:Tell him of the great dream-dawn, of the panpsychism,: Swirl sent. She was becoming agitated. Matters of faith always did that to her. *:Tell him, tell him, erm... actually, could we check the news? We, we didn't check the news.:*

"Erm," Sparkle said. "Aesthetics, I suppose. The Delighted Ones have the full plan, of course. We're too small to see it in full."

"Frankly?" Hargie asked.

"Yes?"

"Your guides are sinister fucks," he said.

"Hargie!"

:Feral moron.: Swirl said. *:Sis, tell him that—:*

:Swirl, just go,: Sparkle sent back. *:You're not helping. You're getting weird.:*

Swirl didn't reply. She was gone. Gone a little too fast.

"Fuck's sake, Stukes," Sparkle said. "You're talking about my culture here. My people."

Silence, thick and stuffy, lingered with the smoke.

"You want to watch movies?" Hargie said.

"Yes, I want to watch fucking movies."

He used his neuralware and brought up a screen that shivered into life inches below the ceiling. An action story: intelligence agent who'd had his head replaced with some sort of gun. Incomparably awful, but an awful she could enjoy.

"Understanding's a delusion," Sparkle said. It just came out. The smoke was everywhere in her head now. It made everything about the mind, but a mind that couldn't handle everything. No wonder Swirl had bailed. "In the final analysis, I mean. Understanding worlds, people. Not even ourselves. Nothing's connected, you know?"

"Too many damn outlooks," Hargie said.

They watched the movie, then another. He pulled another cigarette from the cupboard.

At some point, Hargie said: "Hat was Father's."

Some time after that, she fell asleep.

Six

AEWYN NUKE HAD TOLD Hargie to fix himself up. Insisted, in no small measure. That kind of deal. So Hargie had shaved, styled his hair, unwrapped the shiny brown suit in his wardrobe aboard *Princess* and put it on.

He looked himself up and down in the mirror. Yep: total prick.

But needs must. He'd bounced back this morning, had set himself to work customising *Princess* soon as he awoke.

He hadn't seen Sparkle since last night, when they'd snoozed watching *GunHead Jones IV*. Probably back in her room. Odd to think he'd feared her days ago, suspected her of being shadowed by the Great Foozle, devourer of ships. Now he watched movies and napped beside her. Go figure.

He walked out of his temporary bedroom and into the docking bay, heading toward the lift. He left his hat.

Princess Floofy's makeover was in progress. A cloud of hoxnites blurred her hide as if she were on some ill-connected neuralware screen. Pretty soon she'd be green, bright green, with a whole new array of bumps and preplanned bruises. Fresh ID too, courtesy of Aewyn: *Lady Fussington* out of Psiax Minor. Getting the drugs back to Fractile wouldn't be a problem. Theoretically.

"Hey," came Sparkle's voice behind him. He turned around to see her stumbling out of the hallway of the living area, simultaneously trying to holster her gun and not fall over. "Wait for me."

Woman looked like shit. She couldn't stand straight. Withdrawal had turned her bow-legged.

"Sorry," he said. "Should've explained. They're not expecting anyone else."

She glared at him. The dark rims around her eyes were particularly unnerving: they made her forehead look looming, almost bulbous.

"Don't mess me around, Stukes," she said. "Do I look like I want to be messed around?"

"Look like you'd melt if sneezed on," Hargie said. "Get some rest. I'll be back soon."

"Fine," she said. "Get shot. Or worse. I'm here to protect you, remember?"

"From what? A puppy on crutches?"

Sparkle pulled out her pistol and spun it in her hand with alarming ease. She pointed at him and pretended to fire. She re-holstered. "How's that, puppy-dog?"

"Melodramatic," he replied. "Look, I ain't gonna burn you, tune? Not going anywhere without *Princess*. Hell, if I do... consider her a down payment."

She laughed. "Oh, that ship's a deposit, all right."

He couldn't stand it when people laughed at their own jokes.

"Screw you," he told her. "*Princess* saved your life enough times." He shook his head. "You were nothing like this last night."

She frowned, her eyes thin slits. "What happened last night?"

"Don't you remember?"

"I..." She stopped, closed her eyes as if in pain, then said: "Will you please shut *up*!"

"What?" Hargie said. "I didn't say anything."

Her eyes went wide, almost panicked. "I... just... look, just scram, you little rat. Scram and fetch my leaf."

"Oh, scram *and* fetch your leaf?"

"That's about the size of it," she said. "You're my little errand bitch, Stukes."

"Hey, I'm Fractile's errand bitch." It had sounded good before he said it. "Screw this, screw this in its deeply weird toes. See you later." He walked over to the lift doors. "Oh and we watched movies last night, you amnesiac freak."

"I know!" she shouted. "Of course I know..."

He got in the lift and lit a cigarette.

RESPLENDENT UPON A silver chaise longue, the Ashemi gazed at the domed vault above. The vault rose high and slender into shadow, its malachite walls decorated with some naturally fluorescent purple stone. It occurred to the Ashemi that being in this dining hall was akin to being inside a hollow lilac, a vast and empty bud that would never bloom. From where had that image arisen? Why lilacs? His forgotten mortal life, perhaps, before his ascension to the Geode's depths? Before Ashemihood?

"Of course," the aged house seneschal Topaz, the one who'd first greeted him, was saying, "the Savards are a noble line, descended from the pilot families themselves."

The Ashemi did not reply. He kept his new statueform's face aimed at the dome above. Best to let these people, these admiring mortals, stew in expectation. He watched geode-beasts swim through the air above, denizens of the lilac dome: shoals of tiny oneiropomps, flat-bellied monomantas, a selachian upon its lonesome patrol. A tailored ecology of fauna from another reality, the Geode, armoured and domesticated for service in the mortal universe. Not a little like himself.

"Though now a decayed line," Topaz continued after a silence, "they have brought forth remarkable family members in recent centuries. One might only mention the poet—"

"Savard," the Ashemi said, choosing that moment to meet Topaz's eyes, to acknowledge those around him. Each of the other five dinner guests froze upon their couches, their mouths histrionically wide. Good. "I thought I recognised the name. The love poet, yes?"

"Yes, your Ashemi," Topaz said. "Magnificent odes, too. Odes dedicated to... Pheoni the Appropriate, as a matter of fact."

"Topaz," the Ashemi said through sculpted lips, "why are you telling me this?"

"Because..." The old woman, dark-skinned like all Zahrir women, looked about at her fellow Triune notables. "Because Pearl-Swirl-Sparkle's betrayal of, of Pheoni the Appropriate was wholly unlike their family. Wholly unlike."

"You'll forgive me, Seneschal Topaz," the Ashemi told her. "I am freshly risen from the Geode's depths, sheathed only in this insipid sculpture and deracinated of any and all memories of that other dimension, save only what knowledge our divine mistress has deigned pertinent to my investigation. Clearly I am discombobulated and fatigued. I do not see how the verse of a long-dead poet affects anything."

Topaz looked from couch to couch, then at the floor. "My apologies, your Ashemi." She bowed her head, her white dreadlocks hanging like a willow tree.

"The facts themselves," the Ashemi said. "We wrestle with the facts themselves." Peculiar, lying upon a couch without feeling its form or warmth. Life as a moving sculpture was lived at a remove. "Who oversees this house's wards? Who watches them?"

"We, your Ashemi," said a young man, pale-skinned like all Zahrir males, hair a silver-blond bowl save for two lengths cut like daggers that hung before each ear. "I, Gleam, maintain security here. My headbrother, Glare, sees to the students' final year of training."

"And your other headsibling?"

Gleam shrugged. "A beast-technician. He has no portfolio here."

"Gleam," the Ashemi said, "what happened two years ago?"

Gleam squinted. "I had thought your Ashemi would be in possession of the relevant details and memories."

"I am," the Ashemi said. "I should like to hear it in words. Concise words."

Gleam placed his cup on the table beside his couch. "My brother Glare says Pearl-Swirl-Sparkle were his greatest students. Pearl, particularly. We admit—have long freely admitted—that we may have given Pearl far too much latitude regarding this building's memory lattice."

"May have?"

"Your Ashemi," Gleam answered, "we failed. We shall never expunge this stain."

"Plainly," the Ashemi said. "Continue."

"The facts are scanty," Gleam said. "Pearl accessed the lattice on some fundamental level, stole some information, and then expunged any memory of what that information even was. Pearl's headsisters—Swirl and Sparkle—had their own memories expunged of all detail of the crime: no one, least of all themselves, have any idea of the degree of their accessory. They were exiled to feral space, waiting for a sign of divine forgiveness."

"And of Pearl?"

"Pearl used the memory lattice to penetrate the tether-prison," Gleam said. "His personality is sealed within one of the prison's opals." He looked around. "Thus far, none of us can access him."

The Ashemi let silence breed. He reached a silver-taloned hand out to his couch-side table, took a handful of leaf and crushed it. He opened up his wrought-iron ribcage and poured the leaf dust into the snapping blue flames of his heart furnace. He felt the room become that little more vibrant, that little more real.

"People," he said, "a fear hangs over you. A muted terror. You know this, as do I. This fear comes robed in a question: how could a mere student, no matter their brilliance, ever hope to bamboozle such an august establishment, indeed, upset the very warp and weft of what should and should not be possible with regards to a mere human and their use of the Geode?" He inclined his head to one side. "Well, I have news: it isn't possible."

He had expected a sharp intake of breath from all the dinner guests. None came. Perhaps they had been expecting as much, as convicts expect the blade.

"No," the Ashemi continued, "this takes a Hoidrac hand. A Hoidrac patron to help out dear, brilliant, noble Pearl. Unfortunately, not Pheoni the Appropriate, the Hoidrac to which this planet has long paid homage. Rather..." He held the pause. "Mohatoi Embossed."

"The gods forever war," Seneschal Topaz muttered.

"Such histrionics," the Ashemi chided her. "The Hoidrac never war amongst themselves. That's a human curse. The Hoidrac merely vie to outshine."

"Of course, your Ashemi," Topaz said, bowing like a grey willow again.

"I should like to inspect the Trinity House now," the Ashemi said. "I should like to see this opal."

"HERE YOU ARE, DICKHEAD."

"Appreciated." Hargie took the beer out of Aewyn's hand. "You're one of the good ones, you spiked-toothed deviant."

"I knows it."

They sat by the window, the place they always sat when they came to this bar. Padded seats, low music and lower lighting. Stink of yeast and tobacco. A view of Old Town's maintube outside. Hargie took a sip and watched folk pass. Native Calranese, mainly, short and blond. But every kind of person wound up here scratching for work, all of them lost-looking, saffron ghosts beneath the tunnel city's sodium lights. Kushua: capital of Hailmogambo crust, lowest place in all Desolation Row.

"What you strung out about, Harg?" Aewyn asked.

"Me?"

"Gazing out that window like a nihilist goldfish, you are.'

"It's... my customer," Hargie said. "Sparkle."

"Found her to be a nice enough lady," Aewyn said. "In her way."

"Psycho." Hargie made a wide-eyed face, pointed at his temple. "Mood up and down like an olden-day space lift. Made worse by having none of that rinky-dink drug of hers. She's a fiend. Fuck it. I'm glad we're sitting here, glad we're making her wait."

"Mood up and down, eh?" Aewyn said. "No call for that now, is there, Mr. Bubbleman?"

"It's different from the jumpjunk, Aewyn."

"How so?"

"That's what I'm trying to figure," Hargie said. "Sometimes I swear she hears things I don't say."

"Part and parcel of having a snatch, that."

"No." Hargie rolled his eyes, went to adjust a hat on his head that wasn't there. "I mean... before I left, she replied to something I didn't say, you tune? I dunno. Forget it."

"Your woman's got you all tuned out," Aewyn said.

"She's not my woman," Hargie said.

"Yeah but you're gunning to fuck her, right?"

Hargie looked him in the eye. "No woman I don't," he said. "What's your goddamn point?"

They both fell silent. Hargie looked out the window again.

"Your sister," Aewyn said eventually.

"Sick fuck."

"No," Aewyn said, shaking his head. "New topic, man. I keep hearing about her from bubblers staying at my girls. She's a player now. Riding on yer rep, mind, but still."

"She'll grow out of it," Hargie said.

"Look, why don't you go back home, eh?"

"I get that a lot," Hargie said. "Mainly before the fists."

"Seriously, man," Aewyn said. "You'd be the fucking, I dunno, bubbleking or some shit."

"Swore vengeance, remember?"

"Ratshit," Aewyn said. "Everyone who offed yer dad are dead, probably. We both knows that. Just say you topped off some last big guy. They love you, man. You'd be running that gaff in seconds, you would."

"You just want someone who'll pay your debts," Hargie said. "Mauve son of a bitch."

Aewyn leaned back against his seat's backrest. He smiled a sharp and melancholy smile.

"Yeah," he said. "Shit. Even me family treat me like a piss-taker now."

"Sound judgement."

Aewyn laughed bitterly. "Fuck off."

Hargie thought better of pushing the matter further.

"So," he said, "when we meeting this guy?"

"Whenever you like, man," Aewyn said.

"Nearby?"

"Exceedingly," Aewyn said.

"So who is this asshole?"

"Oi, be nice," Aewyn said. "He just stood you a drink."

Aewyn pulled a lemon-shaped silver box out of his coat and put it on the table.

Hargie looked at him. He picked up the box and unscrewed one end, peeked inside. It looked the part. At least the part Sparkle had described to him: see-through lilac-coloured leaves, their veins faintly glowing. Hundreds of them.

"Hey," Aewyn said, "where's me thumb-love?"

Hargie placed his thumb against Aewyn's and sent him Fractile's money.

"Tidy," Aewyn said.

"Somewhere a bookie cheers," Hargie said.

"Not if I can help it."

"Question," Hargie said. "Why didn't you tell me up front?" He looked down at his suit. "Shit, why'd you get me dragging up?"

"To get you out of that stupid hat, for starters," Aewyn said, sipping his drink. "More importantly, get you off that fucking ship. Proper night out, you and me. When's the last time we had a real cruise, eh?"

"I dunno," Hargie said. "Sparkle's scratching the walls back there..."

"Make her wait. You said so yourself. Come on; druggies curse a dealer while they wait, worship him when he arrives. Be a learning curve for her."

Hargie stroked his chin. He wasn't used to no stubble there. He thought about Sparkle. She was in a bad place. He wouldn't want that for himself, so—

"I knows what you're thinking," Aewyn said. "You're letting that bubble philosophy fuck with you. That 'how would I feel if I were them' bollocks."

"Empathic rationalism," Hargie said.

"Yeah that shit," Aewyn said. "Okay, let's run with that. How's she feel right now?"

"Like her mind's pissing red."

"And that made her treat you like what?"

"A red-piss potty."

"So if you were her—a *future* her, and you looked back on it all—wouldn't you see you—which is now Sparkle as you, mind—as providing a valuable lesson in the long term? About how not to treat others? I know you, Hargie, and you want to do right by people, even when you're some hypothetical foreign drug-fiend lady."

Hargie sipped his drink. "That's the worst argument since democracy."

"Oh come on, what d'you expect? Closest to philosophy round here's how to steal copper wiring without getting shot. Come on; you and me, man." He raised an eyebrow. "Bet she slagged off *Princess Floofy*. Am I right?"

"She called her a 'deposit,'" Hargie said.

"A what?"

"You heard."

"Shit, pal," Aewyn said. "Bang out of order, that."

Hargie finished his glass. "Screw it. Let's get shit-faced."

Aewyn grinned wide. "That's me boy."

"SPARKLE," SWIRL SAID, "are you using our right eye?"

"No," said her lips. "I wouldn't... oh wait, I am. Why am I doing that?"

"Withdrawal. Involuntary response," Swirl said. "Stop it."

"Involuntary, huh? I've got a real nerve..."

Swirl ignored her sister's sarcasm—at their age it was like muscle memory—and lay back on the bed. Too dizzy. She closed her eyes. She missed Lyreko's arms around her. His was definitely the best bed she'd lain on outside of the Harmonies; the bed she lay on now was a close second, the bed on *Princess Floofy* a continental shelf-drop below both. Swirl enjoyed making lists. Arrangement was a sort of meditation.

"Swirl?" her lips said.

"Yes, Sparkle?"

"It's been two hours."

"He'll be back," Swirl said.

"You were very rude to him."

"Seriously, Spark, is there something going on with you two?"

"I'm not the feral-shafter, darling," Sparkle said.

"What about that woman when we first arrived at the rig?" Swirl said.

"Reconnaissance," Sparkle said. "Stop derailing. We shouldn't have pissed him off. You're the tactical one, you should know that."

"It *is* tactical," Swirl said. "He's going to do the job whatever, may as well keep him on his toes. He'll be back soon enough."

"Maybe." Sparkle laughed inside their skull. "It was funny when you called him an errand bitch."

"Yes," Swirl said. "The deposit line was better, though. Thanks for feeding me that."

"Please, you'll make us blush."

Pain stabbed inside Swirl's guts. She rolled on her side and curled up.

"Oh, please..."

The pain went.

"Feel like we're dying," Sparkle muttered.

"Hardly news," Swirl said.

News. Swirl remembered last night, her paranoid urge to see the news. She opened her eyes: still uncoordinated, painfully dizzy. Body control breaking down. She closed her right eye and stumbled off the bed and on to her feet. "Where's the handheld?"

"Lie down," Sparkle said.

"I just want to see."

The handheld lay on the floor atop Sparkle's ghastly red fur coat. Swirl sat back on the bed, switched the thing on and—with her right eye shut—dialled up the memestream.

For a moment, her body felt entirely one again, glued whole by terror.

"Fuck..." she felt and heard Sparkle say.

A composite picture of their shared face stared back at them. A good one: security forces must have rendered it from whatever footage when they'd visited Freightways. They had one of Hargie too, less good. His hat had come in useful after all.

"I don't get it," Sparkle said. "This is an intersystem newsfeed. We wouldn't make that for outrunning a security detail."

Swirl rolled the page along. Bounty... big bounty. Transpired they were wanted for questioning over the destruction of the rig back in Eucrow. It mentioned the deaths of more than eight thousand.

"We have to call Hargie," Swirl said.

"Eight thousand..." Sparkle muttered. "That's aw—"

"Snap out of it," Swirl said. "What's Stukes' ID?"

"What?" Sparkle said.

"His neuralware. What's his ID so we can call him?"

"...No idea."

Swirl growled and fell back on the mattress.

THE TWO MEN MADE THEIR way along the esplanade of Old Town's maintube, shuffling past shift workers and pooka-heads, whores and evangelists. On the corner was an old convenience store Hargie would get smokes from whenever he visited. Now it was a blasted skeleton, its breezeblock innards sprawled across the pavement. Black speakers sat in the windows of what remained of the second floor, belching out smudgecore beats. Two Clan

Nuke soldiers with compaction rifles lay against them, nodding their topknot scalps to the rhythm. They drank soda through canine gas masks.

"Where we going?" Hargie shouted to Aewyn. The speakers would have annoyed him if his ears weren't still ringing from the club they'd left.

Glancing over his shoulder, Aewyn replied something like 'consolation' or maybe 'constellation'.

A tall woman wearing a houri-field approached Hargie. "Intercourse?" she asked.

"*Intercourse*?" Hargie said.

"Intercourse," the woman repeated. Her smiling lips shifted in shape and colour, so too her eyes and nose. If you paid and linked, she could shift to whatever you most desired, but you'd be a desperate soul to do it: half the streetwalkers were infected, would wreck your neuralware with viruses.

"No thank you," Hargie said.

"Intercourse!" she said, and wrapped her arm around his shoulders.

"Get off," he said, pushing her away. Aewyn was ahead of him, fading into the crowd. He left the woman behind, shouldered past drunks and ship crew.

"Hargie!" Aewyn turned around and shouted.

"I'm here."

"We're both here." Aewyn pointed at an obsolete shuttle that had been converted to a building. Women and young men leaned out of the exhaust ports, smoking roll-ups and pouting at no one.

"Consolation," Aewyn said. He grinned and the red diamond tattoo on his cheek rose.

"Aw, shit," Hargie said. Goddamn *intercourse*. "Friend, we ain't teens no more."

"Speak for yourself. C'mon, boy; bound to be someone in there looks like her."

"Fuck you," Hargie muttered beneath the music.

"What?"

He shook his head, then nodded his assent. At least he'd find some quiet there.

It would be free, Aewyn told him inside. To the Clan and friends it would always be free. Hargie's head hurt. Things were starting to spin.

The madame was all piled-up hair and cheap perfume, and her girls lined up. Hargie tried to let Aewyn choose first—that way Hargie could sit out and smoke in the lounge—but Aewyn was insistent that Hargie pick first. He did so, didn't really look.

In the cramped red room, he realised the woman was younger than she'd looked in the lounge.

"How you wannit, sir?"

He slumped onto the bed. "Sit on that chair over there."

She did so. "Now wha'?"

"Dunno," Hargie said. "Check your 'ware, maybe. Give me twenty minutes. Rest my eyes." The ceiling spun clockwise above him. "Just this kink I got..."

"Sir," she said. "Twenty minutes."

He'd fallen asleep. Confused, he got up and looked at her. She gazed at the floor, checking out her neuralware as he'd asked.

"Hold your thumb out," he said.

She did so. He pressed his thumb against hers and paid 100 rupees. He'd expected—hoped—she would smile. Call him decent, a good man. She never even looked up.

He sat in the lounge and smoked liked he'd planned to. Girls and rents lounged around him, silent and placid. He could have left—wanted to—but he had to say bye to Aewyn. The booze maybe, but he didn't want to see him again. Was it possible he'd, well, outgrown his friend? He didn't want to grow up. To most that meant family, a home. To Hargie? Fuck. What?

Aewyn strode into the lounge. "That's it," he told Hargie. "Completed the set now, so I have."

"Damn hooker nerd," Hargie said. "I gotta go back."

"*No*, man. Clubbing, man," Aewyn said.

"Next time," Hargie said.

"*Man.*"

"No," Hargie said. "She's... she's waiting."

"Leashed, you are," Aewyn told him.

"She's my crew, Aewyn." Hell, maybe she was.

"You don't do crews, you friggin' hermit."

"Maybe I do now," Hargie said.

"And maybe she's gone." Aewyn gazed at the ceiling. "She's gone, pal."

"What you mean?"

"No clue, eh?" Aewyn shook his head. "Watch the news, you self-absorbed bastard. There's a bounty on the pair o' you."

Hargie leaped to his feet. "What?"

"Sorry, man," Aewyn said. The boys are picking her up, be shipping her to Freightways. Freightways' bounty."

"Fucker!"

Hargie swung out, aiming for Aewyn's jaw but connecting with his cheekbone. Aewyn stumbled back, whores and rents screaming. Hargie went to grab Aewyn's collar, but the other man pulled out a handgun. Hargie froze.

"Stupid bastard," Aewyn said, pointing the gun and cradling his face. "Never carry a gun, do you? This is Desolation-fuckin'-Row!" He eyed the crowd. "Out! Out, the frigging lot o' you! Now!"

They did so.

"Asshole," Hargie said. "Stinking Calranese shitwad."

"What?" Aewyn said. "What now? She ain't your woman. She's a psycho: you said that. Wouldn't be doing this if she meant shit to you. Fuck, there's a bounty on you, Harg. I could double me money here, but I won't. S'why I got you all dressed up, isn't it? So no one wises up. No selling out Hargie Stukes. Promise. Owe you too much. Fuckin' love you, man."

"Then why?" Hargie said. "Ah, fuck you, I know why."

"Yeah," Aewyn said. "I can laugh off debtors but not me own clan. Family, isn't it? Won't abide a piss-taker. Sparkle's head stops me being arse-up in a sewer. Plain as. Your *pal*."

"Put that fucking gun down, 'pal'," Hargie said.

"No chance. And don't think I won't scatter your head over that pot plant there if you come at me. Clan'll be taking her by now. How you gonna smack the Clan, you twat? Eh? You can stay at Sophi long as you like, fix *Princess* proud. I won't say a word, we both know that." He grimaced, his sawn fangs gleaming pink in the light. "Just fucking *walk*, will you? Walk it off."

Hargie took a long breath, stared as he did so. "One day."

"Yeah," Aewyn said. "One day."

Hargie turned and ran out the shuttle bordello. He'd wasted time. If he ran, maybe...

SHE FELL TOWARD CALRAN, her mind one with the insertion-craft's telemetric and visual sensors. A part of the craft.

A series of temperaments reached her. Long-range Kollective transmissions were difficult in and above this world. Whatever the alien builders had done to Calran's core singularly affected Konsensus technology on some as-yet undetermined quantum level. There was a time lag, and so Zo and her cadre's reports arrived as missives.

Melid was pleased to find Zo had located and tagged that bubbleman, Hargie Stukes. A remarkable piece of fieldwork; Melid would hate to emote as much to Zo when their kollectives merged.

The Domov, Conybeare, had lost the bubbleship's signal as it entered the underside of the floating crust locals called Hailmogambo. Apparently the bubbleman had risen up into the crust's interior somehow, emerging in the old quarter of Hailmogambo's largest tunnel-city. Likely signal loss was due to the sheer volume of rock, rather than deliberate removal of the locator tag. The woman remained unaccounted for.

The woman. Swirl or Sparkle. Hard to evaluate, everything about her. Melid brooked no mysteries.

The woman's Harmonic origin was an unexpected matter. That fact had injected consternation and several competing reevaluations into the mission. Specifically, it had caused disagreement between Melid and Conybeare itself, Conybeare being an amalgamation of everyone involved—including, ultimately, whichever unseen element of the Instrum's power web directed this mission.

Closer to Calran now. She could feel a gravity well's seduction against the hull of the craft, the rising heat of Calran's naked core.

The Harmonies lay far up the galactic spire. More to the point, they lay beyond standard Konsensus territory and influence. Beyond the Fugue.

(ah, the rush of ozone upon the skin of her hull, the embrace of Calran's stratosphere)

The Fugue came into effect about half way along the galactic spire. The Konsensus remained uncertain as to the cause, but long-distance communication through Kollectiveware became impossible. No one had ever entertained colonisation out there; a local kollective might function well enough, but removed from the Kollective-at-Large, it would be prone to toxic individuality. Worse, kancerisation.

Melid and everyone concerned had thought Swirl-Sparkle an agent of relatively local Worlder power: Luharna, say, or Vartiga, or the Calran Combine. If the woman returned to one of those worlds, the Instrum could follow her. Yet now, if one assumed she was heading toward her far home, the mission's time became limited. Following her into the Fugue would be foolhardy, perhaps impossible.

Obfuscation everywhere. Scalpels, Harmonies, the leaf-drug: all obscure, shrouded in their disparate ways. Illik had sought some link between the scalpel-entities and the leaf. The incident back on the rig had proven him likely correct. Fatally so. Illik would have some hypothesis by now, would have forced all these new facts into lucidity. Melid knew herself no worthy successor. She needed Illik's wisdom now, more than ever.

Melid's request for more resources had been denied by Conybeare before she'd even vocalised the thought. Instead, it had elected to alert and reinforce the western fleets of the Instrum along the Fugue's border. A pointless task, to Melid's way of thinking, but obfuscation was the primary outward policy of the Konsensus. Any large-scale operation in so central a Worlder system as Calran endangered that mandate. No mission could justify it.

No matter. Melid's small cadre would proceed as directed. The Konsensus had long triumphed against formidable odds.

Hailmogambo rose toward her. Its upper surface was shadow, its sides red in the exposed core's light.

"Corpses," she whispered. "Crows."

"SHE'S GOT A GUN!" A voice shouted. "A gun!"

Swirl had thrown their shared, thus-far still living body down behind a waist-high graphene crate, back first. It had hurt, though Swirl clearly worked through the pain to a degree Sparkle had to wonder at.

Sparkle used their augmented vision to glance around while Swirl reloaded. They were facing the east corner of Sophi's bay's granite walls, tight up against it, about two metres to spare. The left wall of the corner had fresh ammo marks in it. The right wall had a corpse at its base.

Sparkle studied the corpse. Young man, Calranese. Shaved head and topknot, smoking hole in his chest courtesy of Swirl. Sparkle had taken his face for blemished or wounded when he'd first attacked. Now she could see his face was illustrated with a tattoo. A red diamond.

:Clan Nuke,: Sparkle sent to her sister. *:Aewyn's betrayed us.:*

Swirl ignored her, checked the gun and looked about. Soldier stuff.

:His gun,: Sparkle sent. *:It's a big rifle thing.:*

"Tarantella," Swirl replied, eyes darting, making Sparkle ill. "Needle gun."

:Yes, but should we use it?:

"Shut up," Swirl said. "And stop moving our right eye. Need it right now."

:Involuntary, remember?: Sparkle sent. *:It's getting worse...:*

"Close it shut, then," Swirl said.

The crate rattled. Light flashed against either side of it, danced off the walls beyond.

Silence. Glowing needles littered the floor.

Sparkle closed their right eye.

:There you go.: She felt the cheek muscles on her right side move to the words of her intra-send.

"Hey!" A female voice, croaky. "You there, girl!"

Swirl didn't respond.

"This will be easier," the woman shouted, "if you just surrender. Freightways want a word. Nice people, Freightways. You won't be harmed."

:Ask them about Hargie,: Sparkle sent.

"Shut up," Swirl muttered.

"Don't fret about our Kezzy," the woman shouted. "Kezzy was a proper twat. Could've shot him meself, love."

:Hargie,: Sparkle sent.

"Where's Hargie?" Swirl shouted.

The woman was silent a moment. Then she shouted: "No idea what you mean. Nice to hear from you, though. Appreciated."

"Makes sense," Swirl muttered to Sparkle. 'If they had him, they'd use him.'

Sparkle pictured the layout of the bay.

:Swirl,: she sent, *:I've an idea.:*

"Hey," the woman shouted. "I don't like games, girl. Prosaic is what I is. Prosaic like a fucking hammer. Innit, boys?"

Needles bounced off the crate.

"You got fifty seconds," the woman shouted. "Choose fucking sagely."

Swirl whispered to Sparkle: "Your idea?"

:I think there's a pile of hoxnite cylinders near them.: Sparkle sent. *:Just to the right.:*

"Yes?" Swirl said.

:If that gun of yours can pierce them, they'll fly out like smoke.:

"Kill them?" Swirl said.

:No, they're inert unless programmed,: Sparkle sent. *:But they'll choke and blind them. Then we make a run for* Princess' *hatch.:*

"Fine, let's do it." Swirl rolled around to face the back of the crate. 'Wait. We can't pilot the thing. We run for the lift."

"Love," the woman shouted, "you're taking the piss now, love."

:Wait,: Sparkle sent. *:They came from the lift. There'll be someone in there.:*

"I'll improvise," Swirl told her.

:That's so not your personality type.:

"We go in three," Swirl told her. "Brace yourself."

Sparkle kept imagining needles in her body. Where would they hit? How would it feel?

"One..." Swirl counted. "Two..."

"Come out, girl!" The woman yelled.

"Three."

Swirl leaped up, torso above the crates. She didn't fire.

:What?: Sparkle sent.

"The arm!" Swirl said. "You'reworking the gun arm, Spar—"

The pain was a giant fist crushing Sparkle like a plastic cup. The air glowed.

:Idiot,: Swirl sent to her before they hit the floor.

THE ASHEMI AND GLEAM strode along the corridors of the Trinity House; the walls, floors, and ceilings were an unbroken swirl of chequered tiles. Triune students stopped as the Ashemi passed, the younger ones gawping, the older wise enough to bow their heads.

No doubt they would tell their children about this day. The presence of an Ashemi, a human made blessed servitor, implied the will of the Hoidrac themselves. It implied an exceptional once-human, too: entire generations could live and die without any of their number selected for Ashemihood, for immortality.

"I do not suppose you have ever left this place," the Ashemi said to Gleam through still and gilded lips. "Student, adept, then security..." He gazed at a young student, who duly ran away. "Then head of same."

"Not since I was five," Gleam said. "Not for any length of time."

"I rather sympathise," the Ashemi said. "In a sense, I've never been anywhere but here myself."

"No personal memories," Gleam said, nodding. "Your kind's condition when you revisit this reality."

"You say that like I'm cursed."

It felt good, towering over every single human being. The Ashemi wondered if he had been tall in his pre-Ashemi life, whatever it had been, in whatever century. Perhaps he had not; perhaps a memory of eternally having to keen his neck upwards remained, floating in the murk of his id.

Perhaps his divine mistress, Pheoni the Appropriate, intended it that way.

They stopped at the doorway to the tether cell, its frame a fifteen foot arch carved from one piece of ivory. A communic was built into the doors' black wood; Gleam pushed his face into its fluid metal—horizontal yet never spilling—and the doors melted open. A spiral staircase descended into a blue haze below.

The stairwell descended into a chamber like the inside of a shell, its surfaces mother of pearl. A great fresco above: a painting of Pheoni herself in symbolic dragon-headed form, the bipedal shape in which Hoidrac typically manifested before humanity. The fresco portrayed a moment fitting for this place: the Dissenter's exile. A Hoidrac cast out from its realm by its own peers, by Pheoni and her consorts, falling toward an isolation unknowable to mortal minds. As with all representations of the Dissenter, its face had been scratched out, save for the mouth. The Dissenter's grin unnerved the Ashemi.

A hundred small alcoves indented the walls, each set with opals the size of human heads.

"The tethered," Gleam explained.

"Hard to imagine a prettier prison," the Ashemi said. "Where is Pearl?"

Gleam led him across the room to an opal that glowed pink and red from one moment to the next. The pendants and talismans that hung from the Ashemi's leather mane rattled as he walked. They echoed in the chamber like the warning of some unseen serpent.

Inside the opal, at its equator, a gold-green spiral turned.

"Like a galaxy," the Ashemi observed. "Fitting. An individual's consciousness is a galaxy. A universe. Limitless, in its way."

"Ashemi," Gleam said. "It is a common fallacy that an entire personality can be contained within such opals."

"It's 'your Ashemi', Gleam."

"Apologies, your Ashemi."

"Continue." He did not look at the mortal. He could not look away from the opal.

"The deepest root of a human's personality—its mindless firmament—must remain within the body itself," Gleam said. "Without that, the higher personality fragments instantly, becomes an unaware morass of memory and sensation."

"So this is connected to Savard's body?" the Ashemi asked. "To the sisters? We're talking light years, man. I appreciate ships and people wyrm through the Geode daily... but to maintain a constant connection?"

"This House is one great amplifier, its towers' firmaments interlaced with the largest memory-lattice on Zahrir." Gleam paused. "With all respect, your Ashemi, I thought you would know this."

"Yes," the Ashemi said. "You would, wouldn't you?"

Has she even sent me to investigate? he wondered, gazing again at the fresco of Pheoni, her skin, hair, and clothing pure white. With Hoidrac it was hard to tell. The Ashemi could just as well be her unwitting performance piece, an ironic statement. A jape.

He looked at Gleam. "Why would anyone place themselves in a prison?" the Ashemi asked him. "Even one comely as this?"

"As you said, your Ashemi," Gleam said. "He likely did so at the behest of our great mistress' rival."

"Mohatoi Embossed."

"Only he could have the power to manipulate this situation," Gleam said. "Any human working here without the patronage of another Hoidrac would be detected and annihilated by our divine Pheoni."

"But why this?" the Ashemi said, pointing at the opal. He looked at Gleam, who seemed bored, as if this were a chore. "Why not just leave this world under the shield of Mohatoi, go to one of his patronised worlds? Culakwun, say."

Gleam sneered at the name of Zahrir's rival planet. "You have a theory, your Ashemi?"

"Something inside Pearl, a memory, perhaps," the Ashemi said. "Too noticeable for it to be taken out of the House."

"And so Pearl holes up inside here," Gleam said.

"A fortress. A siege. We see he is here, and yet we cannot get to him." The Ashemi shook a silver-taloned finger. "He waits for a relief force."

"He waits," Gleam repeated.

"Culakwun," the Ashemi said. "Is there an Envoy for Culakwun on this planet?"

"There's an Envoy in this very House," Gleam said.

"What?"

"We have Envoys in their palace-salons." Gleam shrugged. "Both worlds like to keep their rivals near."

"Or rub each other's noses in it. A saying of the ancients," the Ashemi explained when Gleam frowned. "Take me to their Envoy."

"Of course."

The Ashemi gazed at the opal once more. What secret could its mind-spiral clutch?

He reached out to touch its glassy surface. Gleam slapped his hand away.

"How dare you!" the Ashemi said.

The persona-bindi upon Gleam's forehead had changed from green to red. Gleam's brother: Glare.

"Apologies, your Ashemi," Glare said, his face blank, rigid. "Touching the opal might break its connection to the building's memory lattice. It might kill Pearl."

The Ashemi tilted his head. "Then you are forgiven. But I wonder... why could we not smash the thing and be done with the matter?" He laughed bitterly.

Glare didn't reply.

Seven

BOTTLE IN HAND, HARGIE staggered down the tunnelled streets of some new city, that prefab sort hatching all over Calran. Blueprint metropolis. No past, all function. He didn't know its name. He'd just stepped off at a station.

New concrete bathed in halogen yellow. The locals passed him by, eyeing his bottle. The wrong people drank at this time. Bet your ball sack, Jack.

They seemed to be from all over human space. Only thing connecting these citizens was poverty. Hargie hoped that that connection was enough for some new thing to bloom. Clan Nuke preferred their immigrants divided, ensured it with pay in one hand, guns in the other. The Clan Nuke were but a local segment of the Clan Combine, but oh-so-fucking indicative. Indicative of anywhere Hargie went.

He came out at a freshly-made river, its banks concrete and compressed waste. Hargie leaned against the rail and looked out. The orange lights of the street behind him rippled upon black waters. The riverbank opposite couldn't be seen. No lights out there. Cave wall.

He'd felt better, that's for sure. He'd done worse things in his life, but... he'd felt better.

He hated Sparkle. He'd called her 'crew,' for fuck's sake. How'd that happen? He'd kept from people, had ridden alone, and whenever the jumpjunk rushed his veins, he'd shared in the laughter of the stars. Way to be.

He threw his bottle into the rippling blackness and watched it float. *Who were you, girl?* he thought. *Who were you?* He winced, closed his eyes.

"Intercourse?" a female voice said over his shoulder.

Hargie turned around. It was the tall streetwalker from Old Town. Her voice, at least. Her real face was unknown, her appearance a shifting deluge of classically attractive features. She had a hell of a patrol, Hargie knew that much. The pair of them must have been a hundred miles from where they'd first met.

"Lady," Hargie said, "you've come a long way."

She said nothing.

"Look... your tenacity's tribute to the ol' capitalist ethic," Hargie said. "But don't you think I wasn't a likely john the first time you asked? Because I sure as hell ain't now."

"She means intercourse with me," came another female voice.

Hargie looked to its source. A tall, almost spindly woman walked toward him. She had short black hair and cheekbones sleek as knives. She wore an elegant but dated dress over a weird black bodysuit. He'd seen that bodysuit before.

A gun barrel pressed against his ribs. The streetwalker. He looked back at her. Her houri-field had stopped. Illik's daughter. She still had that stupid teeny-fan hairdo with its angry pigtails. Same brutal smile.

So the game ends here, he thought. If only he knew what he'd even been playing.

"Well?" the woman in the dress asked him.

Hargie looked at her. "You'll have to buy dinner first."

WORLDER FOOD. AWFUL, simply awful. Melid had ordered skewered kebabs of some kind; Illik had once told her they were similar to compacted insect. Illik could sometimes be wrong.

"Not eating?" she asked the bubbleman, Hargopal Stukes.

He looked at Zo sitting between them, wolfing down something brown and sticky, making a mess. "Let's leave that to the professionals," he said.

"The woman you travelled with recently," Melid said.

"Yeah, I remember. She could grasp the idea of cutlery."

The man looked toward the busy restaurant's shaded observation windows: the planet's naked core filled the bottom third, darkness the middle and the underside of 'Old Tel', Hailmogambo's neighbouring crust plate, above. Stukes' face was placid, beyond Melid's ability to read. No kollective connection. Another talking corpse.

"Swirl," Melid said. "I want to talk about Swirl."

"What?" He didn't look at her. Very annoying.

"I mean Sparkle," Melid said. "I misspoke."

"That so?" Still he did not look. She got the feeling he was used to being interrogated. How intriguing it would be to place him in sensory deprivation.

"We only wish to help, Mr. Stukes."

He looked at her, finally. "Oh, you want to help? First, get your friend here a bib. Second, tell me who the fuck you people are. Aside from creepy walking broomsticks, I mean."

"We're from the Harmonies," she said. It just came out. There was no Kollective-at-Large, no Domov or Instrum to stop her. Just Zo's surprise. "Not from the same world as your friend, I should add. But of her side."

"Ratshit," he said. "Why'd you try to kill her back on the rig?"

"Not even slightly, Mr. Stukes. My associate here was trying to save her, even going so far as risking walking along a wire in deep space. But you saw that."

"Saw her fail, too," Stukes said.

Zo looked up from her meal. She issued annoyance at his statement. It intensified when she felt Melid's pleasure too.

"But she did try her best, Mr. Stukes," Melid said.

Zo grumbled into her food, spat out some gristle-like substance.

"Your pal, Illik," he said. "He died because of Sparkle. Something to do with her. I'd have thought you'd want revenge."

She felt him study her face with his lifeless eyes. Melid kept her expression blank. They could detect emotion in faces, these creatures. Were good at it, better than Konsensites. It was all they had.

"Mr. Stukes," Melid continued, "Sparkle has got herself into deep trouble. She is a good, if difficult person—I'm sure you know that—and it's vital we bring her back. Her family are very concerned." Worlders: fools for their gene tribalism.

"If you're working for her family," he said, "how come you know screw-all about her? Riddle me that." He took a curly thing off his plate and ate it.

"Good question, Mr. Stukes." Melid was beginning to find she despised this male more than any puppet-person she had met. "The answer is compartmentalisation. If myself or my associates were captured by Freightways—"

"Freightways?" He stopped chewing. Yes; she had a hook in him now, she was sure of it.

"Well, who else? They've put the bounty out on you, have they not? Of course they say they do it for the common good, but we both know they lie, do we not, Mr. Stukes?"

Stukes paused. Then he nodded.

Pleased, Melid continued: "We in the Harmonies possess our own form of faster-than-light travel: the lockwyrm." She'd had the foresight to research, and was now thankful she had. "It is of a wholly different kind to Freightways' freightboxes, but in final effect much the same. This is the great game, Mr. Stukes: Freightways wishes to destroy its rivals—I shouldn't need to tell a bubbleman that—and monopolise a new market. The Harmonies."

"How's Sparkle fit into this sitcom?" he said.

"She's the daughter of a... technocrat." Melid was enjoying this exercise of ironics, this lying. Like combat with mouths. "So extortion, most likely. Either that or cutting her brain open to see what they can find."

Stukes' face creased up. Melid rather enjoyed the sight.

"Well," he said, "I guess..." The man chewed at his lower lip, as if fighting to stop his eyes from weeping. Melid liked that. Clear, unmistakable as a thought passed in the Kollective.

"You guess what?" she asked.

"I guess you're too late, huh? Clan Nuke got her, I went back and they'd taken her."

"Went back where?"

"Not your fucking business," he said. "Not your... Look, it's over now." He looked out beyond the observation window again. "Sparkle's gone."

"Actually, no." Melid let the words sink in. "We've been listening in on Clan Nuke transmissions for a while now. They have Sparkle; we know that, Mr. Stukes. It seems Clan Nuke are averse to using code words. But, oddly, they have yet to inform Freightways of their acquisition. We're not certain why."

"No," he whispered, looking about the room. "No, that makes sense. The longer they wait, the higher Freightways raises the bounty. Heck, it's what I'd do."

"We have a plan, Mr. Stukes," Melid said. "We have the intelligence and the operatives. We can rescue her. But we need you."

"How?"

"As bait," Melid said. "I won't lie. You've a bounty too, remember?"

"Fuck that," he said. "Not for you freaks."

"But you like her, yes?" Melid said.

"She's crew," he said.

Melid lay back in the seat of her chair. "And yet, from all we've been able to ascertain about you, you travel alone. You keep alone. I cannot imagine that, Mr. Stukes. I cannot comprehend why anyone would ever wish to be alone. Where we come from, such a thing is impossible."

"Have you met most people?" Hargie said. "Best thing about 'em is if you squint, they look like bowling skittles. Try isolation. Good for the soul."

"What a bad mood, Mr. Stukes. I think that's just alcohol and big talk, don't you, Zo?" She looked at the Field-Instrum.

"Bravado," Zo said, grinning. The lower half of her face was slick with russet sauce.

Melid leaned forward. "No one likes to be alone, I'm certain. We simply did not evolve that way. Your lifestyle is strong and pure, but it's starting to collapse. It's been diluted by her impurity." Ah, metaphor. "You just don't realise yet."

"Opened a fortune cookie lately?" he said.

"I know what it is to lose someone, Mr. Stukes," Melid said. "Trapped forever in a tightening circle. How could I let it happen? Was it my fault? You're remarkably fortunate to have us. Few people get a chance to amend their regrets."

Stukes shot up from his seat, surprising the two females. He looked set to do something. Yet he remained standing, silent amid the restaurant's chatter.

Melid leered like some mythical predator. She couldn't help it. "Do you really think you can climb in your dirty little ship," she hissed, "fly away and still be the same? After all this?" She smiled and leaned back. "No... you're no idiot."

He massaged his eye sockets. "I need to piss," he said. He walked off toward the toilets.

"You failed," Zo said.

"We have him." Melid emoted an iron certainty.

"We're from Harmonies now?" Zo said, her disdain fluctuating into incredulousness.

"It worked."

"Domov will think bad..."

Zo stared at Melid a moment, then focused her attention—and her tongue—on licking her plate.

SPARKLE, FACE PRESSED against warm rock, could hear the lapping of calm water. She smelled the sea. *Home,* she thought. She opened her eyes.

The ultimate home. She lay face down upon the granite jetty that led out into the smooth sea of her and her siblings' imagination. She got up.

The jetty was pleasant under her feet, baked by the morning sun. The sun cooked her skin beneath the pink shift she wore, danced over the lazy tides beyond, far off into the blue horizon. Sparkle smiled.

Her sculptures-in-progress stood upon the jetty, all in file along one side. Abstracts in ruschito marble, giant amber, porphyry. Sparkle had come here to carve them whenever Swirl and Lyreko had sex. Of late, they had remained untouched. A shame, now that she thought of it. She rubbed a palm against the surface of the marble piece: smooth as the inside of a cheek. Three faceless bodies merged at the waist into a vortex. Uninventive, but her favourite.

Something bad had happened. She couldn't recall what. She turned around to look at the villa.

Serene as ever. For a moment she had feared the villa wouldn't be there, or be a singed ruin or the like. She wasn't sure why she thought that.

The villa's pink-hued roofs and bluish domes wavered in the heat haze. Many Triunes crafted great castles or star-palaces or atmospheric towers for their head-residences. Not Sparkle and Swirl. Or Pearl. A large, comfortable villa between two low cliffs. Erratic and lumbering in design, a gilded shambles facing a calm sea. A silent beach. What need for more?

Sparkle made her way along the jetty toward the villa. She crossed the hot sands, felt the grains between her toes. Halfway up the beach she sensed someone watching her. She looked about. There, up on the right-hand cliff. A tall figure, its body a slender hieroglyph framed by the rising sun.

She ignored it, kept walking toward the villa. Nothing but a shadow-memory, after all, residue of a mind long severed from her own. Shadow-memories happened occasionally, not that that made it less unnerving.

The entrance to the villa was wonderfully cool, and Sparkle could hear music. A springed instrument, its harmonic strikes and rattles echoing through shaded halls. Swirl was here.

Both of them here. A rare thing. The last time any of them weren't alone in the villa was back when Pearl...

Swirl stood over her springed instrument in the music lounge, playing it with clawed gloves. She wore a shift like Sparkle's, but blue. Her hair was blue. The instrument was a series of brass springs of increasing lengths and thicknesses, arrayed in a line upon a mahogany base encrusted with sapphires. An invention of another species, a fellow Admirer-race of the Hoidrac. Humans had to wear prosthetic talons to play.

"Swirl?" Sparkle said.

Swirl ignored her: played faster, harder.

"Swirly-girl?"

Swirl began to hurl her claws at the springs, no precision, again, again. Sparkle covered her ears.

"Swirl!"

Swirl yelled and kicked the instrument over. It bounced against the tiles with a tremendous clatter. She spun around and glared at Sparkle. "What?"

Sparkle stepped back. The springs' reverberation lingered in the air.

"Sister... why are we both here?"

Swirl looked down at the upturned instrument. She sighed and began to remove her claws.

"I've been trying to ascend," she said. "I've tried this last hour or more. Nothing. I can't get out."

"A coma," Sparkle muttered. "We're in a withdrawal coma."

"Withdrawal," Swirl said. "Yes. That and the copious voltage that tore through our nerves. Remember?"

It came to Sparkle then. The troopers bursting in. The firing, the pain. She closed her eyes and tried to ascend. Nothing.

"You're right," she said.

"Of course I'm right." Swirl shook her head, her blue dreadlocks swinging. "By the Delighted, you're an idiot."

"Don't take this out on me," Sparkle said. "We both made mistakes."

"Your one with the pistol wins out."

"This coma," Sparkle said testily. "I really hope it's not one of those thirty-year ones..."

Swirl looked up and around, as if that had any bloody bearing on where the waking

world might be. "I don't want to think what they're doing out there," she said. "To our body."

Sparkle felt suddenly cold. "I wish Pearl was here," she said. "Pearl always—"

"We don't talk about Pearl," Swirl said.

"Well, you know what, Swirl? Maybe it's time we fucking did."

The sharpness of her own words cut her.

Swirl frowned. She stopped. Footsteps above, in the floor above. The two sisters looked at one another.

"Just the shadow-memory," Sparkle said.

"The shadow," Swirl echoed. "That's all we have of Pearl now. Accept it, Sparkle."

"It's not enough," Sparkle said.

"Far too much. The man was a traitor."

"But—"

The villa began to shake. No earthquake: the air itself shifted. Sparkle felt her muscles twitch. It was clear the same was happening to Swirl. They stared at one another.

"Our body," Swirl said. "It's struggling."

"Feral bastards!" Sparkle said.

Swirl became transparent. "We're ascending."

They lay on a hard bench against a harder wall. A dark room, a cell? A man—Aewyn Nuke—gripped their right wrist. Their left fist flew out and punched him on the cheekbone.

"Ow!" He let go, fell backwards out of view. "Fuck's sake..."

:Nice work,: Sparkle sent.

:Been waiting to do that,: Swirl replied.

Sparkle tried to get up, only to find Swirl was attempting the same. They flailed on the bench like a maimed insect.

:Stop it,: Swirl sent.

:You stop it.:

Sparkle heard Aewyn get to his feet. "Told you, Pa," he said. "Woman's a right frigging cacobant, she is."

"Now, now, boyo," said another male voice: same accent as Aewyn's, but deeper. Older. "Must be something you deserved that for, eh?"

:Let me do the talking,: Sparkle sent to Swirl.

"Apologies, good lady," the older voice said. It came from the shadows at the far end of the cell. "Usually we offer better lodgings to our guests. Me name's Pa."

"Hewwo, Pa," Sparkle said. It came out slurred. She could only move the right side of her mouth.

"Hear that, Aewyn?" Pa said. "Proper class, that is. Now... let's be 'avin a closer look at you."

Sparkle heard the hum of grav-repulsors. Something like a giant yellow egg floated out of the gloom toward her. On either side of it marched a guard with a compaction rifle, their faces tattooed with red diamond insignia.

Sparkle didn't really take them in, being too focused on the hovering metallic egg. It had a head—of sorts—just below and before the egg's peak. A jawless human skull varnished with mummified leather-yellow flesh, each eye socket stuffed with a hydra of sensors. Sparkle wanted to be sick.

"What a lush lass you are," an amplifier below the wretched deaths-head transmitted. "If I was only five hundred years younger..."

"You'd still have to borrow a cock, eh, Pa?" Aewyn said, nursing his cheek.

"How's about I chop yours and make her a necklace?" Pa replied. "Where's your romance , you fucking twat? Shut up."

"Wha' a famiwy..." Sparkle said.

"Ha," Pa said, "'what a family' could be our motto, it could. But don't fret: we've no plan to make you add to it or any o' that nastiness. Keep you fresh, darling. For the Freightways, see?" A thin line of drool rolled down from the skull's teeth. "That's why I had the lad here inject your wrist with some of that leaf. Little bit of what you fancy does you good, eh? Should give you enough body-time to do your business in the hole over there. Threw a laxative in that leaf-mix: clean out your tubes so you won't mess yourself when you pass out again."

"Gimme fuww dohhse..." Sparkle said. "Cahn ehscaee..."

"Eh?" Pa said.

"Something about giving her a full leaf dose, Pa," Aewyn said. "She can't escape the cell anyhows."

"What?" Pa said. "Oh, no, no. Why... one of you ladies in there might be an escapologist."

Sparkle gasped. "Wha' you mee?"

"Don't come at me with that, girl," Pa said. "I know about you Triunes. Harmonies been sending 'em this way for centuries. Neat trick; people are too blithe to notice, ain't they? But I notice. I've had a long time to notice a lot of things."

"What you talking about?" Aewyn said.

"Whole party in that pretty head, boy," Pa told him.

"What?" Aewyn said.

"Nevermind , you daft shithead." The egg turned to face Sparkle again. "Your little boss on Freightways—that Fractile—he's dead, love. Not our fault. I knows that much."

:No...: Swirl sent.

:It gets worse,: Sparkle replied. *:You feeling what I'm feeling?:*

Sparkle looked at Pa. "Buisshnehhss..." she told him.

"Oh," Pa said. "Right you are. You'll make it to the hole, I'm certain. Tenacious, you Triunes. Come along, boys."

Pa hovered around and headed for the cell door, his guards following. Aewyn remained standing there, watching Sparkle and Swirl attempt to move.

"Aewyn, you dirty fucking bastard!" Pa said. "Come on, now."

Aewyn sighed and followed his patriarch.

TO ANYONE ELSE IT MIGHT look like madness, sticking around safehouse Sophi. Especially with Hargie currently butt-naked. Clan Nuke troopers could come in and grab him as easily as Sparkle.

Yet, despite himself, Hargie trusted Aewyn. The things around Hargie—money, property, people—were fair game to Aewyn Nuke. But not his friend. Not Hargie's inviolate self. The thing about Aewyn Nuke was, once he let someone in, connected, they became treasure. Only treasure he held onto. That and he owed Hargie, big time.

Princess Floofy sat resplendent and disguised. Fresh hexagonal plating, artificial dirt, a green paint-job Hargie couldn't stand. A temporary sacrifice.

He brought up a window in his left eye and accessed *Princess'* camera. He looked at himself standing before the diagnostic console, a little man. He focused in on that man's red, red eyes.

He deleted the window. He checked the readings on the old-fashioned console. Red light flashing: impurity alert. He'd never had one of those before, not with hoxnites. They converted anything.

He pressed the button, and a small black box emerged. The console assured him the contents were safe to handle. He pressed the same button and the box opened with a pneumatic hiss.

At first he thought the box empty, but he put his hand in and felt something hard and thin, like a statue's finger. Hargie lifted it out. As he did so, the object shifted colour, blurring into the tone of whatever lay behind it. He placed his free hand behind the object and, sure enough, it shifted to a light tan. Captivating. Batladder.

The console couldn't read it.

A tracker? No doubt. Whoever had made the object clearly had no wish for it to be seen. And had it been a weapon, he wouldn't be gazing in wonder now. Yeah: tracker.

Freightways or Aewyn? No: Spindly Gang. Bet your ball sack, Jack. Those freaks had followed *Princess* all the way from the rig.

Hunters par excellence. He'd already suspected they'd stuck a tracker on him the first time the freaky-haired girl had waltzed up in a houri-field and pawed at his person. But his ship, too? Strategic and tactical, the whole burger.

He was glad for his bout of paranoia earlier, which had included at least four showers. Before he'd reached the lift down to Sophi, Hargie had run into an alley, stripped off the damn suit Aewyn had told him to wear—underwear too—and walked naked to the lift doors like a nonchalant madman. No one out on the street had batted an eyelid. Not a fuck bestowed. You could trust Calran for that.

But if the object were a tracker, why hadn't the Spindlies just come here, to Sophi? Too deep into Hailmogambo's rocky belly maybe, or too near the core. Good. Hargie was safe, Aewyn permitting.

He showered, dressed, put his hat on and planned. Then he packed what few things he'd left in his quarters and took them back onboard *Princess*. After that, he went to Sparkle's quarters. He packed her stupid furry coat and her useless red shoes.

She'd want them.

MELID WATCHED HARGIE Stukes from across the ring-shaped table. They were in the back room of a bar in Kushua Old Town, owned by one of their sleepers. Not that Stukes knew that. He and the asset—the latter now residing in the cell in the basement—had been led through a back tunnel.

The bubbleman's eyes darted between Melid, seated before him, and Doum and Zo either side of her.

"So," he said.

Melid let his word hang. Instead, she replied to the download package from the Instrum they had received an hour ago. As an amalgamation of all the attitudes of every individual given access to what had now been deemed 'the Sparkle concern,' Conybeare the Domov displayed dissatisfaction and perplexity at Melid's choices and lies. Feigning allegiance to the Harmonies? No Instrument operation informed outsiders of their origin, real or fictional. It was not in the manner of the Great Hiding, its zero-explanations policy. That way, any Worlder exposed to the Instrum and not subsequently liquidated would be suspected of schizophrenia.

Melid's choices being irreversible, the Instrum awaited further postings with focused interest. The statement came attached with something like intimidation and—somewhere deep within that, Melid felt certain—a slight trace of admiration. She hoped it wasn't her own hubris reflected back at her.

Hargie Stukes began drumming his fingers on the table surface.

Melid began her reply. *Focus noted*, she cognitized into the transmission package, *I have and shall continue to operate in accordance with the limited resources available*. She attached these sentiments with the report entire and sent them. They would be with Conybeare within thirty minutes, thanks to the time lag Calran's exposed core imposed.

Melid felt Zo's surprise. The message was, by any measure, curt. Yet Zo's feelings soon diluted into her continual cynicism of Melid.

Stukes stopped drumming his fingers when he eyed Doum staring at him.

"Sorry," Hargie Stukes told Doum. He checked his fingernails.

"The operation," Melid said.

"Great," he said. "Straight to business."

A lie. Clearly Stukes didn't actually think that. He thought the opposite, that he'd been made to wait. A lie intended to be seen for a lie: Melid had learned of this phenomenon during ironics training. It was called sarcasm.

"Image," Melid said, and a holograph materialised above the circular hole in the middle of the table.

"Old fashioned way, huh?" Stukes asked. "Why not just link our neuralware?" He squinted. "You, er, got neuralware, right?"

"If we linked, you might trace us," Melid said. "Please pay attention."

A model of the Nexus Vault hovered in the air before them. Like all of Calran's floating continental plates, Hailmogambo's vanished alien engineers had hollowed out a titanic spherical cavern at its very epicentre. The cavern was ancient and igneous, rich with cliff-sized chunks of diamond.

Hailmogambo's Nexus Vault had been adapted by humanity as a central transport hub. A loose tapestry of some hundred flyer lanes converged in the cavern's centre, symbolised in the hologram with faint, flashing lines. The flyer lanes issued from tunnels that speckled the cavern's walls.

"Close up on the Doughnut," Hargie Stukes said.

"Pardon?" Melid said.

"Upper third of the cavern," he said.

"The Imperial Villas." Melid said.

"The Doughnut, yeah."

Melid did as he asked.

The upper hemisphere of the cavern was almost entirely of diamond. It shone glumly, as if moist. Humans had had their way with this feature also: its entirety had been carved into a brutally decorative relief of countless hanging villas, docks, factories and who knew what else, a process begun by some insane emperor and dutifully completed by the great-grandson of his regicide.

"Hailmogambo's seat of power," Melid said.

"More like the backseats of the school bus of power," Hargie said. "The Clan Nuke only own the northwest side. At least three other clans around the diameter and the Clan Combine itself own the Hanging Palace at the pole, making sure all the local clans play nice."

Melid closed in on the Hanging Palace: a baroque nightmare carved around a hole leading up and out of Hailmogambo. A freeway into space.

"See?" he said. "Doughnut hole."

"Our likely escape route," Melid said.

"True. But the last thing we want is to wave our dicks at that particular hornet's nest. Pissing off Nuke is enough of a pastime without inviting the other clans."

"On the contrary, Mr. Stukes," Melid said, "the intense proximity of so many rivals works in our favour. From our interception of their security transmissions, it seems they haven't made the High-Combine aware of their prisoner and her bounty. Perhaps they wish to build a relationship with Freightways that might confer them advantage over their peers."

"Sounds like Nuke."

"If we're detected," Melid said, "they won't wish to bring the other clans' attention to the matter. More likely, they'll interpret our presence as an interclan transgression. A fallacy causing Clan Nuke to place trooper units along their territorial perimeter, diluting force effectiveness."

"This 'detected' talk don't fill me with hope," Stukes said. "Being I'm 'bait' and all."

"We consider all possibilities."

Melid adjusted the hologram once more, closing in on the... Doughnut's northwest side. The Seat of Nuke, their target. It hung over the cavern like a titanic and baroque buttress. At its summit was a loading bay and general docks, below that the Clan's palace proper, and beneath that some complex with flyer lanes passing into and through it.

"You haven't been entirely honest with us," Melid said, "have you, Mr. Stukes?"

"Honey, I give what I get." He pushed back the brow of his absurd hat. "But I don't get what you think I give. Or not." He pulled a cigarette out of his jacket. "As the case may be..."

"What are you even talking about?" Melid said.

"My sentiment exactly."

Melid let out a long breath. *Insufferable.* "I'm talking about your time as a prisoner within that facility." She indicated the hologram. "A whole year."

Hargie Stukes lit his cigarette and breathed out. Zo coughed.

"Shit," he said. "You loons ain't even got a floor plan, have you?"

"What makes you think that?" Melid said.

"Wouldn't be rooting around in Nuke's prison files. Wouldn't be licking me up for the lowdown as you're surely about to do."

"There are holes in our overall picture, admittedly," Melid said.

"We're a room of cadavers."

"Mr. Stukes, I assure you we'll acquire comprehensive knowledge once we're on the ground. You have no clue as to the extent of our technology." She smiled. "We only wish to know where the prison cells are located."

"Well, that I know," he said, tapping ash onto the floor. He paused, frowning a moment, then said, "Up top, at the back of the bay. Ready for, er, transport and such."

"Makes sense," Melid said. "Flyer theft; that was your crime, yes?"

"Favour to a friend," Stukes said. "I took the rap and he made sure I got looked after. Had a good run of the place."

"Aewyn Nuke?" Melid said.

"Bet your vagina, Jemima."

"So you're familiar with the dock's layout?"

He made a balancing gesture with his hand. "So-so. But mainly they had me working down at the wash."

"The wash?" she asked.

Stukes pointed at the complex beneath the palace, with all the flyer lanes passing through it. "Had me working the hull-cleaning machines. They make a tidy profit, what with all the passing traffic." He shrugged. "Not that that's any use to you guys. As for the palace itself... been in Pa's court once or twice. Haven't seen much else."

"All potentially useful," Melid said. The disdain rising from Zo and Doum at Hargie Stukes was increasingly noticeable. Melid empathised. "And it's as we imagined. You and our recently acquired asset shall make yourselves known at the palace. From there they should escort you up to prison cells nearby the bay. We'll locate Sparkle, extract her and you, and leave on one of our craft that will be waiting in the bay."

Hargie laughed and shook his head. He stood up. "For a while there," he said, "I really thought you the super-efficient black-ops conspiracy I'd dreaded you were. Call this quits before someone gets hurt."

"You're pulling out?" Melid couldn't hide a smile. She'd been waiting for this. She sensed delight in Zo, too.

"Fucking reluctantly," Hargie Stukes said. "But sanely. This is your shadowy plot? I been more convinced by plots of porn flicks. You think you'll park a ship in that bay with no one noticing? Don't even get me started on 'make yourself known at the palace'. I mean, what as? A pool cleaner?"

Melid laughed. So did her two Field-Instrums.

"What?" Stukes said.

Melid expressed the order. At once, ten assault-instrums in stealth armour materialised. They stood in a circle around the room, their rifles trained on the bubbleman.

"I repeat," Melid told him, "you've no clue as to the extent of our technology."

The cigarette had fallen from Hargie Stukes' mouth. For once—wonderfully—he was bereft of words.

HARGIE WALKED DOWN the basement stairs, the woman beside him, Doum just behind.

"He's quite talkative," the woman said.

"You got the right guy," Hargie said.

She opened the metal door and the three of them entered the cell.

"Hey!" said a familiar voice from the gloom: Aewyn Nuke, strapped to a heavy chair. "What you want? I'm worth a proper frigging ransom 'round here. What you want?"

"Sock for that mouth," Hargie said.

"Aw, shit." Aewyn looked down. "Looks like it's that day."

"Came quick, huh?" Hargie said. "Thing is..." He leaned in. "I'm not your 'jacker. These guys are. They just got me to point, buddy. Given the predictability of your sins, that ain't no epic quest."

"Hargie, man..." Aewyn whispered to him. "What they want?"

"Sparkle."

"What? Oh, and how am I supposed to do that, then? You think I can just waltz up to Pa and ask for her back? He'll tell me to fuck off and suck one, he will."

Hargie turned to the woman. "Hey," he said, "what we call you?"

"Emissary," she said.

"Cosy," Hargie said. "Okay, 'Missy, tell him the plan."

She did so. Hargie watched Aewyn's reaction.

"Aw, fuck," he said once she'd finished. But at least he hadn't noticed the holes in it, or didn't mention them.

"So?" Hargie asked.

"So I'm hardly faced with a wealth of options, am I now? Suicide alley." He looked around the room. "For all of us." Aewyn shook his head. "That Sparkle slag, she's fucking broke you, man."

"She trusted me," Hargie said. "Remember trust?"

"That's your reason?" Aewyn said.

"Maybe. Or maybe I'm just tired of sticking to nothing, looking for killers I'll never find. Of getting punched out on a bar room floor and expected to be grateful." He felt a rage from nowhere, chewing up his stomach. "Well, fuck that."

"Fucking arsewater," Aewyn said. "You and me, man: the same. Floating down life's sewer, sticking to nothing. Hard as tungsteel, us. Trouble is, when it hits we don't even recognise the fucker, eh? We make hard-man excuses."

"What you squawking, y' blond douche?"

"Back in the bar." Aewyn looked him in the eye, smiled his wolf-sharp smile. "All you ever talked about was her."

Hargie thought about that. He preferred turning around and walking instead.

"Do as you're told, Aewyn," he said as he reached the door. "You might live."

BACK HOME IN THE HARMONIES, no one ever talked about leaf withdrawal. It didn't happen.

Sparkle lifted the mallet up high and brought it down upon the sculpture. Pain shivered up her arms. Barely an indent. The tides around the jetty laughed at her efforts. She hated tides. Swing a mallet at tides, they only came back again. Laugh again.

Withdrawal comas? Don't make Sparkle laugh. Wasn't even a thing back home, withdrawal comas.

She readied herself, and took a side swing this time. Glanced off. No damage. Stupid. Sparkle growled.

Bound to happen, wasn't it? Out in deep feral space, dependent on the ever-thinning tentacles of a badly-coordinated obscure drug trade? Overseen—no less—by hapless pricks like Fractile-Radiance-Shine? Bound to happen. May as well have never left home, may as well have thrown Sparkle in a cell and fed her nothing but piss. May as well have shot her.

Sparkle yelled and threw the mallet. It bounced off the top of the sculpture, out of her hands. Splashed into the waves, and the waves laughed.

"Sparkle!"

Sparkle grimaced. Bloody her. Bloody cock-face blue-hair misery-cunt. A withdrawal coma, it had transpired, stretched time. And sharing it with that horrendous shit-for-brains stretched time further.

Sparkle turned around slowly.

Swirl stood on the beach-end of the jetty, trying to look friendly, trying to stop her face cracking into its usual scowl.

"I'm sick of your face," Sparkle told her.

Swirl shook her head and smiled like a patronising bitch-faced bitch.

"Come on, sister," she said, "let's go back inside the villa, eh? Let's talk."

"What?" Sparkle said. The sea air was boring her sick. "So you can call me *idiot*?" She kicked a sculpture. "Fuck's sake, why can't you swear, woman? Just call me a shithead like any reasonable sentient being. 'Idiot, idiot, idiot': all you ever say."

"I do not," Swirl said.

"Yes! Yes, you do. And even when you're being nice you always say..." Sparkle put a voice on here. "You say 'fine'. 'Fine' like the condescending 'idiot' that you are."

"Well..." Swirl blinked, looked about. "You say..." And she did a voice here. "'Mm-yes.'" "What?"

"'Mm-yes,'" Swirl repeated. "You do. When you're acting all brainier than me. Than everyone."

"If that were true, I'd be saying it in my fucking sleep," Sparkle said.

"We're wasting time," Swirl said. "Let's go back in. Let's talk."

"Rather go psychotic in the fresh air, thanks."

Swirl's face grimaced then twitched, as if she'd stopped herself saying something.

"Moron," she said finally. "S-sorry. I didn't mean that. Sparkle... we need to meditate. Pray to the Hoidrac. It's our only chance."

"Oh, you pious piece of..."

Sparkle stopped. Swirl's face had gone funny. She was gazing beyond Sparkle, to the horizon.

Sparkle turned around and looked.

Out on the horizon, reaching far up into the sky, loomed a hairline fracture. A crack of incomparable blackness.

"We're coming apart," Swirl said.

Sparkle turned back around and trotted down the jetty toward her sister.

"Come on," she said. "Back inside."

Eight

THEY SAT IN THE BACK of Aewyn Nuke's flyer, Melid's pistol pointed at the back of his seat. She and her immediate cadre, Zo, Doum and two Assault-Instrums, wore their suits—helmets included—with the stealth function on.

"Still can't believe it," Aewyn was saying to Hargie Stukes, who sat next to him up front. He jabbed a thumb toward Melid and the others. "It's like there's no one back there."

"Crap on the plan and you'll soon believe," Hargie said.

"Yeah, yeah, I fucking knows it," Aewyn said, adjusting the flyer's altitude. "It's just, y'know, there's gotta be a civilian angle for that tech. Make billions, you would."

Sickening. Melid looked out her window, down at the titanic cavern's floor a half kilometre below. A gunmetal city there, all pipes and barrels speckled with a million tiny lights. Banks of fog curled and snaked between the pipes, rose above the barrel-towers, reached for the many traffic lanes that flew high above the city, lanes drawn out by the countless lights of racing flyers. Intersecting, glittering.

"Baby suits," Aewyn said.

Melid looked up.

"What now?" Hargie Stukes replied.

"Civilian angle: baby suits," Aewyn said. "We can't see 'em in the back there, right? You got new parents, long flyer journey, baby flapping around and screaming and that: stick 'em in a stealth suit. Nice relaxing journey then, isn't it? Baby suits."

Stukes seemed to think about this. "Dandy bachelor was a shrewd career choice, Aewyn."

"Aw, come on, man; I'm shitting uranium here." He sighed. "You gotta let me gabble."

Melid lay back against the opulent seating of Aewyn Nuke's flyer. 'Luxury' flyer: a sickening concept of a sickening people.

"Hey," Aewyn said to Stukes. "How about the porn industry, then? I hate it when the man's arse gets in the way."

Hargie Stukes cackled at that. Aewyn laughed too, but then he began to weep, and Stukes slapped his shoulder.

"Tune up, man," Stukes said to him. "S'gonna play just smoosh. Smooshie-fine."

Hargie Stukes planned to betray them, Melid was certain of it. His bubbleship, the enigmatically named *Princess Floofy*, had come to ground. They had lost the tracker tag's signal for days, no doubt due to *Princess* hiding deep within Hailmogambo's rocky depths. Now it skulked a half-mile below them, below the city, hiding somewhere in the misty sewers of the cavern's respirator complex. Likely, Stukes' plan was identical to the one they'd agreed upon, right up until they extracted Sparkle and got to the bay. Then he'd have his ship fly up on autopilot and collect Sparkle and himself.

Melid hadn't the numbers to send a cadre down there. They were already stretched, covering both Stukes' entry into the Nukes' Seat of Power and the docking bay above: eight stealthed Assaults and the equally invisible shuttle they'd flown in on. No, *Princess* could wait. Extraction of Sparkle was everything. And simply knowing of *Princess*' proximity negated its surprise.

"Better answer that," Hargie Stukes said to Aewyn. A call on their linked neuralware, it seemed.

"Put it over the speaker," Melid told them.

"Whoa," Aewyn Nuke said to her. "Frit me there, love."

The speaker came on, its pop and crackle filling the flyer. "Identify yourself," came a rasping female voice.

"Aewyn, isn't it?" he said. "Permission to land, all that shit."

"Scanner says you're not alone in there, boy," the voice said.

A cold wave rolled down Melid's spine then, one that mixed with the general apprehension her cadre's shared psyche exuded. Disconnected from the Konsensus-at-large, she had thought fear would get the better of her, independence being one step from cowardice. But within a trained cadre, she found, a fear shared became a fear diluted.

"Oh, that," Aewyn Nuke replied to the voice. "A little present. Pa'll smile when he sees. If he had a jaw, I mean."

"Ooh. Who is she, then?" the voice said.

"He, actually."

Melid felt the cadre relax at that. Stealth maintained.

"Not over comms," Aewyn continued. "Enemies all around, isn't it? The Doughnut has ears."

The female voice was silent a moment. "Well, all right," she said. "But I'll have to send some boys out to meet you. No offence, love."

"None taken, aunty."

The flyer adjusted attitude and headed down. Melid could see the Seat of Power: a nightmare vision, like a melting skull carved from diamond. Its countenance shone blood red in the cavern's muddy light. A crown of black gravity spikes lined the skull's forehead, and above that rose the enormous docking bay, its contours those of a bullet's exit wound. Far below, Melid could discern the many lanes of flyer traffic waiting to enter the flyerwash complex beneath the Seat of Power.

Apprehension curdled inside her. No Kollective-at-Large to fall back on. All choices fell on her. She felt her cadre pick up on it. Melid dismissed her apprehension with a mannered flourish.

Aewyn and Stukes had fallen silent, their bonhomie fading as they descended toward the skull's mouth: the Court of Nuke's private landing bay. Untrustworthy at their very root, these Worlders, these puppet men. Each with an obscenity inside: individualism. It made them weak. It made them dangerous.

HARGIE STEPPED OUT of the flyer, his hands in the air. Dust, carried on the cavern's winds, danced across his face.

Four Clan Nuke troopers stood waiting: hair in topknots above dog-faced gasmasks, meshwork armour and torso hox-plating.

"A'right, boys?" Aewyn greeted them.

Their officer nodded.

"Bounty on this boy, isn't it?" Aewyn pointed at Hargie. "Coming in quietly. He's a pal, mind. Go easy, eh? Pa'll wanna see him."

The officer nodded and, with a wave of his Calbourne T11's barrel, gestured that they move along the walkway toward the great doors.

What the fuck am I doing? Hargie thought. He had an urge to run, scream, heck, throw himself off the walkway's edge and drop half a mile.

He screwed his act back on tight. Deep breaths.

"C'mon," Aewyn said.

They proceeded up the walkway, the officer and two of his troopers following. The dust collected in Hargie's mouth and nostrils, the winds' constant hum in his ears. He'd be glad to get inside, sort of.

Hargie had no idea where the Spindlies were.

MELID AND HER CADRE stood still against the side of Aewyn's flyer. Any movement increased the chances of being seen. Their suits' surfaces had enough work replicating the flying sand and dust.

The Clan Nuke officer and two of his troopers turned and followed Stukes and Aewyn toward the Seat of Power's double-door entrance. Two other troopers remained, guarding the pad the flyer had settled on.

The cadre waited on Melid's signal. Too long, and they'd miss their chance; Stukes would be in the building and the doors would close. Adrenalin rose in their linked nervous systems as the seconds rolled by.

The two troopers on the landing pad turned away from the flyer to scan the horizon.

Melid signalled, and the cadre fell forward on all fours. Their suits took the strain, muscleform fibres contracting around their biceps and thighs, wrists and ankles. Now quadrupeds, they loped off along the walkway, bellies to the ground, rifles on their backs.

"What's with the lighting?" Melid heard Aewyn Nuke shout over the wind.

"Bloody virus, isn't it?" the officer shouted back. "Hit all the lights along North Doughnut."

Melid's cadre already knew about the lights.

They were nearly a stride behind the two men and the troopers. Melid heard the sound of wheezing pistons: the doors opening ahead.

Zo urged alarm, and the cadre froze on the walkway. Melid poured her concentration into Zo's eyesight. It was Zo's task to take the rear and crawl backwards, lending the cadre 360-degree vision. It immediately paid off: one of the troopers back on the landing pad had turned to cast his view over the walkway.

The cadre waited, panting. By the time the trooper had turned around again, Hargie Stukes and the rest were passing through the great doorway and into a burgundy gloom.

Melid emoted action to her cadre, leaped to her feet and charged straight for the closing doors. The two Assaults were soon a stride ahead of her, Doum to her right, Zo strides behind. If the troopers on the pad turned, the cadre's backs would be riddled with mag-rounds.

The two Assaults made it through, their camouflaged figures out of phase with their surroundings. Melid made it through next, then Doum, almost catching his bulk between the closing doors.

The doors shut. Something smacked down on her right shoulder, nearly causing her to topple over. A shimmering outline dropped down in front of her: Zo. She had leaped between the doors over Doum and Melid, using Melid's shoulder like a stepping-stone. Zo became fully visible when she hit the floor, dropping into a crouch.

One of the troopers turned around. Zo's helmet, still rippling back into invisibility, hovered centimetres from the trooper's armoured crotch.

"What?" the officer asked him.

"Thought I heard something," the trooper said, gazing straight through Melid. "Fuck it."

They turned and walked. Melid's eyes adjusted to the darkness: a vast hall of smoked diamond pillars and cracked archways, fat shadows and stretched light.

They were in.

IN SWIRL'S MUSIC LOUNGE, they found another hairline crack. It bifurcated the chandelier, cracked the air above it, and disappeared into the ceiling. No doubt, Swirl thought, it came out once more in the room above.

"Don't touch it," Swirl said.

Sparkle tutted. "And I was just about to build a stepladder"

Swirl glanced at her. Sparkle's sarcasm was cracking, too: the way she said it, the hint of panic. A sister could tell.

"If only Pearl were here," Sparkle said. "Pearl knows all about the Geode."

"Shut up," Swirl barked. Anger raced through her bones, an instant rage. "Pearl betrayed us. Betrayed our world, betrayed the Hoidrac. He left us to suffer in exile."

"I know!" Sparkle yelled in Swirl's face. "You think I *don't* know?" She pushed Swirl, but Swirl shrugged it off. "But he's my brother. He's my brother and I love him, you sanctimonious fuckwit, you fanatical fuck! He kept us together. He kept you in check."

"You're losing it, Sparks," Swirl said. "You hate being trapped, you always have. You can't think straight. If we can't think, we're going to die in here, you hear me? Just be quiet."

"We *are* going to die in here." Sparkle waved her arms around. "Shit, we might not even be real. Ever think of that, fuckface? The Big Lie might not be a lie. Pearl could be the real person and he just imagined us. We're delusions."

"Don't say that, don't ever say that. Of course we're real, girl. You're hyperventilating."

"You fucking dream." Sparkle's breathing quickened. "I'm going to die with a stupid bloody dream." She began to mewl. "Not even a sexy one."

"Sparkle!" Swirl shouted. "Stop it! Calm down! By the Eye, you're useless! Useless and weak and—and I wish you weren't my sister. I wish I was alone."

The fist hit her cheekbone. Not painful, but Swirl hadn't seen it coming. She staggered back, tried to right herself, and her rear collided with the springed instrument behind her. It didn't topple, just made a dull ring.

Sparkle hit at her again, but Swirl was ready and she blocked. Another punch, and she brushed it out of the way.

Sparkle kept on pummelling. Uselessly, noisily.

Swirl rammed a fist into Sparkle's belly. Sparkle jackknifed, moaned. Swirl jabbed to the side, the kidneys. Sparkle tottered sideways.

One in the face. Right in the face. Sparkle fell on her back.

"Anymore?" Swirl bellowed. "Get up!"

Sparkle didn't move. She said nothing, her stomach racing up and down.

"You need me," Swirl told her. "Because you are useless and you are weak, Sparkle Savard. Always were." She booted Sparkle's thigh.

Blood was pouring from Sparkle's nose. Swirl had cut her cheekbone open. It would all heal soon in here, relatively.

"Outside and in here," Swirl said, catching her breath. She felt herself shaking. "I can break you." Anger regrouped in her. "Look at me!"

Sparkle brought her shaking hands to her face. She said nothing. She sobbed.

"Right," Swirl said. Her legs began to tremble. "I have to work out how to save us."

She walked out of the room, down the hall, the sound of her sister's tears shrinking to silence.

Out onto the beach. She waded into calm waters, lapping tides. She studied the fracture in the sky. She couldn't think about it. She thought of all three of them, playing here as children. They hadn't fought like that since then. And Pearl, Pearl, always there to break it up.

HARGIE'S NEURALWARE asked to take 58 rupees from his account a second time. He accepted. This was gonna cost, whatever happened.

"You cool, Hargie?" Aewyn said to him as they walked the court's long gloomy length.

"Sorry," he answered, "lost in thought."

The hall of the Court of Nuke was longer than a sports field. They passed pillar after pillar; fat things carved with skulls and interconnected swastikas, that ancient symbol of genocide and rebirth. Some pillars were covered in scaffolding and plastic tarpaulin. Wafts of day-old incense filled Hargie's nostrils.

Darkness between the pillars. The lighting had taken a pounding from whatever virus had hit. Occasionally a ceiling lamp would flicker, casting light that twisted and refracted through diamond curves. Hargie saw—or thought he saw—the silhouettes of armed guards.

He thought he saw a dog.

THE CADRE SPREAD OUT between the pillars: Melid, Zo and an Assault to the left, Doum and the other Assault on the right. According to Hargie's description, this would place the first group near the lift to the docking bay, where the prison cells were. The second group would provide visual and, if needed, covering fire. Melid hoped the lift was as large as Hargie Stukes remembered.

Doum spotted a trooper with a dog, a gen-rabid breed with wires in its snout. Melid watched through Doum's eyes. The creature lay idle on its owner's leash. Melid didn't relax. Monstrous things, dogs. A Worlder perversion. Stealth suits were undetectable to standard canines, but field data was scantier with improved breeds.

Doum passed behind them unnoticed. His vision alerted Melid and Zo that the dog-handler stared directly at a gap between the pillars they would soon cross. A light flickered there: two seconds on, 1.8 seconds off.

Melid and Zo waited, then belted across the clearing. No reaction.

Hargie Stukes' group was ahead now, almost at the open space at the end of the hall: the throne itself. Melid counted forty heat signatures ahead, maybe forty-three. A concerning number.

Doum and his Assault companion had reached their positions along the edge of the open space. From the shadows of pillars, they watched a line of troopers standing at attention.

Bright lights up ahead, talking, the hum of a generator. To walk out before the throne, into the lights, would be suicide. One could stand still in bright light and remain invisible. Moving into it was another question.

The Assault on the far left of the cadre had circled around the space before the throne and located the entrance of the dockyard lifts. Swift work. Zo made her way to his position.

Melid took in the scene around the throne. The throne's diamond bulkrippled gold in the glare of the four upturned strip lights that had been set up in pairs on either side. No one sat on it.

The throne squatted upon a large dais, its wide low stairs cut from different coloured gems. Ruby, Melid's suit's sensors told her, amber and zircon and jade. Young men and women crawled and shifted on their haunches at the base of the dais. They wore nothing but loincloths and grey body paint. They seemed despondent, bored.

Before the dais were two sofas with a comfy chair between them. A yellow man-sized egg sat buried amongst cushions on the chair. 'Pa' Nuke, the clan's patriarch: a severed head upon its life-support system, hanging on to life and power with the frenzy of centuries. Melid had seen the reports; she had no desire to get a closer look. This tyrant's logic alone repulsed her.

Men sat on the two sofas, their thighs splayed wide, fists holding cigarettes or bottles of alcohol. Laughing, swearing, looking to Pa. Behind the sofas were three other men around a small table. They played cards. Melid could see nothing in this entire vignette that resembled the Konsensus.

"Here he is," came a distorted voice: Pa's, through his amplifier. "The prancing prick."

"Awright there, Pa," Aewyn Nuke replied.

"Who's this with you now?" Pa said.

"Fucking Hargie Stukes, isn't it?"

"HARGIE, YOU LOVELY little bastard," Pa said, scanner-filled sockets gazing out from his beloved old recliner. "Been years."

"Looking well, Pa," Hargie said. "What's your secret?"

Pa's amplifier rattled with laughter.

"Cheeky bastard," Pa said. "Make me laugh, you do."

Hargie suspected Pa had had some official do, thus the concubines and guards hanging around. Pa liked to bring up his old sofas after that kind of gig, 'skutch up' with the boys and a few beers. Hargie recognised most: Bozza VonBenchod and the Hinter twins; Stagnant Frank; Moonjesus. Fun guys if you got on the right side of 'em. Hargie recognised one of the guys gambling at the table, too. Asshole had his back to Hargie. Hargie liked it that way.

Pa's skull cocked to one side, lending its horror a weird sort of jauntiness. "You know there's a massive bounty on you, right, boy?"

"Why he's here, Pa," Aewyn said. "Wants to hand himself in." He slapped Hargie on the shoulder. "Thinks we may as well have the bounty, isn't it?"

"Does he now?" Pa said. "Harg-boy: don't think I'm not touched by this noble gesture. But how's it someone like you—fast as a rat and nobody's twat—should be desperate to throw his own recidivist arse to The Man, eh?"

Hargie looked down. "Sir, I..."

He stopped. He felt suddenly stupid, useless as those catamites and concubines Pa kept around for tradition's sake alone. He couldn't play this. Just a put-on, a sting, but still he couldn't play it.

"He loves her, Pa," Aewyn said. "The girl. Rather take the rap than run."

A chuckle came from the gaming table. Asshole.

Pa was silent for some time. He saw clear through this rinky-dink ratshit hokum, Hargie knew it.

"Met some stupid fucking bubblemen in my time," Pa said eventually. "But you win the lap-dance, boy, hands down." He rose up from his cushions and hovered toward Hargie. "Look at me."

Hargie did so.

"This the truth?" Pa asked. His sensor-lined eye sockets bored into Hargie, his jawless skull a *memento mori* Hargie didn't need.

"Guess," Hargie said.

"Why you love her, son?"

"I dunno, I..." Hargie hadn't expected this. "Brilliant. She's just... an explosion. Fuck, I dunno, I... I mean she's, like, a fuck-up and shit, but... I need that explosion. And now I've seen it I can't just..." He shrugged. Talking sappy shit in front of these men, these cutthroats he'd once joked with. "I'm tired of sailing through dark, Pa. Tired."

Fucking ratshit.

Pa's sockets turned away from Hargie, and he was thankful for it.

"See that?" Pa said to Aewyn. "Romance, that is. Not like you, you spoilt shred of bell-end."

"Aw, Pa," Aewyn said. "I'm not fucking spoilt."

"Useless too," Pa said. "Good thing your balls are in a bag, eh? Fucking lose 'em otherwise."

"Aw, Pa..."

"Pa," said that asshole at the gaming table, never looking back. "May I speak?"

Pa turned his rotund metallic form to face Asshole. "Of course, Vict."

Nugo Vict got up from his chair, made a real movie of it. Vain bastard, Nugo Vict. Long black hair swept back, neat little chin beard. He wore leather trousers and a ribbed waistcoat that showed off his biceps. The love of his life he kept strapped to his chest: a custom Haltzberg-Schpitzer in its velvet holster. The pistol's black grip glistened in the strip-light air, so too the chrome studs on his neck.

"Vict," Hargie said. "Always a displeasure."

Vict ignored him. "I do not trust this man," he said.

"Colour me shocked," Hargie said. He looked at Pa. "This fool still your bubbleman?"

"Vict runs all me bubblemen now," Pa said.

"Always was licking for that job," Hargie said.

Vict grinned. "Cream rises."

"Shit floats." Hargie looked the man over. Nugo Vict had never liked Hargie's popularity with the Nukes. Both bubblemen, but when did that ever count? "Say, Vict: still taking cuts from your boys' pay?"

"See, Pa?" Vict said. He walked around Pa's chair into the space before the sofas, five feet from Hargie. "Lies come naturally to this garbage. To his kind." Vict was of another diaspora to Hargie. Purebred, too, from an ancient family. Educated. "Are we really to suppose a man like this would take the hard road for the sake of love? Or even take a hard road?" He laughed. "He's working something."

"Oh yeah?" Aewyn said. "Rectum rammed with anti-matter, is it? He's been scanned. No weapon. Fucking harmless."

"You forget his tongue," Vict said. "Man's a braggart."

Hargie gave Vict a stare, a real mean-low. "Quit driving us all 'round town," he said. "What you talking about?"

"Your 'reputation,'" Vict said. "It's more self-inflated than an AI dirigible. A competent pilot, granted. No ace."

"When's the last time you even looked in a cockpit, you preening bitch?" Hargie spat.

"You know what he tells everyone?" Vict asked Pa, pointing at Hargie. "Says he once..." He chuckled, shook his head. "...Wrecked a Falcatta ship with a chuck charge."

"It happened," Hargie said. "People wanna talk, that's their business."

"Yes," Vict said. "It's the utter lack of evidence really clinches it. The grav-wave from a chuck doesn't have the power to break ships. You're a fucking liar."

"And if I strapped a potato gun to my chest, people might think I was hot shit too," Hargie said.

Vict tapped the grip of his pistol. "I've evidence that'll refute that. Care to see?"

"Boys, please," Pa said. "I do the idle threats round here."

"Pa, sir," Vict said. "Apologies. But as you said: why would a rat throw itself into a trap? Perhaps he's something arranged with Freightways—"

"Fuck you," Hargie said.

"Perhaps they'll release him once we hand him over," Vict said, "pump him for information and pay him off."

"They'd give him a better backstory," Pa said. "You've seen their adverts; they're a creative bunch." His dead metallic eyes gazed at Hargie once more. "No. I've lived eight hundred years and sown an age of sadism, fathered Aewyn here's great-great-fuck-knows-what granddad. I'll kill a man for nothing and think even less of it. But even I can look in your eyes and see what you've become: a cunt for love, my boy. A cunt for love."

Hargie shivered, pulled out his smokes, took one from the carton and lit it with his finger. "So what now, Pa?"

"I know what you're hoping. You're hoping for my pity, that in my age and wisdom I'll let you an' that lass go. Not 'appening. I recognise tenderness, but I don't succumb to it."

Hargie nodded, though in truth he never thought Pa'd do any of that.

"Take heart, boy," Pa said. "Freightways aren't us. They have to play by the book, isn't it? Shareholders and tha'."

"Just means they use a silencer, Pa," Hargie said.

"Fucking drama queen."

Hargie smiled. There was a silence in the humid air.

"Hey," Aewyn said, "I'll take him down the cells, shall I, Pa?"

Aewyn was playing the game. Hargie hadn't dared hope he'd carry it this far. Seemed invisible killers were a warrantee of compliance.

"All right," Pa said, "but take a guard, you little fucking whazzock."

Shit. Some asshole in armour? Shit.

"Hey," Hargie said. "Bet laughing boy there's gagging to show us the way." He pointed at Nugo Vict. "Point that tiny pistol at something not a urinal."

One of the boys, Stagnant Frank, laughed.

Vict frowned. Smart, Vict, but easily taunted. His weakness.

"I don't kneel to you, you minuscule wretch," he said, eyeing Hargie's height.

"That what your woman Liza used to say? Before she dumped you for A-boy here?" Hargie pointed at Aewyn.

"Yeah," Aewyn said. "Like squatting on a kidney bean, Liza said about you, Vict. 'Pedophilia from the waist down': her words exactly. No joy." He grinned. "Soon rectified, eh?" He grabbed his crotch and shook.

Laughter all around the sofas. Even Pa chuckled. You could trust in wang jokes.

Vict grimaced. "You know," he said, "my greatest wish is to see—"

"Your own dick?" Hargie said.

"No!" Vict said. "I mean the day you two—"

"Buy you some tweezers?" Aewyn finished.

Laughter bounced off the pillars. Moonjesus hooted. "All right," he said.

"Right." Vict pulled his H&P from its holster. "Downstairs. Now."

"S'what he told the surgeon," Hargie said to Aewyn, nudging him in the ribs. The pair of them giggled like boys and started walking.

"You go, Vict," Pa said, laughing. "Truth is, you're boring the shit outta me."

"No worries," Aewyn whispered to Hargie between laughs, slapping his back as they walked away from the boys. "We'll shit him up in the elevator."

Not ideal, but better than one of Pa's troopers. Vict had no armour, after all, and he was shit with that gun.

But he still had a gun. And now, possibly all the will in the galaxy to waste them.

DOWNSTAIRS? THE CELLS were upstairs. Melid had thought it a... saying or something. An ironic.

But they were walking off to the right. The Dockyard's elevator lay left, so...

So Hargie Stukes had lied. Betrayed them like she thought he would. Just never this early. So obvious. So blatant and Melid had, had...

Her confusion merged with the cadre's. They waited on an order.

Follow them, she ordered Doum and the Assault accompanying him. *Now*.

The two males ran towards where Hargie Stukes and Aewyn Nuke seemed to be going, trying to head them off, keeping to the pillars' shadows as best they could. It slowed them down.

Melid watched through Doum's eyes. Doum watched Hargie Stukes and his two companions pass through into some doorway in the Hall's wall.

Doum stopped in the shadow cast by the last pillar before the door. His breathing became Melid's own. A blur passed Doum: the Assault, running for the door before it closed. Too much light there. Melid ordered him to—

Shots rang out. The Assault's belly burst and he flew up, hit the wall. Youths on the dais screamed. A dog barked. He held there a moment and then collapsed, his stealth-suit powering down. Melid felt the life pour from him, then nothing.

"Thought there was someone," she heard Pa say. His rotund metal body had produced a savage-looking rotary cannon. Smoke rose from its barrel. "Check the body."

Two Nuke troopers ran over to the corpse, the rest covering them. "Pa," one of them said. "Looks like some hi-tech shit, Pa."

"The invisibility's somethin' of a clue, eh?" Pa replied. "Twat. Break out the pulsers. Now!"

Melid blinked and sent out the terminus command.

"Shit!" said the trooper who stood over the corpse. "Fucker's dissolving, he is."

"Hey!" Pa said to the room, his voice amplified. "Hey! Who comes creeping into Pa's parlour? I know you're out there. Come out now and we won't slice your spuds off."

Melid said nothing. What were pulsers? What were spuds? She had to think.

"Clever gadgets you have," Pa continued. "None of your Desolation Row tat, is it, now? I'm guessing you fuckers are either Freightways... or a bunch of cunting Triunes. Which are ya?"

Triunes? Melid put it out of her mind. She called out to the second cadre up in the docking bay, ordered them to extract, redeploy to the 'wash' below, presumably where Stukes was going. Where he had intended to go all along.

Then what? What?

Doum emoted to her. He had found a hatchway beside the door, safely shadowed. Still a risk. Only time for Doum.

Take it, she ordered him. *Will cover*.

This was it then. Combat.

AEWYN IN FRONT, VICT behind. Hargie would have preferred matters the other way around or, better still, both men ahead of him as they walked down the short corridor to the lift. He'd no idea how he'd take out Nugo Vict and his damn pistol. He didn't know if he could trust Aewyn not to turn either, now they were out of the hall. He suspected the only thing keeping this short-lived triumvirate stable was that Aewyn detested Vict.

At least the Spindlies had failed to get in. If they had, Vict would be a corpse by now. Maybe Hargie, too. His brazen lie had worked. Spindlies were killers, sure, but no wise-guys.

A dull thud sounded through the corridor.

Aewyn stopped and faced the other two men. "What was that?" he said.

"Vict's balls dropping," Hargie said.

Aewyn didn't smile. He looked over Hargie's shoulder to the metal door they'd just come through.

"Just the elevator coming up," Vict said. "Wet the bed, little boy?"

Aewyn didn't reply. Usually he would have. He looked at the door behind him a little longer, then turned around and kept walking.

"It's smoosh, friend," Hargie said to him. Shit, when did he ever call Aewyn 'friend'? But Vict didn't pick up on it.

The elevator was small, its walls mesh. The three of them barely fitted. Aewyn's aftershave mixed with Vict's, and Hargie wished someone would have the decency to fart.

"You know," Vict said as the elevator headed down, "I truly hope it is love between you and that woman."

"So you can begin your healing process?" Hargie said. He grinned at Aewyn beside him, but Aewyn was staring up at the elevator's ceiling.

"No," Vict said. "Because you'll have to watch her suffer. Pa's wrong: I've worked with Freightways. I've seen what they do. Wipe away those commercials and you'll find a beast that would make Desolation Row weep."

"I ass-slap you now and you've an excuse, that it?" Hargie said. "Fire that gun o' yours? For once? That your plan?"

"Too much like mercy," Vict said.

"You're one sad—"

Another dull thud, somewhere above.

"Bastard!" Aewyn shouted, and he launched himself at Hargie.

"Wha'-the-fuh-"

"Hold him!" Aewyn shouted to Vict. "They're killing Pa up there!"

Hargie could barely see, Aewyn's chest pressed against his face. He tried punching Aewyn's gut, but had no room.

"Stand back," Vict said, and Hargie saw him pull out his gun.

Hargie couldn't grab it. So he shoved his hand in Vict's face and activated the lighter in his index finger. Vict howled.

The elevator lit up twice, roared twice. Aewyn ducked, let go. Freed, Hargie lunged forward and pummelled the shit out of Vict's face, a month's built-up rage. The fifth punch and Vict's head smacked the mesh wall, and he dropped.

"Fucker," Hargie whispered. The side of his neck felt hot. Wet.

He looked down to see Aewyn gazing up at him. A piece of his neck was missing. The hole spat crimson over his dandy jacket.

"Fuck." Hargie dropped to his knees and tried to press his hand against the wound. "I'm sorry, man. Gonna be smoosh, hear me?"

Hargie felt palms around his throat. No strength, but all the will in the world.

"I'm sorry, man," Hargie said. "Please..."

Aewyn bared his spiky teeth, slick with blood. He stared into Hargie's eyes.

"Aewyn, please..."

Aewyn hissed. His head rolled to one side. His torso toppled over onto Vict's legs.

Hargie winced. He covered his eyes with a palm, and it slicked his face with blood. Aewyn's or Vict's. He wasn't sure.

The elevator stopped, and the door opened with a pinging sound. A woman screamed. Hargie grabbed Vict's pistol. Out in the white corridor, a woman in a lab coat held up her hands. He pointed the gun at her.

"Please..." she said.

"Neural and I shoot," Hargie said, stumbling up and out of the lift, over bodies. "I got a scan-app." He didn't. "I'll know." He wouldn't. "Where's Sparkle?"

"What?" the woman said.

"Woman. Pink dreadlocks. Now!" The last part came out high-pitched. Hysterical. He must've looked psycho.

"Pa'll kill me," the woman said.

"And I'll take you surfing." He placed the muzzle to her forehead. "Move, fuckster!"

The woman squirmed, nodded. He followed her, pistol at the back of her skull.

Aewyn dead. All gone to shit. He couldn't focus. This wasn't his best moment.

ZO SPRAYED THE COURT with compaction fire. Chunks of trooper and sex worker splattered against sculpted diamond. Melid used the cover of Zo's carnage to aim.

She fired. Pa Nuke didn't even wobble in the air. She aimed again, this time for his deaths-head. Too late: the thing was armoured now. Melid ducked round the back of the pillar. Shots reverberated off it, diamond shards flew.

She reached her vision out to Doum: he'd made it through the hatch and now charged down a stairwell. Good work.

Fall back, Melid told Zo through their kollective.

Incoming, Zo replied, *move*.

Melid ran into the gloom, away from the court. She heard something bounce against a pillar behind her. She threw herself on the floor.

Flash of blue. Neither blast nor sound. She leaped up again and ran.

Something wrong with her suit. Her kollectiveware told her her left leg was visible. These pulsers were electromagnetic grenades, clearly. Another flashed in detonation, back and to her right.

Zo informed her they were flanked. Compaction rounds sang above their heads. She wanted to rain murder upon Conybeare for the lack of resources here. And genocide upon bubblemen.

Needles bit into her thigh, dragged her down on her side. She clenched her jaw and winced. A gen-hound had its jaws around her visible leg, shaking it. Her suit's fibres hardened there, mounting a defence Melid knew would soon wither. Venom would follow.

She'd lost her gun. She looked, swept her arms over the floor around her. No trace.

Melid refused to die this way. She growled agony into action. Shaping the muscleform on her index finger into a spearpoint, she rolled over and drove it into the dog's skull. The beast snorted, slumped.

Melid sprang up again, running from the flash of another pulser. Her suit pinged the location of her pistol: ahead, between two pillars.

Heat signatures to her left. Two troopers. She dived, snatched up the gun and switched to area-effect. The troopers, seeing a disembodied leg, lifted their rifles. Melid fired first. The troopers burst into mist. Effective, but it had used all her rounds.

Melid's awareness reached out for Zo. Seven metres behind her, suit denuded of stealth. Zo kept laying down fire, eliminating heat signatures every few seconds. Melid's estimation of the female rose exponentially.

A trooper ran between Melid and Zo. The trooper spun towards Melid, gun ready, and Melid froze.

He didn't fire, hadn't spotted her visible leg. The trooper turned about to face the sound of Zo's gunfire.

Melid charged at his back. Her spear-finger would do nothing to pierce the man's armour. She had no gun. She had no idea what she'd do at all.

She yelled, jumped, and threw herself on the trooper's back, arms around his face. The trooper fired into the ceiling. It rained diamonds.

She spied Zo running at them both, rifle ready. If Zo fired, the round would pass through both trooper and Melid. Melid didn't trust Zo not to.

Zo's barrel sharpened. She drove the bayonet into the trooper's helmet, between Melid's forearms. It punched out the back, narrowly—surgically—avoiding Melid's face.

Melid let go and the trooper collapsed.

"Fall back," she told Zo. They did so.

Another row of pillars. Only another row after that before the locked doors they'd sneaked through earlier. No exit.

Melid set her vision to X-ray. There: a manhole on the floor before them. A wide pipe below.

"There," she said to Zo between Zo's shooting, expressing the manhole's existence to her. "You open. Give gun."

"You open," Zo said. "I gun."

"I stealth. Give."

Zo looked at her. Then she passed the rifle and dived at the hatch.

Melid took Zo's old position and aimed around a pillar. No one. Pulsers detonated in the shadows. Inspired, Melid took her empty pistol and threw it in the direction of the court. Trooper rifles spat at where it landed. With luck, that would buy time.

Open, Zo emoted.

Go.

Zo clambered into the pipe first. Melid followed, replacing the cover above her. Tight in there, but room enough to crawl. They started making their way, who knew where, along the pipe.

"Back there," Zo said. "Saved me."

"Sometimes," Melid said to Zo's suited rear, "I useful."

Zo giggled. "Fun."

THE CORRIDORS SHONE white and too wide. Hargie didn't know how long he could hold this scene: gun to the back of a woman's head, fear of invisible Spindlies shooting them both any given moment. Brow tight with a pal's drying blood.

"Not too far," the woman said.

Too cocky for Hargie. Maybe she'd neuraled for help. He'd counted on her believing his lie about scanners. Dumb, now he thought on it. He could force her to connect with his own 'ware, lock hers down, but it was too late. And a violation. On a par with, say, kidnap at gunpoint.

"Here," she said, pointing to a single armour-plated door. "She's here."

Hargie stepped closer. He felt a breath on the back of his neck. He yelped, jumped back and aimed Vict's pistol at what transpired to be an air conditioner. The woman screamed.

"I'm sorry," he said, targeting her again. "Y'see, there's these invisible..."

Her eyes widened.

"I'm..." He shook his head. "Just open the door."

She did so, and the pair of them stepped through.

A cell, ancient looking, stone walls at odds with the white sterility outside. Sparkle lay on a bench by the wall, her eyes closed. She looked unharmed. Hargie went over and shook her. No response.

"Drugged?" he asked the woman.

"Opposite," she said. "Withdrawal."

"The leaf. You got leaf?"

"In the dispenser." She pointed to a device on the wall.

"Get some," Hargie said.

The woman went over and placed her hand over the dispenser. It made a rattling sound and a small black object popped out. An applicator.

"Do it," he told her.

She walked over to Sparkle and pressed it against her neck. The applicator made a hissing sound. Sparkle's eyelids twitched, then nothing.

"What's wrong?" Hargie asked.

"Takes twenty minutes," she said. "Usually."

"Ain't got that."

The woman pointed at the bench Sparkle lay on. "It comes off," she said. "Got grav. You can push it along."

Hargie nodded and the woman detached the bench. It made a humming sound as it floated on air. He grabbed a handle that had popped out and dragged the thing—light as nothing—toward the open door.

"I'm gonna lock you in here," he said. He thought a moment. "How do I do that?"

"Just close it manually," the woman said.

"Thanks. And, erm, don't neural for help for ten minutes."

"Wait," the woman said. "Could you shoot me in the leg? Please?"

"What?"

"Flesh wound: flab of my calf," she said. "Then they might not kill me for this, see?"

"You shit me."

"Promise I won't neural. Promise." She waved her hand over the dispenser and more applicators fell out. She injected one in her neck. She put her leg up against the wall. "Please."

Hargie sighed. Bile simmered in his stomach. "Sure."

He aimed at her calf, switched to low setting and fired.

Her kneecap flew off. The woman collapsed and screamed.

"Fuck!" Hargie shouted.

"It's fine, fine." She reached out for another applicator on the floor, wincing. "Just go."

Hargie did so.

Desolation Row. What a world.

SWIRL BRACED HERSELF. She'd made a mistake. A bad one.

She walked down the corridor to the music room. Likely Sparkle would be elsewhere now, her room, maybe. But best to start where things had ended.

This would be difficult, uncomfortable. Sparkle would have lots of comebacks. She could turn the knife, that one. And Swirl still had no plan of escape.

She stopped at the doorway to the music room. Sparkle was kneeling on the floor in there. Swirl couldn't see the right side of Sparkle's face. She wanted to see if it had healed.

Sparkle stared at the far wall.

"Sparkle?"

She didn't reply. Didn't move.

By the Eye, Swirl thought, *did I break her*?

Swirl stepped toward her.

"Sparkle?" The withdrawal. Had to be. "Talk to me."

She could see the blood on Sparkle's lip, long dried. She hadn't bothered to clean herself.

"Spar-ki-dar?"

Sparkle moved a finger. She pointed ahead.

Swirl looked.

A woman. Young, her skin inhumanly pale, eyeball-white. Her white hair undulated, coiling upward as if she were descending through water. She seemed a childhood memory, though not Swirl's. Something glanced on a summer's day and recalled decades later. Exactly that, yet now imposing itself on the present. Her eyes were silver orbs framed with white lashes. No irises. A face of such unbelievable beauty, Swirl knew she'd forget it the moment she looked away.

Swirl dropped to her knees beside Sparkle.

No more withdrawal, Swirl thought. A full comadose of leaf. Someone out there had applied too much, administered a portal's worth. A gateway for...

A Hoidrac.

The woman smiled, a hint of pewter fang.

The woman glided toward them. Her dress was woven bees' wings, or something like bees' wings. Flakes wafted into the air as she moved, the dress never decaying.

She passed Swirl and Sparkle. Swirl had thought the woman would touch them, had trembled for that. Instead, she glided through the door Swirl had just come from, silent as the void.

A hand shook Swirl's shoulder. She gasped. Sparkle. She was gazing at Swirl, open-mouthed. The dried blood on her face had become an ancient symbol. Swirl could not recall its provenance.

Swirl motioned that they should both follow the woman. She got to her feet, made the Loican sign, and headed for the door. The woman had already gone. The sisters followed her wake.

"Pheoni," Swirl muttered.

Sparkle looked at her.

"Pheoni the Appropriate," Swirl said. Pheoni, foremost patron of Zahrir. To see her...

Outside on the beach, Pheoni wandered toward the jetty. Pieces of her wing dress danced in the air, the breeze carrying them toward the sisters. A piece touched Swirl's forehead. It stung, then soothed the pain with a pleasure far more eloquent. Swirl sighed.

Pheoni glided onto the stone jetty. For a moment she was a silhouette before the sun: inhumanly thin, two horns rising slender from the skull. Talons. The moment passed and the woman-aspect returned.

The statues along the jetty melted as Pheoni passed, reforming into the visions Sparkle's chisel had no doubt sought but never achieved. Inhuman, the Hoidrac, but all human dreams and glories a bauble to them, a mere facet of their immeasurable totality.

The crack in the sky began to heal.

The sisters followed, stepping onto the jetty. Swirl kept her eyes averted from the reborn sculptures. Too much beauty, too much. She kept her eyes forward, upon that most exquisite object of all.

Pheoni stood at the end, looking toward the horizon.

Swirl realised Sparkle was no longer beside her. She looked back to see her sister caressing the contours of one of the statues: a porphyry vortex rising into three conjoined figures.

"Sparkle..."

Sparkle didn't respond. Tears ran from her unbeaten eye.

Swirl had to drag her own gaze away, towards the end of the jetty once more. Pheoni still stood there, but now she gazed back at Swirl. That face. That... mask.

Then, as if her body and arms were fixed to some board, Pheoni fell backwards. Into the water, fast as a hammer's swing. No splash.

Swirl couldn't wait for Sparkle. Sparkle wasn't meant to follow. Hadn't the strength to pass those statues.

Swirl belted up the jetty. She dived into the waves.

HARGIE PUSHED HIS STRETCHER with its sleeping passenger. He recognised the corridors now. He even passed the concrete cell they'd cooped him in when he'd done his sentence here. Good times, good as they could be. Paid to have one of Pa's clan as your buddy.

Pa. Hargie had seen a friend die, punched a man senseless, and kidnapped a woman this last hour, but for some reason Pa's words preyed on him most. He didn't love Sparkle. What fool could? Sure, she made a guy think. Pretty women did. When she smiled, got that funny-crazy look. He had a thing for funny-crazy, his lifelong curse. But then there was serious-crazy, and Sparkle could tune to that, too. Hargie had no time for serious-crazy. Not one momo. No sir.

Another lab-coated technician walked past. Never looked up. Said nothing.

Hargie sped up his pace. He should have taken that woman's lab coat earlier, washed his blood-stained face.

Spark's face was beautiful asleep. Regal. He felt better looking at her. Felt strong.

Concentrate.

His neuralware requested he pay another 58 rupees. He accepted the charge.

His window was closing. He pushed harder, ran.

CRAWLING THROUGH THE tunnel behind Zo, Melid reached into the kollective and gazed through Doum's eyes.

Doum had reached the bottom of the stairwell. Melid sensed the burn in his legs, his breathing. Thirty flights.

Doum ran down a white corridor. He stopped at the cells. Looked around. So many.

No time, Melid called to him, *find the wash facility. Head them off.*

Melid felt Zo's approval. Zo's attitude to Melid was in flux, Melid could feel it, though what final equilibrium it might reach remained obscure. The two females crawled on.

Doum's view: a corridor, a turn right, another corridor. Scarlet dappled the pristine floor. Blood.

Doum turned another corner and saw a man loping and stumbling ahead, hands to his own face. The blood was his.

Nugo Vict, the bubbleman who'd marched Hargie Stukes off into the elevator. Small penis, allegedly.

Before Melid could order Doum to interrogate, Doum smashed into the man. Vict went flying into a doorframe and dropped, either dead or unconscious.

No matter. Doum was on the right track.

Melid noted where Vict fell.

GEODE BEASTS SWAM THROUGH the warm currents, their luminous forms—fist-sized, translucent—a pulsing carnival of geometries. Down here, the sea was not a creation of the sisters' shared brain like the villa. Down here was an estuary between that brain's uniqueness and the ageless ocean of all minds.

It still felt like a sea this close to the surface, one impossible to drown in. Below her, in the black depths, Swirl knew things became another medium entirely. The Geode's outer edge, its skin. The Geode: dimension of sentience, the unified id of all life. Playground of the Delighted Ones. It bled into Swirl's neural waters above. Mingled with them.

She could not see Pheoni. She spied a scintillating luminescence below, like a serpent made of countless silver lights, floating just above the true abyss.

Swirl dived, swam. Shoals of Geode-beasts scattered as she thrashed her limbs. Nothing like the beasts in the Trinity House back home, bound in alloy hides and pressed into the service of humanity. Wild things, they knew only the Geode's skin, occasionally rising up—as now—to the lowest depths of an individual's subconscious so as to feed on spent moods, used sensations.

Darker she dived, darker. Only the strip of luminescence below cast any light.

Swirl swam into this luminescence: a conglomeration of millions, possibly billions, of shining marbles, or something like marbles. They glowed silver, pale gold, metallic red and blue. Some circled around one another or spun in groups; others floated alone. She found she could pass right through them.

Stars. Yes. She swam through a portrait of the western galactic spire.

Down, down through the interstellar replica, down, down until she emerged from the galactic plane's southern side.

No up nor down now; the sea Swirl had dived into had given way to space. Nothing but a psychic eternity and the light of replica stars.

Swirl stopped, looped around. She gazed down upon the galactic spire's curling length.

A new glow: it began as a flicker somewhere towards the core-wards end, close to the plane's equator. Swirl watched as the reddish glow spread, a fire leaping from star to star.

:Humanity.:

Pheoni's voice, a susurration, a thousand whispers coalescing into a thought.

The fire represented humanity in ages past, reaching out from its lost and half-mythical world, seeding a thousand more beneath alien suns. Many of these fires choked and perished, others disappeared amid the void. But many survived, pouring their success onto stellar neighbours.

Swirl turned her head toward a region further along, toward the spire's peak. When the human flame reached there it cooled, mixing with a cerulean blue: the benevolent rule of the Hoidrac, the Delighted Ones. The birth of the Harmonies' human district.

Swirl's gaze was drawn—she wasn't certain why—back to where humanity had first arisen, an unremarkable yellow star. A black ring, somehow darker than the space around it, circled humanity's birth-sun.

Soon, all the stars neighbouring that sun had their own black ring. A plague of nothingness, ever spreading.

The Spindlies. Swirl simply knew it, had known that nothingness from back on the rig, back when the Geode had burst into reality and Illik had dissolved into her.

Left behind, Swirl thought, *the Spindlies were left to die. Our ancestors left them.*

The blackness contaminated all stars in its way, all through the region of feral space, that vast and tragic portion of humanity without Hoidrac guidance. To each star system, a ring of pure nothing. Here was a human power larger in volume than any known, its infection of human space almost total.

And hidden, its growth unseen and unchecked. How? Where could the Spindlies possibly hide?

The nothingness approached the blue light of the Harmonies. There it stopped, as if checked by the potency of the Geode's strength as its essence leaked from the Harmonies' star systems. Swirl saw that both were antithetical to each other, intrinsically blind to the other's nature. It was why the Spindly pestilence here was rendered in a total and terrifying black. The Hoidrac could not read it, could not read them...

The horror of it. Through accident—she'd dare not imagine design—the Spindlies were no part of the Geode's hyper-spacial fabric. Somehow, they had walled themselves off from the great subconscious, from the awareness-plane of all life in the universe.

:Blasphemies,: Swirl whispered, or tried to whisper. Here it came out more like the mental conversations between Swirl and her head-siblings.

She felt something tiny in her hand, where the mark had been. She opened her palm.

A world, or half a world, floating above her palm: Zahrir. Its snow-washed southern continent faced her. Swirl's home.

Above it, the Wound. The Wound was a flat sea of blue flame where a northern hemisphere should have been.

In ancient days the Hoidrac had 'pierced' Zahrir, making of it an eye-world. Zahrir's southern hemisphere was no different from any habitable planet, but Zahrir's northern hemisphere lay within the Geode itself, unseen.

There was an island: the Mendicant's Isle. It sat directly upon Zahrir's equator. You simply had to visit, to walk far enough, and you could physically enter the Wound's flames, the gateway before another reality.

A walk Swirl would have to make. Of course. No ingestion of leaf, no comadose, could bring the hidden truth her body carried—some unknown yet vital part of the Spindlies—into the hands of the Delighted Ones. Swirl would walk into unreal flame. Her duty. Her fate.

:If I fail?: Swirl asked the stars.

The miniature of her home-world began to crackle. She watched its continents smoulder, the seas boil.

A roar filled her ears. Her world didn't burn alone. All the stars, each replica stellar body in the galactic spire. She could feel a trillion screams racing through her bones, the tearing asunder of titanic fleets.

War. War on a scale no human had ever been asked to conceive. The galactic arm aflame. One all known space—all humanity—now sleepwalked into.

Swirl felt a rush of power.

HARGIE RAMMED THE STRETCHER at the primitive doors to the Wash. The doors swung open, and he galloped into a humidity rich with detergent.

He'd prayed no troopers would be there, their rifles hungry, and some goddess must have listened, because there weren't.

There were, however, a whole lot of indentured workers. Busy-busy-business as usual here. Heck, maybe he'd gotten away with this. If he kept up his speed.

The Wash was a long concrete room: a raised level all along the left, concrete pillars all along the right. The spaces between the pillars looked out into the great cavern of Hailmogambo itself. Grav fields fifty metres beyond kept the high winds from entering.

Hargie slowed so as not to draw attention. He pushed his lucky hat forward and looked down. Hide the blood. Nothing he could do about the blood on his jacket. Prisoner-workers ambled by, pushing crates of suds or hoxnites. That helped him mix in, the only difference being he was pushing a comatose. Weird what people missed.

Pneumatic wheezing and rattling to his right, sounds he'd hoped never to hear again. He glanced in its direction. Hanging cables trundled along on a rail just beyond the pillars. They would stop and then, with a great hiss, water vapour erupted from below, the vapour's source just out of sight. Flyers at the end of those cables, their chassis in the grips of giant callipers, getting squeaky-shiny clean. Fifty-eight rupees a wash. Sweet business.

He kept walking, desperate to just break and run.

Hargie turned right, narrowly avoiding a moving crate, and came to a space between two of the pillars. Beyond the pillars, the great cavern's eternal night was awash with microscopic lights. The transportation heart of Hailmogambo. He checked his neuralware: four minutes. Shit. He would do this.

Shouting, somewhere behind him.

Turning, he saw workers topple, and crates crash over for no visible reason.

No, almost visible: a moving blur. A spindly, running in its stealth-suit toward him and in no mood to take shit.

Hargie pulled Vict's pistol from his pocket, aimed at the patch of blurred reality hurtling towards him. He didn't want to kill. He aimed low, fired twice. The blur went down and rolled.

The shape got up again, ran again, stealth faltering, a fractured figure of a human. Meaty, shorter than most Spindlies. Fucking Doum.

He aimed higher: groin height. Fired, missed. Fired, hit Doum's hip. The man spun and fell on the Wash's floor. The stealth-suit shorted out. Doum lay still.

Hargie breathed out. Workers were screaming and running. Hell, why not?

Nuke troopers, five of 'em: up on the raised level, coming through a doorway. They'd seen Hargie and were—

Two of the troopers exploded into chunks. The rest ducked and took positions. The fuck?

More Spindlies, blurred movement and rifle fire at the end of the Wash where Hargie had come from. Had to be that squad from the docking bay high above. Fast bastards.

More Nuke troopers, coming in from another doorway up on the rise. They took positions, threw pulser grenades.

None at Hargie, being of no immediate interest. But he had nowhere to go, standing against a sheer drop into the cavern like he was. And nothing to hide behind, save Sparkle's stretcher, of course. But that just felt ugly.

Keep smoosh. Any minute now. A hiss, and water vapour fogged his view.

Someone grabbed his wrists.

"Mouse!" Doum bellowed through his visor-less helmet's mic. "We go home now, mouse!"

The fuck? He'd just put Doum out. The agony in Hargie's arms said otherwise.

"I break your arms, mouse!" Doum said. "Slowwwly!"

Pain. Hargie dropped to his knees and yowled. Doum was pushing Hargie's elbow joints the wrong way. Snap soon. Quarter mile drop behind, no backing away. Hargie tried to aim the pistol at Doum, but he couldn't get an angle. He fired into the air.

Doum ignored the shots. Doum laughed.

Doum let go. He grunted. He stumbled backwards. Hargie saw a bare foot slam into Doum's hip wound. Another slam, and Doum yelled.

Doum swung a fist at his attacker, but they dodged, dipped under it, came up and drove a fist below his helmet. Doum dropped on his back, limbs splayed.

"Say hello to Lyreko," Sparkle said. She slammed her bare heel into Doum's throat and twisted. The cracking sound made Hargie want to puke.

"Hi," Hargie said to Sparkle. "You always wake up this hardass?"

"You've got it on lowest setting," Sparkle said, indicating the pistol. She had her business mood face on. "What's the plan?"

"I... need a minute."

"Idiot," she said.

MELID AND ZO RAN THROUGH the doorway, and Zo shot three troopers in the back. Three shots.

Sparkle and Hargie Stukes were on the Wash's floor below, a sheer drop directly behind them, trapped. Their bubbleship was still in the sewers of the city far below.

Instrum Doum lay at their feet, his limbs splayed. Life signs still, but fading. Melid felt a twinge of... *something* from Zo. Zo held it down.

Melid ordered the second cadre to circle Sparkle and Hargie Stukes, ordered everyone to de-stealth. The look on the two Worlders' faces was delectable.

"Drop the pistol," Melid barked. "Surrender."

"I know you people!" Sparkle shouted. "I know what you are!"

"Then you'll know to surrender," Melid said. Sparkle must have accessed whatever was inside her own mind, whatever it was of Illik she'd absorbed.

"Never," Sparkle said. "I am a citizen of the Harmonies, blessed of the Hoidrac. And soon, monster, we shall be your greatest nightmare!"

"I see," Melid said. "I suppose we'd better kill you now, then."

Mirth, hidden and silent, rippled through the cadre. A compelling ironic; Melid was rather proud of it. In truth, they would kill the Worlders later, after context-appropriate vivisection.

"Wait," Hargie Stukes said, waving his pistol-free arm, shouting over the sound of pressurised vapour and passing chains behind him. "I'm not."

"What?" Melid said.

"Not, you know... Harmonious. I'm a bubbleman." He pointed the pistol at his own head. "And there's one fucking thing you clearly ain't factored about bubblefolk, friends."

He fell silent, looking over his shoulder at the death-drop behind. Weak little Worlder. Slave to gravity. He wouldn't have the nerve to shoot himself.

Wait, why was he threatening to shoot himself? What unknown did he know?

"Yes?" Melid asked. Some data in his head, perhaps...

He gulped. "Well, let's put it this way... see, it aint... the man with a gun to his head. Oh no." He looked over his shoulder at the drop again. "It's, er... the gun with a, er, man to its—"

Stukes grabbed Sparkle's waist and pulled her backwards. Sparkle screamed. They disappeared over the edge.

The cadre stared.

Melid took a deep breath. Mission ended, if not ideally executed. So be it.

Zo ran down to Doum. Melid let her.

Impressive, these bubblemen, Melid had to admit. She hadn't thought a Worlder capable of such will, such spite in the face of the enemy. Worthy of a Konsensus human. Almost.

The walls roared. The space between the pillars ahead filled with something metallic and green and smeared with cleaning foam. It rose up, a decoupled chain swinging away from it.

A ship's hide. *Princess Floofy*.

But the tracker had indicated *Princess* was far below, down in the cavern's very...

Oh, but Stukes had clearly found the tracker, hadn't he? Made use of it, left it down there. Melid grinned despite herself. Brazen little shit.

In two seconds, the ugly bubbleship was a shrinking sphere, a silhouette off, off into the cavern's depths.

Melid felt fingernails digging into her palms. If not for her suit, they would have bled.

SWIRL CHECKED AND AIMED the Haltzberg-Schpitzer in front of the long mirror. A fine pistol. Far better than the Raic-9 she'd had before. Worthy of her, as far as feral tech could be. Worthy of a Hoidrac's chosen servant.

Quite the thought. She held back a shiver.

"That Nugo Vict person clearly had taste,' she said to the mirror in her and Sparkle's quarters. "Though we must buy a holster, next place we visit."

Silence. Like being a monomind. Was this how it was for them? The thought troubled her. She pretended to find some dirt on the pistol and rubbed.

"You know," she said, "I think Hargie did an incredible job. Don't you think? Not just at the Wash, I mean. Getting us out into space entirely. I'd have thought Freightways and the Nukes would have been right on our tail, but..."

She put the gun on the chest of drawers.

"Sparkle, I know you're not in the villa. I'm sorry. How many times do I have to say sorry?"

Nothing.

"Look, I had to do it," Swirl said. "Had to. You were hysterical. Simply..."

Nothing. She walked away from the mirror and sat on the bed. She couldn't look at herself. Not with pink dreadlocks. She wished they were blue again.

"Sparkle, we have bigger problems now, don't you think? The entire galactic spire teeters on war and most of its inhabitants aren't even aware."

:What's the point?:

"What?" At least she was speaking.

:What's the point of fighting when my side is your side?: Sparkle sent. *:What's the point?:*

"Sparkle..."

:You're a socially inadequate lump of sadistic shit.:

"Fine," Swirl said.

:You're not my sister.: No anger. Calm as the sea by their villa.

"That's—"

:You're not my sister,: Sparkle sent. *:I don't want you, I don't need you. When I am outside here, I want you in the villa. Same the other way around. We don't talk to each other. We can send textuals to say when we're going out or in.:*

Swirl stood up again. "You don't mean that."

Nothing.

"Fine," Swirl said. "Fine. Right. How's this? I'll stay in the villa the next few days. Free rein for Spar-ki-dar, eh? I won't pop my head up till you say."

Sparkle sent nothing, but Swirl felt the warmth of Sparkle's mind rising, waiting to take control.

"Fine," Swirl said. "I'll go, then. Fine."

Swirl stood on the beach before the villa. The crack in the sky had vanished. The statues were gone.

Alone.

Sparkle, she reminded herself, was a fickle thing. She would change her mind within hours.

She would.

AS SOON AS SWIRL WAS gone, Sparkle went to the kitchen and ate a cupcake. She ate two. She remembered Swirl had upped her exercise regimen and so she went back to the fridge and ate a third.

She wanted to seize life. To gorge. Events hadn't changed her, they had only succeeded in accentuating her vices. She didn't want to think of the wonders she'd seen, didn't presume their meaning, had no use for their mire. Keep moving, Sparkle, live and get home. But then she thought of Swirl's fists and an emptiness inside followed. She knew that emptiness too well. She knew always to evade it.

She took a shower. Then she went back to her quarters and put on her red dressing gown. Removed Swirl's dire attempt at cosmetics and did her own. She exuded a little perfume from her neck and pits: her own formulation. Swirl never let her use it.

Sparkle left her quarters and made her way down the corridor, bare feet on the dusty grill floor. She got the final cupcake from the kitchen.

The door to the cockpit was open as usual. Bright lights, bare metal walls.

"Hi," she said.

"Hey there." Hargie didn't look up. He sat there in his seat, staring at the wall.

"You having... one of your downtimes?" Sparkle asked.

"Little. Not so bad."

She hung by the doorway, uncertain.

"Could you make the stars happen?" she said. "I'd like to see the stars, Hargie."

The walls of the cockpit rippled and everything, everything all around above and below, became deep space . A large yellow star smouldered just above where the air conditioner had been.

"Where's that?" she asked him.

"Calran system, still. Hiding... out on the edge."

"I see," she said. "I brought something for you."

She walked forward. She sat—uncomfortably—on the arm of Hargie's pilot chair.

"Cake," she said, holding it up. "Existence's saving grace. Take your hat off."

He looked at her a moment. Up and down. Shock and awe. Sparkle was one hell of a tactician at this, mm-yes; forever a move ahead of her opponent's thinking. He took his hat off and dropped it to one side, not once breaking eye contact with Sparkle. Naturally.

"Here," she said. She broke a piece of the cake off and offered it to him. To his mouth.

Hargie stared at it.

"Do you fear me?" Sparkle asked. "I wouldn't want you to fear me, Hargie."

"I don't get you," Hargie said. "Not slightly." He leant in and ate the morsel.

"I'm human, Hargie. Like you. The distance between worlds isn't so great." She had cream on her fingers. "Lick it," she said.

He looked at her.

"We're not so different," she said. Her smile was like a circling raptor, like the swoopquill birds of home. She could see it in his face.

His mouth surrounded her fingertips. A pause and then a single suck. She felt it ignite her belly and her skin. It surprised her, the power. Such a long time.

"Your hair's crazy," she told him. "I rather adore it."

Balancing on the chair's arm, she dropped the rest of the cake and reached out, stroked his hair. Brown and russet and red. She leaned in, rested her face in its thickness. Surprisingly clean. She held herself there, sensed his breath quicken. Slowly, she moved her face down the side of his head. She closed her eyes, caressed his cheekbone with her own.

"Why?" she heard him whisper.

"You saved me," she said. She wasn't really thankful for that at all. She hadn't even thought about it.

"Shit, no," Hargie said. "You ain't no fucking trophy—"

"Shh."

She drew her face around to his, caught his top lip between her own. She let go. Held his gaze.

"I've seen you look," she said. "Because I've looked." She kissed him, once, twice. His lips caught hers. Soon his tongue pushed its way into her mouth, the gentlest visitor.

She drew her palm down his chest. Tighter than she would have thought. Old scars: two cigarette burns on his pectoral, one on his stomach. Lower, her fingers penetrating the gap beneath his loose belt. Hargie shivered.

She cupped the thickening length. Not huge, but chunky. An eager, almost cheerful thing, mm-yes. She worked her hand back and forth. Slow, firm. She kissed his forehead.

Fingers—callused, yet careful—touched just beneath her collarbone, slipped under her gown. They moved and soon her right breast was theirs, his index finger circling her nipple, bringing it alive.

"Feral," she said, and she grinned and kissed him again. "Beast."

Sparkle stood up, stepped away into the gloom. It pleased her to watch his face, the disappointment.

The temporary disappointment. She undid the knot at her midriff and let the night dress fall. She stood naked under the digital sun's far-off light, still as her statues upon the jetty.

She put the statues out of her mind.

Hargie played a calm face, but Sparkle knew better. Swirl may have worked this body into shape, Sparkle thought, but only Sparkle knew how to use it.

"Clothes off, Captain." She grinned. "Prepare to be boarded."

He was already taking off his shirt before she'd finished speaking. His trousers and underwear got stuck around his boots. Sparkle laughed and helped them off.

"You're beautiful," he said.

She didn't reply. She clambered, theatrically, onto the pilots chair, over him. Button and lights dug into her shins. Kissing, tongues, harder this time. She felt fingertips drift between her legs.

"Uh," she said.

"Yeah," he said.

"Oww."

"What?"

"Look," Sparkle said, "the, er, ambience here's incredible; stars etcetera. But my shins hurt. This chair's arms..."

"Right," Hargie said. "Bedroom?"

"Too prosaic," Sparkle said.

She got up and took his hand. Laughing, almost running, she led him along *Princess'* corridors. The pipes made a rumbling sound as they often did.

"Jealous, your girl," Sparkle said over her shoulder as they ran.

"She'll forgive me."

She stopped at the doorway of the lounge. The lights were off.

"Here's good," she said.

"You hate that sofa," he said.

"I'm remarkably negotiable." She kissed him. "Come see."

Hargie gulped.

She fell back on the horrendous mess of a sofa and dragged him down with her. He buried his head in her neck, grabbed her shoulders. She closed her eyes, felt stubble make its way over her collarbone, felt his erection twitch against her belly.

Swirl would know now, she thought. Sat in the villa, watching the skies above turn iridescent with adrenalin and hormones. Swirl couldn't do a thing.

Lower, lips racing over her stomach and down between her legs. He slid his palms under her buttocks and she pressed her thighs tight around him. She gripped his hair. *These war-plotters be damned*, she told herself between pleasure's waves: Spindlies and Freightways and Hoidrac. All of them. *Demur you, blades of every power*, she thought. *Demur to Sparkle, wet as dawn's grass...*

"Now," she told him, pulling him up. "Quickly."

"Want it?"

"*Now.*"

He manoeuvred his hips between her thighs. She stroked his back. She felt him prod at her, missing his target.

"Junk comedown," he said. "Focus all shit." He let out a long breath. "Been a while."

She smiled, and her smile felt natural.

"Come here," she said. She took his penis in hand. "Push."

She drove her hips up to him and he pushed, and the tip slid in. More pushes—firm, gentle—and he filled her. Nice, just right. She grasped his buttocks, directed his rhythm.

"Yes," she said. "Mm."

He pumped at her, harder, his face lost in her dreads.

"Faster," she said, pressing her nails into his back.

Five more thrusts, six, seven, and then he shuddered, moaned. Relaxed.

"Oh," Sparkle said.

Silence fell in the lounge's gloom. They held their embrace.

"I'm... rusty," his voice in her ear said. "And you're a beautiful thing."

Gently, she pushed him off and he slipped out, already softening. She sighed.

"When I said 'quickly' I didn't mean..." She shook her head. So long she had waited while Swirl and Lyreko had hip-banged again and again and... this was it?

"Sorry," he said, and touched her cheek with his hand.

"Well, okay," she said. She moved his hand away and stood up. She went over to the table, lifted the cloth and wrapped it around herself.

"I need a cigarette," Hargie said.

"You need a manual."

Hargie said nothing.

For a silly-evil moment, she thought about storing Hargie just to spite Swirl. Five of their body's seed-palettes were still empty. Imagine: "Here, Swirl: preserved feral jizz. Deal with it. I'm off to the villa." But she triggered her gland instead and killed twelve billion ambitions. Perhaps Hargie wasn't compatible anyway. Big galaxy.

She brushed her hair back. "I'm going to find the rest of that fucking cake."

"Hey," Hargie said.

She turned to face him. He sat with his arms around his knees, legs drawn up. Pitiful.

"Whatever," he said. "Forget it. Whatever you want."

His eyes studied her face. He was trying, she thought, to see her side of it. No: she knew he was. She knew him better than she thought. How very peculiar.

"Fuck it," Sparkle said. Before she could think, she offered him her hand. "I believe in second chances."

"Really?"

"Yup." She shrugged. "Tenth, too."

MIDNIGHT. HARGIE STUMBLED through the dead forest, the rifle in his hands. Toward the ancient cemetery.

Fifteen. Heart pounding. Shorts and vest.

This time round he had his adult mind, adult perspective. Worse when it came like that: on a rail, trapped in a late-night-movie repeat. He knew what'd happen. Had happened.

Man, and so real this time. Lucid: that the word? Hargie could feel dank earth between bare toes, the itch of rain-logged twigs. The rain had come only hours before, rained hard. Droplets fell from the trees into young Hargie's hair.

The dead trees thinned out before the cemetery. The cemetery was old, real old. Human settlers who must've died out one by one, buried each other. No one alive could tell you who they ever were. But they'd made strong headstones. Good as the day they were made. Eighty maybe, parked out in straight lines.

His father's body hugged one of them. Tied by the wrists, kneeling, chest tight to the headstone's carved words. A language no one living knew.

Hargie stepped out into the moonslight. The rifle felt heavier now. Other rifles lay about, their dead owners beside them. Six in all. Freightways men. Hired guns.

He'd seen them all die. His father, all of them. And he had run.

Now he'd returned with the rifle. Why? What could he have possibly hoped to do? Adult Hargie watched his own stupid, childish progression. Stepping toward Father, walking around, knowing the sight would haunt him for life.

Father's torso was bare. Fat sagged over his belt in a way it never had in life. Father had always been moving.

His jaw rested on the top of the headstone. Above that was the top of his mouth and above that, nothing else. A bloody hollow, black in the moonslight. Black splatter rolling down the gravestone ahead.

One shot, and the closest thing bubblefolk had had to a leader was gone. Hargie's father. One shot.

"He'll suffer," Young Hargie muttered to the trees beyond the graves. "I'll make sure he suffers."

He thought he saw movement out there. He lifted the rifle, squatted.

He waited a moment, two graves away from his father's corpse. He wouldn't cry.

He moved forward, scuttling over the wet grass, bent over, using gravestones for cover. A needless precaution. It was one of the Freightways men, crawling for the shadows. Dragging himself. The man was like a slug, leaving a black wet trail behind him.

Hargie lifted his rifle. No thoughts. Roar, recoil. The back of the man's neck flew up, became a hanging flap. He stopped moving.

Funny: the silence that followed was louder than the roar.

:A curious sport.:

The voice came from behind him. Wrong sounding, like a man's and a woman's compressed into one.

This had never happened before. It didn't go like this.

Hargie turned around.

No one. Just Father, his lower face—nothing else—resting on the headstone. Dead men all about.

Father's mouth grinned. *:A curious cycle, this.:*

Blood ran from the mouth as it spoke, ran down the gravestone in a thin line.

Hargie dropped the rifle.

:Brave boy, oh sweet boy, we have not long,: Father's grin said. *:I penetrate, violate. I abuse certain proximities.:*

No. Too damn... this wasn't fair.

"You're not Father," Hargie told it.

:A vignette: Daddy's brains daub moonslight stone. I steal it. I appropriate, boy, I smear shit on your walls.:

Hargie couldn't run. He wanted to run.

"Are you... the Foozle?" he asked. Spirit of the void, eater of ships.

:I'll take that name. I chew joy and spit out holocaust. Give me filth, give me infection, sing of incest and shrapnel, torn foetus on barbed wire.: It laughed then, a single bark.

"I don't want this," Hargie said. "Please."

:That slit you fuck,: Father's mouth said. *:That you r-r-rape so blindly with its consent: Beware.:* Father's body shuddered, vomited a dark jelly. *:Hmm,:* the man-woman voice said between spitting, *:what did that brain-glob control, we wonder? Love? Compassion? Pissing?:*

"Please," Hargie said. He couldn't look away. "Please."

:Oh, little boy, when you fuck *her, little boy, when she smiles and jests and swoons and slathers you, little boy... do not trust her.:* The grin vanished. *:Never then. Trust only her cold and piercing eye. Trust her disdain.:*

"Dream," Hargie said. "Just a dream."

:Perhaps. One that's followed you a while.: The grin returned, alien smile on familiar lips. *:Dreams bear prophesy, or so fools claim. Here's one, you deformity: return home and you'll greet your father's killer.:*

Hargie turned and ran, into the dead woods.

:Am we a riddle, sweet boy?: the Foozle-Father-thing called to him. *:Am we a riddle?:*

HARGIE JOLTED AWAKE. Darkness all around, a pressing black.

He was in bed, in his quarters. A nightmare. Nightmare logic. Nothing more.

He rolled over. The other side of the bed lay empty. He remembered Sparkle. Had he dreamed that too?

He reached out: the sheets were still warm.

The feel of the nightmare remained, if not the details. Cold, revolting. He lay there, frightened some part of the nightmare might return. For some reason, he was sure it would.

3. Qur'Bella

Nine

THE ENVOY—NAKED SAVE for a silk loincloth—arose to greet them as they walked out onto the tropical roof garden.

A studied move, the Ashemi thought. *Theatre*.

The Envoy was an Ingresine: the rulers of the breed-world Culakwun. Consequently, he was preternaturally beautiful. More significantly, his breed-class were fitted with two extra spinal discs from birth. He stood as tall as the Ashemi, though his height had a different, serpentine quality. The Envoy knew how to use that height.

"Greetings." He bowed his head with its black coiffures. "We are honoured, your Ashemi."

The Ashemi immediately disliked him. The man's expression was openly insincere, a disposition mirrored in his companions: a gaggle of fellow Ingresines who lay upon stone chaises longues and made no rise to bow.

"A pleasant roof garden," the Ashemi said. "A whole tower to yourself."

"Thank you. We've done what we possibly could with the place."

A blizzard raged beyond the force field: a white torrent that glanced off the field's sides and steamed off its dome. Inside the field, the garden was humid. At least the Ashemi assumed so. He couldn't feel heat. But the palm trees, violet orchid blooms, and Gleam's perspiration suggested as much. Geode-fish swam through branches.

"I'm here about the matter of Pearl Savard," the Ashemi said.

"Really?" the Envoy said. He rested one hand against his hip, curved his long waist in a manner faintly quizzical. "I *am* surprised."

One of his cronies—a female with kohl-rimmed eyes—giggled into her drinking bowl.

"I'm certain your friends," the Ashemi said, "are aware I am no mere Zahrir official. I am personally sent by this world's very patron: Pheoni the Appropriate."

The Envoy turned around to face his companions. He stretched his arms wide. "Quiet! Desist!"

They obliged—though most, the Ashemi noted, hid smiles behind wine bowls.

The Envoy turned to face him once more, a thin smile upon his face. "Apologies."

An audience, the Ashemi thought. *He plays to his crowd.*

"Why should questions about Pearl surprise you?" the Ashemi asked.

"Because I've already been questioned." The Envoy gestured at Gleam. "By the brothers there."

"And?" the Ashemi said.

"And I did not have to answer," the Envoy said.

"Now you do."

"Ashemi," the Envoy said, quite bored, "I am honoured by your presence, but not beholden to it. My own world's patron, Mohatoi Embossed, protects me. Diplomat's privilege." He gestured to a youth, who brought him a wine bowl. "Forgive my candour."

"I appreciate it. Candour makes this encounter pass with alacrity." The Ashemi stepped closer. "You, sir, stride as if your patron owns this world. He does not, though certainly your master can work his powers in the shadows, can cloud mere human minds and ensconce souls inside opals."

"You ravish all reason," the Envoy said.

"But he cannot contend with his rival in daylight," The Ashemi said. "Not on his rival's world."

"Really, now."

"Do you not recognise my presence as a sign of Pheoni's determination in this matter?" The Ashemi said. "Do you truly believe I am the last card she is willing to play?"

"I believe she is angry," the Envoy said. "She's been hoodwinked and humiliated by this Savard affair. So it seems."

The Ashemi said nothing. He merely gazed, making use of his own lifeless countenance.

"Very well," the Envoy said eventually. "Mohatoi or Pheoni, they are all Hoidrac ultimately. And we their servants."

"Ultimately."

He saw Gleam look at someone stepping out from behind a palm tree, a scythe pistol at their waist. A *Phosomuj* guard: one of Culakwun's many pure breeds, sired from numberless generations of psychopaths. Armour black as nightmare sheathed its body.

No threat to the Ashemi: his own body's demise would only mean a return to the Geode. But Gleam was clearly concerned.

"A display of power," the Ashemi told Gleam, loud enough for everyone to hear. "And a saving of pride."

The Envoy chuckled and sipped. "Pearl came to me."

"This is new," Gleam told the Ashemi.

The Envoy ignored him, passing his empty bowl back to the youth. "He wanted sanctuary on Culakwun. Pleaded, said he would be persecuted."

"And?" the Ashemi said.

"Nothing. What possible use was he? Twenty-four, still in the Trinity House. Brilliant, perhaps, but no information to offer." The Envoy inspected his long nails. "Nothing worth disturbing our two worlds' *renowned* friendship."

A thought struck the Ashemi. "Pearl's sisters," he said. "Did they speak?"

"No," The Envoy said. "I suppose they merely watched. Or he drugged them somehow, or used some inhibitor. I'd be fascinated to know."

"That's confidential," the Ashemi said. The Envoy mouthed the words as the Ashemi said them.

He'd been hoping to discover more about Swirl and Sparkle, the sisters. Under interrogation, they had proved unwitting to their brother's plot. It was clear, however, that their memories had been wiped for hours before Pearl's escape. Whether they had been mentally overwhelmed by their sibling or consciously involved in the last stages, no one knew, least of all themselves. A humiliating position. Exile had been a mercy.

"I suppose I should tell you," the Envoy said, "we had Pearl traced after he left."

"You kept that secret," the Ashemi said.

"Well, I *like* secrets. But for an Ashemi I'll forgo one. Pearl took a teardrop from the Trinity House to his parents' cottage out near the Husks."

"When did this occur?" the Ashemi said.

"Hours before his betrayal." The Envoy pouted and cocked an eyebrow. "He met someone there. A feral."

A feral? "You have my attention."

"Thought I would," the Envoy said, and two of his companions stifled laughter. The Ashemi couldn't comprehend their irreverence. "The feral represented Freightways, one of their *executives*, is that the word? Such an ugly language."

"The..." Gleam frowned, searched for the terms. "...interstellar travel company? *That* Freightways?"

"Same," the Envoy answered him. "My dear, *darling* little three-head."

"Don't bite," the Ashemi told Gleam, only to find the persona-bindi on his forehead had blinked from green to red.

"He'll know when I bite," Glare said, looking at the Envoy.

Freightways? The Ashemi could not fathom it. He was aware of the company—Pheoni had curiously seen fit to let him retain that memory—but could not see Freightways' intentions here. There was no need for Freightways in the Harmonies: the Geode with its lockwyrms served as a far superior means of transport. The Geode's limitless energies towered over feral tech in all things.

"You mock," the Ashemi said.

The Envoy's layabout friends made swooning noises. He himself undulated his long torso, made a hurt face. "I don't know what you mean."

"Are you honestly suggesting mere ferals aided Pearl?" the Ashemi asked. "That the filthy and masterless could delude the Hoidrac themselves?"

"Of course not, Esteemed One," the Envoy said. "But perhaps they dally with some Hoidrac hand as yet unseen. Have you thought on that? Want to know my theory?"

"I would never deny a host," the Ashemi said.

"It's all symptomatic of a greater malady besetting this planet," the Envoy said. "A culture built on multiple personalities? Frightfully jejune."

"Really," the Ashemi said.

"And the result? An insistence on mucking with life outside the Harmonies, sending out little Triunes to push leaf everywhere. We Culakwun merely keep back and stay beautiful. But this lot..." He gestured at Gleam "Well, some of that...*ferality* they insist on playing with is bound to rub off. I'd be investigating the Trinity House's own staff."

"I thank you for your hospitality," the Ashemi told him. "You will see us again."

"I do not doubt it," the Envoy said, and all his companions broke into laughter. They didn't bother to hide it this time.

"You will see us again," the Ashemi repeated, this time to the companions. They broke into fresh mirth. One of them dropped a bowl. The Ashemi found he detested these Ingresine scum.

"Forgive them," the Envoy said. "They're having a good time." He eyed the Ashemi up and down. "Someone has to."

'MM-YES...'

Agreed, Hargie thought, the fur of Sparkle's coat smothering his face, her shoulder blade pushing at his nose. That was her sign. It would be her, not him. This was for her.

Sparkle was sitting on him, and he sat on a bench by a footpath that followed the river. No one around, early morning, silence behind them in the summer-green trees.

Sparkle leaned forward, never losing rhythm. Hargie breathed deep, cleared his mind, took in the riverside. The wide waters crawled, were almost still, patches of green algae all over. And... damn, oh, she was speeding up.

Concentrate. Eyes on the view.

A storage unit on the other side, empty vehicle park. No one. Oh, but fuck, she was... no, no. Beyond the park, the minarets. Oh. He could hear the dawn call to contemplation, an undulating whisper in the summer heat. *Hold it, man*, they sang, *hold back*. Look at the sky. Sky never failed to unnerve him.

Still looking down, Sparkle raised a hand. Hargie took it, closing his fingers between hers. He pulled his other hand out of her long skirt and slid it around her stomach.

A dog trotted by.

The owner followed. Oldish man, overweight.

Sparkle didn't stop and, these days, Hargie knew why: her eyes kept screwed shut at her peak, always. Her peak.

The man's eyes met Hargie's. His face was placid. He nodded. Hargie looked away.

Sparkle's spine arched back, her shoulders pushing Hargie back against the bench. Right then she screamed, that odd, sweet cry of hers like a question.

The man walked on, never breaking stride.

Sparkle was bent forward again, taking deep breaths. The man had vanished by the time she got around to standing up.

"Come on," she told Hargie. "We'll be late."

They buttoned up, then walked along the river, arms around each other's waists, she staggering and delirious-looking, he with his still twitching, unscratched itch.

"Nice to have sky over our heads for once," Sparkle said. "Been two years for me. Fucking rig..."

"Skies are lies, honey," he said. "Thin blue curtains. Gimme a hull anytime."

This was their life now: screwing and running. Insane. Hargie feared he was having the time of his life.

He'd never known such a woman. Funny, proud; an intellect that dwarfed his own, but one she wore lightly, half the time. It even took the jumpjunk comedown's edge away. Seemed her brand of crazy slotted with his own. There was the trick. That and the incessant fucking.

She was ruining him. She was making him.

"Hargie," Sparkle said, "there's something."

Hargie nodded.

"You deserve to know where you stand," she said.

"Don't sweat," he said. He'd pictured this coming. "Just a journey. Good times. Pay me off and I'll dust, go hide." He shrugged his shoulders, made too much show of it. "Different lives, tune? Different lives."

"Let's not talk about that," she said, stopping by a weir where the river bent. "I'm not talking about that."

"Well, what?' He put his palms on her shoulders. Didn't she ever get hot in that coat?

"I've been very... up, this last week or so. But you've probably noticed I have, well, let's call them pronounced mood swings."

"You shock me," he said.

She play-slapped his arm.

"Seriously, listen," Sparkle said. "There's times I'll just 'flip', as your people say. Become this cold, bitter person." Her nose wrinkled. "Just this humourless, anal bully of a bitch."

"I wouldn't say—"

"Oh, do," Sparkle interrupted. "Please. But here's the thing: when I get like that, keep a wide fucking distance. No moves; you won't be thanked. I might even hurt you." And she leaned in and hugged him.

"Shit..." he said. *Shit*. He'd seen her kill a man. He held her, stroked the back of her head. "Talk about it?"

"I lost a brother," she said. "We've... I've never been the same since. I'm not ready to say any more."

"Shit."

"I know."

He realised she'd kept an even keel this last fortnight, since the escape. Even their arguments were a breed of fun, fierce but never bitter. Not like weeks before. He'd put it down to their newfound... well, give it a name.

Had she been fighting these last days, holding back the pendulum? That time she'd got up and left his bed as he'd slept: had she *flipped*, then? Night of that dream, now that he thought about it. Something about that forgotten nightmare picked at him now. He pushed it away.

Hargie leaned in. "When you figure me a hypocrite?" he whispered in her ear. He leaned back and smiled.

"Pardon?" she said.

"First time you saw me comedown: you stuck your head round my door, made sure I was smooshy-keen, all right. Pictured life through my eyes. That's rare. I've been all over and that's rare. The same, you and me. In the head, tune? Me up and down, you left to right. No middle to either. And screw the fucking middle. The middle stinks."

"Hargie—"

"Honey," he said, "this difference between us, it's just worlds. Like you said. Just worlds."

She pulled back a little and looked at his face. Her eyes were moist. "Thank you."

"Shit, I got that right?" he asked her. "That where we are now?"

"Let's..." She looked across the waters. "Let's call it a mutual addiction." She smiled.

"Sure."

They kissed to the murmur of the weir.

"Earlier," Sparkle said, "you didn't, er..." She raised an eyebrow and looked down. "Did you?"

He grinned. "Puts me ahead. By two."

She put on a mock frown, walked away in the direction of their appointment. "Don't think for one minute this is over."

Hargie grinned and followed.

SPARKLE'S IDEA, QUR'BELLA. Hargie, bless his tobacco-reeking hide, might have thought of dives like Alnar, or one of the system's outer rigs, but never a leafy tax haven like the system's prime world. Interstellar bounties didn't count on Qur'bella, not while you could prove you had credit and kept discreet. That gave them a few days, at least. Enough for a little homework. A little fun.

They walked along the Rue Al-Bukhari, arm in arm, working through the crowds, seeming like lovers to anyone watching, no doubt. Amusing. You couldn't love a feral; they were too physically possessive, insensate to life's wider palette. Hargie just made things interesting again. And she'd long deserved that, trapped behind Swirl's persona back on the rig. Now her sister could keep behind the curtain, could wait for her call.

"Fucking sky," Hargie said out of nowhere. He gazed upwards, above the many crenellated roofs and glass domes, to the summer sky. "Creepy."

"Don't you bubblemen have a world?"

They passed a bistro: executives ordering hashish; tourists; a few of the Mecatheist faithful drinking coffee after the dawn call to contemplation. They refined Qur'bellan coffee through some kind of artificial mammal gut. She'd read that somewhere, mm-yes. Millions of obscure facts, barnacles on the hull of her mind. All useless until they weren't.

"Lost our world long ago," he replied. "Then we tried another. Happened when I was a kid. Dead world." He frowned. "Wasn't to be."

"Space creatures," Sparkle said, studying the bubbleman.

"Guilty as charged."

Sparkle didn't ask anymore. Hargie was open enough about his years in space, but he shut down about his childhood. She didn't even know his age; early thirties, she guessed. Those tiny burn marks on his arms and torso: he'd shut down when she'd asked about those, too. She suspected the two were linked.

"We're here," he said.

Pierr Lazann: Bespoke Gene Analysis. Discretion Paramount & Guaranteed.

:We're here,: Sparkle sent to Swirl. Swirl had textualed Sparkle earlier: a note to ask for permission to watch the consultation. She had a right, Sparkle supposed.

:Thank you,: Swirl sent, the first words she'd said to Sparkle in weeks.

Sparkle sent nothing back. She leaned in and kissed Hargie's cheek. Surprised, he turned his head to kiss her mouth. She thrust her tongue between his teeth.

"C'mon," Sparkle said to him when they broke off. "Let's go in."

Swirl made no comment.

White marble inside, crisp air and a fountain. The receptionist wore gold lipstick and a transparent hijab. "Good morning," she said. "You've an appointment?"

"Tuffley," Sparkle replied. She could smell sex on herself. Paranoia perhaps, but she upped her perfume. "Jon Tuffley." She nodded at Hargie. "That's him."

The receptionist stared into the mid-distance, checking her neuralware. Her eyes widened, just a little, then her gold lips sank back to a smile. "Could you wait here, please?"

She didn't wait for an answer. She walked off into a back room.

:Keep alert, Sparkle,: Swirl sent.

Sparkle ignored her.

"Eyes up, hon," Hargie said to her. "The vibe here..."

"Of course." Sparkle gazed around the reception, though clearly the pair of them were over-reacting. Discretion was everything in places like this.

A man in a cream suit stepped out of the doorway the receptionist had gone through. "Mr. Tuffley?" he asked Hargie. "I'm Pierr Lazann. If you would follow me."

They did so, and found themselves in a glass-walled office overlooking the river and the city's majjidplex. A minaret shimmered in the distance: hoxnite clouds, restoring the aged features. Lazann offered them seats.

"I wanted to meet whoever owned this sample," Lazann said, lowering himself into an oddly familiar seat. From the Harmonies, Sparkle realised, Torochoi style. Not cheap. "I pride myself on having never asked a client for the details of their case. This is the closest I've ever come to losing my pride." He smiled.

"Your pride's safe, brother," Hargie said. "Believe."

"What Mr. Tuffley is saying," Sparkle told Lazann, "is we too must keep our client's confidence."

The client being Illik's burnt and severed hand. They'd sliced a little off and incinerated the rest. Unpleasant, but it seemed in step with this new outlaw life.

"Quite," Lazann said. "I jest. But what you have here... well, it's without precedent."

"Lay it out, Laz," Hargie said.

Sparkle shifted in her seat. It annoyed her that Hargie couldn't adjust to this kind of company. Lazann was the finer sort of feral.

"The full report, I'll neural you," Lazann said. "But what we have here is the most comprehensive, the most elegant and inspired restructuring of the human genome. No laboratory I have ever liaised with could create this. They could not even retro-engineer it." He shook his head. "Do you know much about the effects of zero-g on the human body, Mr. Tuffley? Ms., erm..."

"Ohlson," Sparkle said. "And, no, I cannot say I do."

"Of course not," Lazann said. "The invention of artificial gravity millennia ago rendered it an academic question. We've an embarrassment of riches, one we've long taken for granted. But someone..."

"Yeah?" Hargie asked.

"Someone has solved the issue. Perfectly stable muscle cells, superior blood cell production, a cardiovascular system bordering on the uncanny. An immune system that no virus could hope to invade. Incredible joint flexibility, and probably a sense of balance that would embarrass even the greatest dancer."

"What are you saying, Mr. Lavann?" Sparkle asked.

"Your sample is from a being adapted to life without gravity. They wouldn't function on a world like this. Not without technology I couldn't begin to imagine."

:That's how the Spindlies go unseen,: Swirl sent to Sparkle. *:Deep space, unseen. That, coupled with their stealth technology…:*

"Their nervous system too," Lazann said. "The spine marrow would produce some synthetic electromagnetic chemical. I can't hypothesise why."

"Thank you, Mr. Lazann," Sparkle said.

Hargie held his thumb out. "So what? I pay now?"

Lazann chuckled. "No, sir. You pay downstairs. What should I do with the sample?"

"Burn it," Sparkle said.

They stepped outside and Hargie lit a cigarette.

"Real space creatures," he said to the sidewalk below his shoes. "Spawn of the Foozle..."

"Foozle?" Sparkle said. "The spacers' bogeyman, yes?" She grabbed the flaps of his hat and pulled on them. "Poor baby."

"Ah, shove it up your ass," he said, and smiled. "Your pretty, pneumatic, deity-validating ass..."

He went to grab, and Sparkle let him.

:You're putting yourself through this to get at me, aren't you?: Swirl sent.

Sparkle grinned, leaned in and kissed Hargie.

:I adore him, Sister,: she sent, *:adore him with the heat of a trillion supernovas dunked in mustard.:*

:Very funny,: Swirl sent. *:I swear, if he hurts you, I'll—:*

:Have something in common with him?: Sparkle shot back.

Swirl fell silent.

FIELD-EMISSARY MELID slammed her foot into the dummyform's featureless head. The figure flew back and hit the training-core's curved wall, its muscleform body collapsing, then reforming again.

It flew back at her, pushing off from the plated wall, flying head-first toward her midriff. Melid spun away, but the dummyform's black arm rounded about her stomach. It rammed the air out of Melid. Winded, she got yanked along on its mindless trajectory.

It would drive her into the other wall, flank first. Melid shoved her arm between its thighs, hooked the left one, and lifted. The dummyform hit the wall with its back. Melid let it take the hit, throwing herself against its mass.

She punched at it. Formless now, but she didn't stop: punch, kick, punch, kneading the muscleform. She yelled.

A presence behind her issued amusement. Zo.

Melid turned in the air to face her.

Zo floated at the doorway on an axis horizontal to Melid's own. She smiled.

Melid issued a formal greeting. She disengaged the dummyform's combat program, and its black mass peeled from the wall and slithered through the air. It settled in a spherical nook beside others like it.

"Unexceptionable," Zo said. It came with none of her usual disdain.

In truth, Melid was relieved Zo had ceased her snarling bout of sex with Doum in the ship's onboard fuck-core. Her supervision of Doum's convalescence kept pouring into the whole crew's psyche. Melid really didn't need it.

"I angry," Melid said. Everyone felt the truth. Why not press it into language?

"You angry," Zo replied.

Field-Instrums like Zo and Doum were hard to read. They didn't think like everyone else. Parts of them were missing—their self-preservation, their long-term planning, empathy—while other parts were unique to them, and wholly indecipherable to the greater mass of Konsensus citizens. Identified in childhood and removed from the general scheme of things, their talents were a blessing. But their proximity...

Melid ceased her train of thought. Zo was picking up on it, delighting in her discomfort.

Melid took a combat stance. "Practice."

Zo grinned. She pushed herself off of the doorway's handles and glided toward Melid.

Melid flexed, found she couldn't move. Frozen, utterly fro—

Melid's nose exploded in agony. She cartwheeled backwards, her shoulder slamming against the wall. Zo grabbed and held her. Melid's movement came back.

She could barely see, eyes streaming with tears. She gripped her face, felt blood bubbling out between her fingers, into the air.

"Conybeare," Zo muttered in Melid's ear. "Keep you controlled. Best you know."

Melid wanted to murder Conybeare, that accretion of collected mind-shit. She wanted to kill Zo too, hand of Conybeare. She stared into the other female's eyes, exuded a melange of hateful feelings.

"Anger good, Emissary," Zo told her. "Keep."

"You sickness."

"Yes. And you good. Promising." Zo smiled, radiated respect. "Wouldn't show you just now... otherwise." She stroked the blood off of Melid's upper lip. "Not deserve this."

"I failed," Melid said.

"We failed: Konsensus. Mission: under-resourced. All dead if not you. Hard mission. Wrong blame."

"Conybeare hear you, Zo," Melid said.

"Zo Field-Instrum." She pointed at herself. "Not care. Doum think same." She unconsciously exuded a recent sex-image, and saw no reason to suppress it once she'd noticed.

"Towel," Melid said.

Zo darted across the training room and brought her one. Melid took it.

"Why show?" Melid asked, pressing the towel to her nose. "Could tell."

Zo giggled, issued delight.

Unusual this, Melid thought, Conybeare giving subordinates the power to freeze her limbs. An extreme measure. They had worked alone on Calran, had become their own tiny kollective, temporarily adrift from the Kollective-at-Large. It scared—for lack of a better term—the Konsensus as a culture, and its military wing, the Instrum, in particular. The one fear: kancerisation. It hung over their people's entire history.

Melid chuckled. She was used to it. Her home kollective—Silvercloud—had long been suspected a kancer-in-waiting. There was its intermittent connection with the rest of the Konsensus, of course, and the proximity of the Scalpels. No matter. It fell to Silverclouders like herself to prove their home kollective true.

"Enough anger," Zo said, cartwheeling toward Melid like some energetic child. "Fun now?"

Melid looked at her. "Fun."

MELID AND ZO FLOATED into the ship's brig, moods amused and faces stern.

The red tiled, torus-shaped brig had one inmate. Naked he stood, tethered to the side of the central pillar with muscleform bands. He didn't look up. His long black hair undulated in waves, caressed by air conditioning.

"Perhaps some gravity," Melid told him in Anglurati. "Since you have been so good."

Gradually, weight made its presence known and the two females descended to their feet. Melid felt the fibres of her bodysuit harden in response.

The man groaned as the bands dug into his armpits.

"Feel at home now?" Melid asked.

Melid had thought Conybeare and the Instrum would have had this Worlder shot out of an airlock by now. After all, Melid and her cadre had been relegated, placed on mere search-patrol, like sixty-eight other hunter-killer craft hoping to stumble into *Princess Floofy*. Yet the Instrum permitted Melid's cadre this little foible. This Worlder.

"Mr. Nugo Vict," she said. "Can you hear me, Mr. Vict?"

He lifted his head up, squinting at Melid from beneath his brow. He seemed surprised by Melid's broken—but already healing—nose.

"Please," he said. "Ransom. They'll pay."

Melid didn't reply. She reached out and, oh so gently, lifted his penis between two gloved fingers. "I wouldn't say that was small," she said. "Would you, Zo?"

"Seen bigger," Zo said.

"Well, naturally. But it's certainly not small. Not like that nasty Hargie Stukes claimed, eh, Mr. Vict?"

Vict said nothing. His face said it all. Silly corpse-puppet-thing. She turned the penis left and right, always threatening to yank, but never quite.

"Of course," she said, "you can never really tell until full tumescence, can you? That's the ultimate decider."

"No better," Zo added.

Melid let go, wiped her gloved fingers against one another. She was enjoying this, putting pain in a dumb thing. It released frustration in a socially responsible way.

She exuded to Zo to say something horrid.

"Emissary," Zo said, "can we rape him? Like the Worlders do to each other?"

"I don't know, Zo," Melid said.

"Oh, please..."

Absurd, of course. Elegant, too, using a Worlder deviance to torture a Worlder.

Vict gulped. "But you're..."

"Female? Irrelevant. Zo here likes to—what's the word?—carve sex holes into males. Don't you, Zo?"

Zo lifted a hand and shaped the muscleform on her suit's index finger into a serrated eight-inch blade.

"My willy," she said, and giggled.

Urine streamed from Vict into a drain below.

"Oh, Mr. Vict," Melid said. "Fortunate the gravity's on..."

"Please," Vict said, sobbing. "Do anything..."

"Would you hunt Hargie Stukes for us?"

Vict's expression transformed from self-pity to something like hunger. Impressive. Very impressive.

"A bubblepilot to hunt a bubblepilot," Melid said. "You're a very good one, so we're informed."

"I..." Vict said. "I want to be useful."

"Fear and vengeance are a heady mix, are they not?" Melid stroked Vict's left neck stud. Smooth, shiny. She'd wanted to touch bubble studs for some time. "And we can make you very rich. Richer than Pa ever allowed you. And best of all..." Melid let the sentence hang.

"You might not die," Zo completed.

"FUCK YOU!" SPARKLE shouted down *Princess Floofy's* passageway. From her cabin. Wouldn't even come out to look at him.

"And a fuck back at ya!" Hargie shouted back from the open hatchway of the cockpit. "Bouncing off your arrogance, once round that big head o'yours and right in your fucking ear!"

She'd washed his hat. No asking. Just washed. Like that.

"Nice," came her voice. "I was trying to be nice, you grumpy scrotum-rash!"

"I'll tell you what's nice: your little plan."

"What plan?" she barked from her pit.

"You wanted an argument," Hargie shouted. "It's mana to you! So you washed Betsy when you know I'd hate that and you'd come out looking the victim. You're a genius, a mastermind of bicker."

Silence down the passageway, Sparkle working through his words. Yeah. Damn right.

"Betsy?" Sparkle said. "That's what you call your hat? Oh, ha ha ha!"

"S-Sometimes. Fuck you!" Hargie hit a button on the doorway and it whirled closed. Just him and the cockpit. Way it should be. He slumped down in his chair.

Bigger problems. He had bigger problems. Feds everywhere. Every Falcatta fuck from here to Andromeda. Turn left: bounty patrol. Right: Freightways broadcast with bitch-face's bitch-face slapped on it. Everything draining Hargie of tricks, of ideas.

Almost.

Too long cramped up. Sparkle couldn't handle it, was finding ways to twist the knife. At least on the rig she'd had places to go.

Hell, she'd ruined him. Simple as. He cradled his head in his hands. He heard the door whirl open behind him.

"Fuck..." he muttered.

She looked down at him. She'd changed clothes: combat trousers and t-shirt.

"Argument over," she said.

"Over?" he said. "Over when you say sorry."

"Let's put our..." She chewed on her lip. "...understanding to one side and concentrate on the situation. We're a team here."

Damn woman! Freak. No... no. Another little plan. Laugh at him, call him over-emotional. Hargie no bite.

"Sure," Hargie said. "Well, keeping low on Qur'bella only bought time for the Feds and Freightways to get their act together."

Sparkle nodded. "I thought Qur'bella an unsound plan."

"It was *your* plan!" He shook his open palms at her. Now she'd laugh.

Sparkle's eyebrows arched. "Yes," she said. "Yes, it was."

"Wow," Hargie said. "That an apology?"

"Fine," she said. "Whatever. Please, Hargie, continue."

"Well, okaaay. Okay then." He breathed out. "We're pushed into a corner: someone must have got their mitts on *Princess*' signature and we're setting off sensor-buoys soon as we jump into a system. Been going round in circles, almost coming back to Qur'bella. Almost."

"Almost?" Her face all analysis, all frost.

"You're, er..." he said. "This is one of your moods. Right? Business mood?"

"Moods?" She seemed to think about the word. "Yes, I suppose it must be." She pursed her lips. "So, you know, hands to yourself."

"Yeah, you said."

"Yes. Yes I did."

Crazy woman. Drug fiend. Hundred-percent-proof bat-ladder.

"Soooo..." Hargie said. "I've jumped us to somewhere neither Feds nor Freight dare go."

"Where?"

He blinked and the cockpit walls turned to deep space. Before them lay a bright silver nova, gold light issuing from its insides. He'd hoped never to see it again.

"A nova," Sparkle said. She was bathed in the golden light, the blackness of deep space behind her. "Should we be as close as this?"

"If it were a nova, no," Hargie said.

"Well, what is it?"

"You know hoxnites, right?" He took a cigarette out and lit up. "Nanobots fixed to do one job, whatever job, and that's it. Done." He breathed out. "There's reason for that. You programme nanobots to do lots of jobs, to adapt, reproduce? You get this."

"All this is hoxnites?" She gestured at the stellar cloud. "It's got to be millions of kays wide, or some such."

"Not Hoxnites: nanites," Hargie said. "Carefree, do-as-they-please nanites. Most dangerous thing in the universe. Heard of the Utgian Oligarchy?"

"Who?"

"Were," he said. "They did this. Must have been desperate: broke every galactic law. The galactic law. Happened three hundred years ago and if anyone escaped, no one's saying why. You're looking at the entire Utgian system, scrambled. Nanites using every atom to replicate themselves."

Sparkle walked forward and studied the image. She turned around to look at Hargie, silver and gold framing her near-silhouette. "And no one's doing anything about it?"

"Qur'bella are," Hargie told her. "S'why they have all the tax breaks and shit. Got a whole fleet here. Used to throw fusion at 'em, but the nanites worked out how to convert that, too. Now Qur'bella use some freeze-stuff, painting over any clouds that break loose. It's working, short term."

"Insane," she said. "We're insane."

"Got a better idea?"

She shook her head. Of course not.

"This Qur'bellan fleet," Sparkle said. "Won't they know we're here?"

"I've got a special scrambler code," Hargie said. "Courtesy of a... pal of mine. Local man. Thought we'd go knocking." He looked her up and down. "Freshly cleaned cap in hand."

"Who's this 'pal'?"

"Sung Eucharist."

Sung-fucking-Eucharist.

Ten

SWIRL GAZED AT THE old space station. Even she could tell this feral tech was of an earlier age. The thing looked like a funeral wreath of solar panels.

"What is it?" she asked.

"Utgian border installation," Hargie said from his chair. "That and ten like it are all that's left. Some of them are even deserted."

"How do you mean?"

"Squatters in some," Hargie said. "Live outside a monster's cave and people leave you alone. That's the rationale."

"That nanite cloud's too big a monster than I'd care to live next to."

"Kinda proves my point." Hargie frowned a moment, blinked. "Contact. We're in." He took a long breath.

Princess started to move. Having the cockpit's walls become the view outside was perfectly wonderful when you gazed at things from a distance. On a docking approach it was nauseating. The outer edge of the station whirled side to side as they neared, made worse by the fact that Swirl felt no corresponding motion. Ancient solar panels parted to let them dock. Swirl could see other bubbleships nestled in the station's copious arrays, like a litter suckling on a beast.

:Top left,: Sparkle sent. *:The box.:*

Swirl was startled by the send. She had barely received any of late.

:What about it?: she sent back. The thing seemed a regular sort of shipping box.

:The circular exhaust at the near end,: Sparkle sent. *:The Freightways we visited had the same. Swirl, it's a tiny Freightways box.:*

:By the Eye, you're right,: Swirl sent. *:How do you remember these things?:*

:Neurons, darling. Look them up.:

"Hargie," Swirl said, "that's a Freightways box up there."

The bubbleman nodded. "Nothing to fizz about. One reason Eucharist and I fell out of touch. They made him a shy little Freightbox for his shy little enterprise."

"What's this... enterprise?" Swirl asked.

Hargie focused on docking.

:Who is this Eucharist person?: Swirl sent to her sister.

:Hargie'd risk Freightways itself,: Sparkle sent, as much to herself as Swirl, *:to protect me?:*

Swirl groaned beneath her breath and massaged her eyelids.

Idiot. Still, at least she was communicating.

SPARKLE WAS SURPRISED to see Hargie had taken his hat off to sit at the long wrought-iron table. A gloomy hall, this, and cold. Black mahogany panels stretched vertically from ceiling to floor all along the room's length, making Sparkle think of a millipede's segmented hide. She could smell wood polish, saw motes of dust drift through the air. Everything was sombre. Cobwebs would have completed the ambience.

"So, Mr. Eucharist," Hargie was saying, "that's why we're here. That's how it falls. Rest you've probably, y'know, seen on the news." He swallowed, looked Eucharist in his chrome-yellow eyes. He'd told him most of what had happened.The leaf drug, the Spindlies, the escape from Calran. Most of it. "And here we are."

Sung Eucharist was a big man. Not fat; muscular. Sparkle could discern formidable biceps and pectorals beneath his loose-flowing robes. His female bodyguard, standing to the right of his high-backed chair, seemed a spear beside a mighty shield. Eucharist's shaved head caught the nanite cloud's light that glowered through a shaded window running the length of the dining hall. His skin was almost impossibly white, whiter than the men of her homeworld even, almost silver. His long beard—braided and black—flowed down from his chin like a waterfall from a mountain, a mountain in an ornate throne.

"We've..." Sparkle felt her lips move: Swirl in the head seat. "We've got money. We will have money..." Swirl faded off.

Frigging imbecile. Sparkle didn't voice her disdain. She knew her sister knew her well enough.

Eucharist ignored her.

"Hargopal," Eucharist said finally, his voice thick and dark like a river of tar in some lightless underworld, its accent hypnotic, lyrical. "Hargopal Stukes."

"Yeah," Hargie said.

Eucharist looked at the scar-faced bodyguard stood beside him. "You recall Hargopal Stukes, yes?"

The guard shook her head. Sparkle realised she was a Falcatta. Twisted bubblefolk, sired from kidnapped bubblewomen generations past, raped for their remarkable genes. So, bubblefolk and Falcatta both worked for Eucharist. Sparkle had been led to think that an impossibility.

"Hargopal Stukes," Eucharist said, laying his chrome irises upon his subject once more. "Bubbleman extraordinaire. Gifted smuggler. Defeated by his own ethics. Deemed this place a... 'black web.'"

"I brought the shipment back to you," Hargie said. "Plenty would've dumped that shit into a star." He coughed and shifted.

"And telling you did not. It seems these 'ethics' stretch only as far as Hargie Stukes' personal horizons." He looked at them both. "Or his own preservation."

"Yeah," Hargie said.

"Quite a bounty," Eucharist said. "On each of you."

"Paid bounties always come with attention," Hargie said. "You taught me that, Mr. Eucharist."

"A bubbleship, then?" Eucharist said. "That might be worth something. Salvage. No crew found."

Hargie looked down.

:Let me take over,: Sparkle sent to her sister. *:Now.:*

Swirl did so without comment.

"Mr. Eucharist," Sparkle said. "There's been a mistake. Hargie rather had me under the impression you were no dullard."

Eucharist looked at her as he might a piece of lint upon his sleeve.

"Why..." Sparkle said, dressing her hesitation as a significant pause, her tongue but one step ahead of her thoughts, "...would you discard a fountain of wealth for the price of a mere bubbleship? Which, I suspect, you know the price of all too well." She smiled. "Why don't you spare us this theatre?"

"If you'll spare us the desperation," Eucharist answered.

"Desperation? You jest." Sparkle pointed at herself. "This is smugness you see, surely? The self-preening audacity of someone who knows they have the final offer." She leaned forward. "And who senses her host senses it too."

Eucharist turned to Hargie.

"Where did you find this person?"

"Flip it around," Hargie said. He scratched his chin.

"Snacks," Sparkle said. "I'd like some snacks."

The two men looked at her.

:Sparkle,: Swirl sent. *:Stop trying to kill us.:*

"Least you could do," Sparkle told Eucharist. "I'll bet you have far classier morsels than those in the hold of his ship." She pointed at Hargie, her eyes still on their host. "Wine too, should you have it. Medium dry, but I'll settle for dry."

"Of all lost Earth's customs," Eucharist said, "the right to a last meal was by far the most civilised."

Cold rippled in the pool of her belly, yet she kept her face a mask. The House had trained Sparkle for these moments as much as it had trained Swirl to kill. Hopefully training was enough.

Eucharist gestured at the Falcatta woman. The guard left. Eucharist looked at Sparkle again. "Continue."

"Appreciated," Sparkle said. "You displayed no curiosity about the leaf drug Hargie mentioned earlier on, sir, when he outlined our travails. Now I'd wager you are one of the few feral individuals with a grasp on the existence and extent of that trade."

"By 'feral,'" Hargie said, "she means—"

Eucharist silenced him with a look.

"I'm an established merchant," Sparkle said, "within the leaf nexus. I personally know the head of our northeast operation."

"Fractile is dead," Eucharist said. "Murdered."

"Yes... *yes*," Sparkle said, "And I'm certain a businessman of your acumen sees the power-vacuum therein. The trade, of itself, does not have to be overseen by a Harmonic. Indeed, the Harmonies increasingly prefer local agencies. My voice carries weight. And, er..." She gestured at Eucharist. "Well, to insinuate more would be patronising."

Snacks and wine arrived. Shelled, nut-like things, and a glass of—by the Eye!—vintage saddaric from back home. Eucharist kept a gorgeous cellar here in nanite hell. Sparkle feigned mere satisfaction. The Falcatta guard returned to her position beside Eucharist.

"How can I be sure," Eucharist said, "I would hear from you again?"

Sparkle pretended to chuckle. In actual fact, she had just shuddered from the marvellous quality of the wine, its flash flood of Zahrir memories.

"Well, you can't," she said. "I could show you the large quantity of leaf I keep for personal use, but what does that prove?" She took another sip and shook her head. "No. The truth is, it's really two options. Isn't it?"

For the first time Eucharist smiled, a little. He shrugged his thick shoulders.

Sparkle pressed on. "One: you sell our bubbleship and space our corpses out into infinity's great paper basket. An—"

"Your drugs, too," Eucharist said.

"You'd space my *drugs*?"

"I'd sell your drugs," Eucharist said. "After I spaced you."

"Right." Sparkle took a breath. "Where was I?"

"Being spaced," Eucharist said.

"Er, quite. So you'd have the price of a secondhand ship. What's that, Hargie?"

"Spare change to Sung Eucharist," Hargie said. "Pocket dust." Sparkle could sense him getting animated. "Eucharist don't play low stake. Not-no-never."

"That a fact?" Sparkle asked Hargie. "Well, then there's option two."

"Fix up the ship," Hargie said. "Restock, give us a new ID; a *good* ID, like only you do, sir. Then let us fly. Cost you nothing, almost."

:Is this working?: Swirl sent to Sparkle. *:Actually working?:*

"The Harmonies honour all debts," Sparkle told Eucharist. "And remember those who help it. We are an empire far richer than every feral world combined, our territory wider than you could know. Our technology is unique: a synthesis of humanity's and a bi-dimensional superspecies. Beyond replication, beyond defeat. And should we ever choose to stir, well..." Her eyes held his. She popped a morsel in her mouth. "Just a thought."

EUCHARIST CLAPPED HARD and slow. A phenomenon, Hargie knew, that could go many ways. Hargie's grandaddy had been terrified of Sung Eucharist. Given Hargie was a grown man now and Eucharist hadn't aged a fucking day, Hargie understood why.

"A thought indeed," Eucharist said, and he placed his palms upon the table. "Leaf. The drug from nowhere, people are calling it."

"And now it can be from you," Sparkle said to him.

Hargie studied Sparkle. Initially he had thought her bent on irritating Eucharist, some elaborate suicide-by-proxy act that'd drag Hargie with her. But he'd soon settled on a more likely set of reasons: Sparkle was foreign, arrogant and, yes, utterly bat-ladder. But now...

Now it had all come together. All her eccentricities, vanities, coalescing on this one moment, this deal. Like a mess of iron filings waiting for a magnet. Hargie wondered if everybody was like this where she came from.

"Very well," Eucharist said. "But I raise the stakes. I require a show of good faith."

"Yes?" Sparkle said.

"It transpires our bubbleman's ethics may actually prove useful," Eucharist said. "My pilots in the Psiax Quartet are trying to renegotiate terms."

"Screw that," Hargie said. "I ain't crushing some poor striking assholes. Hargie don't grease that action."

"You think my hands eternal fists?" Eucharist said. "My hands were open to *you*, remember."

"He thinks you a handshake that slowly crushes," Sparkle said to Eucharist.

Eucharist bore his chrome eyes into Hargie, switched their gaze from formidable to avuncular. Hargie hated that more.

"I would ask you to mediate," Eucharist told him. He gestured a hand in the air, as if groping for the words. "Bestow... fresh insight. My people are already in talks."

"That all?" But it was never all.

"There's your family's name of course," Eucharist said.

Shit. That.

"Your family?" Sparkle asked. Shit.

"He's never told you?" Eucharist asked her. "Hargopal?"

Hargie lifted his hat off the table and pretended to inspect it for dirt. He shrugged.

"What?" Sparkle said.

"His father led the solidarity movement," Eucharist told her. "Brought all the diasporas to its banner. Impressive, especially for a lower family. Their surname wasn't even of the bubblefolk; a 'stat' surname, I believe they call it."

"Why didn't you tell me?" Hargie heard Sparkle say. He didn't look up. "So what happened?"

"They claimed a new, semi-habitable home, a world," Eucharist said. "Stukes senior even persuaded the more sentimental star-nations to donate terraforming equipment and expertise. The Freightways corporation had other ideas, their interstellar business preferring all bubblefolk inchoate and bickering. And they knew plenty of them could be bought."

"No shit," Hargie muttered.

"They broke the solidarity movement," Eucharist said. "Executed his father."

Sparkle drew breath.

"Yeah," Hargie said. All he could think to say.

"Darling," Sparkle said, "why didn't you—"

"Trap," Hargie said to Eucharist, ignoring Sparkle. "Lead us like sheep to your bounty."

"I do not chase bounties," Eucharist said. "I'll be taking quarters on your ship. No guards."

"You'd have your gun," Hargie said. "You always have a gun."

"And then I'd have a ship I could not pilot," Eucharist said.

"There's the returner," Hargie insisted. "I know you know about that." He wouldn't call him *sir* anymore.

"The returner?" Sparkle asked Hargie. "They exist?"

Shit. She had an ugly way of looking things up on her handheld.

"Activating said returner would lead me to a great quantity of bubblemen eager to know why I was in possession of your ship," Eucharist said to Hargie. "You're grasping for excuses, boy."

Hargie slumped back in his chair.

"My return home is pressing," Sparkle said. "This all sounds like quite the detour."

"You clutch to the misconception that this is negotiable," Eucharist said. "Besides, the coordinates I'll give you are little more than a lightyear away."

"Hargie?" Here it came. It hadn't taken her a second. "Hargie, I know this is difficult for you. But, please—"

"You're just the gift that keeps on giving, ain't you?" He felt his teeth grit. He slung his hat on the table.

"Well, if you'd have dignified me with just a little of your past..." Sparkle said.

A silence fell. Damn galaxy, everyone in it wanting things their own way. Sung Eucharist understood that, owned the playbook. Sparkle had opened a deal, dragged them both up from begging, and Hargie was grateful for that, impressed. But this game was now their host's. All he'd had to do was figure Sparkle's levers. Eucharist had Hargie then. He always knew how. But for what, exactly?

"All right," Hargie said. "We do this quick."

"Naturally." Eucharist turned to Sparkle. "My guard will escort you to your quarters."

Sparkle peered at the Falcatta woman.

"Lady," Eucharist said. "I would speak to Hargie alone."

"Of course." She emptied the last of her glass and stood up. "Hargie?"

He looked at her. Sometimes her face was the most human thing imaginable.

"Thank you," she said. She turned and left the hall.

Great. That look of hers exposed him before Eucharist.

The man himself stood up and, stately as an orbital rig, made his way around the table toward Hargie. Then he sat on the table's corner next to Hargie's seat and looked out the long window, to the slumbering gold of the nanite cloud. It lit his pale features in the gloom. Hargie had watched him gaze at the synthetic nova more than once, and always with the same look. A frown, like he was staring at an impossible puzzle and was more frustrated by it than he'd care to admit.

He breathed out, looked down at Hargie in his chair. Old uncle Euchy.

"Entangled with a Harmony woman, I see," he said. "Mirrachish by birth, if I'm any expert." He frowned. "Or perhaps from Zahrir..."

"She's just a job," Hargie said.

"Your job calls you 'darling'. They're witches, these Harmony women. And their men warlocks." He looked up at some decoration or other on the hall's walls. "For your half-educated purposes, at least."

"Expert, huh?" Hargie said.

"They are children of humanity, as are we all. But they surrendered to an alien way, to its protection and comforts." He looked at Hargie once again. "I respect them for it, in truth. A strong suit for that inevitable game."

What the heck did he mean?

"All a game, huh?" Hargie asked. He took a cigarette from his pocket and lit up.

"Certainly." Eucharist paused. He breathed out. "Hargie, I know of these... 'Spindlies' you mention, those who follow you. They call themselves the Konsensus."

What? Shit. How could he just drop this shit? "What are they? Cartel? Pirates?"

"I cannot say. But they are everywhere, my boy. Hidden within asteroids. Spread thin, I think, but something unites them. Something of mind."

"They're Totalists?" Hargie said.

"Totalists are primitives beside them," Eucharist said. "The greater part of humanity too. The Konsensus' ships are jump-capable, like yours."

"What?" It was like Eucharist had just announced he was a dildo cannon. Revelation atop revelation, tossed out like confetti. Sung-fucking-Eucharist. "No way."

"We can only assume they solved the matter independently," Eucharist said.

"But that would make them..."

"Capable of conquering the stars?" He seemed to consider the issue. "Perhaps. And your Sparkle upsets their hive. Perhaps she already comprehends this and chooses not to tell you." He leaned in toward Hargie, wafting away smoke. "Perhaps she is the most dangerous woman in the galaxy."

"Leave a toilet seat up and I guarantee it," Hargie said.

Eucharist gazed toward the doorway Sparkle had exited through. "Focused. Charming." He made a gesture, as if trying to fish the right word from the air. "Sensual."

"She's something, all right," Hargie said.

Eucharist looked back at him, seemingly disappointed. "And the others?" he asked.

"Others?"

Eucharist's gold-yellow irises searched Hargie's face.

"Nothing," Eucharist said eventually. He smiled. "I meant other women before her. It's been a while since we've talked."

Odd question. Sort of thing poor dead Aewyn would've asked. Never Eucharist.

"Oh, you know..." Hargie replied, picking up his hat. "Focused. Charming." He took a cashew from Sparkle's bowl. "Downloaded."

SWIRL KNEW SHE'D BE spending the night in their brain's villa as soon as she saw the double bed. Sparkle didn't comment. She got right on with cooing at its four posters and silk sheets.

From the side of their shared sight, Swirl could see antique weapons upon the cabin's walls. She wanted to inspect them.

:Still my time, sis,: she sent. *:You've jumped my shift. Again.:*

"Still not talking to you," Sparkle said. But she relented and let Swirl take over. Fair was fair.

Corporeal again, Swirl strode over to the weapons hanging from the walls. Ornate things like meat cleavers. Impractical, yet charming. She touched them. Well made.

:Boring,: Sparkle sent.

"Thought you weren't talking to me," Swirl said. "Anyway, I'm grabbing what body time I may before your gentleman caller slouches in."

:I can tell him to go,: Sparkle sent. *:He's just a plaything. You remember how it was, dear, surely.:*

Had Swirl been this irritating when she'd taken Lyreko as a comfort and diversion? Surely not. She'd always made time for her sister, let her take control whenever it'd been possible. But none of that counted now. Not since the fight. Since her fists.

:Actually,: Sparkle said, *:I suppose there is something I want to talk about.:*

It broke Swirl from her grim reverie. "Yes?"

:Hargie mentioned 'the returner'. I've been researching bubbleships. It would seem returners aren't some public myth. And Princess Floofy *apparently has one. Which must make her very old indeed, mm-yes.:*

Swirl wiped dust off the cleaver's blade. "I see. This will all make sense soon, I take it?"

:It's, er, well, it's like a button,: Sparkle sent. *"Somewhere in the cockpit. And anyone can hit it, if anything happens to the pilot. A one way ticket to a Desic.:*

"Still waiting on the sense cavalry here, sister," Swirl said.

:Home of the bubblefolk,: Sparkle explained. *:Desics generate some powerful bubble signature, so they say. Returner allows a straight run home to one. At an expense.:*

"Expense?"

:Kills the ship,: Sparkle sent.

"Could only improve *Princess*," Swirl said, jokingly.

:Agreed,: Sparkle sent. *:Can't stand the hox-plated cow.:*

"But I get your meaning. We find it, we have a last-ditch escape. You never know." She wrinkled her nose. "Could you not just ask Hargie about it?"

:Did you see his face in there?: Sparkle sent. *:He only said it because he thought we'd—I'd—have no clue what he meant. No, sister, best he does not know how much we know.:*

"Cold, Sparkle," Swirl said.

:Hargie's a sweet creature,: Sparkle sent. *:He loves* Princess. *We get cornered, he may not have the resolve.:*

"Our mission comes first," Swirl said.

:Naturally.:

Swirl could kill a human in a blink, had long trained to do so. But there was something in soft, ditzy Sparkle that unnerved even her. Sparkle could rise from infatuation to adoration, then downwards into ambivalence in the time Swirl took to merely regard someone. How many weeping faces had Swirl seen back at the Trinity House? How many broken hearts screaming at Swirl to see Sparkle? And they had been Harmonic citizens. What mattered a dirty feral? Swirl almost felt sorry for Hargie Stukes.

:I don't trust Eucharist,: Sparkle sent. *:Best we find the returner. Soon.:*

"We can't get inside *Princess* without Hargie knowing," Swirl said.

:We can do the next best thing,: Sparkle sent.

"Of course. How—"

There came a knock at the door.

:Answer it,: Sparkle sent. *:I've got to drop into the villa, arrange things. Take minutes.:*

"It'll be Hargie," Swirl said to her sister.

:Probably just wants sex,: Sparkle sent. *:Hold him off.:*

"What?"

:But act like me.:

"Deny a rutting beast *and* act like you?" Swirl said. "There's a contradiction in terms."

Sparkle had vanished.

Idiot. Swirl answered the door.

Hargie. Puppy eyes staring out from beneath his hat.

"I kinda snapped at you back there," he said.

Right. Sex, then.

"Fine," Swirl said. She realised she was being too Swirl. She added a Sparkle-ish giggle. It must have looked weird, but Hargie didn't comment.

"Shoulda mentioned my past, too," he said. "Owed you that." He put his hand on her shoulder.

Swirl stopped herself from flinching. His hand stayed there, which, considering alternatives, was fine by Swirl.

"Fine. Perfectly fine." She thought about it. "Neither of us have lives for looking back upon."

"Guess so."

"I'm sorry about your father," Swirl said.

"Don't." He looked away from her, gazed at his hand on her shoulder.

"You don't have to tell me anything," Swirl heard herself say. "Really."

His eyes met her. They needed her. Strange, to be this close to someone again. His hand felt warm on her shoulder. He leaned in. Swirl didn't move. She felt his breath. She...

:I'm back:

Swirl jolted. She faked a coughing fit.

:Good idea, coughing,: Sparkle sent. *:Bought time. Let's swap.:*

:What?: Swirl sent back.

:Go to the villa, the constructery,: Sparkle sent. *:I've left diagrams.:*

"You all right?" Hargie was asking. "Slap your back?"

Swirl gestured she was fine. Leaning forward, she gave ascendency over to her sister. Faded, fell...

...and found herself stood in the villa's cool hallway. No more cracks anywhere, good as new.

By the Eye, she'd let Sparkle take the driving seat again. She would've stood her ground, told Sparkle to do her own work, if only Sparkle hadn't stumbled on her and Hargie...

Animal instinct. She and her sister shared the same hormones, after all. You had to expect... blurring... occasionally. Very occasionally.

Well, she was here now. Get to the constructery, search for the returner, get back and take over again before any funny business kicked off.

The constructery lay in the basement of the villa: a humble enough cellar, when not active. But when Swirl or Sparkle stepped inside, it could become a simulation of any place the sisters had ever visited. Currently it was *Princess'* cockpit. Sparkle had set the simulation to a high filter, displaying the notional construct of the cockpit in Sparkle's higher, rational mind, or Sparkle's version of a rational mind. The cockpit was convincingly realistic when you focused on a particular part of it, but a silent hurricane of colours at the edges of your sight.

The default setting. Barely any use. Sparkle had meant the lower filter.

'Low,' Swirl said, and the cockpit became fragmented, bloomed pink and scarlet.

Swirl had once heard awareness described as the lady of a great castle, asleep on her throne. Servants from below stairs came to her, woke her when her attention was required, but otherwise the castle carried on happily enough with her dozing. The lady merely *thought* she was forever awake, assumed she oversaw all.

The lower filter sewed back together all the memories discarded as useless by the lady; that is to say, Sparkle's higher mind. The visual result was a cockpit very different from that of the higher: it seemed made of motes, those blobs of colour that distracted the eyes after looking at light. And yet, counterintuitively, it was somehow more real than the higher mind's reconstruction.

Black silhouettes flickered all around her: stark interpersonal memories that appeared with whichever filter you happened to use, though Sparkle had edited most of the details out. Swirl could see a shadow she suspected to be herself during the descent toward Calran, holding back Sparkle's panic attack. Two other silhouettes flickered in and out, one atop the other in Hargie's chair. Swirl sighed. She knew her sister had been rushed for time, but a little more editing, dear...

An object materialised in Swirl's hand. She inspected it: a silver metal disc, wide as her palm. On one side was a smaller disc at the centre. It clicked when she pressed it. A button.

The returner. Or a simulacrum of the same, composited from several likely visual sources out on the memestream. Sparkle was good at that; no Pearl, but good. The goal now for Swirl was to find anything even slightly resembling it within this stitched-memory cockpit.

"Transpose," she told the constructery.

She watched an arc of blue light explode silently from her own head and coat the room. Swirl's own subconscious construct; it filled the cracks and gaps of Sparkle's. The cockpit scintillated pink and blue, an iridescence like peacock ore, like beetle wing: a composite of the two sisters' awarenesses. The two colours never blended.

More moving silhouettes appeared, Swirl's own interpersonal memories of the cockpit. A panic-stricken Sparkle emerged, completing the memory-shadow of Swirl restraining her. Another silhouette of Hargie appeared in his chair. Almost an antithesis of the love-making Hargie, this Hargie stared mutely up at a disembodied pair of shadow arms pointing a shadow-pistol. Swirl's memory of her own actions the first day they'd boarded *Princess*.

She started looking around, gazing over the walls and fittings, holding out the replica of the returner and waiting for some answer. The chair was the logical place to look, but she would save it till last. She didn't want to think about those two.

Swirl checked the row of console things at the fore-end of the cockpit. Perhaps the returner lay on one of them; she hadn't seen the consoles used for anything else. Their surfaces producing no clues, Swirl got on all fours and checked under one. She immediately cursed her own idiocy. Why would she have any memory of the underside of something she didn't even know the use of? Sparkle might have been on all fours here before, though...

Swirl shivered. An uncomfortable thought. Why was she having these uncomfortable thoughts? That classic self-disgust, maybe, at recognising an opportunity to exploit a person ignorant of one's Triune nature. Hargie had touched her earlier, and Swirl had let him. If she had permitted anything further, she would be a criminal, a gross abuser. And so she wouldn't have. Hadn't. But it was the recognition of the possibility—that she could *think* that—that made Swirl feel... *ill*. Yes, ill.

She checked the ventilators, the pipes, the pile of bric-a-brac against the wall. Nothing. Fine. She would inspect the chair.

She ignored the silhouettes as best she might, keeping her sight on the chair's arms. Nothing resembled the returner. Hardly surprising—Swirl had seen the arms' dials and buttons enough times—but her instincts wouldn't let go. An emergency would require the returner as near as possible to the pilot's seat.

A bright flash of pink on the chair caught Swirl's eye. The right arm's end: it flashed pale scarlet every time the silhouette-Sparkle's knee collided into it. Swirl walked around and looked at the end of the arm. Odd: the arm was an inch longer in the pink collision than it was in its blue state.

Yes: clambering onto Hargie, Sparkle had inadvertently nudged a secret compartment the slightest touch ajar. Her subconscious—here rendered in pink—had picked up on it. No doubt Hargie had noticed some time later and sealed the compartment shut. Swirl's subconscious memory—the blue in this reconstruction—had never seen it any other way but sealed.

She lifted the replica in her hand to the chair arm's end. It could fit. Swinging upward on a hinge, perhaps.

Swirl grinned. She and her sister were a formidable team.

Upstairs again, she walked by the music room. She was a little too scared to go back in there since the Hoidrac's apparition. The air in there seemed somehow volatile, too full with... *potential.*

She carried on walking and sent a knock and a request to come up. Sparkle did not reply.

Outside, above the sea, the sky flickered with an aurora borealis of rainbows. Somewhere out there, Swirl's time-shared body was sexually responding.

Swirl sat down in the hot sand and grunted. Here for the duration again. Maybe she should take up sculpture.

MELID STARED AT THE grass. The grass, she could cope with. Green, wiry: like the paddyroot of home. Deep breaths. The light was strange, the light of a sky-soaked sun.

Concentrate.

She looked up from her feet. Up, slowly, up, off into the far horizon. The land not rising up, not curling over and embracing itself, cocooning all within. The blue emptiness filled the upper half of the horizon. No rock or metal or muscleform to nail the air down, to keep it in.

All skies, Melid thought, *are the faces of death.* She braced herself to look up, right up, into the belly of the sky.

The simulation vanished. Melid was staring at a plated ceiling.

Emissary.

Conybeare's voice in her head.

She looked down. The Domov's avatar stared glacially at her. She had developed negative feelings toward this composite intelligence which, naturally, Conybeare and all the individuals that comprised it were aware of. A childish attitude, one she blamed on her exposure to Worlders.

"Conybeare," she said.

The Domov expressed that the following encounter between them would require a greater use of verbalisation, given the concepts and facts involved.

"Like the Worlders," Melid said, intrigued. "Proceed."

It vocalised in Anglurati: "At 0900.08.08.04 standard, a Worlder craft colloquially deemed a 'bubbleship' used its gravity manipulator to jump within the system of kollective a/025 'Aetherdown.'"

"*Princess Floofy?*"

"Designation unknown," Conybeare said. "The bubbleship ejected its refuse and jumped out of system. Aetherdown kollective's sensors registered a primitive radio transmission amid the detritus."

How like a Worlder Conybeare is, Melid thought, *in its refusal to emote.* A one-way tunnel: the Domov was wholly aware of Melid's emotions.

"Instrum operatives located the signal to a small airtight canister," Conybeare said. "On its surface were instructions written in Anglurati, informing us it would not play a message until receiving a certain live fingerprint. Yours."

"Mine?" Melid said.

"We cloned your hand and accessed it," Conybeare said. "Prepare to receive."

Melid closed her eyes.

A visual recording: black backdrop, size and dimensions uncertain. Arclight Annie popped up into view, making Melid start.

"Hellllluuuuuuu!" Arclight Annie said or, at least, a distorted voice pretending to be Arclight Annie. Its glass eyes glared at the viewer with unsurpassed menace.

Arclight Annie was a popular toy amongst Konsensus children. Melid had played with them herself. Its gangly limbs now danced, not from some Konsensite's thoughts, but by what looked like primitive electrical wires.

"Helluuuuu!" it said again. It spoke in Anglurati, not emotic jiang. "Helluuu to lil' miss Melid, Melidy, Melidy, Melidy Silvercloud! Are weeeee gonna have fun or what? Come home, Lil' Miss, come home! There's lots to see at Silvercloud, if only you spyyyyyieee with your little eyeieee!" It began to dance. It began to sing. "If only the Instrum could see, could see, all of the things that'll be, be, be!" It stopped abruptly and leered into the camera. "Goodniiighhhhht!"

The recording stopped. Melid opened her eyes.

She looked at Conybeare. "This was fashioned by Worlders?"

"Presumably," Conybeare said.

"How do they know my name?"

Conybeare said nothing, choosing to exude a *well-you-tell-me* sentiment.

The exposure was overwhelming. It wasn't outside the bounds of reason that Melid was the only Konsensus name known to anyone outside the Konsensus. She took deep breaths. This was more alarming than staring up at a sky.

"How..." She stopped, breathed deep, collected herself. "How would Worlders get their hands on a puppet?"

"Puppets are dissolved after use and their matter reclaimed," Conybeare said. "A Konsensus citizen would have to give one to an outsider. The Kollective-at-Large would have recorded a memory of that. Alarmingly, there is none. There is also the matter of your fingerprint."

"My hands were never bare," Melid said. "On every mission I've worn the suit. How... how could I not? On Calran I would not have been able to move, not in that gravity."

"On Calran we could not observe you the entire time," Conybeare said.

"I haven't individualised!" Melid shouted. "Nor kancerised!" She wanted to swing out at Conybeare, mere projection though he was. She didn't care that he picked up on that. Must she always go through life suspected? To hail from Silvercloud was to be suspected whatever you did, however hard you toiled. "Check! Read mind!" She'd returned to speaking jiang.

"That has already occurred," Conybeare told her, unaffected by her bellowing. "You appear wholly in step with the Konsensus."

"Yes," Melid said.

"Though individuals have evaded detection before. That is how kancerisation begins."

"How?"

Conybeare said nothing, exuded nothing.

"Well," Melid said, swapping back to Anglurati. "What now? I assume I lose Emissary status." She shivered. "At least. I'm known now."

"Not as yet," Conybeare said. "You and your cadre shall proceed to Silvercloud."

"What?" Melid said. "Upon the order of some Worlder?"

"This Worlder seems to know the existence and location of at least two kollectives. They appear to keep that information to themselves, otherwise we would have had to order two major habitats to auto-annihilate by now." For the first time, Conybeare blinked. "Your presence at Silvercloud will bring this crisis to a head, however that transpires. This is preferable to inaction."

"Yes." It was all Melid could think to say. They would surely annihilate Silvercloud after she was done there.

"If it should be the case you are mentally compromised," Conybeare said, "Field-Instrums Zo and Doum can neutralise you."

"I am aware of that," Melid said.

"The Instrum shall take especial care with your thoughts and experiences while you visit Silvercloud: sensitive information shall be kept from Silvercloud's local kollective, whilst quotidian thought and emotion shall remain so as to not arouse suspicion. You and your craft will claim to be on rest-visit."

"A visit home," she said.

The Domov had vanished.

"Home..." she whispered in emotic-jiang, to no one.

Eleven

SWIRL GROANED. LYING in bed on board *Princess*, her eyelids glued together with sleep, she wondered why she groaned and why she was awake.

Something beeping. Things didn't beep back home in the Harmonies. Ferals beeped. The beeping didn't stop.

"Fine," she muttered. "Fine." She turned anger to action and leaped from her bed.

A light flashed on a little box on the wall. She'd never bothered to find out what the box was for, but now that its light flashed in syncopation with the beeping noise, she knew it to be the enemy. She slapped the box and a screen materialised in the air above.

The screen said: *cockpit presence required.*

"Idiot," she said to the screen. "Stupid sentence structure."

The bleeping had stopped, at least.

:What the fuck are you doing?:

Now Sparkle was awake. Idiot central.

"Telling this, this *thing* to behave," Swirl said.

:Why?:

"Because." She massaged her eyes awake, coughed. "Because it's an idiot."

:Right,: Sparkle sent. *:Now we've a pre-emptive strike policy with inanimate objects, how about we let the toilet know where it stands? We're bursting here.:*

"No," Swirl said. "Cockpit."

Sparkle fell silent, considering the matter. *:You've been in Feral space too long, dear.:*

Ten minutes later Swirl was stomping down the corridor toward *Princess'* cockpit. She'd taken the measure of shoving her pistol—Nugo Vict's pistol, beautiful thing—down the back of her trousers. One of Sparkle's long blouses did the job of obscuring the bulge. With Sung Eucharist on board, it had been Swirl's default setting.

She stopped before the cockpit door. Two days' travel. Not once had she had a chance to check the chair's arm for the returner. Either Hargie would be in there, Hargie and Eucharist were in there, or the hatch door was locked. The latter suggested Hargie wasn't comfortable with *Princess*' passenger either.

:Well,: Sparkle sent. *:Go in, then.:*

"Wait." Swirl lifted the back of the blouse and placed it behind the butt of the pistol. Ease of access. She had a gut feeling, ever growing, that Eucharist had played his card.

The hatch whirled open and she stepped through. Hargie sat in his pilot chair, quite still, the walls around all gloomy and metal. Eucharist was beside him on one of the fold-out chairs, the embroidered tails of his long black coat hanging down to either side. The grandeur of the man and the cheapness of his seating produced an absurdity Swirl tried to ignore. No gun, it seemed. Swirl could settle for that.

"Good day," Eucharist said.

Swirl nodded. "Hargie?" she said.

"Hey," Hargie replied. He raised a lazy hand. He was coming down.

"We've come out of jump?" Swirl asked.

"Indeed," Eucharist replied, stroking down his long beard absentmindedly. "We're awaiting rendezvous. Sleep well, I take it?"

"Well enough," Swirl said.

She walked over to Hargie, keeping to the other side of his chair to Eucharist, never showing her back.

Hargie looked up at her, smiling. An expectancy left him when he met her eyes. Clearly he'd guessed her 'mood'. He looked down at his legs in their brackets. "Man," he said, "jumps ripped it outta me. Gravity well here."

"I'm going to need you primed," Eucharist said. "Here." He pulled a small square like a plaster from his robes and offered it to the other man.

"Thanks," Hargie said, and took it.

Swirl snatched it from his hand. She glared at Eucharist. "What is this?"

"Up-patch," Hargie said. "An upper."

"Quite safe," Eucharist said, "if one limits one's intake."

Swirl ignored him and looked to Hargie. "You don't know what's in this, Stukes."

"S'standard patch," Hargie said, his voice slurred. "Smoosh, tune?"

She sighed. The two men had a way of making her feel like an ignorant foreigner. She handed the patch back to Hargie and he unpeeled it, slapped it on his neck.

"You were a lot more trusting two days past," Eucharist said. "You even requested snacks."

"And?" she said, shrugging.

"An observation." He smiled and his chrome irises studied her face.

"Hargie, how about you throw up a visual?" she said.

"That's my Sparks," Hargie told Eucharist, brightening already. "Everything plain, straight up."

"Focused," Eucharist replied.

"I'm not anyone's anything," Swirl said. She hated it when men talked like that. Men weren't like this back home.

The cockpit's walls transmuted into deep space. They were high above a titanic blue-white star. A disc of ghostly light issued from its equator.

"Hardly any rock here," Hargie said. "Who'd live around a lone wolf?"

"Around a Wolf-Rayet star?" Eucharist said. "Someone with copious insulation, clearly."

"Coordinates?" Hargie asked.

"Not yet," Eucharist said. He looked up, accessing his neuralware. "Another eight minutes. For the time being just... bubbleship."

"Bubbleship?" Hargie said.

"Fly around aimlessly," Eucharist said. "Loiter with intent. Bubbleship."

"Loiter any direction?" Hargie said.

Eucharist chuckled.

"Wolf-Rayets," he said, gesturing at the star. "Beauteous things. I'm told they make natural fissures between our reality and the Geode."

Swirl studied him. "You're the first non-Harmonic to mention the Geode. I'm impressed."

"If one's to live in the galaxy, one should take an interest in how it works," Eucharist said. "Its usages."

:Remarkable man,: Sparkle sent to Swirl. *:Ravenous intelligence.:*

:By the Eye,: Swirl replied, *:you're like a dog with its penis out.:*

Sparkle didn't respond.

"Stop here," Eucharist said minutes later.

Hargie did so. "You sure now?" he asked. "Plenty good patches of nothing we ain't tried."

"Who'd want to live out here?" Swirl said.

Hargie jolted in his seat. "Spindly ships," he said. "Four, right on top."

"Does that answer your question?" Eucharist asked Swirl. "Konsensus stealth technology really is impressive, is it not? I've begged, but they never give me the recipe."

Swirl drew her pistol and aimed at the bald chrome-eyed bastard. "What is this?"

"Remuneration," Eucharist said, calm as the sea by Swirl's villa. He pulled a black object out of his robes and spoke into it. "Transmit flight path."

"Tell them to go," Swirl said. "Or I part your cranium."

"They'll destroy this ship," Eucharist said.

"Do it."

"Lamentably," Eucharist said, "I am the only means you have of getting out of this trap."

"Jump," Swirl told Hargie.

"Point blank," Hargie said, his face a grimace. "Wouldn't have a chance." He looked at Eucharist. "Right, fucker?"

"Let history judge me, boy," Eucharist said. "If it can find me."

:Swirl,: Sparkle sent, *:the returner.:*

Swirl dived at the chair's arm. She pulled at its end and it flipped up. The returner.

The button was missing. Just a hole at its centre.

:Shit.:

Swirl met Hargie's eyes. His face was oddly serene. Almost disappointed.

"Hargie," Eucharist said. "You should receive coordinates in a moment. I recommend you follow them."

THE BLIZZARD SEASON had passed, or so Gleam had told the Ashemi. It had seemed a short time indeed. A week? Strange seasons on Zahrir. Strange people.

They trudged through the fallen snow, up toward the cottage on the hill. It was early morning, the moon low and ghostly in the blue sky.

"Well, this is it, then," Gleam was saying, struggling to keep up with the Ashemi's long strides. "Either we will have our truth or know the Envoy lies. And if the Envoy should lie..."

"Then the Envoy lied," the Ashemi replied. No breath emanated from his own mouth. It fascinated him. "It wholly depends on how intimidated he was by my appearance on this world. It's as likely his mockery was heartfelt as much as bravado. We've no idea how much his patron Hoidrac is willing to protect him."

"Or his estimation of same," Gleam said, practically panting now. "If you want my opinion—"

"It is not required."

"Your Ashemi."

In the silence that followed, the Ashemi could discern the call of some local fauna, a high ululating sound. The cottage lay before them at the hill's peak. It was larger than the Ashemi had expected, its slumping grey walls fitted with wide circular windows of stained glass. No illumination. Behind it the Husks—a mountain range of peculiarly warped stone—carried the sun as an altar carries its sacrifice. Strange mountains. And a stranger race who lived within them.

"You do not trust me, do you?" Gleam said between pants. "You never do." He coughed. "I mean... thus far."

"I don't question your intent," the Ashemi said. "But every human in this matter is potentially compromised, their memories victim to the moods of powers vastly greater."

"Some might call that paranoia, your Ashemi."

"Paranoia has no enemies, no threat," the Ashemi said. "No, whatever your opinion, it's best you don't voice it. At worst, you may be the puppet of our patron's rival, Mohatoi Embossed, at best... I'll have considered it already myself."

"Appreciated, your Ashemi," Gleam said.

They came to the cottage's front door and Gleam stamped his boots of snow. He knocked.

"A parochial life out here," Gleam said. He wiped the snow from his greatcoat.

"Perhaps an enviable one." The Ashemi pictured the summer fields of his mortal childhood. It was all he could recall of life then. Summer fields. Blooms. Warmth's memory.

The ululating sound was far louder now, coming from somewhere behind the cottage.

"Corquills," Gleam said.

There was movement in the door's window. A man answered, pale-skinned as every Zahrir male, powerfully built. His friendly expression disappeared when he saw his visitors. Something like anger replaced it, albeit briefly. Resignation followed on its heels.

"Can I help?" he said.

"You may bow," the Ashemi replied. "I am sent by Pheoni the Appropriate, mortal."

"Yes," the man said. He bowed his head. "Yes..."

"We're here to see the parents of Pearl Savard," Gleam told him.

"Of course," he opened the door to them. "Silver's in the back garden." He gave Gleam a look. "No need to remove your coat."

The man led them toward the back garden and then left. The garden shone white in the sunlight. The ululation of those animals, the corquills, reverberated against the garden's stone walls.

Snow sculptures, multicoloured and slender, rose from the white blanket. So did flower sculptures, abstract and of all sizes, their ice-cold matter vibrantly dyed: scarlet, tangerine, cerulean blue. Strange bird-like creatures, their feathers a shiny blue-black, would land and take off from these flowers. They hooked themselves to the sculptures with four limbs like those of some hairy insect, and shot dark tongues into the holes at the centre of the blooms. A man in a long coat stood watching them, his back to the visitors.

"Excuse me," Gleam said. "We're looking for Silver Savard. We were told she was here."

The man's shoulders slumped upon hearing him. He turned around.

"That would be me," he said. 'The Savards produce many binary-gendered multiminds. Half the year I'm physically male."

"You don't look a Triune," the Ashemi said, pointing to Silver's light brown skin. "You don't even resemble a citizen of Zahrir."

"Your Ashemi," he said, bowing almost begrudgingly, "I've only recently transitioned. Another week of treatment and I'll be pale as this land."

The Ashemi gestured at the snow-forms. "What are these sculptures?"

"There's no need to prevaricate," Silver said. "I know why you're here."

"I'm genuinely interested."

Silver laughed bitterly. "Yes. Our guests always are. They're snowflowers, several breeds."

"Breeds?" the Ashemi asked. He was fascinated.

"Algae in the snow; they reshape it after the blizzard season, colour it. Attracts the corquills." He studied the Ashemi as the Ashemi did the snowflowers. "My children love the snowflowers. Or loved. I really don't know."

"Pearl?"

"Pearl particularly." Silver walked closer. There was a long bruise down the right side of his clean-shaven face. Surgery, the Ashemi guessed, a month or so past.

"Where's Coral?" the Ashemi said. "The father?"

"Here," Silver said. He tapped the side of his head. "Inside."

"You're *siblings*?"

"That offends you." Silver said, barely curious at the Ashemi's reaction. "We Savards have always maintained standards."

"Ashemi," Gleam said, almost embarrassed. "It's a common enough practice. Fresh genes are sourced to prevent deformity."

"More I don't know," the Ashemi said.

"I suppose," Silver said, letting out a long icy breath, "I shall have to forgive the term 'common.'"

The Ashemi felt a strange melange about this Silver. Sympathy, disdain. He pointed at the man's bruised face. "You're injured."

"A fall," Silver said. "I slipped feeding the corquills."

The Ashemi thought of the man who'd just let them in. A powerful man.

"Perhaps your, er, brother, Coral," he said, "could give us his account."

"Coral does not leave our skull," Silver replied. "Events broke him." He looked at Gleam. "Your crony there knows that."

"Then perhaps your other sibling..."

Silver looked down. He ground one foot against the snow. "My prenatal scrying ruled out Triunism."

"A mere biune." The Ashemi turned to Gleam. "You didn't tell me that."

Gleam looked at Silver with a subdued grin. "I thought it better from Silver's mouth."

Animosity between these two Zahrirans, then. Likely Gleam's prior investigation had proven troublesome for both. The Ashemi decided to move matters along.

"Pearl visited you," he said. "The night he imprisoned himself."

"I've been through this too many times," Silver said.

"No, you have not," the Ashemi said.

"I've made my recollection of it available," Silver said.

"You've made a *replinisense* available," the Ashemi said. "In it, you and Pearl embrace, he says he must go and cannot explain why. A lie. Fabricated by your son and placed in your mind to shield what you truly recall of that night. The Culakwun Envoy had Pearl tracked here. We know there was a feral."

Silver didn't look shocked. Likely he'd always known this moment would come.

"I'm still proud of my son," he said, gazing at the Ashemi with defiance. "Few could manipulate Geode technology so well, could fool worlds. Brilliant. All my babies, brilliant. But him..."

"Continue," the Ashemi said.

Silver pulled his coat tighter around himself. "We hadn't spoken for some time. He had chosen a lover neither I nor Coral approved of. A Culakwun, a monomind. One of the Envoy's staff. Pearl says, 'Mother, a stranger is coming, arriving in a public teardrop. But first you must accept a replinisense I've constructed, to obscure your true memory of this from outsiders'.

"Well, I'm suspicious. But his father laughed. He always indulged Pearl's brilliance. 'What's it matter?' Coral says. 'We'll still have the true memory, we'll still know.' He thought Pearl was showing off. I thought his lover had put him up to something, his Culakwun scum."

"But you were wrong," Gleam said.

"Arguably," Silver said, knife-glancing the Triune. "So he takes out his device and patches our memory over. Well, readies our minds for a *future* memory. It's then I scream. Coral gasps. In the replinisense our son is hugging us, telling us he is going away. He does not know when he'll return. 'Where's Swirl?' I demand. 'Where's Sparkle?' Sparkle, you understand, being my little spoilt one. 'Building', Pearl says. 'Hidden in our mind-villa, building something I've asked them to.' He looks scared then and I know he's lying. But I say nothing."

"A mother's love," Gleam muttered.

"It was *their* skull," Silver shot back. It occurred to the Ashemi that Silver was directing at Gleam all the venom which reverence forbade him drenching the Ashemi with. "My children were *adults*, adepts of the House." He let out another misted sigh. "Then a teardrop lands by the cottage, as yours did just now. Imagine our surprise: a feral man."

"What did he look like?" the Ashemi asked.

"A caricature," Silver said.

"How do you mean?"

"Of their aristocracy. Of their..." Silver waved a hand, searching for words. "*Executives. Bizness* suit. Big smile. Insincere." His mouth trembled with disdain. "Mongrel genes. I let Coral take ascendancy; he was the diplomatic one. The feral said he represented some company—one of their '*money*' generating guilds—and he offered a hand to shake." Silver closed his eyes. "In retrospect I'm doubly glad Coral didn't take it. He could've so easily..."

"Why 'doubly'?" the Ashemi asked.

"He was no feral." Silver shivered. "Not slightly. Well... Pearl said he had some information. Stolen from the Envoy by Pearl's lover. Or someone his lover knew. I..."

"What was this information?" The Ashemi said. The corquills had gotten louder.

"Useful to these ferals, perhaps. A lockwyrm homing signature, the coordinates... I don't know... one of their crude space ships."

"Strange," the Ashemi said through inanimate lips, "this talk of lockwyrms and the Geode used at the behest of ferals. Blasphemous, almost. Why didn't your son and this individual ask you to leave the room? Why witnesses?"

Silver shrugged. "I don't know. The feral was garrulous about it. Said it would give his company, guild—*whatever*—some advantage. 'Take out the opposition,' he said. Back then I assumed his belief in the replinisense Pearl had given me and Coral was total in its ignorance. Now, however, given what occurred..." He bit his lip, stroked his head. "It must have desired witnesses."

"It?" the Ashemi said.

"Pearl handed over the information and..." His breathing quickened. "It manifested. The skin fell away."

"What?"

Silver stooped, shivering more than the frost required.

"A Hoidrac. Manifest. Took my son, into the opal. Must have. My babies..." He winced.

"A Delighted One?" the Ashemi demanded. 'Posing as a feral?' He felt an incredible anger. The heresy. The very thought.

"Broke Coral," Silver said. "Broke *me*."

"You lie," the Ashemi said. "You're mad."

"No face." Silver dropped to his knees in the slush. "Teeth..."

The corquills bickered louder, faster. Hell's choir.

"Which one?" the Ashemi said. "Which Hoidrac? Mohatoi Embossed? Him?"

Silver shook his head.

Not Culakwun's patrons, then. An impious thought came to him, one worth asking.

"Pheoni the Appropriate? Her?"

Again, Silver's head shook. He rocked back and forth.

"Who?" The Ashemi had to shout over those damned creatures now.

"*Jhatain-Oukael*," Silver chanted. A wince, a high moan. "*Jhatain ia*."

"What?"

Silver took three deep breaths, braced himself and stared at the Ashemi.

"The Dissenter! The Dissenter itself!"

The Ashemi swung the back of his fist and struck the man's face. Silver collapsed on the frozen lawn. The corquills took to the air in fright.

The Ashemi studied his own fist. Blood upon gilt knuckles.

"He's alive," he heard Gleam say.

He looked down to see Gleam kneeling over Silver. He'd lifted the man's head and the Ashemi could see both wounds. The old bruise left by Silver's partner, the fresh red one left by himself.

"Symmetry," the Ashemi said. It was all he could think to say.

SWIRL RAN BACK INTO the cockpit. The walls were still on VR setting: an immense asteroid ahead, a lumpen fist of glacial silver. Gigantic white plumes rolled from the thing: ice, steaming away from the ancient rock's surface. Behind the tailed asteroid lay the blue giant's equatorial disc. *Princess* and the rock were level with the disc's edge, two mites before its ethereal vastness.

"You've hidden your gun," Eucharist told Swirl.

"Silence, idiot," she told him. Swirl had indeed hidden the pistol; a hopeless act, most likely, but still. Then she'd taken the supply of leaf and hid that too, careful to take a few leaves and hide them upon her person. Then, at Sparkle's panicked behest, she'd hid a few *in* her person and now dearly hoped the plastic bag wouldn't break. Addiction, as the ferals would term it, had its own logic.

"So we're crashing into this thing?" Hargie asked Eucharist. "That their plan? 'Accident' like with the orbital rig?"

"All will be clear soon enough," Eucharist said.

A diamond of red light appeared on the rock. It grew, widening until Swirl could see a scarlet-lit cavern within. A sleek shadow—presumably one of *Princess'* escorts—entered it, its sharp angles blurring in the red gloom.

"Memoryform rock," Eucharist said. "Given these people's prosperous strategy of concealment over the centuries, it's arguably their greatest invention. One cannot siege a fortress that is not there."

"Or escape a prison," Swirl said, frowning at that wretched bastard.

4. System L47:23:15

Twelve

"HERE," EUCHARIST TOLD Hargie, pointing a finger at some bump in the cavern's black, plastic-looking wall.

Hargie said nothing. He positioned *Princess'* right flank tight against the wall, almost bumping into it. He wondered whether the bubbleship would have bounced straight off whatever that substance out there was. Sure as damn wasn't the inside of any normal rock. There were Spindly ships docked against the cavern's opposite wall. Their diamond-shaped hulls were as sleek as ever, but now they had weird black tumours growing out of their midships. He didn't pay it any mind. He was trying not to pay much of anything any mind.

Princess hovered by the wall. Hargie felt a tingle down his right side: something touching *Princess'* hull. Instinctively he drifted to port a little, but whatever it was kept touching.

The wall was reaching out. He could see it on a screen he'd brought up on his neuralware: the bump on the wall beside *Princess* was growing, stretching, running like melted wax over the bubbleship's hull.

Hargie shuddered. His neural represented this groping tendril's presence as a cold honey consuming Hargie's right side. Damn. Everything about these Spindly rock-fuckers was wrong. Creep-edy-dah-dah wrong.

"What's going on?" he heard Sparkle say. She must have been staring at the image on the cockpit walls, the black tar rolling across the VR image of their surroundings, covering *Princess Floofy*'s equator.

"It's docking with us," Sung Eucharist said.

"We're docking with *it*," Hargie said, suddenly more pissed off than he already was. "Not 'docking with us', shithead. You know, I truly fucking hope it was worth it, Sung. What they paying you in, exactly? Orphans?"

"Stay calm and we'll all make it out of this," Eucharist said, smiling at Hargie like an indulgent uncle. "I imagine."

"Right now your word's worth a quarter rectum. Half, tops."

"Come now," Eucharist said. "Chicanery is your people's very lifeblood. It's not my treachery but my imagination that riles you."

"Riles?" Hargie said. "Let me—"

"Open the hatch," Eucharist said.

"F—"

"Open the hatch before they crush this ship."

Hargie did so, fear rising in him, the insect in the web.

They waited in silence.

Slop, *slop*, came a sound from down the corridor, *slop*, *slop*.

"I'll wager you wish you'd kept your pistol," Eucharist said to Sparkle. He stood up and straightened his long coat.

They came through the door. Hargie thought them serpents at first, black and faceless. But as they slithered and rolled through the doorway, he could see they met in a central body, a nightmare nexus between squid and spider and melting plastic.

The same stuff as the walls outside, Hargie realised, as the Spindlies' suits. The horror's tentacles stuck and peeled themselves off the floor and ceiling, a locomotion that seemed at once needless and elegant. Two more of the things poured through the doorway.

"Get up," Eucharist said to Hargie. "And relax, the pair of you. They are here to escort us."

Hargie got up, to see Sparkle step back when the first horror budded gun barrels and a laser sight. The weapons hummed.

"No sudden movements," Eucharist said. "They are controlled by people."

"That meant to reassure us?" Hargie asked.

"Not slightly," Eucharist said.

Sparkle yelled. Her wrists and ankles were in the grip of the first horror's tentacles. It drew her toward its body's centre.

"Don't fight," Eucharist told her. "It's near-zero gravity outside. These machines will carry us."

"What?" Hargie demanded. "When were you gonna tell us this?"

The two remaining horrors made their way toward the two men, selecting one each. Hargie gulped, stared at the mass of fluid plastic coming for him. Its tentacles didn't feel slimy when they wrapped around his wrists, but dry and warm, like inflated party balloons. They circled his legs, his shoulders, his ribcage.

He felt himself lift off the ground. The horrors carried them out of the cockpit and along the corridor. It was comfortable enough, but something in their undulating motion made Hargie feel sick.

Before he knew it, they were out of the hatchway and out of *Princess*, floating down a tunnel of the same black shiny material, an artery with walls like crude oil.

No gravity. The horrors had ceased using their tentacles, were speeding down the dim-lit pipe under jet propulsion.

Wrong, creepy-wrong. He suddenly wished he were back on Import, getting thrown to mutant mutts by small-town shitkickers. A fucking golden age.

THE TENTACLED MACHINES released them in a small disc-shaped room of bright lights, or at least a room brighter than the gloom they had travelled through. Swirl blinked. She was aware of standing on nothing, of floating. She could see a silhouette. Maybe two.

"Welcome, Sung," a female voice said. "Welcome, friends."

:Well, this isn't good,: Sparkle commented to Swirl.

Swirl's eyes adjusted to the glare. Silver walls. A woman floated at the centre of the room, unmistakably a Spindly despite not wearing one of their uniforms. She wore a grey trouser suit and her black hair up in a roll at the the back of her head. Her face was delicate, her eyes thin, burning with a violet intensity. Her lips were sensuous and full. Somewhere behind her a man, his dark beard a fierce triangle, rested against a wall. Both of them had bare feet.

"Utile-Theoretical Kend," Eucharist said, swimming through the air toward the woman and grasping her arm affectionately. They began to spin gently around one another. "It has been far too long. I trust the project runs well and safely?"

"As can be expected," the woman, Kend, said. "The day we foresee approaches." She looked over at Swirl and Hargie. "Thanks to your efforts in bringing our guests here."

"The word's 'hostages,'" Swirl told her. "You need to practice your Anglurati."

Kend's face lit up to hear Swirl talk, as if Swirl were some antique clock Kend had finally managed to fix. "Swirl Savard," she said. "A pleasure to meet you. You've come a long distance since the orbital rig."

:Shit,.: Sparkle sent.

"Her name's Sparkle," Hargie said, balancing himself with a wave of his palms.

"No, I don't think so," Kend told him. "She's been operating under the name Swirl these last two years. Haven't you, Swirl?"

"A cover," Swirl said, though she was sorely tempted to claim her sister's was the cover name. She looked at Hargie. "Sparkle is my actual name."

Hargie frowned, his eyes darting left and right. "Come to think of it," he said, "both sound kinda ridiculous."

"They don't have the dignity of *Princess Floofy*, admittedly," Swirl said.

"I imagine..." Kend said, her expression vaguely nonplussed, "...you are wondering why you are here."

"Knife prods, mostly," Hargie said, nodding at Eucharist.

"Long journeys make him nettlesome," Eucharist told Kend. He swam toward the wall; he seemed unnervingly accustomed to the medium they floated in. Eucharist positioned his rear against the wall next to the silent man. It was only then Swirl noticed the black circles along the wall. They were of the same substance as the machines and the Spindlies' suits. She watched one of them adjust around Eucharist's bulk, holding him to the wall.

"I should first disabuse you of your fears," Kend told Swirl and Hargie. "Though we are of the Konsensus, we are not those in pursuit of you.

"We are your friends," Kend continued, "though you are ignorant of this fact. To that end, there's really no reason for you to hide the leaf drug inside your vagina, Ms Savard." She turned to Hargie. "Nor you the quantumphetamines within your anal passage."

"Obliged," Hargie said.

Kend looked to Swirl again. "Indeed, we desire you to put it to good use."

:Please tell me she means the leaf,: Sparkle sent.

"How so?" Swirl asked.

"But I forget my manners," Kend said. "Would you two like a seat?"

"Fine here," Hargie said.

Swirl decided she'd risk one of the black wall discs. She'd been wrapped in the stuff only minutes before, so why fear it now? She leant forward in order to swim toward the wall, but succeeded only in cartwheeling upside-down.

"I got this," Hargie said.

Swirl felt hands slide underneath her arms, righting her into a horizontal position. Hargie kicked his legs off his tentacled machine and they floated slowly forward. He obviously had experience in zero-g. They'd never trained Swirl for it back at the House. If she ever got home, she told herself, she'd suggest the idea with extreme prejudice.

"I'll help," Kend said. She and Hargie dragged Swirl to the wall and secured her into one of the circles. A strange sensation, but at least she was static.

"Phew," Hargie said. "That'd be a lot easier without all that jumpjunk in my ass." He looked at Kend. "Please continue."

"Of course," Kend said, swimming backward through the air. It was only then Swirl noticed a random scattering of bumps on the floor. They rose up to meet her, were sensitive to her feet's proximity. Kend used them to kick against or curl her nimble toes around, an action balanced by the sure dexterity of her upper body. Natural to this creature of zero-g.

"You are presently guests of local kollective Silvercloud," Kend said, coming to a stop at the centre of the room. "Believe me when I say that is the only kollective you would wish to be guests of."

"Sorry," Hargie said. "Not feeling it. All I seen of your people is murder and fugly fashion choices."

"We have our charms," Kend said.

"You can be killed," Swirl said. "That's endearing."

"The citizens of Silvercloud are not the same Konsensites who are chasing you." Kend shrugged. "Not all of the time, at any rate."

"I don't understand," Swirl said.

"We are rebels," Kend said. "I think that's your word. You see, a kollective is more than a collection of individuals. In each of us lies an ancient bio-program, bestowed upon our ancestors by their masters from humanity's origin world. It aided our survival in the local void back then, and it is the secret of our unseen interstellar success now. We are a shared mind lightyears wide.

Each of our citizens has flung down the walls of their skull for a greater good. It has been that way for millennia."

"I don't get it," Hargie said. "Everywhere I go, the galaxy's full of people who can watch each other shit. What's the deal?"

"That's not the attraction," Kend said, unperturbed. "We generally choose not to watch someone else's bodily movements. Isn't custom enough? And if a citizen should wish to experience that or any other act through my senses, who am I to hinder their curiosity? No, that would be impossible in any typical kollective. And a waste of Silvercloud's newly acquired gift."

"And what is that?" Swirl asked.

"A relative solitude of mind."

"Their great crime," Eucharist said.

"Indeed," Kend said, and she smiled at Eucharist like he was the only sane person in the room. She turned to Swirl and Hargie again. "The people who chase you belong to the Instrum. The Instrum began as Konsensus citizens elected to deal with the outside. The 'outside' being you people: the Worlders. The Instrum masterminded the great hiding. But, over centuries, they have become controlling, a superego to the id of the Kollective-at-Large. They fear difference. And that is a problem for both our peoples."

"I don't understand," Swirl said. "If you share all your thoughts, how is it you can keep secrets from this Instrum?"

"Silvercloud has always been at a remove. This rock's orbit passes through the stellar disc's radiation every nine standard days. Nine days in, nine out. During this transit, Silvercloud's mental kollective is blocked from the Kollective-at-Large, becoming its own localised kollective. These past three hundred years it hasn't been a problem, aside from giving 'Clouders a reputation for eccentricity. We intend to keep it that way."

"And we're in this... lock-off period now?" Swirl asked.

"We're almost out of it. That's why—during the last 'lock-off"—we asked Sung Eucharist to act quickly after he reported your arrival at his installation."

"A pleasure to help," Eucharist said, his countenance still.

"So in a couple o' hours," Hargie said to Kend, "we all get busted by that crazy Emissary bitch and her cronies? When your neighbourhood klicks back into the, the... mainframe... the game's up? The Instrum'll know." He squinted. "You're going to explain, right?"

Kend breathed out. "This would be so much easier if we could share thoughts."

"Fuckin' creepier, too."

"Some twenty years past, Silvercloud suffered a major accident." Kend blinked, and a diaphanous hologram emerged beside her, a see-through diagram of Silvercloud. All the infrastructure—tunnels, chambers, ports—lay within what might be termed the asteroid's northern hemisphere. "An attempt was made to excavate a tunnel in the southern zone and install an observation suite. There was an unforeseen fracture—my people understand better than anyone how space hates life—and three hundred of us died. Only one citizen survived. Illik. I believe you met him."

Swirl nodded. She wasn't sure how much Kend knew of Illik's explosive death.

"He survived by blocking off the observation suite's sensor barrel." Kend pointed at a thin tube highlighted in white. It ran right through Silvercloud's southern hemisphere, alone in the solid rock. "The observation suite blocks even the Kollective program, so as to protect itself from impurities. For the first time in his life, Illik's mind was alone. There was just him and what the suite allowed him to see around our sun. Like any of us, he found such an experience... excruciating, yet unique. He knew, with work, some new truth might be extracted from the pain. He also knew, as soon as he would be rescued, the phenomenon would be lost, diluted among the Kollective. Rationalised and forgotten."

She stopped speaking, tilting her head to one side. Swirl was sure Kend was in mental conversation with the silent man sat beside Eucharist.

Kend nodded to no one and continued:

"Illik knew it would be days before help might arrive, if at all. He used the suite's laboratory to grow a memory-spine: the Kollective's equivalent of a server. Illik programmed it so that, upon his reconnection with Silvercloud's kollective and, more importantly, the great Kollective-at-Large, the spine would convince everyone that Illik had merely sat and waited for help, albeit temporarily insane from his solitude. False, overriding memories. Even Illik would be convinced.

"The memory spine grew, down in the now blocked-off suite, as Illik intended. Eventually it compromised the entire kollective of Silvercloud: during the disc transit, when Silvercloud was blocked from the Kollective-at-Large, all citizens were free to think how they like, to share or not share their thoughts as they pleased. They just didn't realise they could. When a transit period ended and Silvercloud joined back with the greater Kollective, everyone's recollection of the transit period would be replaced by synthetic memories. For the most part, that didn't really matter: no one but Illik knew they had the freedom, as I said. But it gave Illik the chance to persuade likely individuals to his cause." She smiled. "I was among the first."

"How many in your little club now?" Hargie asked.

She looked at him. "All of us. It took a lot less time than any of us imagined, though a few had to be silenced, were lost to 'accidents'. Our rebellion is constrained by time, my friends. Currently, I conspire. In forty minutes, I shall be a good little citizen of the Konsensus: I will not remember your arrival, or even who Eucharist is. I will not know you are being kept here. Our lives are such that we must collude against ourselves."

"That's insane," Hargie said.

"Perhaps," she said. "But it is pleasant to have the opportunity."

:Logically,: Sparkle sent to Swirl, *:that must mean we are in this observation suite of hers. If we were anywhere else, we'd be noted as soon as the locals defaulted back to dickhead setting.:*

"This is the observation suite," Swirl said to Kend.

"How perceptive," Kend said.

"Many layers, our Sparkle," Eucharist said. Something about it put Swirl on edge.

Kend waved at the hologram and the white line of the observation suite grew, branching into a complex of tunnels and chambers. A close-up. "We've had the time to extend our secret retreat. Welcome to your new home for the next nine days. Longer, should you wish it."

:Wait a moment,: Sparkle sent. *:Why did they build the observation suite in the first place? What did they want to observe?:*

:Good point,: Swirl sent back. "So why build the suite?" she asked Kend.

"Good point." Kend smiled. "The Scalpels."

The hologram of Silvercloud vanished. In its place emerged something else entirely.

A crude rendition of that most beautiful of objects. It floated in space above the Wolf-Rayet star's equatorial disc. For some reason, the object's surfaces were rendered in a flat grey. But even without the colour and the dazzle, the mind-rending blend of Geode energy and material matter, the thing was beautiful. Reduced to geometry, to angle and curve, one sensed some universal truth expressed in its form, exposed like a bare shoulder from a dress.

Beauty beyond awe, and, as the sisters had known since childhood, beauty was but one of its weapons.

"The Scalpels," Kend said, gesturing at the hologram. "Their kind come here every nine days, presumably to bathe in the energies of the Wolf-Rayet star. Illik may have realised his own individuality trapped alone in the observation suite, but it was gazing at these ancient beasts, at their unique visual aspect, that made him want to hold on to that individuality. To gift it to others."

Swirl smiled. "You don't say."

She caught Hargie in the corner of her vision. He mouthed some word. 'Foozle,' perhaps.

"Swirl," Kend said.

:Sparkle,: Sparkle sent.

"Sparkle," corrected Swirl.

"Sparkle," Kend said, "you can end your dissimulation."

"I'm not." Swirl hid a shiver. "Really I'm not."

"We know you Harmonics are aware of the Scalpels, though presumably you give them another name."

Swirl relaxed. "Kharmund," she said.

Kend grinned. "Illik was right. They are a common sight, yes, in the Harmonies? Comparatively, I mean?"

Swirl nodded.

"Good," Kend said. "And your drug, the leaf... you can communicate with them using it? Your scientists have mastered such?"

Swirl laughed. "Something like that."

Kend looked over to the silent man and smiled. She looked back at Swirl.

"That's all we wish of you. I have personally designed machinery, a Kollective-based transmitter that requires a nervous system acquainted with leaf to make contact. At least we think. We hope." She wrinkled her nose in a manner that seemed childlike to Swirl. "None of it is invasive, I assure you."

"What then?" Swirl asked.

:Swirl,: Sparkle sent, *:tell them nothing. We know nothing.:*

"And then, well, we'll know," Kend said. "We have to know. It's not something we can explain. The Scalpels' physical aspect is a question. We risk everything for the answer, whatever it may transpire to be."

"And then?" Swirl said.

"And then the answer itself determines our next move." For the first time Kend looked uncomfortable. "At worst, we wipe our minds of our experiment, destroy this hidden installation. Return to our regular existences."

"Rather pointless, isn't it?" Swirl said.

Kend shook her head. "What Illik began, we must all finish. We must. And if all memory of a truth is lost, well, better it existed than not."

:Yep,: Sparkle sent, *:That's the awe-slap, all right. And far from the first time. Looks like the, er, 'Scalpels' are as effective as ever.:*

:Of course,: Swirl sent back.

"They are more than beasts," Swirl told the room. She met Kend's eyes. "Come here. Bring your hologram."

Kend did so, swimming through the air like some fish eager for a hook.

:Swirl, don't tell her shit,: Sparkle sent. *:Better still, make up some shit.:*

:No, sister. We were destined to come here.:

:Swirl…:

The hologram was within arm's reach. Swirl brushed her hand through it, as if its pixels might confer on her the grace they tried to replicate.

"You people see star-beasts," she told Kend, "and in that, at least, you are correct. The Kharmund are beasts from another universe: the Geode. They emerge from its very depths." She pointed at the Kharmund's surfaces. "This, its exterior, is an armour, created by our rulers the Hoidrac. It permits the Kharmund to exist here in the tangible universe. But what you comprehend is not the whole of it. They do not come here alone."

"How do you mean?" Kend said.

"The Hoidrac bind them. They blend into them. Make them their steeds."

"The Hoidrac are a myth," Kend said. "Illik said so."

"Poor creature," Swirl said. No condescension. Swirl's pity was felt. "The Hoidrac are aliens become gods. They perspire myth in their mere being, yes, but they are real. So very real. The Kharmund are the ultimate expression of Hoidrac power: exquisite in appearance, capable of hell."

"They are craft? Combat craft?" Kend said.

"A crude but fair analogy. The final effect is the same. The ability to bring willpower and destruction wherever desired."

Kend gazed at the holograph as if had only just materialised. Swirl knew that look: a rational mind in rapture. Long had Kharmund conquered worlds this way.

"Did you think you were the only ones who'd thought to hide entire fleets?" Swirl said to Kend. "The Hoidrac hide in plain sight. They allow locals to weave their own explanations, their own myths, for the wonders they see."

"Hoidrac, Konsensus," Eucharist said. "Two prowling fleets unseen, practically atop one another. Is anything possible save war?"

"You knew the truth of the Scalpels?" Kend asked him.

Eucharist smiled. "I merely extrapolate."

Swirl continued. She wouldn't let Eucharist seize Kend's open-mindedness.

"You don't have to let your dream of privacy die, Doctor Kend. The Hoidrac can protect you. Embrace them, and they will set your people free. They always do." Swirl smiled, a tender smile. "I want to help you do that, Kend."

There, in Kend's eyes: a hope that had never dared blossom, that didn't even know it could. Kend broke the gaze and, blinking, looked at the silent man. She nodded.

"We have to leave now," she told the room. "You will remain here for the next nine days. There will be gravity comparable to your usual medium. Mister Eucharist will show you around."

Kend turned and swam out of the room, bare toes pushing off the floor's rising bumps. The silent man followed her, only once looking back at Swirl.

The room fell silent.

Swirl closed her eyes. Purpose, holy purpose. The Hoidrac had a plan for her. For everyone.

THEORETICAL KEND TOOK her position: a seat-pit two along from social core 43's hatchway. Yan squeezed himself into the seat-pit next to her along the room's hemisphere. The transition back to the Kollective-at-Large would find them alone in here, talking about a science expedition to close-view the Scalpel when it arrived.

Scalpel! Ha! *Kharmund*. She knew their name now, their nature. But not for long. And not for the next nine days.

She couldn't concentrate on these matters with Yan beside her. Currently they were sharing a two-way kollective all their own, as the ancient birth-Worlders must have done millennia ago, as it had been meant to be used. Yan's fears and mistrusts were bleeding into her. They could feel Silvercloud's kollective in the distance, its benevolent warmth. Forever there, yet never intruding.

"Don't trust her?" Kend asked him, expressing the notion of Swirl—no, Sparkle Savard.

"Like a hull-rupture," Yan said.

"Unused to Worlders," she replied. "Like living corpses. Will adapt." She issued a professional sympathy at him.

He demurred from it. "She'd make traitors. Would try."

"Traitors already," Kend said.

"Only to Instrum." And he met her eyes, stared with a passion matched by the sentiment he issued. "Not to Konsensus, not true-values." He emoted a conceptual then: a cold and slivering other, an alien force staining passageway and bulwark. "The Harmonies," he explained.

"Foreign, yes," Kend said. "But each Harmony-world: own philosophy. Independent. Protected by Hoidrac: Silvercloud thrive. We could be us. No fear. Hope-example to all kollectives."

"We had plan," Yan said. "Adhere."

"No; different now. New contexts. This mind-independence alters." Yes: it altered everything.

"Plan: contact Scalpel, learn," Yan said. "Then terminate Worlders, hide new knowledge to-be-found, wipe ourselves." He breathed out long. "Plan."

"No, no," she said with such force a globe of saliva sailed from her lips. "Contact Scalpel, make alliance. Protected, we grow. Grow new Konsensus." She emoted a polite immovability. "New plan."

Yan emoted frustration. No: anger, held back, fighting against the twin drag of his emotional and physical desires for her, long held and occasionally requited.

"This..." he said. "This ends with contact. No more. Each moment risk. If Instrum visit? Physical-visit Silvercloud?"

"Silvercloud remote," Kend said, soothe-emoting at Yan. "Physical visit?" She answered herself, issuing amused derision.

"This wrong," Yan said, calming yet implacable. "This wrong, Kend."

"Truest-friend, Yan," Kend said, and she could feel he felt her love. "We Silvercloud. All Silvercloud debate. Decide."

Yan went to speak, but both their bodies were overridden by the memory-spine in the secret installation. Kend watched her own limbs and Yan's drift into new and exact poses, so that their bodies would not betray the lies—indeed, a vast alibi of unimaginable detail—to the rest of the Konsensus, or at least those parts of it that might care to look. Silvercloud had passed through the blue giant's disc, and reconnection with the Kollective-at-Large loomed near. They would be a different Kend and Yan seconds from now. A different Silvercloud.

Kend felt Yan issue another conceptual at her. It was composed predominately of respect, but also a—

Kend felt satisfied with the expedition's roster. Some old, some new.

"Good work," she told Yan. "Productive."

Yan issued assent.

"Reconnection to Konsensus complete," he noted. "New downloads."

"Oh," Kend said, shimmering a pleased delight. "Visitors arriving, five days: Melid."

"Melid." Yan smiled, exuded nostalgia. Such a pleasing curiosity, Melid.

"In Instrum-craft."

They shared prides: friend-pride, home-kollective-pride.

Melid. An Instrum Emissary now. Yes. A fine thing to meet Melid again.

Thirteen

"GRAVITY'S LIGHTER," Sparkle heard Hargie say. He stood against the plated wall of the... well, Sparkle had started to think of it as the common room.

She looked up. Yes; the smoke from his cigarette billowed wider.

"To avoid detection," Eucharist said from across the scarlet metal table. He never looked up from his solitary board game. "Silvercloud is reconnected now, returned to the happy herd, all looked over by that benign shepherd the Instrum. This is as much gravity as our hosts dare." He stroked his long beard. "But enough to keep each pawn in its place." He looked set to move a piece, but decided against it.

The common room was a hollow disc, wide and shallow, the grey plating of the table repeated every-bloody-where. Hexagonal exits led to bathrooms and sleeping cabins Sparkle hadn't had the resolve to inspect yet.

"So what part of your fiendish plan," Sparkle said to Eucharist, "prevents me and chimney boy here from beating your brains out against the walls of our shared prison?" Her shoulders ached. They had since the anger had subsided and the self-recrimination had kicked in. And the air in here: too stark. Too sterile. At least Swirl was back in the villa. Sparkle couldn't handle her current piety bout.

"I'm your way out of here," Eucharist said, more interested in his damn game.

"You keep saying that," Sparkle said. "But you're trapped as much as us."

"An honoured guest, I'll thank you," Eucharist said. "My ship comes in nine days' time. To leave now would draw the senses of the Konsensus and ultimately the Instrum." He glanced at Sparkle briefly. "What kind of guest would I be then?"

She'd give anything to break this man's calm. No fists, no shouting. A whisper and a smile. She couldn't think of anything.

"Eucharist," Hargie said. "How'd you fall in with the Spindlies? Eyes meet over a bleeding corpse?"

"A week ago you were calling me *sir*," Eucharist said. "You came begging."

"Then ain't now."

"Silvercloud did their research," Eucharist said. "I was local, or local enough, and I'd already had dealings with the Konsensus."

"Somehow that doesn't surprise me," Sparkle said, rubbing her shoulder.

"I'm sympathetic to Silvercloud's cognitive quest," Eucharist said. "And they pay well for my sympathies." He gestured around at the walls. "I provided the gravity spikes here. You should thank me."

"You're a tool to these people, Eucharist," Sparkle said. "They can kill you as much as us when all this is done."

"I think not," he said. "You see, my girl, they have asked me to complete their..." One hand gestured in that irritating way it did whenever he searched for a word. "...Indiscretion. Whatever they discover from contacting those alien craft, they will pass the data to me and then wipe their minds of the entire matter. Then it will be my duty to ensure this data—deracinated of anything incriminating—falls accidentally within Konsensus awareness." He smiled. "I am content to be a tool. To be played. Somehow, I think you do not feel the same."

She breathed out, kept the frustration in check.

"Hargie," she said. "Get over here."

"Why?" he asked.

"Massage my shoulders."

"What?"

"Please." She looked at him and raised the best smile she could.

He put the cigarette out on the metal sideboard and walked over. His hands felt good through her shift, his breath against her scalp was a small sanity. She dipped her head forward and her dreadlocks swung out gently in the lighter gravity. She closed her eyes.

"You bested me, Eucharist," she said. "I thought I was the player, thought I'd hooked you to my will." Her lips pulled tight against her teeth. She relaxed them. "You played me."

"You played better than most," she heard Eucharist say. "I was impressed. Your honesty impresses further. Too many are blinded by pride."

She gazed at him, her head still bowed. "Make no mistake, 'sir'. I tell you this so that you know I won't be played again."

"The game continues," Eucharist said. "It always has."

He seemed to think for a moment; then he pointed at his game board and looked at Sparkle.

Sparkle shook her head. "Oh please, no."

"You don't play?" Eucharist said.

"Have our current conversation and play chess?" she said. "I'd be happier if the cliches stay on your side of the table."

She closed her eyes again. She couldn't face chess with she herself the piece of too many players. First Eucharist and now Swirl, currently—and thankfully—practising zero-gravity moves in the villa. Swirl had set their course: a destiny, some half-seen divine crusade to patronise their captors. To save them. Sparkle had been too stunned to counter her, hadn't really taken it in. Established now. Sparkle would have to pay the notion lip service; anything else might give away their truth or seem insanity.

"By way of conversation," Eucharist said, "what are we to call you?"

She didn't open her eyes. "Anything as long as you bow."

"Kend called you Swirl before," Eucharist said.

"I told you: a cover name."

"And 'Sparkle'?" Eucharist asked.

Hargie stopped massaging her shoulders. His hands remained there, tight.

"You're looking at her," Sparkle replied to Eucharist. The palms kept still on her shoulder blades. "What, Hargie? What?"

A pause. "I'm dumb," Hargie said. "It's a dumb question."

"What?"

"Why 'Sparkle'?" he asked. "That's an Anglurati word. Your people don't speak that."

She opened her eyes and looked straight up. She could only see the tip of his hat.

"Issaressi," Sparkle said. 'In Tu'la'lec, I'm Issaressi.'

"You never told me your name."

"I did: Sparkle," she said. "What's the issue here?"

"Bubbleman, bubbleman," Eucharist said. Sparkle looked down to see Eucharist waving a placating hand at Hargie. "You misunderstand. For the people of the Harmonies, particularly Zahrir, the meaning is the name. Not mere syllables."

"You know my world," Sparkle said. She could feel her shoulders tense once more. Fear in her bones. Secret world, Zahrir.

"I visited once," Eucharist said. "The Seat of the Tri-Seneschal. The Husks mountain range. And, albeit briefly..." He smiled here, met her eyes. "...The Trinity Houses."

She leaped up and brushed Hargie's hands away. "Headache," she said. "I'm..."

She pushed past the chair she'd sat on and walked away.

He knew. Eucharist knew. Something Swirl had given away, surely. She made it to a hatchway and leaned against the wall.

"You okay?" Hargie's voice, far off behind her. Like a judgement, all these monominds judging her.

"Yes," she said. She would have to tell Swirl. Tell...

Played again. Eucharist knew, and knew Hargie didn't know. That was it; that would be Eucharist's leverage. And she could tell Hargie, yes, and Hargie wouldn't believe her, would think her crazier than he already did. And the telling was worth execution back home.

"The woman needs rest," Eucharist said.

Her body tensed rigid. She spun around and looked at the two men. Oh, she could spit fire at Eucharist. She really could. Spit witty acid and leave him speechless.

But nothing came, nothing that sounded good in her mind. She gazed at Hargie. He was still standing by the chair, his face placid. She held out her arm toward him. *Come*, she mouthed. She forced her rage into a pose of fragility, made her eyes and lips soft, wanting.

Hargie took on that frozen stance Sparkle had always found funny in men, as lust saturated their dignity.

"Issaressi," he said. Then he picked up his cigarette pack off the table and walked toward her.

This, at least, was a victory over Sung Eucharist.

An easy one.

THE TRICK, SWIRL FOUND, was to think ahead to the next surface, and to push off from there and think of the next. Thankfully the glasshouse behind the villa was long and thin and its glass unbreakable, or unbreakable enough for her current purposes.

She couldn't recall how long she had been practising. Trapped in the secret installation, her hosts oblivious to her existence these next few days, she could see little point in anything else. There would come a time when her practice would pay off. A truth of her life.

She pushed herself off the glass ceiling and the bushes drifted toward her. She had to stop thinking of ceilings and floors, of up and down. The Konsensites did not think that. The soles of her shoes connected with the soil and she tensed, pushed against it and flew up. No, outward.

This was it, where her life had been leading. Her exile to Feral space had been a lie: she'd been a sleeper, an agent incognizant of her placement. Perhaps, she wondered, her brother Pearl's crime was a cover too. Not conscious, of course. The Hoidrac had played to his inconsistencies and vanities. Down in the Geode's very depths, they saw the things humans were blind to, planned centuries ahead.

Help Kend and her rebels contact the Kharmund. The Hoidrac, most likely Pheoni, would free them, take Swirl and Sparkle home and—dare she think it?—compel the siblings together again.

She connected with the ceiling, felt a greater force against her palms and knees than she'd expected. She ignored it, gripped hard to the transom with one hand and aimed a figurative pistol at the gardens below. Above.

Sparkle might be a problem. Often was. She had doubts, believed matters to be mere coincidence. Absurd. Sparkle's lack of faith was absurd. They had talked about it, in the few moments here when Swirl wasn't training and Sparkle wasn't rutting away fear. Sparkle feared the coming Kharmund. The great armoured star beasts didn't offer lifts, she had told Swirl. And the manner of Hoidrac that chose to ride Kharmund: unpredictable, volatile. Even the world-patrons, the foremost of all Hoidrac, seemed to keep Kharmund-riders at a distance.

Swirl held onto the glasshouse ceiling. She closed her eyes and felt the heat of an imaginary sun beat upon her skin. Sparkle was no problem. Swirl had been too kind to admit that to herself, but it was true. Firstly, Swirl had set the agenda here on Silvercloud, had voiced assent. For Sparkle to say otherwise when she had use of their shared body would risk discovery. Secondly... well, Swirl was the stronger, physically and mentally. A fact. That ugly scene in the music room had proven thus, much as Swirl was ashamed of beating her sister.

Sparkle would be needed. Swirl wasn't so arrogant as to think this mission was hers alone. She thought of that other moment on the jetty, when she had followed her alien goddess into the depths and Sparkle had remained, trapped by her own awe at the Hoidrac's sculptures. Such awe would be required, doubtless. Sparkle's intelligence and incredible memory would perform some unseen purpose in the next few days. She was their heart, warm and soft. Swirl was the armour that protected it.

Swirl laughed. She loved her sister.

MELID PUSHED HERSELF along the docking tunnel, handrail to handrail, Zo and Doum behind her, three Assault-Instrums behind them. She felt part of them nowadays. That sentiment reflected back at her whenever she thought about it in their presence. Melid needed that now, returning home.

They were dressed to look like members of the Instrum: muscleform suits, peaked caps of ancient humanity's martial officers. The Instrum only ever seemed to dress like that when visiting civilian kollectives.

The hatchway ahead stretched open, and Melid and her cadre poured through into the greeting-core, its scarlet lighting brighter than the tunnel. The air tasted familiar enough, a rich melange compared to that of a craft. The gravity, however—slightly heavier than a craft's, due to Silvercloud's rotation—struck Melid as alien. Time changed all things.

Kend and Yan were there, floating at the centre of the core. Their shared sentiment of nostalgic love hit Melid first. She could have cried.

Only then did Melid notice something like fear. Trepidation. The two Utiles sensed holes in her, barred zones within her memory and psyche. Melid was an Emissary now, full of things common Utiles were not permitted to know.

"Calm," Melid said. "Please calm. I am me."

"Forgive," Kend said.

"Forgive," Yan echoed.

For a moment, Melid assumed she had allayed their fears. In truth, they had poured toward Zo and Doum. To Kend and Yan, these two were little but strutting holes, almost Worlders in their unknowability. The lives of Zo and Doum were a patchwork of little but restricted facts.

"Happy to return," Melid said, trying to regain her hosts' attentions. And she was. She was happy. "Long journey."

"Indeed," Kend said. "Rest your people. Silvercloud welcomes."

"I know."

Fourteen

"WELL? HOW WAS THAT?" Hargie asked.

"Distracting," Sparkle said.

"What d'ya mean, 'distracting'?"

"We're beneath a hive of killers, Hargie. Distracting is the ideal."

He rolled off of her, sticky skin peeling. "Next time go straight to 'ideal.'"

He reached for a straight from out of his jacket pocket that lay next to the black rubbery bed-thing they lay on. He lit up: a bright point, lonely in the low red light of the room. Tasted good.

"Do you have to do that here?" Sparkle asked, wiping perspiration from her collarbone.

He offered her the smoke. She smiled and took it. She coughed, then handed it back.

"Would've been easier with a touch more gravitas," Hargie said.

"You mean 'gravity,'" Sparkle said. "Least I hope you do."

"Huh. Always thought they meant the same thing."

"You lay, you learn," she said.

"Learn too much with you." He tapped her damn-cute nose. "How do you think our hosts go about it? In Z-grav, I mean."

"The Konsensus? Probably shot sex after a show trial. Too inefficient." She looked at him. "No gravitas."

Sex was no longer a luxury. Not these last eight days. It was a shield, a fortress. The mixed scent of their bodies against the plastic-smelling air only reminded Hargie of that. Things had changed: only months before, anything but his hand had seemed a fable, a personal folktale. Now here he was, the most beautiful, brilliant woman naked beside him. Eight days of fuck-to-forget. Joy still there, but the edges shorn off. And his neuralware couldn't access shit. No respite from others. From himself.

"We'll get out," he told her.

"So Eucharist says."

He winced, played it off as the cigarette. He didn't like Eucharist and her, their whole hate-fascination-know-it-all ratshit. She moaned a lot louder here, more than before. Freaky Spindlies hadn't fitted a proper door on this cabin, and he was sure she was overacting so Eucharist might hear. He didn't want to even guess the reasons.

"We'll get out of here and get a real bed," he told her. "No more cabins. A world, like what you're used to. Harmonies."

She said nothing.

He threw the cigarette away and rolled toward her, the bed's rubber grumbling.

"Well?" he said. "What d'ya think?"

Her eyes met his, eventually. "You know, I can always feel when you come."

"What?"

"Seriously, I've never felt that with other men." She laughed, reached out and waggled Little Hargie. "You're a damn nail-gun, sunshine. Surprised my pelvis hasn't detonated."

"Shit," he said. "You do this. Every time I bring up us. Get all crude and shit."

She took her hand off of him. "What are you, a PG rating?"

"Sparks..."

"By the Eye, you can be histrionic sometimes," she said.

"Fuck history," Hargie said. "This is us."

She sighed and muttered something in her own language. She looked at the ceiling.

"Yes, Hargopal," she said. "This is us."

"Shit, just say it's physical," he said. "I can do physical. Hell, I'm King Physical."

"It's physical."

"...'Kay."

They said nothing.

"If," Sparkle said, "you want to simplify things beyond recognition."

Hargie threw his head back on what passed for a pillow. "Fuck."

"You know," Sparkle said, "back home we don't have conversations like this. We don't quantify." She sighed. "We don't chide women for being crude, either. Fucking feral."

"Yeah, real hot shit, the Harmonies," Hargie said. "Bet you can't wait to get back to lounging and laughing at the rest of us. Ferals. Primitives."

She got up fast. Hargie thought she'd just straight up and go, but she sat on the edge of the bed. She stared at the wall. Away from him.

"How can I?" he heard her say. "I'm not the same person who left there. You people wrecked me. I wrecked myself. Only thing I have in common with the Harmonies is the bloody leaf."

He studied her back, smooth and deep burgundy in the scarlet light. Her head bowed, and Hargie told himself he wouldn't weaken. Not yet. Not nearly.

"See, this is what I don't tune," he said. "Couple days past, you were spinning these people some destiny. Convinced them the Harmonies are gonna save them. Now this. What's your problem?"

"It's five foot tall and wears a stupid hat," she said. "Sometimes in bed."

"It's like you're, I dunno... three people."

"Three?"

Her tone shook him. He couldn't read it. Anger, fear, amusement. All these things.

"Why... yeah, sure," he said. "Your moods. And one of you I'm plain wild about. There. I ain't proud. Plain wild, and fuck what you think. Hell, ten minutes ago she was here and I'm sure, for a moment, she was wild back at me." He was tired of lying down. He sat up. "And that other one? Your 'business mood'? The one who don't touch me? Who treats me like shit? I'll take her. If it means I get the first, I'll take the second. At least she's consistent. Reliable. She ain't my enemy." He poked her shoulder blade then. "This is my enemy. You leave me to hang and you leave these poor Silvercloud stupes to hang. Just a pretty nothing when you get like this. Self-pitying." He took a deep breath. "And you're getting worse since we've been here."

"You're so fucking boring," Sparkle said. She got up and stumbled into her knickers, threw her fluffy coat on. "Your theories are boring, Mr.-fucking-therapist."

"Always walk away," he said.

She turned around and glared at him. He felt naked. Which he was.

"So much for your people's philosophy," she told him. "So much for your 'empathic rationalism'. What a joke!"

"Done your homework, huh?" he said.

"What is it, now? 'Everyone's basically like you if you try hard enough to understand'? Shit."

Hargie laughed. "Get that off a leaflet?"

"Oh, yes, sorry; 'statistically, you'll never meet anyone who isn't nice deep down'. And that's why bubblefolk are soooo feared and respected in galactic politics. It's a stupid, saccharine wet tissue of a philosophy, Hargie, amid a selfish, sociopathic galaxy. Abso-frigging-lutely asinine. And you know what?"

His fists had clenched. He unloosened them. "What?"

She ducked and came up again. The next moment, one of her loopy-scoop shoes flew at him. It bit just below his left eye and flew off, hitting the wall.

"Fucking... ow!" He cradled his cheek. Some blood. A cut.

"I want to believe it, you stupid prick!" she shouted. "Me! I need to believe it!"

Her eyes seemed to almost shiver as she glared. It was as if she awaited some answer. An exact answer. One Hargie didn't know.

"Where's the fun in this?" Sparkle said. "Where's the... fuck it."

And she walked out.

INEVITABLY THE MOMENT came, as if her brain could no longer hold the joy, collapsing out and rippling across the Kollective. Melid could not have stopped herself if she tried. She could sense them out there: the general mass of Silvercloud paid little regard, but among them pulsed aroused minds. The typical swarm of adolescents, of course; also two idle adults, all of them basking in Melid's tides, her ecstasy conducting their own. Her gift to them. A quiet duty of communal life.

Time slowed and she gave herself up. She let herself not think. Melid simply existed, a bundle of cooling pleasure adrift in the endless mindframe of the Kollective-at-Large.

"Melid?" Kend's voice.

Melid smiled, suddenly aware of her body, the tingling warmth, her eyelids still screwed tight. Kend's arms, too: tight around her thighs, her breath hot against tenderest flesh.

"Pleased," Melid said. "Grateful." It had been some time. She had not allowed herself with the cadre. Her muscles felt as if they had melted.

"Old friend," Kend said. "Long time."

Melid opened her eyes and watched Kend rise from between her legs and slide her torso over the surface of Melid's own. Face to face, they kissed. Melid tasted herself upon Kend's lips, bathed in the affection and respect from Kend, saw it matched by the look in her eyes.

They held one another. The silkform around their separate bellies unloosened and merged with each other, holding the two females together and in place at the epicentre of the fuck-core. Melid emoted to the walls, and some twenty other lengths of white silkform snaked through the air toward them. She felt their fabric lengths drift and roll across herself and Kend, caressing hot skin. Kend sighed.

"Unexpected this," Melid said.

"Why? Nothing new." Kend kissed the bridge of her nose. "Friends."

"Gaps in me," Melid said. And she evoked the Instrum, the barricades it placed across whole zones of her being. "Different now. Changed."

"No." Kend stroked Melid's cheek. "Still same. Yet proud now."

Melid felt it to be true and squeezed Kend's shoulders, kissed her neck.

Kend laughed. "Also duty. Duty! You needed this. Observe yourself."

Melid did so. Kend was right: the edges of Melid's mood had softened, expanded. It pulsed slowly. The act had unwound her. She hadn't realised how much she had needed touch.

"There greater gap in you," Kend told her. "Loss of Illik: concern me."

"In you too," Melid replied. "All Silvercloud."

"Greatest in Melid. Please: mourn-share. Together. Now."

"No." Melid looked away. "Not time."

"Not healthy," Kend said.

"Not time. Must... finish mission."

Kend tensed, hungry for more knowledge, wary of the Instrum's intervening in this gentle moment. The pair of them sensed the miasma around them—compassion, pheromones, sweat—begin to disperse.

"No, no, no," Kend whispered. She stroked Melid's hair, drew Melid's head in to her chest. "Forget, forget. Not ready: I see this." Their shared emotions kindled once more, a little.

"The Scalpels," Melid said, lips brushing against the softness of Kend's left mammary gland.

"Situation unchanged," Kend said. "Scalpels still visit. We watch? When next arrive?"

Melid could only nod. Kend wiped moisture from Melid's eye and cooed, humming the melody of an old creche rhyme. Melid remembered Kend singing it to her long ago in the creches, when Melid was little more than a babe and Kend a visiting teenager. Had Kend not become a scientist, Melid had always thought, she would have made an excellent nurture-technician.

Melid looked up. "A mission. Why came here."

She waited for the Instrum to lock her off, even paralyse her. Nothing, though doubtless they watched.

"We can talk," Kend said. She was surprised as Melid. She made a show of shrugging, herself aware the Instrum watched. "Talk."

Melid told her of the message dropped off by the unknown bubbleship, the words of some Worlder through the guise of a puppet that had directed the mission here. She didn't mention the rest of the mission, and Kend didn't pick up on any of it. The barricades were clearly still up in that regard.

"Think, Kend," Melid said. "Anything unusual? Anything change here?"

"Nothing. Silvercloud always same."

"I know," Melid said. She frowned. Nothing, absolutely nothing. The cadre had scoured all of Silvercloud's recent memories only yesterday. It could all have been the day Melid had left. No change.

"Maybe Scalpels," Kend said. "Puppet mean Scalpels? Not Silvercloud?"

"No: Silvercloud." Melid thought a moment. "Silvercloud outer surface, maybe. Asteroid surface. Probe maybe, or hoxnites." She looked at Kend. "Surface last surveyed? Comprehensive survey?"

Kend stared ahead, accessing the information. Melid could have done that herself, but politeness forbade her.

"One month, five days," Kend said. Her professionalism had obscured her recent affection. "Begin new study?"

"Begin."

They waited, wrapped in silkform snakes, their hands still. They said nothing, expressed no sentiments. Melid felt Kend's stomach breathe against her own. In, out.

The survey results came to them. Nothing remarkable. Nothing changed.

"The southern installation?" Melid asked.

"Nothing there," Kend said. "Caved in. You know this."

Indeed, Illik had told her many times of his near-death there. Of all the deaths. Falling rocks were second only to the void. Both great-killers.

"Survey it," Melid said.

Kend did so. They waited again.

"Nothing," Kend said. "No more installation. Just cave-in."

"I go look," Melid said. "Physical search."

Kend shook her head. "Impossible. Hatch opens, yes. Rocks beyond. No access. Nothing to access."

"Then open hatch," Melid said. "Just... look."

Kend laughed. "Strange one, you."

"Certainty. Always."

Kend made a salute like the armies of old Earth. "Field-Emissary!" she said.

"Taunting!" Melid said and she laughed. "Taunting, oh you!" She slapped Kend's shoulder playfully. "No, no, must check. Silvercloud disconnect soon. Get information now."

She reached out through the Kollective to her cadre. Almost all of them were in fuck-cores themselves, meeting the locals. Morale: important, since Calran. Perhaps the search could wait an hour or so.

"Wait," Kend said. She looked at Melid with serious eyes. She drew her palm down Melid's body. "Please wait."

Melid grinned. She grabbed Kend, licked her neck and squeezed her buttocks. Kend rippled surprise, delight. She squealed.

"Permission," Melid said in Kend's ear. "Permission: invite Yan."

"No need permission," Kend said, her interest perking up at her colleague's name.

"Not asking. Giving. I am excuse."

"Yan friend," Kend said, half-protesting. "Just friend."

Melid issued a forgiving exasperation. "Just call."

Kend kept an odd self-denial regarding Yan. She always needed a third party, ideally more, to discard it. Her friend absolved, Melid worked her way down Kend's torso, the silkform that held her obeying her movements. Down, down. Chest, belly, lower. The essence of the Konsensus, after all, was mutualism.

SPARKLE FOUND HER SISTER in the glasshouse behind the villa. She stood a while in the doorway unnoticed, watching Swirl dance through the warm air above the rows of blooms. Swirl had a sword, and when she wasn't throwing herself from all the surfaces, she was swinging the blade at imaginary assailants.

"There's better ways to prune, Sis," Sparkle called to her.

Swirl stopped in mid-air, mentally removing the momentum of zero-g. She floated.

"You should try this," Swirl said, looking down on Sparkle like some arbiter. "It'll come in useful."

"I implode on contact with useful," Sparkle said, remembering to smile. "You know that. Besides, why bother? You're clearly very good at it now."

Even at that distance Sparkle could discern Swirl's frown. "What do you want from me?"

"Come down here, for a start," Sparkle said. "Bad enough I'm having to be conciliatory; why add a crick in my neck to my woes?"

Swirl hung in the air a moment, searching for some comeback that never materialised. She drifted down to the path between the blooms. Sparkle walked over to meet her.

"Are you all right?" Swirl asked her.

"When am I less than magnificent?" Sparkle said.

Swirl chuckled.

"I showed Hargie the door," Sparkle told her. "He was starting to get..." She curled her lip. "Serious. Wanted to know 'where we stood.'"

Swirl blinked. "Men are so cruel."

"Tell me abou... hang on, you're being sarcastic."

"You think?"

"Serious, Swirl," Sparkle said. "Bloody serious. That's up there with 'sensible footwear' in terms of Sparkle-repellant."

"I see where this is going," Swirl said, inspecting a nearby bloom with her free hand. "Just like in the Academy: some poor wretch weeping at our door and me having to tell them to go."

"I'm not a teenager anymore," Sparkle said. "I'll just... act like you if he bothers me. Swirl-by-proxy."

"Well, if it's any help, I'm sorry to hear this," Swirl said. "I know Hargie meant, erm..."

"A competent shafting," Sparkle said.

"A competent... etcetera... to you."

Sparkle braced herself. The perfumed reek of the blossoms stung at her temples. "There's something else."

Swirl looked at her. Sparkle wished her sister didn't have that blade in her hand. Impossible to be murdered in this imaginary villa, of course, but temporary dismemberment wasn't outside the remit, which only made the blade more frightening.

"He may know," Sparkle said. "About us."

"What?"

"He said it was like we—the single persona we try to project—are like three people," Sparkle said.

"Three?"

"I'm two, you're the third," Sparkle said. "At least I think that's what he meant." She shrugged. "Prick."

"Then he's just being poetic," Swirl said. "In his way. Plenty of feral people have wavering personalities." She eyed Sparkle up and down. "The beauty of our condition is it's beyond the ken of feral experience. They don't have the Geode to induce it. They don't even know what the Geode is. Stop panicking."

"There's Eucharist, too," Sparkle said.

Swirl frowned.

"He knows, and he wants us to know he knows," Sparkle said. "And he's drip-feeding Hargie suspicions. Bastard." She kicked at a cobblestone on the path.

"You're paranoid," Swirl said. "He would have used it against us by now."

"He... said he's been to Zahrir. He knows. And why not? After all, Pa Nuke bloody knew. We're so assured of our cleverness, aren't we? Triune arrogance." Sparkle eyed the blade. "And I'm sick of it, Sis. I'm sick of this lying and—"

"Hold it in," Swirl said, almost growling. The shock of it made Sparkle step back. "Hold it in or I'll have to kill Eucharist, do you understand? I'll have to kill Hargie."

"You wouldn't."

"It's my function, Spar-ki-dar." She placed her hand on Sparkle's shoulder. "Pearl's the Geode specialist, you're front of house. I'm the killer."

"No," Sparkle said.

"Why should you care? He's just a diversion. Another feral." She grinned, more determined than pleased. "You're wise to discard him. Otherwise I'd have to snap his neck." She clicked her fingers. "Painless. Because you'd inevitably tell him. Inevitably."

Sparkle shook her head. *No*, she mouthed.

"Keep him at a distance, eh?" Swirl said. "Then we can leave your little plaything at the border with his life."

"Why?" Sparkle said. "Why are you doing this?"

"Why?" Swirl said. "Because next to the Hoidrac, Hargie is less than dust. And because I have to ensure you survive." She reached out and stroked Sparkle's hair. "And not just for my sake."

Sparkle stared at her own feet. It occurred to her that, while sex had been a mental defence against her current situation, Swirl had had no such recourse. Nothing to fill the hours save spiritual fervour and murder-practice. But she was far from insane. That was the scary part. Swirl was entirely herself, brought into frightful contrast by her current situation.

And she was the only means out of here. The only means Sparkle could trust. Nothing mattered save survival.

"Well," Sparkle said, throwing another smile out, natural as breathing, "this is all academic. Hargie's an idiot. An outcast. I've quite thrown him away." And it was true, perfectly true. "You and me, Swirly-girl. And when we get back, Pearl too."

"Pearl too," Swirl repeated.

Sparkle looked about the flower beds, their lunacy of colour. "Pearl adored this place," she said. "Knew every flower's name."

Swirl dropped her sword onto a soil bed and gently hugged Sparkle. "We have to remain strong," she said.

"Naturally," Sparkle replied, spitting out one of Swirl's blue dreads that had swung into her mouth.

"Tomorrow Silvercloud disconnects," Swirl said. "Three days later, the Kharmund arrives. The Kharmund, sister. Your faith is quiet—I understand that—but you have it."

"I love the Hoidrac," Sparkle said.

"How could it be otherwise?"

THE LOCAL KOLLECTIVE informed Melid she had just conceived. She pressed on down the tube, handrail to handrail. Never losing rhythm, she looked at Kend pacing beside her and saw her recognition.

"Oh, Yan," Melid said to Kend. "Typical."

"Yan," Kend said. "Credit to Konsensus."

Behind them, Yan rippled with pleasure. The three of them shared a brief torus of delight.

A pleasing thing. It sheltered her friends from the shadow of Zo's and Doum's proximity. The two of them followed at a slight distance, their pistols holstered but ready. Weapons were a rare sight in Silvercloud.

One minute until disconnection, the Kollective told them. A hatchway stretched open and they passed through. Beyond was the tube leading to the disused elevator.

Strange, Melid thought. She felt Kend pick up on her reaction.

"Air fresh here," Melid said. "Illogical: unused tube. Any recent visit?"

Kend blinked, accessing Silvercloud. "No. Not two years."

Then surely? "Non-Kollectives."

"Worlders?" Kend said.

"Maybe," Melid said.

"Be detected," Yan said behind them.

"Maybe," Melid repeated. She ordered Zo and Doum forward, toward the hatchway before the elevator hall. They did so, drawing their pistols. Melid felt Yan and Kend's fear as they passed.

It seemed Melid, Kend, and Yan had to request an override together. An understandable level of security, though Melid wondered if she was being paranoid.

Twenty seconds to disconnect.

The hatchway stretched open. The lights beyond warmed up. A mezzanine, quite pristine, as if a single moment had been made eternal. No, something wrong with it. Again, no stale air. Something about the place, the drift of the motes under the lights maybe, or something, whispered of recent use. Zo and Doum propelled themselves inside, and the others followed.

Melid looked at the lift doors. "Halt," she told the two armed Field-Instrums. "Call reinforce—"

Disconnecting.

Melid came to, her face against the cool plated floor. Something was wrapped around her, holding her arms tight against her body, her legs pressed together. She could hear shouting.

She opened her eyes, craning her neck to take of this new scene what she could. She saw Zo, swearing and screaming, struggling against the black, segmented tentacles of a serv-unit that had coiled around her. In another tentacle it held Zo's pistol. Melid could hear Doum growl and struggle too, no doubt receiving the same treatment. The hum of a serv's reactor just above her told Melid she had fared similarly.

Kend floated into Melid's vision, coming to rest on all fours on their shared surface, her face inches from Melid's own.

"Melid?" she said.

The Kollective was gone. Silvercloud's local kollective, too. Only Zo and Doum to cling to. And they were frightening, an inhuman tumult of rage. Melid struggled against the coils.

"Melid..." Kend repeated. "Remember." Kend offered a connection, one that tasted familiar, some submerged dream-life.

"Remember," Kend repeated. "Choose us." She nodded toward Zo. "Death for them."

It came in fractures, half-drowned by the screaming feedback of Zo and Doum's unleashed psychoses. They clawed at her, at the universe. She wanted them gone. To get away...

Home. She could remember. The hidden installation, the Scalpel project. Her real childhood.

"Please," she heard Kend say.

Melid accepted Kend's connection.

The rage vanished. In its place came a serenity long forgotten. Melid relaxed. She could feel Silvercloud, the other Silvercloud. The other life. Kend and Yan's warmth nearby, the distant lights of twenty thousand other people above her like stars. Each one at a remove, offering only what they wished to offer of themselves. A controlled communion.

I am a traitor, Melid realised.

"Kend," she said. "I'm home."

"Home." Kend bathed Melid in Silvercloud's love.

SAT ALONE IN A NEARBY social-core, Melid sucked at the drink pouch Kend had given her.

What parts of her life, her childhood and adult life before she joined the Instrum, had been real? What fabricated? She'd spent the last hour sifting through her memories—real and constructed—of Silvercloud. It seemed she possessed two memories of any one moment spent during Silvercloud's disconnection. Though the actual events had precedence in terms of her immediate recall, she could access the forgeries if she concentrated. Her generation's eleventh birthday, for instance, had fallen on a disconnection day. She'd had two eleventh birthdays: one a simple trip to see the Scalpels, another a cover story. A party in a social-core with far too many guests. In retrospect, it must have made an alibi for a lot of people.

Melid shifted in her seat-pit. She remembered reminiscing over a scalpel encounter with Illik and her class. Not real, not wholly. The thought processes had been altered to hide Silvercloud's traitorous mentality. To think: a conspiracy so clandestine that most of the time, no one knew they were in it.

"How Melid feel?" she asked the empty room. She didn't know. Melid had grown up in Silvercloud's secret. She believed in making contact with the Scalpels, whatever the cost. She was sure she believed it, had believed it intently right up to the moment she had left Silvercloud six years ago. Then she'd been wiped.

"Six years," she whispered, sipping her drink.

Kend entered. "Melid," she said. She issued kindness, warmth.

Melid hesitated. She hadn't truly shared with anyone since the disconnection, though it was far from the horror Worlders lived by. Melid could still feel the presence, the reassurance, of other minds. That was the beauty of Silvercloud.

She hadn't engaged with anyone directly since she'd had time to come to terms with her decision. She had panicked earlier. She'd no idea where she stood.

"Glad you join," Kend said.

Melid connected with Kend's emotions, issued her own gladness. Kend smiled.

"Glad," she replied. "But next? After next reconnect?"

"Silvercloud programme. Never fail."

Melid winced. "Too hard. Dangerous. Am deep in Instrum. You kill me: safe. Kill cadre. Programme memory: accident." Melid closed her eyes, drank in the wide psyche of Silvercloud, lost herself within it. "Safer."

Kend laughed, issued more kindness. "Melid, no." She held Melid's head in warm hands. "No. Unnecessary. New factors here."

Melid opened her eyes and looked at her. "New factors?"

"Mm-hm." Kend leaned in and kissed Melid on the lips, long enough to calm her, to let endorphins run. Satisfied, Kend stopped. She kept her forehead against Melid's. Each one's eyes became the universe to the other.

"Before next reconnect," Kend said. "Silvercloud communicate: Scalpels."

Melid's breath heaved. Kend giggled and kissed her again.

"How?" Melid asked.

"Worlder," Kend said. "Here. In southern installation."

Melid sighed. "Eucharist," she said.

"Yes... but others too."

Melid felt Kend evoke a visual between them—no one else. Melid closed her eyes and received it.

A grey room, a social-core. Kend's vision. Dark-skinned woman with pink hair. Talking, no sound. Sparkle Savard.

"No," Melid, said and she broke away from Kend, stared ahead. "Bad. Cadre chase her: my duty." She looked at Kend again. "Killed Illik."

"Illik?" Kend shimmered shock, soon swallowed by a resolve Melid couldn't fully read. Unnerving. "Then we use her. Destroy."

"Kend—"

Kend placed her hand on Melid's shoulder. "Sparkle knows Scalpels. Knows truth: Harmony god-craft."

"No gods." Melid laughed, a cackle seasoned with anger.

"To them gods, rulers," Kend said. "Aliens to us. Scalpel come, her mind communicate." Kend smiled. "Finally! You want? Always want... yes?"

Melid nodded.

"Good," Kend said. "Good. Then kill Worlders before reconnect. Collate information, dump place findable. Wipe our minds." She poked at Melid's belly playfully. "Konsensus learns. All happy, yes?"

She felt Kend study her. Melid concentrated on nothing but her love of Scalpels.

"Let you think," Kend said. With that, she kissed Melid upon her temple and swam out of the core.

Melid was thinking, all right. Thinking three things.

Firstly, it had to be Sung Eucharist who had sent the puppet's message. Who else? He was the only Worlder who knew of Silvercloud, and had long profited from it. But why? Why betray Silvercloud to the Instrum?

Secondly, Kend hadn't picked up on all of Melid's feelings just now. Unconsciously or not, Melid had apparently shielded her ambivalences with shock at Sparkle's presence and excitement at the Scalpels. She hadn't realised the extent to which she could hide her thoughts from others in this illegal kollective. She hadn't had reason to, before now. Perhaps time among Worlders had changed her.

Thirdly? Kend. Kend had made the programme along with Illik. She must have known its full potential by now, what a mind could hide.

Exactly what, if anything, was Kend not telling her?

EUCHARIST HAD HIM SCREWED. Hargie had lost his Empress piece, a champion and a priest. He had all angles covered regarding his Emperor. At least he thought he did. If only his neuralware could access the memestream, he wouldn't have to play this crap.

"I'm no good at this game," he muttered. He hated all of this. The smell of the air here, the nothing to do. For some reason he thought of Sparkle's bare flat stomach. The heat of it against his lips. Gone now. Barred to him.

"I think you are a natural," Eucharist said, looking up from the game board. "Have confidence. Display confidence. The game always follows."

"Got it all figured out, ain't you?"

"I appear to," Eucharist said. "Keep up, boy."

"Appearances can be deceiving," Hargie said.

"They always are." Eucharist's chrome irises gazed down upon Hargie's Emperor. "That's the vital piece," he said. "Remember that, Hargie."

Hargie just nodded. Of course it was the vital piece. Why the hell point it out? "Exactly how dumb do you think I am?"

"An order of magnitude more than our Harmonic lady."

Hargie tensed in his seat. "Care to explain that? Care to explain that with my Empress piece up your nose?"

"She is a, er..." He did that damn thing with his hand, like it was a flower blooming. "Complex person."

Hargie smacked his palm against the metal surface of the table. "She's complex *people*, dammit. Call it what it is."

For the first time since Hargie'd ever known him, Eucharist looked taken aback. "You know this?"

"How can you miss it?," hargie said. "Fuck. I mean she's crazy right? You get crazy people with piles of people in their skull. You hear about it. See it in movies."

Eucharist seemed to relax. He snorted. He reached out and gripped Hargie's shoulder.

"No, boy," he said. 'No. Multiple personality syndrome is a fictional illness, a misdiagnosis. It does not exist in nature."

"That so?"

"Indeed. It is a myth, one that has followed humanity to the stars. And it survives because people hunger for easy explanations. No one really knows anyone else; that's the problem. There is an emptiness between our minds as real as between worlds. By judging someone to be several people, we absolve ourselves of empathy's struggle. Are you really so tired of struggle?"

Hargie said nothing.

Noise came down the tunnel beyond the room.

"Speak of the Foozle," Eucharist said.

Hargie got up and walked toward the hatchway. Footsteps, and plenty of them. A hum too, a whole collection of hums. The sound of those tentacled things.

A woman stepped right in front of him. Spindly uniform. Hargie looked up.

The Emissary.

"Greetings," she said. She grinned wide.

"Shit." Hargie stumbled backwards, fell on his ass. He shuffled backwards instead, thighs pumping, clawing the metal floor.

The Emissary stepped forward through the threshold. "Mr. Stukes," she said. "Of all the places..."

"Gettahwayfromeee!"

She lifted her arm, her fingers pointing at him. He waited for whatever the hell was coming.

Sparkle stepped through the threshold and stood beside the Emissary. She half-smiled.

"So..." Hargie said, trying to control his breathing. "All along. A damn conspiracy..."

"What conspiracy?" Sparkle asked.

Hargie looked from one woman to the next and back again.

"Fuck knows!" he barked. "Just... fuck..."

"Hargie, it's fine," Sparkle said. She had her business mood on. "From what I understand, Melid is on our side now."

"Melid?" Hargie said. "She's 'Melid' now?"

"Always was," the Emissary said. Hargie realised her hand was being offered to him.

Screw that. He got his own damn self up on to his feet.

The Emissary—Melid—stepped to one side and gestured behind her at the corridor that passed by the room. The humming was louder now. Hargie watched as the machines hovered past. The first one had Melid's crony wrapped up in its tentacles, the girl Zo. Her mouth was muffled by a tentacle, and her eyes went wide on seeing Hargie stood there. She hovered on by. Another machine skimmed by and this time it was Hargie's eyes' turn to go wide: Doum, the big guy. How the heckanoony did he still live? Hadn't Sparkle slammed a heel in his neck? Shit. Doum frowned at Hargie, and Hargie was pleased when he skimmed out of view.

More came. Other struggling Spindlies, other cronies presumably. Six, seven, eight. Hargie was too bemused to count anymore. Was all this a plot, one built around him? Two star empires conspiring to drag some lone spacebum off the strip, fuck his mind?

"What is this?" he said to no one.

"A twist," Eucharist said from behind him. "Clearly."

Hargie ignored him. He looked at Sparkle.

"Kend explained," she told him. "Melid's originally a citizen of Silvercloud. When she returned here and Silvercloud disconnected, her old memories returned."

"And you believed that?" Hargie said. "Thought you're from the Harmonies, not the Gullibles."

Sparkle smirked, some thought in her crazy head clearly amusing her.

"You must not fear me, Mr. Stukes," Melid said.

"Then dig out your lobotomy tools." He shook his head. "Actually, forget I said anything."

"Sarcasm," Melid said, with an expression like she'd just recognised an obscure make of ship.

"Yeah," Hargie said. "Hell, ask your friend Sparkle here. She's always faking."

Sparkle threw her palm over her mouth and guffawed.

"What?" Hargie demanded. "What's funny now?"

"Erm..." Sparkle squinted, as if trying to remember something. "Basically, 'I never fake my sarcasms'. It was better phrased inside my head, to be honest. It had an emphasis on you, well... being a poor lover. No offence."

"What?" Hargie said. "You're crazy."

"Define 'crazy,'" Eucharist said from across the room.

Silence fell.

"You know," Melid said out of nowhere, "I actually do have lobotomy tools onboard my craft." She shrugged. "I'm making smalltalk."

Hargie smacked his palm against his own forehead. "What a team."

Doctor Kend, or whatever her title was, walked into the room. She wore a Spindly suit.

"Melid," she said. "You're not helping our case."

"Perhaps not," Melid said. "Mr. Stukes here is not convinced of my good faith."

All three of the women were looking at him. Down at him. Naturally.

"Mr. Stukes," Kend said, "you have my word Melid here is our friend and ally. If she were against our plans here, the rest of Silvercloud would know of it. I know your Worlder disability prevents you from seeing the shared truth of this, but I ask that you trust us."

"Yeah?" Hargie said. "Well, I go by what I see in a face." He looked at Melid's. A face on some tyrant's monument. "I go by what I see."

He walked away from the women and sat back in the chair by the table. He didn't look up at Eucharist on the other side, just stared at the game he had no hope of winning.

"I think," he heard Melid say, "it would be instructive for our guests to see Silvercloud while they are here. To help them understand."

"Some things ain't worth understanding," Hargie said.

"Ms. Savard, then," Melid said. "Perhaps the people of the Harmonies are more accustomed to learning new things."

"Perhaps we are," Sparkle said. "I would like that very much."

"Yan and I," Kend said, "will be preparing our machinery for the Scalpel event. I can request a guide to—"

"I'll do it," Melid said, cutting her off. "Why not? I'm unengaged right now and I should like to see my old home."

Hargie looked up. Melid and Kend were gazing at one another, maybe sharing in that psychic shit of theirs.

"A fine idea," Kend said eventually. She turned to Sparkle. "Would you be happy with that?"

"The irony appeals," Sparkle said.

"In a matter of hours we shall be like old friends," Melid said.

Sparkle didn't reply.

"It's agreed, then," Kend said. "But first, Sparkle, I should like to show you the machinery we will be using in the observatory. You will be required to operate it, in a sense."

"What sense?" Sparkle asked.

"You shall see," Kend said.

"Shall I accompany?" Melid asked.

"That won't be necessary," Kend said. "We shan't be long."

With that, Kend led Sparkle away down the corridor toward where the prisoners were being taken.

Just Hargie, Melid and Eucharist now. Real funhouse.

"So when you gonna betray everyone?" Hargie asked Melid. "I'd like to cram a meal in before I'm spaced."

He got nothing out of her face. Instead, she looked at Eucharist.

"Sung Eucharist," she said. "I saw you once when you visited here. When I was young."

"I know," Eucharist replied. "You did not trust me then, either." He looked back down at his game.

Melid took a breath, studying the two men. "I'll be outside," she said, and left.

"I LIE IN THIS?" SWIRL asked Kend.

"Yes," Kend said.

The thing was like an ancient prophylactic Swirl had once seen in a museum. Far larger, of course, but the same transparent skin, and similarly ribbed.

:It's like an insect wing rolled up,: Sparkle sent.

:Yes,: Swirl replied. *:My thoughts exactly.:*

The room was entirely white, a tone Swirl hadn't seen in Silvercloud before. She was surprised, too, by the lack of any interfaces. No instruments or tools lying about, either. No surfaces, no shelves or tables, for any tools to lie on. Merely a bare long room with a woman-sized chrysalis at its centre.

"And I'll be able to breathe in there?" Swirl asked.

"Naturally," Kend replied.

"Reassuring," Swirl said. "And you're confident this will... broadcast our... my mind to the Kharmund?"

"I think so. Whatever lifelong use of the leaf drug has wrought on your brain may, in theory, attract the Scalpel." Kend grinned. "I mean 'Kharmund.'"

"Has one of you ever tried it?"

"I have," Kend said. "Nothing. It's as if we're not there to them. Or they choose to ignore us."

"I imagine the truth lies somewhere in between," Swirl said.

"That makes no sense," Kend said.

"To a human mind," Swirl said.

Kend laughed. "I cannot begin to tell you how excited I am. How we all are. I wish you could share in it."

Swirl stepped closer to her, placed her hand on Kend's shoulder. Kend shuddered but contained herself.

"We will share much when the Kharmund speaks," she told Kend. "We shall be a sibling people: different pasts, a shared future."

Kend squinted. "What does 'sibling' mean?" She shook her head. "It does not matter; I take your meaning. Do you think you could lie inside this now?" She gestured at the chrysalis.

:No fucking way,: Sparkle sent. *:Not yet. Not til right before the broadcast. Our brain could scupper the deal, Sis.:*

"Is it urgent?" Swirl asked Kend.

"Not particularly," Kend said. "I'm just eager to study a Harmonic's brain. Generations of leaf drug use..."

"I'm sure it's much like any other brain," Swirl said. "Full of fear and contradiction."

:And gloop.: Sparkle sent.

"I'm certain it's more than that," Kend said, and her eyes were like a child's at dessert time. "I'm certain."

"Well," Swirl said. "I'm a mild claustrophobe. The less time I spend in that thing, the better."

"A claustrophobe," Kend said, her eyes even more full of wonder. "I've heard of that."

"Besides, Melid is waiting to show me your world."

"Melid..." Kend said. "I've been meaning to talk with you. About Melid."

"I thought you people had no secrets from one another," Swirl said.

"We don't," Kend said. "Not typically."

:This is not good,: Sparkle sent. *:Melid's an unknown factor once more. Colour me unsurprised.:*

"It is possible not to share everything in a disconnected Silvercloud," Kend said. "Frankly, we are still learning how such a thing works."

"You seem a faster learner than most," Swirl told her. "Exactly what aren't you sharing with Melid?"

"I—we—haven't told her... well, she's still under the impression that this is about making contact with the Scalpels alone. That when this is finished, the data will be placed in some readily discoverable location, and we'll then wipe our minds of all relevant details."

"You haven't told her of the plan? Of the revolt?"

Kend's face twitched. She seemed on difficult cognitive ground.

"Melid is obsessed with the Scalpels; she would risk her life to bring new knowledge of them to our people. But the revolt—"

"Kend—"

"I love her," Kend said. "Love her in ways I do not think you Worlders could ever comprehend. But she has been away with the Instrum a long time, and when she returned..." She shook her head. "She has holes in her mind, barriers common Utiles cannot see past. If we told her the full extent of the plan, your plan, she might not stand with us. I don't know." Her eyes glazed with water. "We would have to kill her."

"I understand," Swirl said. "She's like a sister to you."

"A sister?"

"You accept her for all her faults."

Kend wiped her eyes. "Yes. I've even kept those monsters of hers alive. For her sake. We're keeping them in the plasma chamber here. With the old plan, we could wipe their minds. Now we'll have to..."

"Wipe them out," Swirl said.

Kend nodded. "I'm hoping once things become clear to her, she will see the virtue." "And if not?" Kend looked at Swirl. She didn't answer.

"I find that sooner or later, all things in life become balanced against one another," Swirl said. "Ask yourself what you value more: your friend, or this freedom you experience right here and now? The former I can't advise you on, but the latter will only grow under Hoidrac protection. It will bloom wider than you could ever imagine."

Kend's face flashed that child-before-a-dessert expression again. They'd no poker faces, these Konsensites. Swirl knew herself a social dolt, but even she could read them.

"Melid awaits you," Kend said. "Remember." She walked away toward the portal.

:Interesting,isn't it?: Sparkle sent. *:Front row seats to a new dawn.:*

:Yes,: Swirl sent back, following Kend out of the lab. *:Another people grasp for Hoidrac truth.:*

:I meant the dawn of lies.: Sparkle sent.

THE ASHEMI STRODE THROUGH the corridor of the House's public baths. The steam of the saunas collected on his ornate form, dripped from his black iron ribs. He passed alabaster cubicles thick with steam. From one he heard the syncopated slap of two men copulating, from the next the leaf-frenzied laughter of women. Ahead, from the cubicle he intended to enter, came only silence.

The Ashemi looked inside. The steam wasn't so thick in here. A long window, hanging at an angle between the wall and ceiling, cast sunlight on two stone massage altars below. On the far one Gleam-Glare-Moon lay face down. He was naked and he wept.

"Gleam," the Ashemi said. "About the matter of—"

Gleam screamed and leapt up. He staggered backwards onto his feet, until his back was tight against the wall. He seemed far more concerned with obscuring his body's rear than the front. An interesting choice, the Ashemi thought. The flesh-bound were peculiar.

"Your body is an irrelevance," the Ashemi said. "Our case is paramount."

"I know," Gleam said. At least the Ashemi assumed it was Gleam. He wasn't wearing his persona bindi. He relaxed. "*Our* case? That's new. I've never known you... to put it that way." He frowned. "But I've never known you to walk in on my private time, either."

The Ashemi looked at him. "Why were you crying?"

He wiped his eyes. "I wasn't. My other brother, Moon." He eyed the Ashemi defensively. "He's not used to all this. Beating civilians. Demon gods. He's just a technician."

In truth, the Ashemi wasn't used to beating civilians, either. He wasn't sure why his reaction had been so visceral. The name of the Dissenter had brought it out in him, as well it might many in the Harmonies. The Ashemi had thought himself—whoever he was—more rational.

"Silver is a liar," he said. "Or likely adulterated. No Hoidrac materialises in the waking world. Not in this age and certainly not that... *particular* Hoidrac. Every individual mind in the Harmonies is protected from him. It." He remembered why he'd come here. "But it works in our favour. The Envoy never mentioned he'd had sensitive information stolen. So either he doesn't know, or he omitted the fact."

"Perhaps he wanted us to find out," Gleam said.

"Perhaps. Either way, he has to work with us. I'm tired of this petty rivalry between your world and his."

Gleam shook his blond head. "Others might not share your sentiment, your Ashemi. Culakwun has been petitioning to invade Zahrir for centuries. And, permitted, they could easily." He looked at the Ashemi, spoke slowly: "They merely have to devise a method entertaining enough to—"

"Spare me the banalities," the Ashemi said. "I serve Pheoni, not her favoured pets. But, I tell you, the truth of Pearl's crimes lies with the Envoy. I know it." The light from the high window caught his blue glass eyes. He strode over to the window.

"Come here," he said to Gleam.

"Your Ashemi... could I ask you to pass that dressing gown?"

The Ashemi looked at him. A most nervous expression, Gleam. And yet he stood rather proud, his arms by his sides, genitals uncovered and hanging. These eccentricities were becoming irritating. He took the gown from the hook nearby and passed it.

Dressed, Gleam walked over to him.

"Look," the Ashemi said. "Practically summer out there." The hill peaks were green, near-free of snow. The sun shone at full strength, though he'd no capacity to feel its warmth.

"It is," Gleam said. "Almost."

"These seasons are insensible. Confounded world. At exactly what speed is it travelling?"

"There's more to it," Gleam said. "Erm, tectonics, eccentric orbit. That sort of thing."

"Eccentric? It was winter's end, what? Two days ago? I call that outright deranged. Describe this orbit to me."

Gleam looked down. "I've really no idea, Ashemi..."

"This is your *world*. You know, Gleam, you're remarkably incurious for a security head."

"My purview doesn't stretch to astrophysics," Gleam said.

"Humility, Gleam."

"Apologies, your Ashemi." Gleam closed his eyes, evidently enjoying the sun's warmth. "Earlier I checked public transport records to the cottage. On the day of Pearl's visit."

"And?"

"There was the teardrop Pearl took from the Trinity House, of course. But also another. So at the very least there *was* a visitor, whatever their manner."

"From the Trinity House?" the Ashemi asked. "From here?"

Gleam shook his head. "It was called to a landing patio at the foothills of the Husks."

"The mountains? No one lives out there but..."

"The Anointed," Gleam said.

"I hardly think that secretive order would use public transport," the Ashemi said. "A decoy, surely."

"Let's hope so," Gleam said. "Interrogating the Anointed would be outside even your remit."

"Why don't your brothers ever tell you to mind your manners?" the Ashemi said, quite irritated. "You're becoming like that Envoy." He gazed outside again, at the green hills. "Let's pay him another visit." Gleam winced at the suggestion, but the Ashemi ignored him. "If he does not believe us, we will offer Silver's mind up for his inspection."

"Do you ever remember?" Gleam said.

The Ashemi looked at him. Gleam's gaze was steely, almost blasphemous.

"What?" the Ashemi asked.

"Being human."

"YOU'VE CHANGED, MY boy," Eucharist said. "You know that?"

Hargie looked up from the damn boardgame. "Ratshit," he replied. "I'm static as a rock."

"Yet rocks move," Eucharist said. "Continents drift."

"Piss runs wild. You got a point here?"

Eucharist leaned back in his chair. "'Some things are not worth understanding'. You said that. I find that statement at odds with the famous bubbleman philosophy, your 'empathic rationalism'. I'll grant you modern bubblefolk are the very model of cognitive dissonance, balancing your gullible heritage with an adopted and healthy skepticism, but you, sir, have gone over the edge."

"Fascinating," Hargie muttered.

"I wonder why," Eucharist said. "Being trapped here, perhaps? Among these hive people?" He wagged a gloved finger. "I do not think so. I think it is her. She confounds you."

"Well, she confounded me right outta her bed," Hargie said. "Confound her right into yours if you like. Hargie don't give a zero-g shit." He looked at Eucharist's face but saw no twitches, no tells. "Professional now, me and her. Way it should have been."

"A shame," Eucharist said. "I mean that. You'll fall back into your old ways without her. Your old philosophy."

"Nothing wrong with my philosophy," Hargie said.

"I agree," Eucharist said. "It's the universe that fails it. Trust me: empathic rationalism shall not survive the century. A shadow lumbers forward." Eucharist smiled his kind uncle smile. "I should like you to survive it. I should like the bubblefolk to survive it."

Hargie shook his head. "Do you ever just... I dunno... drink a slurpy-pop, watch a movie?"

"What?"

"Do you 'contend with the abyss' or just wipe your butt like everyone else?"

Eucharist chuckled. "I do enjoy a slurpy-pop. You have me there." He seemed to consider some matter. "Let me show you something," he said, and he stood up. He walked toward the doorway.

"Please not your abyss," Hargie muttered. He got up and followed. *

The land. The land.

A beauty she hadn't known since last she gazed down upon Calran's shattered form. Perhaps before then. Perhaps since home.

"How do these crops flourish in total darkness?" she heard her own mouth say. Swirl was looking at Emissary Melid but, thanks to their augmented eyeballs, Sparkle could fix her own view upon the landscape stretching out from below the plated ledge they stood upon.

"It is not total darkness," Emissary Melid replied. "We take the infrared light from the waste energy the kollective produces and direct it into this agri-cavern."

Swirl had asked another stupid question. If they could see this landscape through the goggles, then there must be some sort of light it worked with. They weren't wearing bat ears, for fuck's sake. A better question might be "What are you planning, Emissary?" or "Where's your shame, murderer?"

"Emissary," Swirl said, "I find this use of waste energy most elegant."

"Our crops were genetically modified millennia ago," Melid said.

"Of course," Swirl said. "My people could learn much from Silvercloud."

And we from you. That's what Melid should have said. Telling she did not. Swirl hadn't picked up on that, but Sparkle had. Normally she'd demand control here, being the anthropologist, the socialiser, but it was vital to give Swirl space. She was their one ticket out of here, after all, the only one trustworthy. Better to let her do whatever she liked.

Mm, but these were tertiary thoughts. The landscape below was everything.

Easily a mile high, perhaps five miles wide, its depth unguessable. It dwarfed the underworlds of Calran, even the great transit. The red light in her goggles soaked everything with an oil-paint authority, a perfect alloy of photorealism and the Cubists of legend. Below her lay a valley of paddy fields, each level with square-carved walls as of an ancient fortress. Level upon level, tens upon tens of fortress walls, a plume of messy black foliage topping the heights of each. A mass of right angles, their sides alternating from light to shadow, the whole a chequered collage of scarlet and burgundy.

Wonder enough. But the wonder repeated above, where the sky would have been. An identical cubic landscape unhindered by gravity's pedantic rule. And all of it, from roof to floor, daubed with pink mists, billowing over crops, snaking between levels, iridescent in the infrared's glow.

The accidental masterpiece of a utilitarian race. Mm-yes.

:Ask if we may meet those who work this land,: Sparkle sent to her sister.

:I don't see the point,: Swirl replied. *:Time's short, and we've already met their leaders.:*

:If the Hoidrac choose to help these people, it's only fitting we should try to understand their daily lives.:

Swirl turned their shared head toward Melid. "Could we meet those who work this land?" she asked.

Melid frowned. "Difficult. They are unaccustomed to Worlder humans. You are frightening to us. The lack of connection renders you..." She half-smiled here. "Unknowable."

Sparkle sensed Melid's honesty hid other, darker truths. An illogical notion, but her notions had long proved trusty.

"Fine," Swirl said. "Understandable."

"Perhaps," Melid said, "you might care to fly over the paddy fields with me? We can take refreshments over on the other side. Local cuisine. I can broadcast to all that we will be there and not to approach."

"How would we fly?" Swirl asked.

Melid's half-smile turned full. She blinked, and a now familiar humming sound echoed from the corridor behind them. Swirl turned, and Sparkle saw two of those black, tentacled machines—the serv-forms—approach. The red light of the paddy fields framed their segmented hides.

Sparkle could feel Swirl's physical fright. Yet Sparkle felt nothing but excitement at something new.

"Appreciated," Swirl told Melid, "but I..."

:Let's do this, Sis,: Sparkle sent.

:We can't fully trust Melid yet.: Swirl replied.

:Funny. You never mentioned that before. Not scared, are you, mighty one?:

Swirl took a deep breath. "Yes," she said to Melid. "Yes, I should like that."

Yes, Sparkle thought, Swirl could do as she liked. But what she liked was easily directed.

HARGIE AND SUNG EUCHARIST stood before a wall of black glass. The rest of the small room's walls were grey plated metal, like everywhere else in this secret installation. Hargie hadn't been to this end before, had had no reason to.

"All right, Sung," he said, looking at the black glass. "Love what you did with the place. Not too showy, not too plain."

"Meet the neighbours," Eucharist said, and he placed a palm on the glass.

The wall flashed white, then became transparent. Behind it lay a disc-shaped room, not dissimilar to the habitat Hargie and the rest were currently living in. The difference was it had a bunch of monsters lolling about inside: Zo, Doum, and all Melid's discarded cronies. Maybe a dozen in all, floating around, lying around or sitting on the ceiling. One of them—a man—was apparently taking a dump in a hole in the wall. They still wore their black skin suits, but their weapons were gone.

"They cannot see us," Eucharist said. "The glass is black on their side."

"Intriguing," Hargie said, and he flipped them the finger.

"Two of them were remotely stunned in a tunnel just as Silvercloud disconnected from the Kollective-at-Large. The rest were stunned inside their docked craft. Including someone you may know."

Hargie frowned.

"I'll get him for you," Eucharist said, and he pressed the glass again.

One of the nearby Spindlies looked up and the rest instantly did likewise, as one. They were all still connected to one another. A tiny Konsensus—Trademark Konsensus, original brand—trapped in this hell-rock as much as the next man, who was Hargie. Irony: was that what they called it?

They screamed and shouted, all in silence, muted by the thick glass. They made gestures offensive in any human culture. Hargie saw a brown flower bloom on the glass' top right corner: the Spindly who'd been taking a dump had clearly joined the protest. Hargie was more impressed than anything: no easy throw in zero-g.

Eucharist drew a circle on the glass with his finger and then yelled at it. Everyone inside clutched their ears and doubled over. Some of them began to spin.

"Appreciated," Eucharist said. He ran his finger down the glass. Hargie guessed this meant he was turning the sound on their side down. "If your... exuberances are quite finished, my friend here would like to speak with the one who is not of your kind."

Eucharist must have switched the two-way on, because now Hargie could hear those freaks all laugh. Zo, who sat at the far end of the cell and who had so far sat smiling, got up from some pale brown lump she'd been squatting on. She shook the lump and it quivered, arms and legs flailing from it, a shaking head. A naked man. Zo had been sitting on a man.

She lifted the man up and, pressing her feet against the wall, propelled him toward the glass Hargie and Eucharist stood before.

It was Vict. Fucking Nugo Vict.

Vict's eyes were wide. He was a bubbleman, knew enough about zero-g not to fight it, he'd only spin and carry on the same course. He put out his hands as he hit the glass and they got smeared in shit. He got more on his arms and a little on his face. He took a while to right himself, streaking the glass still further.

Vict stared through the glass. "Stukes," he said. "What are you doing here?"

"Back at you."

"I woke up on..." His eyes shifted side to side and then he whispered: "These people's ship. Last thing I remember before that was—"

"Killing Aewyn Nuke?" Hargie said. "Recall that, you lowdown slime?"

Vict's eyes screwed up and he winced. "I know... I know I wasn't your friend. I know I was a no-good son of a bitch." He opened his eyes again. "I know it! Just please... we're bub-boys, Hargie. Both of us. Has to mean something, right?" His chin quivered, the hair on it no longer styled. A mad brush. Hargie noticed he had a thousand tiny cuts all on his chest and arms. "Empathic rationalism, right? The philosophy."

"Yeah," Hargie said. "You were all about seeing the other guy's point of view."

"You're a better man than me, Hargie," Vict said. "Always were. That what you want?" Vict's eyes began to water. "Please..."

"Smoosh," Hargie said. "Chill your boots, boy. I'm getting all rationally empathic. Picturing your point of view as we speak."

"Really?"

"Yeah," Hargie said. "I'm picturing you on this side of the glass and me there." He whistled and shook his head. "Can't say it appeals, fucko."

Vict broke down. His shoulders heaved and his features twisted. He started to blub.

"What?" Hargie said, "what are you trying to say now? I need my fucking ratshit fix, boy. Play the hits."

"Fuck you," Vict blurted. "Fuck you. You don't know what these people are like. You don't know what she can do." He began to shake again. "Fuck, man, why's she keeping me alive?" he sobbed.

A black gloved hand—slender and shiny—reached down from above. It caressed Vict's cheek and he screamed. The hand gripped his neck and he froze, too scared to move.

The hand was followed by a brutally cut pigtailed hairdo, in turn followed by an upside-down face, pretty and monstrous. Hargie shuddered. He hadn't seen Zo approach. She must've crawled along the ceiling, quiet as a spider. He'd never been so close to that girlish devil. He was thankful for the glass.

"Found a little friend?" she asked Vict. Even the timbre of her voice was somehow... wrong. The Foozle in lipstick.

"I'm sorry," Vict mewled, "sorry..."

Zo giggled, wiped shit off the glass and placed the same hand over Vict's open mouth. His eyes flashed wide and she giggled some more.

"Hush," she told him.

"I've seen enough," Hargie said to Eucharist.

"I beg to differ," Eucharist replied. "Talk to her."

"What?"

"Talk to me," Zo said. "Dead man." She looked at Eucharist. "Dead men."

"Fuck that," Hargie said. He took a cigarette out and lit it. One of five left.

"Talk to her," Eucharist repeated. "Ask her something."

"This is..." Hargie trailed off. Ah, what the hell. "So, er... what is it you like to do?"

"Kill," she replied. "Kill the already-dead. Put pain in strangers."

"Sheesh," Hargie said. "Surprised your parents let you. I wouldn't even let you go nightclubbing."

"Nightclubs are good for death," Zo said. "Noise. Corpses mistaken for drunks. Getaway easy."

"Don't say?" He looked at Eucharist. "C'mon, let's dust."

"No," Eucharist said, placing his arm around Hargie's shoulders. "You're learning. Ask more."

Hargie tried to budge, but Eucharist's arm was firm, if friendly.

"Why'd you kill?" he asked Zo.

"Duty," Zo said. "Konsensus knows best. Knew when I was a baby. That I'd be good. Good at killing. And lying. Lying to the already-dead."

"No..." Hargie shrugged. "I mean what do you get out of it? Personally?"

"Duty," Zo said.

"No, I mean... fuck it, why? Why enjoy... what you do?"

Zo giggled. Her dainty nose twitched.

"No one ever ask you that before?" Hargie said.

"No. But..." She looked like a little girl working out a big math sum. "I feel... me. Feel complete. In my body." She shook her head and smiled. "And that's how I'll feel when I kill you, Worlder. Dead man." Her eyebrows knit into fierce angles then, her expression a placid lake with a beast looming to its surface. "Remember that."

Hargie cracked a fake smile and blew out smoke. It rolled across the glass.

"I remember your own boss sold you out," he told her. "Wonder how you feel about that."

She said nothing, kept her smile. Behind her, the other Spindlies shuffled and looked over at Hargie and Eucharist. Vict, still with that filthy hand over his mouth, shut his eyes tight.

"I killed an ickle-little girl on Calran," Zo said. "Part of plan to capture you, capture dead woman. Emissary's orders." That thing when you stared at an upside down face too long and it didn't even look human anymore: Hargie had it now, looking at Zo. "Quick. To the head. More being inefficient. But I gutted her after. All over the bed. Around the necks of her dolls. I bit off her nose."

"What?" Hargie tried to step back, but Eucharist held him in place.

"Diversion," Zo said. "Look like local killer." She giggled again. "But pretty. A pretty thing to make."

"Ratshit," Hargie said.

"Am I putting pain in you, dead man? Tell me. I've made people end themselves. Block neuralware, control it and all their friends hate them and they end themselves." She giggled, but this time it curdled to a moan. "Does it hurt you? Me killing ickle-little girl? Am I... mmm... am I making pain? Uh, in you? Hurt?"

Her upside-down face creased with delight, her alien eyes screwed tight. Hargie realised he couldn't see where her other hand was. The other Spindlies began to cheer.

"Huuurt," Zo said. "Hurt you?"

"Cut this!" Hargie yelled at Eucharist. "End it, you fuck!"

"Hurt you?" Zo said. "Hurt you? Pain, p-paiiiiin, uh, hurt, paiiii—"

"Stop it!"

The glass went black. Eucharist let go.

Hargie had to steady his own breathing. Panic attack. Hadn't had one since, since he was a kid.

He breathed deep. He'd dropped his smoke. He squatted to pick it up, but his fingers shook. The smoke just rolled around. He sank onto his ass.

"I am sorry, my boy," Eucharist said. "Truly. You had to see this."

"F—"

"This is how these people are," Eucharist said.

"Not all like her..."

"They use her," Eucharist said. "They are happy to use her as an instrument of foreign policy. Does that strike you as the action of a humane people? A decent people? No, no, boy. By condoning her, they are all her."

"Fuh..." Concentrate on the breathing. Concentrate.

"You think your 'empathic rationalism' can account for her?" Eucharist asked. "For them? It is a noose around your thinking, around your neck. It will not survive the coming age. Deep down you know this, Hargie Stukes. Zo and Melid and Vict and the Nukes shall inherit. Users like Sparkle Savard shall inherit. Not you. Not your kindness. Their time is coming." Hargie felt a palm slam into his back. "Grow up," Eucharist's voice said.

That girl, Hargie thought, *that poor fucking girl.* His vision blurred. Dammit. Dammit, he was weeping.

"You're right," Hargie said, his face already in his hands. "You're right."

MELID DIRECTED BOTH serv-units, her own and Sparkle Savard's, dead centre through the agri-cavern. Faster, the winds singing in her ears, lashing her face, the serv's limbs tight around her body. Melid had not done this since she was a child. Life with the Instrum precluded that manner of thing.

Was that what Silvercloud's modified kollective offered? Guiltless trivialities? Could such things really be of any worth? Melid was startled to find she wasn't sure anymore.

Below, other servs tended the paddy levels, many of them operated by Utile-citizens not present within the cavern, perhaps lolling about in a fuck-core, working as they made love. Those who chose to be present weren't visible from this height, their distant forms lost among the crops and obscured by mist.

She looked ahead to her right at the serv-unit carrying Sparkle. *Strange*, Melid thought, having to do that. With a Kollective connection, she wouldn't have to look.

Sparkle's arms were outstretched, her fingers splayed. Overjoyed. So incongruous with her earlier demeanour when the serv had lifted her into the air. So resolved then, so carefree now.

Melid concentrated, and Sparkle's serv rotated over. She could see the Worlder's mouth widen with alarm. Sparkle drew in her arms. But then she grinned, clearly delighted by the shock of it, a landscape below that was only moments ago above. Melid smiled too. She couldn't help it.

Sparkle stretched her arms out once more. *A bird*, thought Melid, soaring, as in the old visuals of Earth. A crow.

Melid ceased smiling.

She twisted her serv around and accelerated, matching with Sparkle's. The air howled through her senses. She gazed down on the same fields as Sparkle, but they didn't see the same thing. They never could. The infra-goggles she had given Sparkle could only render a half-truth about this cavern. Melid's vision was superior, more real. Countless genetic modifications over generations had seen to that.

Enough. "I'm taking us in to land," Melid said into a communicator: a primitive device Melid had had to dig out and programme into both servs' memoryforms.

"Absolutely!" came Sparkle's voice, half-soaked in the billowing air. "This is amaaaaazi—"

Melid cut her off. She focused, thrusting their servs toward the wall of the agri-cavern, the ferrous cliff-high band that separated the two landscapes. She couldn't make out Sparkle, obscured by the glow of her serv's jets, but she pictured her fear. Scared little crows-bird.

A horizontal slit of light blinked open in the iron wall, widening to a rectangle. She let the wall's safety protocols take over, and issued a warning to all those citizens beyond the slit that a Worlder approached. She attached a sentiment of alien horror—an amalgamation of her emotional reactions on first encountering these outsiders—to the warning. Melid was certain they would land in an empty installation. Within seconds, the Kollective verified that intuition.

They flew through the entrance, decelerating as they did so. Beyond lay the extrusion-spheres.

"This," Melid said into her serv's communicator, "is where our food comes from." If Sparkle's reaction was in any way vocalised, Melid didn't hear it. Melid had already cut her off.

The extrusion sphere was a quarter mile in diameter, an orb's interior plated with hexagonal graphene tiles. Every second row of tiles had a circle cut into its centre, each the rim of an inbuilt vat. The gelatinous contents of each glistened under red lights.

Melid could see and hear the many utiles migrating toward the far hemisphere, away from the approaching Worlder. Their servs remained, attending to and darting between the protein vats.

Melid and Sparkle's own serv-forms landed on the nearer hemisphere's equator band, near a vat full of blue food. The servs uprighted themselves and released the two females from their uncurling limbs. Melid stepped onto the graphene floor and Sparkle, seeing her, did likewise.

Sparkle was grinning. Then she looked down, looked back up again, and her expression had altered entirely. She had the resolved look from earlier, when they had stood on the ledge overlooking the paddy fields. Strange how Worlders could shift like that. A terrifying unpredictability.

"How do I—" Sparkle started to ask. Before she could finish, her feet were already stepping off the ground.

"How do you walk here?" Melid replied. She hid her smirk. Worlders were all about the face. "Like this."

She concentrated, and a row of handgrips on silver pillars emerged from the floor next to Sparkle. Melid did the same for her own immediate space.

"Whichever direction you take, the handgrips will rise to meet you," Melid said. "Of course, being... worldbound... you may not have the upper body strength. The serv can carry you if—"

"I'm fine, thank you," Sparkle snapped. "I've been practising zero-g."

"I see." Where she could possibly be practising zero-g movement since she'd been here was a mystery to Melid. Sparkle had been consigned to the gravity rooms of the installation.

And yet she was good. Not Konsensus-good, but more than capable, bounding from one handrail to the next.

"Where?" Melid said.

"What?"

"Where have you been practising? How?"

Sparkle frowned. She thought about it for some time. "Press-ups," she replied. "Builds upper body strength. You should try it."

Melid accessed 'press-ups' in records. "Not much call for them around here."

Sparkle shrugged. "You mentioned food," she said. "You wanted to show me Konsensus delicacies."

"Delicacies?" Melid said. A Worlder word. She had to look it up. "Yes, I did, didn't I?"

Sparkle gave her a funny sort of look, and Melid realised her own face was giving her away again.

"Follow me," Melid said.

She glided, hand to hand, toward the vat with the blue food inside it. She concentrated on a pipe that jutted out of the side of the great rim. A sucrose-silk bubble emerged from its end, soon filled by blue jelly.

Melid gripped the bubble and twisted. It broke off, perfectly sealed, and she threw it in the direction of her guest. "Catch."

Sparkle caught the bubble. She squeezed and inspected it. "What is this stuff?"

"Our finest mucus," Melid replied. That wasn't true. No one called it *mucus*, but she wanted to see the look on the Worlder's face. She wasn't disappointed.

"Mucus?"

"Blue mucus," Melid said. "Happy eating."

Sparkle kept gawping at the thing. "What... what's it made from?"

"The raw material is amino-acids from local comets and such. But the stem-recipe is ancient as Earth. Insect flesh."

"Insect?"

"Perfect for our ancestors'protein needs." Melid said. "And easily replicated."

"Right. Fine..."

Sparkle stared at the sucrosilk bubble. Silence, but for the churning of the vats.

"There is a perforation," Melid explained. 'You place your mouth over it and—'

'Yes, yes, fine.' Sparkle kept staring at it. She took a breath. "Bear with me one moment."

She stared into the air before her, her eyes wide behind the goggles, and, for the slightest moment, Melid believed the Worlder would pass out. But no. A grin came, a shift in every muscle of her being. She bit into the bubble and drank like the famished. The bubble soon emptied.

"Mmm," Sparkle said, tiny blue spheres passing from her lips. "Got any more?"

Remarkable. This woman was the most... Worlderish of Worlders. Each action defied her last. Melid twisted around and headed toward the vat once more. For a moment she felt an odd sensation, a ripple in the Kollective. It vanished before it really arrived.

Awake too long. Melid poured another bubble. A child screamed.

A scream with no connection. Melid spun about, scrabbling at the hand-pillars. A male child, eight or ten, falling backwards into a cartwheel. Connected now, Melid could feel his terror, the fight or flight.

Terror at Sparkle. Sparkle lurched toward him, handrail to handrail, her movements spasmodic, untrained. Unnatural. Her profile was vicious, lips stretched, teeth bared.

Melid issued a warning to Sparkle. Stupid: how could a dead woman heed that?

Melid gripped two handrails and propelled herself at Sparkle, a bullet of bone and flesh. She circled her arms around Sparkle's centre, shoulder connecting with her ribcage. Sparkle yelled.

"Swurrr! Hel—" but it muffled as Melid grasped at the Worlder's face. Stink of perfume, otherness. Another grasp, and the goggles were off. They hit something: the rim of another vat.

"What are you doing?" Melid asked.

A roar filled her ears. Struggling with Sparkle, she looked up to see a serv carry away the child. Melid blocked out his terror. Others would take care of him.

As the roar became distant, a calm came over Sparkle. "It's fine," she said. "Fine. She was trying to help."

"What?"

"*I* was trying to help," Sparkle said. "Help the boy."

"You scared him," Melid said. "All you could ever do."

"HMM..." SWIRL HEARD Melid say. They were floating in the elevator, down, down into the secret installation.

"What is it?" Swirl asked.

"Another bubbleship's arrived," Melid said. "Docking right now."

"A bubbleship?" Swirl righted herself against the elevator wall. Her zero-g was more instinctive now, less thought-out. "Who's arriving? Who knows about this place?"

"Sung Eucharist," Melid said, and she eyed Swirl like she was an idiot. The infrared of the goggles made it clear in the manner of some abstract painting. "I believe this bubbleship is for his extraction."

"Of course."

Of course. Sparkle would have pointed that out, highlighted Swirl's slowness. Melid was almost a surrogate Sparkle. She was in the villa, utterly upset. The incident with the boy had genuinely shocked her.

"He'll miss the Kharmund," Swirl said.

"Yes," Melid said. "He typically does."

Swirl would have asked more, but the elevator came to a stop and the doors hissed.

"Take the goggles off," Melid told her. "You are accustomed to the light beyond."

Swirl did so, placing them in her trouser pocket. She couldn't see.

The doors opened to reveal the corridor of the habitation space they'd stayed in.

"Careful," Melid said. "Gravity kicks in at the threshold."

The pair of them crossed it with scant dignity: Swirl into her milieu, Melid out of hers. They had to hold each other's wrists in the fight for stability. Neither noticed at first. When they did, they let go and said nothing.

Hargie and Eucharist were in the main lounge: Hargie sat on one side of the game table, Eucharist stood by the other. He wore his long coat.

"Leaving us so soon?" Swirl asked.

"Business on Luharna." Eucharist turned his head and smiled. "A miserable duty," he said, "when one must part from such"—he waved his hand in the air, then found the word—"provocative ladies."

"Spare me," Swirl said.

"Space me," Melid added.

Eucharist chortled. Those strange chrome eyes of his glinted under the halogen lights.

"The truth is, I cannot wait," he said. "The next reconnection would mean I'd have to hide here for the next nine days. I'm a businessman. One whose employees are best not left idle."

"Ain't that the truth," Hargie said. He pulled out his cigarette packet, checked the contents, but didn't take one out.

"Melid," Eucharist said, "I would be obliged if you showed me to the docking bay. Your hatchways do not oblige Worlders."

"Best that way," Melid said.

"Hey, Sung," Hargie said. "You lied."

"Did I, now?"

"Said you'd see us to the other side of this," Hargie said.

Eucharist shrugged. "I'm only human."

"Don't exaggerate."

Eucharist chuckled again and then looked at the unfinished game on the table. In a single move he took Hargie's Emperor piece. He picked it up.

"Move like an Emperor," he told Hargie, "think like an Emperor." He placed the piece into the breast pocket of Hargie's jacket and patted it. "That'll see you through. It has for me."

"You're a fucking education," Hargie said.

"Emperors always are."

With that, Eucharist made his way to the threshold.

"Look after him," he told Swirl. "Whoever you are."

Swirl said nothing. Eucharist followed Melid out and down the corridor.

Hargie just sat there, hands on the table, staring at his knuckles. Her body's very presence unnerved him, she realised. She didn't know what to say. His life was so small compared to the great event. It wasn't a lack of empathy Swirl felt, but an inability to compare scales.

"I'd better get ready," she said. She turned to go.

"Sparkle." He barely finished the word.

She turned around. "Yes?"

He looked up. He studied her. His eyes were redder than she'd ever seen them. Shadowed sockets.

"Doesn't matter," he said. "You got your business front on."

"No, please," she said. "I want to hear."

"Be careful with these assholes," he said.

"I know."

"And... be happy. I just want you to be happy." He broke from her gaze and searched for his cigarettes. He took one out this time. Lit it. "Doesn't matter."

It came to Swirl then. An immense sympathy for this feral, this cornered beast.

His words were saccharine, barely articulate. But Swirl knew his pain. Had known it at Lyreko's death, almost.

"Thank you," Swirl said. She coughed. "I've got to prepare now."

"Sure."

She strode toward her sleeping quarters.

WRAPPED IN A SERV-UNIT'S limbs as it gently propelled him through a milieu he'd never be able to traverse on his own, Sung Eucharist never lost his dignity. Never lost control. Melid, gliding down the corridor beside him, had to admire that.

"It was you, was it not?" she asked him.

"Be specific, Emissary," he replied.

"The message. The doll."

"I do not understand," Eucharist said. "You're too specific now."

"You lie," she said.

"I wouldn't have thought Konsensites experts in that regard."

"I'm an..." She searched for the Worlder phrase. "Eager amateur. We're quite safe, Eucharist. I can block the Silvercloud kollective to an extent I'd never grasped until now. If I concentrate, I can even block direct interest."

They turned a corner. "How can you be certain?"

"You sent a message informing the Instrum—me particularly—that Silvercloud is actively involved in betrayal." She paused. "See? I don't hear the rumble of approaching servs, do you?"

"Interesting," he said.

They were silent until they reached the hatchway to his bubbleship's docking tube. The pair of them came to a stop.

"There's a card in my coat's pocket there," Eucharist said. "You'll forgive me: I cannot currently reach it myself."

Melid let out a long breath. She reached in and took it. The card, cream-coloured and dappled, had a long series of binary upon it.

"After you finish up here," Eucharist said, "broadcast on that signature. I shall answer many questions then."

"Why not now?"

"Because those questions are not apparent now," he said. "I can say no more." The hatchway doors stretched open. "You can let me go now. I can swim the tube well enough."

Melid kept him there, wrapped in those black tentacles.

"I've watched you since I was a child," she said. "I suspect you the worst human in the galaxy."

He looked struck by the suggestion. "Promotion."

"What?"

"Once, I was the worst human in the world."

Gibberish. She wouldn't dignify him with questions. She caused the serv's limbs to unravel, and watched that uniquely infuriating man clamber into the blackness of the tube.

SPARKLE CHIPPED AT the new block, finding form within the basalt. The sun hung high behind her, baking her neck. Sea salt in her nostrils. Sea salt and dust.

The sculpture would be of the boy, with a frieze behind him of the titanic paddy levels. She hadn't encountered the boy there, of course, but the two images had merged in her aesthetic instincts if not her actual memory.

Basalt was hard. You had to work against basalt. The tides whispered as she chipped. They hissed. Sparkle would carve the boy's face at the moment their eyes locked, his face placid. Before...

She'd never guessed she could have put so much fear into someone, so much pain. It had marked her. Sparkle knew herself well and it had marked her, chipped at her substance. Perhaps her more than the boy. So far, the exact nature of this marking eluded her.

"Sister."

She looked to her right, where the jetty met the beach. Swirl stood there, an avatar of the waves with her blue hair and blue shift.

"Sister," Sparkle replied. She smiled. "It's time, yes?"

"We should prepare."

"Naturally." She looked at the basalt block. "I hope I get to finish this."

"You will." Swirl walked closer, up the jetty toward her. "What's it going to be?"

"I don't know yet," Sparkle said.

"What happened to the other statues?" Swirl asked. "The sacred things?"

"Dissolved, I think. Hoidrac touch made them too wonderful to last for long." She sniffed. "I suppose that's wonder for you."

"I suppose." Swirl was silent for a moment. The breeze pressed her dreads tight against the right side of her face. It looked like a thick brushstroke. "Hargie—"

"What's that fuckhead say now?" Sparkle's own anger surprised her.

Swirl paused a moment, then shook her head. "Nothing," she said. "He's said nothing at all. I just thought I should tell you he's prepping *Princess*. If need be, we'll have the option to go. After..."

"The Great Encounter."

"Good term," Swirl said. "Like it."

Sparkle dropped her tool and wandered up to her sister.

"Actually, while we're in here..." She stopped, thought. "Actually, what's our alibi right now? What are we saying we're doing?"

"Toilet," Swirl said.

"Again? Ah, forget it. Look, don't you think it's strange: that boy's terror?"

"No," Swirl said. "We're like walking cadavers to these people. Poor whelp's scarred for life."

"Thanks." Sparkle closed her eyes. "I know." She opened them once more. "What I mean is, how come he wasn't warned? They're all connected."

"The Silvercloud kollective is different," Swirl said.

"Not that different. Never so unique. They couldn't afford to be: the silence would break them, from what I can gather. And Melid sent out a warning, remember? Even if the boy was being irresponsible..."

"An adult would have stepped in." Swirl frowned. "So what are you saying?"

"There's something going on we're not aware of," Sparkle said. "We haven't got the... receivers."

"That's paranoid."

"You can see it in their faces," Sparkle said. "It's their weak spot. Every strength has a weak spot. They don't fixate on faces like we do. Their faces are almost a... vestigial organ, I suppose. Almost. A balancing tail at best."

"I've noticed that," Swirl said.

She'd have made a good Konsensite, Swirl. Her expressions were immensely readable. Her wants. Sparkle knew she was hiding something.

Yet inconsequential, whatever it was. Survival mattered now.

"Come on," Sparkle told her. "Let's go outside and play."

Fifteen

TWO MINUTES THIRTY. The control-core was alive with excitement. It kept pulsing into trepidation and back again, a Mobius strip of heightened sensation. In the core were Melid, Kend, and three other Utiles. Melid swam about, watching, trying not to get in the way. She had no use here save as an observer.

She had much to observe. Astoundingly, the Utiles were using terminals, actual terminals as of ancient times. Kend had explained that these were a safety measure: in an encounter with the wholly unknown, you could rely on nothing. Simplicity was best. It worried Melid, that. Worried the others too, though they'd had long to adjust to the implications. They certainly knew how to use the terminals, which were by any reckoning peculiar things: muscleform growths that bloomed out of the spaces between the wall's vertical ribbing. They made a *click-clack* sound as their users darted fingers over their interface boards. Their screens radiated a serene and purplish light.

"Long time no-seen Scalpel," Melid announced to the core. "Excited."

The others mirrored her sentiment, then focused on their work. It wasn't like Melid to say something out loud like that. But she was in two minds, absorbed with two things, and she would rather draw attention to the first than the second.

The child. Oum: that was his name. The child's terror had been immense. Melid had had to block it out at the time. She still did. It occurred to her that Worlders never felt such horror.

But none of that was the thought she was trying to obscure.

The population of Silvercloud had immediately wanted answers, and were immediately obliged. A fault in the secret kollective's programming, no one anticipating a Worlder presence ever being in the extrusion-sphere. Kend had taken responsibility, being the last surviving architect of the programme and the individual who had first heard Sparkle's request for a guided tour. Her contrition had shone genuine and stark throughout Silvercloud. Everyone had soothed her: no individual could be blamed. Silvercloud had set upon their experiment as one. It would cling to its mistakes as one.

Lies, ironics. Melid knew it.

She knew it because Kend was too good a tech-utile, too thorough a mind. And Melid knew it because she herself could lie. She could keep things, keep big, dangerous things—doubts, questions—from her fellow Silverclouders. Her time among Worlders had afforded her this. The possibility had always existed, perhaps, but she had had no concept before.

She looked about the small core: not a hint, not the tiniest hint in any of the Utiles around her, whether physical or emotic, that her current thoughts even affected them.

Kend: gazing at her terminal as if it contained some baby galaxy, her face lit lilac in its haze. She knew, too. Perhaps she had programmed the hidden kollective that way, or Eucharist had convinced her, or... no, more likely she had stumbled upon it, been transfixed as any scientist might, explored and noted the possibilities. Yes, Kend alone. This was her kollective. That thought, so alien and obscene, chilled Melid.

Kend looked at her.

Melid tensed. She smiled back.

"Come," Kend said. No emotic accompanied the word.

Melid held down her fears, smothered them in expectation of the Scalpels. Excited, she was excited. Giddy. She made her way to Kend using the floor hooks below her.

"Beside me," Kend said. "Lie along. Watch terminal."

Melid did so, their shoulders and hips touching one another.

"Excited," Melid said, as if that word might hide the confusion of thoughts within her.

"Calm," Kend said. "Look."

Melid gazed at the terminal. Sparkle stood in the laboratory, looking down at the body-long device she would soon climb into. She was like a mourner, sombre before a translucent sarcophagus. Hargie and Yan stood some feet away.

"Sparkle, please climb in," Kend said suddenly in Anglurati. On the screen the Worlder woman looked around. "Yan, Hargie, time to leave."

"A moment." Sparkle's voice, weak and hollow over the terminal.

"Quickly, please." Kend blinked and the screen changed: a series of images of deep space. One of the images showed Silvercloud itself, its trail of icy vapour falling into the void forever. The Wolf-Rayet star lurked behind it.

"How many probes?" Melid asked.

"Not probes," Kend said, issuing a teasing delight. "Feel out."

Melid closed her eyes and did so. Out beyond Silvercloud, within its orbit, were some hundred citizens. Of course: probes and serv-units would have only provided a blur when the Scalpel arrived. The eyes of another, shared through the Kollective, would provide a vision of the Scalpels comparable to seeing for yourself, almost.

"Dangerous," Melid said.

"Worth risk."

Melid had to agree.

Five minutes.

A peculiar sort of sentiment emanated from Kend as they both registered the time. A shyness, a tender fear. Melid emoted concern, curiosity.

Kend registered it, yet kept her eyes on the screen. "Thinking. Have... thought." She bit her lip.

"What?"

"You-me," Kend said. "Since return. Feeling change."

"No," Melid said. Kend had detected her. "No. Still same. Still Melid."

Kend smiled, closed her eyes. "No. Melid, soon mind-wipe, soon end hidden kollective. Last days lost. Want say... feelings. Want say important." She shrugged. "Important to me."

"What say?"

Kend craned her head toward Melid in what seemed the most difficult struggle. She met her eyes. "Pair. Want you, me... fond-partners."

Like a kick from nowhere. "Partner?"

"Mmm." No words from Kend, but her emotics were a crackle of delicate, feathery static. The terror of asking, the agony of hope. Genuine.

"Yan..." Melid said, still processing. She felt the others in the room pick up on the emotic singularity between them.

"No Yan," Kend said. Melid could feel the heat of her body, the scent of her skin this close. "Love Yan friend, but. You. You... understand."

Melid laughed at the suddenness. "Why now?"

"Before lost. Before..." she shook her head. "Please, Melid. Please... think."

Too much. The Scalpels, the conspiracies. Too much. Had this been the truth Kend had obscured, that Melid had sensed and sensed wrong? She had no comparison. No one had ever wanted to partner with Melid, to share everything in life. Not even Illik, and Melid had hated him for it, she could see that now. Inside the Kollective-at-Large, Melid had existed at the perimeters of others, a stranger to truest needs. Melid of Silvercloud, Field-Emissary, had never consummated.

Her vision watered, and she hated herself for it. Either Kend was playing her like a puppet, an Arclight Annie, or... the dirt Melid had accrued from wading in Worlder filth had ruined her, had left her unable to trust this beautiful human, this moment. This ache...

"Please..." Kend whispered, barely a breath.

"Want..." It came. "Think... want." And she did. She felt her lips quiver.

"Come." Kend reached out and cradled Melid's head. She emoted the promise of all at Melid, a yielding, embracing all. And they had but minutes, no luxury of hours or days for this consummation. A binding promise. Yet seconds to bind, to tether their ids and egos in briefest ouroboros. To matter to someone.

She looked at Kend's face. She stopped herself. "Wait."

"No," Kend said, "you want. Please now." She stroked Melid's shoulders, caressed her hip with the inside of her thigh. "Please."

"Listen." Melid tried to smile. She emoted all the affection she could. "Want this, but not here-now. Not panicked." She leant in and placed light kisses upon Kend's neck. She felt a vein beneath the smoothness beat rapidly. "But..." Kiss. "Promise." Kiss.

Kend moaned almost silently. "Promise?"

Two minutes remaining. Melid placed her mouth upon Kend's lower lip and sucked gently. Their auras crackled with sexual and mental potency.

Melid let go of Kend's lip, kept her mouth there.

"Watch Scalpel now," she muttered. "Watch history." She reached a hand to one of Kend's own, and they linked fingers. "Together."

Kend smiled. The pair of them looked toward the screen of the antiquated terminal. Kend watched with a new expectation, an alloy of curiosity and joy.

Melid did her best to mirror it. Kend was a liar, a brilliant one. A thought so desolate now, cold as an hour-old tear. Melid tried not to think of it at all. She had so nearly fallen for it. Yet she had seen the lie, the slightest thing, in Kend's face. Like a Worlder might.

But why?

SPARKLE SMILED AND nodded at the two men. She tried not to look nervous.

"Sparkle, please climb in." Kend's voice over some unseen speaker, startling Sparkle. "Yan, Hargie, time to leave."

"A moment, please," she said aloud to the air.

The thing before her looked like death, a cellophane shroud beneath the halogen lights. Time to climb inside...

"Good... luck," she heard Yan say. His Anglurati was poor.

Sparkle nodded, never looking up. "Oh, I've got this," she said.

She didn't have this. And all *she* had to do was climb in to the shroud and close her eyes. Swirl was already in the Villa meditating. Preparing herself. Her...

Her—come on, Sparkle, just admit it—utterly insane self. What was the term Hargie always used? Bat-ladder? Yes, events had turned Swirl into an entire stockroom of flying mammal-themed utilities. What manner of zealot believed they could wave hello at a Hoidrac—a Kharmund rider, no less, a bloody Kharmund—and expect a hello back, let alone a lift back home?

She took the cylinder out of her coat, her hand shaking, opened it. She bit down on a leaf, an entire leaf. Whyever not? Go with the theme, Sparkle, mm-yes, go with it. High-foot this ballet of suicidal-grade stupid to its logical crescendo. How had she let this happen? How had she fooled herself that her insane, fundamentalist, physically abusive sister was the lone golden path to survival? There was no path to survival. Not here, not—

"Hey," Hargie said.

Sparkle yelped, spat leaf ichor down her front.

"What?" Hargie said.

"I thought you'd fucked off with laughing boy!" She took deep breaths. "Fuck's sake..."

"Been standing right here."

"Trying to concentrate," she said. "You're... a distraction."

"I'm gone," he said. "I just wanted—"

She looked up and he stopped talking. His lips went tight, and he turned around toward the door. She had a sudden hatred for the back of his jacket, the angle of his fucking hat.

"A distraction," she said to him. "That's all."

He left. She wiped her chin and gazed at the shrouded tube.

"Now, please," Kend's voice said. It made Sparkle jump again, a little.

"Yes," she said. "Yes."

She stepped around to the entry end of the shroud and bent down. As she placed her palms on its inner gurney, the leaf kicked in. The air around the rim of the entry seemed to warp, sucking in all motion and vitality. A halo of ethereal fangs, gateway to an underworld.

She braced herself and climbed in. The sterile air inside shot down her nostrils, degraded her throat. She should have took her coat off, she realised. Too hot. Slowly, so sluggishly, she rolled over onto her back, the tail of her coat wrapping around her legs as she did so. She took the pipe beside her head and shoved it in her mouth. Leaf sap dripped in.

Close your eyes, she told herself. *Soon sleep, soon you'll be...*

...standing on the beach.

The loopy-scoops had been a mistake. Not made for sand, those shoes. She blinked. They didn't vanish. Her subconscious had clearly become attached to them.

She stumbled toward the villa, an ache growing in her ankles as she struggled not to tumble on the yielding grains beneath. With so much leaf, the villa became impossibly real. The reality she had just left—the corridors of Silvercloud—seemed almost abstract, a cartoon.

But the sky was wrong. There were clouds, there was the sun, but all of that seemed like a reflection on the surface of a shallow pond or lake. Real enough when she looked at it, but if she looked through it, the lakebed, with all its reeds and pebbles, became apparent.

Behind the sky rose a vast cavern of muscleform, that uniquely Konsensus material. Night-black and plastic: black mesh, black studs, black spines that arched the world. A thousand red lights blinked in its firmament, carrying unguessable data. The softer parts of this biomechanical abyss, Sparkle noted, seemed to breathe, though that may have been due to the translucent sky beneath. Whichever, she had taken too much leaf.

She pressed on toward the villa, to her sister. This was no time to be alone.

"A DISTRACTION," HARGIE heard her say as he left the lab. "At best."

Almost snarled, that last part. He wanted to turn around, chew her ears up. He didn't. This was her scene. What she did now mattered, for him and everyone else. Say nothing.

The Spindly man with the beard, Yan, waited on the other side of the door. Hargie had to crane his neck back to meet his eyes.

"Hey there," Hargie said.

Yan barely nodded.

"We go wait in the quarters, yeah?" Hargie asked.

"I wait here."

Hargie nodded. He thought about that. "I'll wait here too."

Maybe Yan was their tap and 'lock man. Maybe when Sparkle finished up, Yan's job was to finish her up, space her corpse. Tap and 'lock Hargie, too. Given the last few days, Hargie was oddly okay with half that. He just wasn't sure which half.

"Yes," Yan said eventually.

"Okay, then."

Had that been a reply to Hargie? Maybe a reply in his head to all his Spindly dicks. Hargie wished Eucharist was still around. The Emperor piece from their game was still in Hargie's jacket pocket. It was made of that black stuff the Konsensus made everything out of. Must have got them to knock out a set for him. He had a way like that, Eucharist. A way that got his self-loving ass out of here and left his compadres choking.

He looked up. Yan was staring at him. *Punch him in the balls*, Hargie thought. Things get heated: bang! Full-square in the daddy-shack. Had to hurt there, even for Spindlies.

No, stupid. Men don't drop when you strike between their legs. Adrenalin sees them through, they handle agony later.

Yan still stared, right through Hargie.

The jaw. That was the smart money. Pop a jaw and even the Foozle would drop.

Shit turned, Hargie would go for Yan's jaw. If he could reach it.

Shit. Yan was wide-eyed. Angry-looking. Shit, what was Hargie thinking? This Spindly could break him. And even if Hargie won, where could he go? They'd probably throw him in a pit with the hell bitch Zo.

Yan's face went funny. He started to cry.

"Erm... Yan?"

Yan looked at Hargie and tried to stop himself. He only wept more.

Hargie hadn't planned for this.

NO SCALPEL. AN HOUR had passed. The room, all Silvercloud's kollective, crackled with an intensity.

"Maybe no come?" Melid said to Kend.

"Always come," Kend replied, "must come."

Kend flicked through the terminal's series of images, though much of it she could have seen with her own kollectivised consciousness. The terminal had become a sort of fetish. There was less and less to cling to as time passed. In an hour, reconnection would occur. At least the last twenty minutes of that would be needed to cover Silvercloud's tracks: reprogram, clean up, hide the Worlders.

Forty minutes, then. Everyone felt it.

"Where?" Kend barked, punching the terminal. The flash of rage went right through Melid. Through the core. Kend stared at the screen once more, her shoulder blades rolling with her breaths.

Melid noticed blood pool between Kend's knuckles. Melid reached out and gently inspected Kend's hand. No lasting damage.

"No more," Kend muttered. "End now. Want... end lies." She winced at the final word, the foreign word. "Find truth."

A brave sort of misery emanated from Kend, like a fabled animal of old Earth. Injured, lame, yet still circling, still ready. Melid could feel her old friend emote that same offer of consummation, but coy this time, a pretence at an unconscious slip.

Melid ignored it. Better yet, she faked a yearning followed by a powerful self-control.

Where had truth vanished to in this place? she wondered. Had it ever even existed?

SPARKLE FOUND SWIRL in her shell-blue music room. She sat atop the grand haspichol at the far end, cross-legged upon its lacquered maple lid. She wasn't meditating, though. She was eating an apple.

"Hello," Sparkle said.

Swirl wore a blue ball gown. Unlike her. A beam of sunlight from a window above lay between the sisters. Dust rolled on within the beam like generations of stars, like lives.

Swirl smiled. No tension in her body. Quite relaxed.

"Apple?" Swirl offered a fresh one to Sparkle. It had appeared in her hand, out of nowhere. Things often did in the villa.

Sparkle walked closer, stopped just before the the ray of falling sunlight. She shook her head.

"Really, sister," Swirl said after taking another bite. "I wonder if there's ever been a fruit you like."

Sparkle thought about this. "Wine," she said.

Swirl chuckled. A chunk of apple rolled down her chin. "You're adorable. But you really should eat better."

"That's your job," Sparkle said. "I'm alcohol duty."

Swirl considered the matter and took another bite.

"I must say," Sparkle said, "I'd never have expected you quite this... calm." She shrugged. "Not ever. Especially not now."

"Perhaps I've reached a plateau," Swirl said. "The struggle and the tension are over." She eyed her sister. "And now I look down. Do you understand?"

"Not really."

"Climb up here," Swirl said. "Sit with me."

"They haven't arrived yet," Sparkle said. "We're broadcasting. Why haven't they arrived?"

"Oh, they have," Swirl said.

"You can feel them?"

"Certainly. Can't you?"

Yes. There had been a change in the air. Or something. Sparkle felt a chill rise in her. She wanted to sit next to her sister. Somehow that seemed safest.

She moved toward the haspichol. She crossed the beam of light and the dust stung her cheek. Sparkle gasped, staggered back, cradled her face. A feeling of increasing bliss, of womb-lost pleasure, rose on her face. She winced.

The dress. Just like Pheoni's dress.

Sparkle gazed up at her sister. The beam of light obscured Swirl's eyes. But a grin was visible: it stretched wide. Sweet juice flowed from Swirl's teeth, her lips shining with its glaze.

Sixteen

"YAN..."

The Spindly must have been pure water, way he was crying. He'd been pouring out salty for, what? Half an hour? The guy was on his ass now, long legs and arms all buckled like a broken insect.

"Yan, man..." Totally outta tune, this guy. Hargie thought about putting a hand on Yan's shoulder. But how might he react? Regular people were corpses to these creatures. "Yan... look, I'm scared too. We're all scared. But Kend's got this figured, right? They got this..."

Yan winced at her name, kept sobbing.

"Ah," Hargie said. "Woman, huh?"

Yan's red eyes darted upwards for the slightest. Then he got right back to weeping.

"Fucking knew it." Hargie whistled, took out his last cigarette. Fuck it. "Guys like us, man, we're too good. Open up our chests and get our pumps ripped out. Then they run. Game's rigged, tune?" He lit the smoke with his finger. "Game's rigged."

Hargie took that damn fine hit, breathed out. "Know what? Fuck her. Fuck her, Yan. She's the loser. Never deserved you. Oh, oh, and just wait, Yan. Just wait till she meets the next guy, I mean some *real* asshole. Tells her everything she wants to hear, all smiles and lies, then burns her. She'll know what she threw away then, Yan." Sharp toke, breathe out. "But then it's too late. She can't have you back. Because you've got pride, Yan. You fly tall, tune? Pride." Hargie shook his head. "You never needed anyone. Never did. And, fuck, she ain't that fine. She ain't all that." He took a drag. Long and nasty. "Fly tall."

Yan's eyes met his.

"Stop talking," Yan said.

"Sure," Hargie said. "You're in a bad place." He shrugged. "I see that."

The lights flickered out. A flash of blue. Weird light, the same as the energy on the rig when Illik had exploded. They came back on again.

"Shit."

THE SCALPEL! THE SCALPEL!

At once, Melid knew the Scalpel had been there some time. Or, at least, some part of it had been, watching from a realm unknown, peering in. Its essence had been around them, seeping in unnoticed until the Scalpel's true manifestation made it obvious, undeniable. A hum long there. Below register.

The emotion hit first. A vast swoon, beginning in the awareness of each watcher, each brave pair of eyes floating in the void, each pouring into the tributary of Silvercloud's kollective and on, one tide, one wave crashing into Melid's senses. Beauty, such beauty. Oh, so... oh!

The shockwave receded and Melid could visualise, could see as she closed her eyes. A Great Sail, type 2-A. Her lips twitched, mouthing words she didn't even register. A kilometer high, its slender, arched and serpentine form trailed winds of time, this universe's quantum foam torn and boiling in the entity's wake. She could hear Kend, galaxies away, sighing. Kend was lost in the Scalpel's beauty. Addicted. Melid barely cared about her.

The Scalpel's snout: tapered and smooth, free of detail, grey. Two sleek horns rose from the head, each trailing past the spinal sail and evaporating into some other dimension. And the sail. The sail! A row of quarter-mile spines descending along the Scalpel's back, membrane between them. Mists billowed from the sail, vapours of Scalpel-light. Of Unreal. Purest geometry. All grey.

"Oh, Hoidrac," she heard Kend whisper. "Oh, Harrrrrmonies..."

Melid flinched. She knew those words. Didn't she? They were... wrong. Somehow wrong. She felt Kend notice her thoughts, dozily fear them.

Before either woman could react more, another explosion came. Another tear in the fabric.

Another Scalpel.

"DON'T YOU LIKE ME, sister?"

"I adore you," Sparkle said, looking down. She was on her knees now. "Delighted One."

"I'm no Hoidrac," came Swirl's voice from the grand haspichol above. "I'm Swirl."

"But my face," Sparkle said. "You... stung my face."

"This mask leaks," Swirl said. "But take heart, sister; no mask is possessed by its wearer. Rather the opposite."

"I don't understand," Sparkle said.

"No."

Sparkle frowned. She felt dreamy. The leaf she'd swallowed. She stared at the tiles before her knees as if they might give an answer. She feared the being, sitting above, falling upon her. Touching her.

"Are we... going home?" Sparkle asked. "To Zahrir?" She gulped, she lied: "Sister."

"Not physically." Sparkle heard the apple core drop nearby. "Impossible without our dear Pearl. The Sliver might erode."

The Sliver? Of course, that piece of Illik inside them. A... blueprint of the Konsensus.

"I see," Sparkle said.

"How much of a believer are you?"

"In what?"

"In our mission, sister," Swirl said. "In the Delighted Ones. In beauty."

"I... can lapse," Sparkle said. "My belief in anything is tidal." She laughed. She wasn't sure why. "You know that, Swirl."

"Sit with me. Up here."

"I'm happy here." Sparkle felt her breath quicken. She felt watched, watched from every direction. "We can awake now. They've probably finished their—"

"Sit with me."

"No," Sparkle said. "I mean, thanks b—"

"You make beautiful sculpture, sister."

"Thank you," Sparkle said.

"Tell me about sculpture. Tell me about lost wax method."

Lost wax method? Sparkle mouthed to the floor. Oh, she knew all about that. Too much, normally bored her siblings with those sort of facts. Too full with uselessness.

"L-lost wax method... is the most ancient, ancient of casting processes," Sparkle said. "Actually. Yes, ancient." She was shaking, she was actually shaking. "A one-shot process. You make a mould—not necessarily of wax, could be plaster, even a force field, I suppose—and you pour the molten bronze, or, or, what have you, and let it cool. Then you..." She gulped, felt her nails dig into her palms. "You chip the mould away. You destroy it. To remove the sculpture within."

A foot swung down from the haspichol above. Slender. Taloned.

"Sit with me."

Sparkle gasped. She dragged herself backwards, loopy-scoops hard against the tiles. The foot was Swirl's again, bare and brown. Sparkle tried to get up, but fell on her bottom. She dragged herself backwards, tiles cold against palms, thighs straining.

Swirl rose from the grand haspichol's lid, the skirt of her blue gown sliding down her legs. The hem never touched the ground. Swirl floated forward, arms wide, dreadlocks undulating as if she were submerged.

"Come," she said. "The Delighted Ones require us. They require us both, Sparkle."

They want the Sliver, Sparkle thought, struggling to her feet. *Just the Sliver. Lost wax method.* Her left scoop snapped. She went over again. Cheap plastic, even in here. The pain of the tiles. She pulled off her shoes and threw them. Not at Swirl, not them. Too scared for that.

"How can you?" Swirl said. "They love us, sister. They elevate us above all humans."

Fuck off. She wanted to scream *fuck off.* But not to the Hoidrac. Evil to think such things.

"No toil, no illness," Swirl said, floating closer. "Everything Harmonic. Every dream yours. Why run? Why ever run?"

No thoughts, just turn, just run. Why consider the blasphemy of running? She spun around toward the exit.

"Always so weak, sister," Swirl said.

Sparkle stumbled from foot to foot and—

Sparkle and Pearl and Swirl so young and skin smooth and dashing down golden beach and noon sun on naked skin and the fun of it the running the thought-dappled joy mm-yes and—

Sparkle's vision shifted between the blue of the music room and the dream saffron of a memory. The beach, the beach by their minds' villa. The visions flickered between one another. But she was running now, she knew it, running for the way out. Concentrate. Concen—

Sparkle behind, always behind, always last allowed, left out, and the splash of the brine was cold between toes at first but warmer as she ran, bath-warm at the knees and the lazy waves slowed her, Swirl leaping and laughing, dark skin baking, chasing Pearl ahead of them all, leading as he liked, muscles marble-white, shining in Sparkle's eyes and wait for Sparkle, wait for Sparkle you two—

Sparkle staggered forward and her palms gripped the doorway's sides. She fell through into the hall, got up, uncertain which way led out. Left, definitely left.

"Don't run," Swirl's voice echoed behind her. "Don't make it like this."

lazy tide stroke thighs, giggles, splashing, warm lurch rising, touching new wisp with a tingle each time and Sparkle was happy to be there, to be a part, to watch them both and Pearl, hey, Pearl, Sparkle points, what's happening what is that happening let me see—

This is what they did, Sparkle thought, her world flickering back to the shaded blue of the long corridor. If you fought, they punched through, found your discomforts, the uncomfortable memories. *Push it out*, she thought. *Keep moving.*

Pearl hunched over like stomach ache, Sparkle worried but Swirl curious and taking command because Swirl was a warrior, stand up, Pearl, stand up and show us and, shaking arms he did and his thing was alive and Swirl laughed, bellowed your serpent's dancing Pearl, a grown up now, a serpent-dance and never asking she grasped it softly, smiling at him so pale and alive—

Sparkle had to crawl-run down the hall. No light ahead. The door to the villa was closed. She hadn't closed it when she'd come in.

Pearl a serious face so sudden and, lip bite, he put pale finger so like his serpent between brown round thighs, caress new black fur—the mirror of Sparkle's, and Sparkle breathed deep to watch, a secret Swirl murmured, just this villa, just here and Sparkle wanted to play, let her—

Sparkle shook her head to free her vision, and her shoulder hit the dark wood of the door. She was at the door. Scrambling hands worked the lock. Come on, come on...

Pearl's hand on Swirl and Swirl's hand on Sparkle and Sparkle's fingers around the serpent's dance and mm-yes no shouting now, breath-heavy and quiet but somehow louder than worlds and tickle, tickle in Sparkle's belly and the lazy waves, booch-shhh, booch-shhhh, booooch-shhhhhhhhh and Pearl's face pained, Sparkle had hurt him, Swirl looking at the water between them like it was a puzzle and a tiny thing, a white thumbnail blossom there, blooming out, diluting, the silence of all three like mourners over a dead thing, then the splash of Pearl turning and running through waves, Swirl's mouth a round O and Sparkle so wrong, so guilty in belly she had hurt him, hurt her brother, ran after him but everything she ever did hurt, only wronged and—

A fist hit her temple. It took a second for Sparkle to realise it was her own. She must have thrown it before she flickered out. The door handle jammed, again, again. But she wasn't thinking: up. She pulled it up. The door opened and the beach was no longer there.

Nothing. Nothing beyond the door. A flat dead blackness. No depth. No stars.

"Fuck you!" she screamed at it. "Fuck you!" The flickering of memory had stopped. Just the shaded hall, the blue of its walls.

She turned around. A silhouette in a ballroom gown floated toward her, long skirt inches off the floor.

"There is wonder," it said with Swirl's voice. "Or there is nothing."

"My mind!" Sparkle screamed at the approaching silhouette. "This is my fucking mind! Mine!"

"How unique," the shadow said, Swirl's voice like a whisper to her ear despite the distance. "You consider that oblivion behind you an option." The silhouette passed under a ray of soft light, and Sparkle thought she saw two slender horns. "How unique."

Sparkle's eyes watered. Terrified of the blackness behind, of the sister-as-mask ahead. Something in her wanted only to embrace Swirl, to plead forgiveness for her sins, her defiance. And the ball gown was so beautiful...

No. No, she just needed a moment. A moment to think. To decide.

A taloned hand seized her face from behind. Sparkle screamed. The hand dragged her backwards, into the black.

The last thing she heard was Swirl: a roar of cheated anger.

WHAT WAS HAPPENING?

Melid concentrated on the view of the Scalpels. The trick was to not concentrate too much, to not get dragged into the wonder. She took pains to deracinate her view, de-render it.

The second Scalpel—smaller, Spine-Sail Type-1—was on a direct course with the first. The first, larger Scalpel laid down a series of web-like energy patterns, of a kind unknown to Melid. A duel? That could happen? Melid's curiosity barely exceeded her fear.

She spent a bare second checking on Kend, lost in the wonder.

The energy webs didn't lie between the two Scalpels. The larger had set them to bloom in the void between the smaller, accelerating Scalpel and Silvercloud itself. A tactic, presumably. Melid hadn't a Craft-Emissary's training, but surely nothing about this extrapolated well for Silvercloud.

She opened her eyes, broke from the vision and looked at her supine friend.

"Kend." Melid shot a sharp emotic at her, a warning.

Kend blinked. She gazed at Melid.

"Watch terminal," Melid told her. Melid flicked through the visuals until it showed the energy webs. Something new: tiny comets of energy, a shower, flying towards Silvercloud, fired from the smaller Scalpel. The webs warped and stretched to stop them. Each comet tumbled into a web and vanished, as if passing into a portal to nowhere.

"Silvercloud: defences?" Melid asked Kend.

Kend looked at her. It was, Melid remembered, an absurd question. Silvercloud had no defensive weaponry. Its only defence, like all kollectives, was in pretending to be space debris.

Melid closed her eyes and watched her de-rendered vision. For a moment it seemed the webs had swallowed every comet. All but one.

The first Scalpel issued a single comet of its own, swift on the trail of the its enemy's. Both on a collision course with Silvercloud.

"Brace," Kend told the room, a command she sent to all Silvercloud.

"FUCK THIS," HARGIE said. "Open the door."

"No," Yan said. "Experiment."

Hargie gestured all around: the newly flickering lights, the gurgling sounds from Silvercloud's pipes, vents, and hell-knew-whats. "Experiment over," he said. "Results stupid."

"Experiment," Yan insisted. "Must experiment."

"Damn your sexuality. Open the door."

Yan's face shifted from determination to surprise. He grabbed Hargie by the shoulders and threw his own lanky frame on top of him. Hargie collapsed, yelled. He hit the metal floor with his right shoulder, pain shooting down his back. He tried to punch at Yan's chest but couldn't get momentum, just made his arm hurt.

"Hey!" Hargie said.

"Quiet, worl—"

The air burst into knives. Blue-light knives, hungry for deeper things than flesh. Hargie felt them tear through his thoughts, his hopes. Through the history of each piece of his clothing, the angles of his breath. His body simmered to an equation, a signature in time.

The only thing that remained a thing was Yan: a silhouette of nothing, his borders impregnable to this new strangeness.

The corridor returned as quickly as it had vanished. There came a sound like an animal keening. Hargie realised it was his own breath.

"Worlder." Yan. Yan was shaking his shoulders. "Arise."

He was fine, he realised. His body, Yan, the walls: all fine. He got up, fast as he could. Just like back on the rig when Illik exploded: same head-hump, same weird.

"C'mon," he said to Yan, "open that door now..."

"Pressure falling," he heard Yan say. "Keep closed."

No. Not this. It wouldn't end like this. Hargie thrust his palm at Yan's shoulder.

He didn't budge. A pillar of stone.

"Please, Yan. *Please.*"

But Yan's face was as cold as all his kind, cold as that fucking door.

Damn galaxy. Everyone seeing things their own way.

MELID WAS ALREADY IN free fall when the second blast hit.

What was it? Nothing like she had expected. Blank, depthless grey. She couldn't see her hands, but she could feel them. She touched her own face: yes, the hands were there. It was as if her eyes couldn't render the air, the light.

Pain in her spine and her vision returned. Melid had collided with the wall of the core. She shook her head, slapped her cheek to bring life to herself. She could still feel all Silvercloud, though much of its kollective slumbered.

Bodies floated around Melid. One of the Utiles—male—fell towards her, unconscious, his thoughts oddly inert.

Melid pushed her back against the wall, held her arms out and grabbed him. He drifted into her, face forward, the momentum causing Melid's breath to heave out. The male's eyelids batted.

She tried to look over his shoulder. "Kend?" she called out. Kend felt unconscious, too. Melid was clearly the first to awake. Instrum gene upgrades.

"Melid?" the male in her arms said. "Danger. Don't reach outside: watchers dying. Watchers in void."

"What?"

His voice seemed to double, as if accompanied by a female's.

"Scalpels at war," the two voices said. "Too much... beauty." The man's lips moved, but the rest of his face slept. "Our watchers die."

"Kend?" She could see her over the man's shoulder now: flat against the opposite wall and upside down to Melid's orientation. Kend's eyes fluttered open.

"Hope for... best, Melid," Kend said. Her lips said the words, yet Melid could hear a deeper voice saying exactly the same thing inches from her ear. The male utile.

No. No, no...

"Kancerisation," Melid muttered. The nightmare of Konsensus history. "Kan—"

The male utile's eyes opened. He seized Melid's throat.

About the Author

JAMES WORRAD LIVES in Leicester, England, and has for almost all his life. Currently he shares a house with a cat and another writer. He works for a well-known brand of hotel, an occupation that never leaves him short of writing material.

He has a degree in classical studies from Lampeter University, Wales. He has found this invaluable to his growth as a science fiction and fantasy writer in that he soon discovered how varied and peculiar human cultures can be.

In 2011 James attended Clarion, the prestigious six-week SF workshop held at the University of California, San Diego. There, he studied under some of the genre's leading professionals and also got to see a lot of wild hummingbirds.

He's had short stories published by Daily Science Fiction, Flurb, Newcon Press and Obverse Books. He also writes screen plays for short films, one of which- Flawless- won the Seven/Five Film Festival Award and was selected for both the Cannes and NYC Independent film festivals. (It was also screened at CERN, home of the Large Hadron Collider).

He's a regular face on the science fiction convention scene. Should you see him at one feel free to say hello.

Connect with James Worrad

Find James on his publisher's website:
http://www.castrumpress.com/james-worrad/

Sci-Fi Thrillers from Castrum Press

Cyborg

By JCH RIGBY

A military science fiction thriller portraying a dystopian future of corporation greed, exploitation and deadly secrets.

It started as just another assignment.

INVITED BY BIG-HITTING corporation ARTOK, combat journalist David Chambers, is visiting the planet Parnassus to report on the 'Human Enhancement Programme' when he witnesses the unthinkable, a crash site of an alien ship. The huge structure contained alien bodies and, more impor-tantly, alien technology, but, before Chambers could digest the scene, a rival corporation invades, and Chambers barely escapes with his life.

Chambers retreats to the safety of his habitat of Orchard accompanied by Richter and his team, but, Chambers is unaware of the extent of the cor-poration's reach. On their arrival, they are arrested, and, mysteriously, only Chambers is released, but, not before he is threatened into silence.

Richter, however, needs to be heard, his avatar reaches out to Chambers with harrowing tales of special forces, secret missions, violence and trickery resulting in the creation of half-humans, half-machines – cyborgs like him-self. Richter recruits Chambers to tell his story and expose the terrifying truth of the corporation's despicable plans for humanity.

But with billions of dollars at stake, the corporations cannot let the story break and will do everything in their power to keep their secrets safe.

More here:
http://www.castrumpress.com